TOGETHER AT THE TABLE

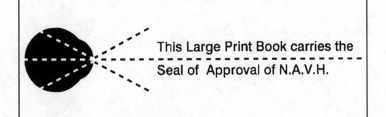

This Large Print Book carries the
Seal of Approval of N.A.V.H.

TOGETHER AT THE TABLE

A NOVEL OF LOST LOVE
AND SECOND HELPINGS

HILLARY MANTON LODGE

THORNDIKE PRESS

A part of Gale, Cengage Learning

GALE
CENGAGE Learning

Farmington Hills, Mich • San Francisco • New York • Waterville, Maine
Meriden, Conn • Mason, Ohio • Chicago

GALE
CENGAGE Learning®

LIBRARY OF CONGRESS CATALOGING-IN-PUBLICATION DATA

Names: Lodge, Hillary Manton, author.
Title: Together at the table : a novel of lost love and second helpings / by Hillary
    Manton Lodge.
Description: Large print edition. | Waterville, Maine : Thorndike Press, 2016. | ©
    2016 | Series: Two blue doors ; #3 | Series: Thorndike Press large print Christian
    fiction
Identifiers: LCCN 2016014472| ISBN 9781410486905 (hardcover) | ISBN 1410486907
    (hardcover)
Subjects: LCSH: Large type books. | GSAFD: Love stories. | Christian fiction.
Classification: LCC PS3612.O335 T64 2016b | DDC 813/.6—dc23
LC record available at http://lccn.loc.gov/2016014472

Published in 2016 by arrangement with WaterBrook Press, an imprint
of Crown Publishing Group, a division of Penguin Random House LLC

Printed in Mexico
1 2 3 4 5 6 7 20 19 18 17 16

*For Sandra Bishop, who remained
invested in this project
and helped give Juliette
a truly beautiful ending.*

And for Danny, who is my home.

PART I

1

As the days grow short, some faces grow long. But not mine. Every autumn, when the wind turns cold and darkness comes early, I am suddenly happy. It's time to start making soup again.

— LESLIE NEWMAN

Dear Neil,

I've started this e-mail several times, and I know that doesn't mean a lot because you've yet to receive a completed draft, but it's true.

We celebrated the three-month anniversary of Two Blue Doors last week. We made an event of it — Nico created three glorious specials in honor of the occasion, and Clementine made this anniversary cake with figs and meringue that still brings a smile to my face. We celebrated with our diners, then celebrated afterward with the staff.

It was bittersweet for me, because any celebration of the restaurant's opening automatically makes me think of you, and the last time we spoke.

Today was Toussaint, All Saints Day. And while patrons came in — some in costume — to celebrate Halloween, I used my break between seatings to put flowers on my mother's grave.

She passed away in September, on what would have been Chloé's first day of eighth grade. "Passed away" is such a weird term, isn't it? I was there — we all were — when it happened. And it seemed maybe less of a passing and more of a leaving. She stopped breathing and she was gone.

You were right. You were right and you knew you were right, and I yelled at you for it. I wasn't ready for the truth, not then.

I was angry for weeks after our fight, at first hoping somewhat spitefully that my mom would pull out and go into remission and I would have been able to say, "Hi, remember me? My mom is in remission."

It's petty. I'm not denying it.

But instead she faded away so quickly, and I couldn't trust myself to write.

Sandrine was here. She really is the best of my mom's cousins. Did you know she was a nurse before she became an innkeeper? I don't remember if that came up while we were in Provence together. Anyway, she was here and stayed for a month, helping when hospice wasn't at the house. I will always be profoundly grateful to her for that.

That last week, we knew it was coming. The hospice nurses warned us that she didn't have much time left. She was in good spirits throughout — at peace with her life, aware of her future. Sometimes funny, sometimes irascible in French, but never in despair. That made it easier on the rest of us, at least as much as possible.

The memorial was nice. Mario, Adrian, and Clementine catered, bless them. The Italian aunts and uncles all flew out, which was great. They cooked and cleaned and wept with my father as he said good-bye to his wife. My father sang Lucio Dalla's "Caruso," and all of us cried buckets.

My mom hadn't finished grieving her own mother's death when she died, so I'm glad they're together. They're likely in heaven making pastry — that's what I like to think about. If I focus on that image, I can smile for half of a second before my face defaults to "blank."

I felt numb for the first month, going through the motions of work. Fortunately for me, restaurant work is a good place to lose yourself, and I'm good at it. Setup, cleanup, management — there's not a lot I'm not involved in. We all work hard but the reviews have been good, with numbers to match. The restaurant has been featured in magazines and newspapers — both regional and, lately, national — as a place to visit.

But I've realized that I only ever wanted to impress three people in my life: my mom, my dad, and my grandmother. And now that we've found success, the fact that I've lost two out of the three steals much of the joy from the success we've obtained.

Is this e-mail too maudlin? I can't tell. But maybe you can't process death without being maudlin. Read it over and let me know. I didn't mean for all this to be so long.

The whole point was to say (a) my mom died and (b) I'm sorry we ended the way we did. Truly. I think we would have both moved on, eventually, but I'm sorry things ended that way. I hope you've found someone lovely (and local), ideally someone highly conversant in bacteria.

(I don't mean that to sound condescending, only that I feel deeply unqualified for such a thing, but I do recognize that bacteria is important. You can't live in Portland and not hear a great deal about probiotics.)

Don't worry about me, I think is what I'm trying to say. I learned how much I can carry on, and there's value in that. I learned that sometimes it doesn't matter if you move on with purpose or move on without, as long as you're moving, some-how.

I hope you're well. I hope you're happy. I pray good things for you.

Juliette

I sat back and reread what I'd written, hardly a paragraph in before I rolled my eyes. I looked over to the dark blankness outside my window and sleeping Gigi on my bed. Three in the morning hadn't done me any favors.

I moved my cursor near the Send button, but once again I felt my right hand drift, saving the draft and sending the e-mail to nest with its siblings, all curled up and cozy together in my Drafts folder.

I took a deep breath and closed my laptop, then rose from my desk before crawling into bed. Gigi sighed and stood, shook herself off, and relocated to my pillow. I placed my face next to hers.

"We're going to go for a long walk soon. You and me and Adrian. A long, proper walk on the river. We'll walk fast enough to keep warm. People will stop to pet you. You'll like it a lot."

Another flutter of the eyelids, but no other indication of anticipation. I patted her curly fur and nestled into my pillow. "That's all right. You'll enjoy it later."

I shouldn't have been surprised when I woke the next morning and realized I'd been dreaming about Neil.

We were standing in the lavender field again, and it felt . . . like I was right where I belonged and terribly out of place, all at the same time. I woke up feeling disoriented, even more so when I took my first deep breath of the day and caught a fragrant whiff of lavender.

Lavender.

My eyes opened fully, and I remembered that today was the day we'd host our first wedding at the restaurant.

I reached for my phone and checked the time: 6:34. I didn't need to get up for another twenty-six minutes, but the adrenaline from the coming event and the residual memory of Neil in the lavender field were enough to encourage my feet to find the floor and get a start on the day.

Another inhale — I really was smelling lavender, but I also remembered that the bride had requested lavender-vanilla petits fours filled with vanilla *crème anglaise*.

I showered and dressed, arranging my damp hair into a sleek braided chignon and

15

dressing in a swingy black jersey dress, the sleeves long enough to keep off the chill. *Tomorrow,* I promised myself. Tomorrow I would wear color and walk Gigi for miles.

After a brisk walk for Gigi, I settled her into her kennel and jogged down the stairs to the Two Blue Doors kitchen.

Hard to believe we'd been open for three months — some days hard to believe we'd opened at all.

I found our pastry chef, Clementine, in the kitchen, lavender sprig in hand.

"Hey! Just finishing up," she said as she set the sprig onto the top of a tiny iced cake. "The petits fours are almost done, and then I'll put them into the walk-in to keep cold."

"They look amazing," I said, leaning over to better examine my roommate's work. Each completed petit four was meticulously iced and decorated with a small sprig of lavender on top.

"Like I said, just about done," Clementine said, pouring icing over another set of bite-sized cakes. "I wanted to get these tucked away before the guys came in and made the whole place smell like onions and seared meat."

"Good plan, though I thought they'd be here by now." I pulled out my tablet. "Actually, fifteen minutes ago."

16

"I'm here!" came a voice from the back door. But it was our line cook Kenny's voice, not my brother's. Or, for that matter, my boyfriend's.

"Hi, Kenny. You didn't see the chef outside, did you?"

"Yeah, he's right behind me."

"What is this, roll call?" Nico asked as he walked inside.

"We're on a tight schedule with the wedding today," I reminded him. "We've got the lunch seating and then a quick turnaround for the wedding."

"It'll be fine," he said, giving me a conciliatory pat on the shoulder.

"I know. It's just . . . first wedding we've done here. This could be a great start."

"We're certainly making good money on it — hey, Adrian!"

I turned to see Adrian, my boyfriend and my brother's sous-chef, enter through the back door.

"Morning," he said with a friendly nod to Nico. "And morning to you," he said to me, dropping a short kiss on my lips.

Nico crossed his arms. "What did I say about kitchen PDA?"

"What, that applied to us?" Adrian held his palms out in a show of mock confusion. "I thought that was about keeping a respectful distance with the radishes."

"Have a good lunch service," I said. "Be extra careful with the petits fours that'll be in the walk-in."

"They're almost done," Clementine called out.

"Good, because I need your station space," Nico called back.

"You can have it when the desserts are done," Clementine retorted.

The bickering continued, of course. I wished Nico would ask her out, marry her, and be done with it. But in the wake of Mom's death, each of us grieved deeply in our own way. In recent months, Nico had spent increasingly long hours in the kitchen, often ignoring life outside of the restaurant. I stayed out of it, at least most of the time. Instead, I readied the dining room. We had a full day ahead.

The lunch rush nearly knocked us off our feet. Since our July opening, we'd made full use of the outdoor seating. I'd worked to make our garden patio as lovely as possible, and our customers agreed. Young trees in planters had graced the corners, while boxes filled with blooming annuals had lined the railing.

We'd enjoyed an Indian summer, but with the end of October came the heavy rains and chill that found the place between my sleeves and gloves. The tree leaves had long turned to rust, setting off the mums in the boxes. White twinkle lights at the top of the trellis and wound into the trees made the dusk and evening hours truly magical, while vinyl sheeting and propane heaters still kept it just warm enough for intrepid diners.

It was great for business, especially for newcomers. People walked by and stopped just for the opportunity to eat outside.

But the business boom also meant increasingly heavy workloads for our staff — and the Saturday lunch service was no different. Nico and the rest of the kitchen staff worked to get each dish plated and perfect, while our servers, Braeden, Patrick, and Mallory, and I rushed to get the orders out quickly.

"Juliette!" Nico called to me after I dropped off an order. "We're low on the brussels sprouts."

"I'll take care of it," I said. I encouraged the staff to push the nonsprout appetizers, but my own tables were having none of it.

And to be fair, it was a dish we'd become famous for — brussels sprouts sautéed with pancetta and a hint of orange zest, served with a poached egg and parmesan on top. My own mouth watered thinking of it, and

I saw fifteen of them leave the kitchen per sitting.

"I've got three more orders for the sprouts. Do we need to cut them off?" I asked Nico.

He looked up from his station. "It's fine. I pulled out the sprouts reserved for the wedding."

My eyes widened. "Yeah?" I asked cautiously. I didn't want to contradict him in front of the staff, but . . .

He read the caution in my eyes. "It'll be fine. I made a couple calls, and the New Seasons at Cedar Hills has the amount we need. I need to get some air anyway — I'll just run and get them."

"Okay," I said, even though I hated the idea. We had too much to do for me to feel okay with Nico leaving the kitchen.

"It'll be fine," he repeated. "Kenny and Adrian will be starting the prep work. And I can look at their bulk dates, because I'm not happy with mine."

I nodded. "Do what you need to do," I said. I knew getting things at a grocery store rather than our supplier would be more expensive, but at this point the important piece was simply having the ingredient at all.

Adrian and Kenny began cleaning their stations before the last of the lunch guests left. I closed out the tabs, thanked the guests, and left Braeden and Mallory to tidy up the dining room while I ran upstairs to eat a bite and let Gigi roam free.

After another short walk to the park and back, I walked back downstairs to get ready for the wedding.

We'd received the call about the wedding two months before. The bride and groom had gotten engaged at the restaurant — an event which may have had to do with our free champagne promotion our first month in business — and called shortly after to ask if we rented out the restaurant for weddings.

We hadn't before, but it seemed a perfect time to start. How hard could it be, anyway? It was catering — which all of us had done — and serving in our own space.

So far, the preparations had been straight-forward. I'd had a sit-down meeting with the couple, Sonnet and Theo, in mid-August.

"We just want something simple," Sonnet had said. "We're not eloping, but we're not having a long engagement or an elaborate wedding. No tulle, no rose petals, no topiaries. Just the two of us getting married and eating good food with family and friends."

No rehearsal, either. "It's a wedding," she'd said. "Not a school play. And we're paying for it ourselves."

I hadn't asked, but it sounded like punctuation in a conversation she'd had many other times with many other people.

Sonnet and Theo chose items off our menu to serve as a buffet — including the brussels sprouts — before meeting with Clementine to plan the petits fours. I charged enough to cover our usual take on a Saturday night and give the servers a paid night off.

Nico, Adrian, and Clementine would do the food prep and setup. I'd run the beverages and keep everything running smoothly; Adrian had volunteered to stay through the event with me and wash dishes after. It was a small enough crowd at fifty, and a simple enough buffet, that we could comfortably run the show with a skeleton crew.

Sonnet and Theo had chosen to have a standing ceremony in the dining room, with reception overflow on the patio; I took a bucket outside and pruned off dead leaves and stray branches, then swept away cobwebs that had formed overnight. After a brisk sweep, it looked wedding worthy.

My phone rang; I pulled it from my back pocket to answer. "Nico, hi. What's up?"

"Hey, Etta. So . . . I'm having some car trouble."

2

Life is too short for self-hatred and it's too short for celery sticks.

— MARILYN WANN

My eyes squeezed shut. "What happened?"

"Alfa died," he said, though it was a little hard to hear.

Of course it did. "It's not dead, it's just resting," I said, quoting my oldest brother, Alex, the mechanic of the family. "Where are you?"

"I'm on 217, northbound."

"You're kidding."

"I'm not."

"Your Alfa has terrible timing. Mine only breaks down on side streets."

"You're living your best life," Nico quipped. "The tow truck is on its way, and I texted Adrian to have him pick me up."

"Are you sure? Adrian's prepping — or if he's not prepping, he will be. I'm tied up here, since I've got the wedding party coming shortly to set up. Did you call Alex? Dad? Sophie? Anybody?"

"Alex and Dad are tied up. Sophie is on dance detail with Chloé — first homecoming, remember?"

"You're right. I can't believe I forgot." I shook my head. That was the restaurant business for you, guaranteed to make sure you miss out on as many milestones as possible.

"Don't worry — she'll take enough photos to make sure you feel like you're there."

"True enough."

"It's just thirty minutes here and back. It'll be fine."

"I'm holding you to that," I said. "Be careful on the side of the road, there."

"I will. Is it raining over there?"

I looked out the window. "Not yet."

"It will be."

"Lovely. Stay safe."

He promised he would, and we hung up.

Adrian met me outside. "You talk to Nico?"

"I did. Hurry back, okay?"

"You worry too much," he said, dropping a quick kiss on my lips. "See you soon?"

"You'd better!" I shook my head as I watched him step down the stairs to our small back lot, climb in his car, and drive away.

Two down. I didn't like it, but my opinion wasn't moving mountains today.

The sound of footfalls on the front deck shook me from my thoughts. I strode around to the front to find Sonnet and a few friends on the doorstep.

"Hi, you guys! Sorry, I locked the front to keep people from wandering in. It happens." I pulled out my keys and opened up.

Sonnet shook her head. "No problem. I parked in front of the restaurant. Is that okay?"

"Perfectly okay."

"Cool. I've got more flowers in my car, and my clothes and stuff."

"Sounds great." I introduced myself to her companions — a sister, Poem, and friends Sara and Meg. "Let's get stuff downstairs, and I can help you out with the flowers."

Poem, Sara, and Meg *oohed* over the space as they stepped inside. We deposited the clothes downstairs and set to work with the flowers.

Listening to the women, it sounded as though they'd made the arrangements themselves from mums and autumn leaves. More leaves were scattered across the buffet table, with gold-painted pinecones scattered here and there like magical objects.

Shortly after, a navy-blue pickup truck pulled up, and a couple of guys, both in their late twenties, unloaded a tall wooden structure from beneath a violently blue tarp. Sara looked out the window. "Hey, look! Will and Zach are here with the chuppah frame!"

I helped the guys to the back-deck stairs, and Sonnet directed them to place it on the back of the deck. Sara gave Will a kiss before shooing him away, and the women headed back to the dining room for final touches.

A quick glance at the lot showed that Adrian hadn't yet returned with Nico, but the rain had certainly arrived.

Not good.

I watched the droplets ripple into puddles for a moment before slipping into the kitchen, where I found Clementine preparing the next day's bread pudding. "They're still not here yet, are they?"

Clementine looked up from her whisking. "Not yet, no. What happened?"

"Nico's car died, Adrian went to pick him up, nobody's back yet, and I have concerns."

Clementine snorted. "What is it with you guys and your Alfa Romeos that break down half of the time?"

"Italians are romantics, and Alfas are the

26

vehicular embodiment of that fact. But enough about cars — we've got to keep this thing on time."

"We'll be fine," Kenny said, pausing in his pursuit of shredding carrots for the Moroccan salad.

I wasn't convinced, but my phone rang before I could voice my opinion. "Adrian, where are you?"

"It's me," Nico said. "I borrowed Adrian's phone. We, ah, we ran into a problem. Or — I guess, the other way around."

"None of what you just said is making me panic any less."

"You know how there's the scientific phenomenon of people driving into things because they're looking at them? Well, add a wet road to that, and you get an idiot crashing into the tow truck."

"You're kidding."

"Nope!"

"You sound remarkably cheery."

"Didn't hit my car, but now they're calling a tow truck for the tow truck, and I can't leave before I give a statement to the police."

"Police?"

"Well, it's enough of a to-do here by the side of the freeway, what with the tow truck and the idiot and the other tow truck on its way. There are road flares and everything

27

on this scenic rain-soaked highway."

My stomach twisted. "Okay. I'm assuming you don't have a time estimate?"

"Not yet."

"I know you tried calling family, but what about a taxi? I mean, what's your time line? If we're serving at six —"

"Plenty of time."

Well, he'd also said that he'd be back in half an hour, and that hadn't much panned out, either. But I knew my brother. He could put a lot of food together very quickly if necessary.

So I practiced the deep cleansing breaths advised by the yoga teacher I never saw anymore — on account of my job — and returned to the phone call. "Keep me posted," I said. "And please, please don't get hit by a car."

"I won't. Traffic's moving too slowly now that the police are here. With the flares."

Perfect.

We said our good-byes and hung up. But before I could discuss the prep schedule with Kenny — and rope Clementine into staying longer — I caught the sound of Sonnet's voice.

She didn't sound happy.

I rounded out of the kitchen to find Sonnet and her friends facing three older women in the dining room. Sonnet caught my eye, her look of panic begging me for help. I couldn't blame her. The three of them in their best wedding boleros, bolts of tulle tucked under their arms, looked like a scene from *Macbeth* gone pastel.

I pasted on my best manager's smile. "Hello. I'm Juliette D'Alisa, manager here at Two Blue Doors. Is there anything I can do for you?"

The center woman stood up straighter and nodded. "I'm Theresa, Theo's mother. We just came by to do a little prewedding sprucing."

That explained it. Sonnet struck me as someone who had no problems asserting herself, but a mother-in-law-to-be? Tricky territory.

"That's wonderful," I said. "Let me get the wedding binder," I improvised. "Just to check off the decorations in the contract agreement."

"Contract agreement?" Theresa echoed.

"Right. When I meet with brides and grooms, there's a list created for the approved decorations."

"It may not be in that list," Theresa hedged. "But it's just tulle. Won't leave a mess — it'll just make it look like there's a wedding."

"Let me check the list," I said, retreating to my office for my wedding notes. I hastily shoved them into a blank-covered binder of ordering accounts before returning to face down Theresa. "No tulle on this list. Is that tulle fire-retardant treated?"

Theresa gave one of her compatriots a nervous glance. "I'm not sure. I think so."

"It's usually marked," I said. "On the bolt. In red."

Lady to the Left checked her bolt. "I don't see any markings in red."

"Oh, that's a pity," I said, darting a quick glance toward Sonnet. "I'm afraid I can't allow you to decorate with untreated tulle."

"But —," Theresa began to protest.

I shook my head. "Fire code for restaurants. Because our space is small, it's a hazard."

From the corner of my eye, I could see Sonnet's shoulders drop in relief.

Theresa looked around the room. "It is a very small space."

"Agreed."

"Cramped."

"The old buildings, you know," I said, sagely. I wasn't going to let myself be insulted by a woman dressed in a cantaloupe-colored suit. "There's some time before the ceremony — I'd be happy to set up a table for you on the covered patio, if you'd like to relax."

Theresa glanced to her right and left. "I suppose we could. We came from Wilsonville. In traffic."

I made a sympathetic face and led them outside. Smooth wood benches lined the edges; I set them up in a corner before retrieving one of the folding patio tables from the basement.

In the kitchen, I prepared a tray with a pitcher of lavender lemonade and glass tumblers. Theresa cast a critical eye, but the others — who had to be sisters, the resemblance was so strong — were impressed by the ice cubes with lavender sprigs inside.

Who wouldn't be?

Once they were safely set up and out of trouble, I went looking for Sonnet.

"We're doing pictures at the park," she said. "Under the gazebo, it looks like, though we've got lots of colorful umbrellas. The photographer will arrive shortly."

"Let's get you somewhere more private to get ready, or I'm afraid you'll have company before too long," I said, tilting my head toward the patio. "Let's get your clothes. You can follow me upstairs."

"Isn't there a residence upstairs?" Sonnet asked, eyes wide. "I couldn't —"

"Escape Theresa? Yes, you could. Do you like dogs?"

Sonnet nodded.

"Then Gigi will enjoy the company. You'll be doing me a favor."

They followed me upstairs, and I felt glad I'd tidied sufficiently the day before.

"This is so nice of you," Sara said as I let them inside.

"It's no problem. And the light is better up here, anyway." I flipped lights on. "At least now it is. This was my grandmother's apartment. She actually owned the whole building."

"She didn't run the bakery, did she?" Sonnet asked. "The one that used to be here?"

"She did, actually."

Sonnet's eyes widened even farther. "Mireille Bessette? Mireille Bessette is your grandmother? She was amazing. I sketched at the bakery some days because I was so inspired by her style. I'm a women's wear designer," she said, holding up a hand. "Not a stalker, I promise."

"Not worried," I answered, suppressing a smile. "And she was amazing, and lived an incredible life," I said. "Today's your day, but give me a call another day and I'd be happy to show you her closet."

"Really?"

"There's a vintage Dior in there."

Sonnet nodded. "You're right. I have to get married today. But next week —" Her gaze lingered in the direction of the closet.

"Next week," I promised.

Once the younger women were well ensconced in my apartment, I headed back downstairs to check on the older women, and finally on the kitchen to see if Nico had made it back yet.

I knew before I swung open the kitchen doors that they weren't. The quiet only served to amp up my concerns.

I pulled out my phone. No missed calls or texts.

I dialed Nico's number and waited; no answer. I redialed with a stubborn tap twice more, his voice mail picking up each time.

Next, I dialed Adrian. Same. I walked back to the kitchen and put my hands on my hips. I had a bride and her friends upstairs and fifty guests arriving in two hours.

So I washed up and got to work.

"Kenny. You've got the Moroccan carrot salad done, but where are we with the brussels sprouts?"

"Everything is prepped. We just need the sprouts."

"Good. Go ahead and start caramelizing

the onions for the goat-cheese toasts, and then get the bacon going — just be sure to undercook the bacon. It'll cook the rest of the way in the oven."

"Yes, chef."

"Clementine, can you take over the grilled crudités? We need to get them chilled by five."

She nodded. "Yes, chef."

"Excellent. I'll start prepping the butternut-squash fritters," I said, rolling up my sleeves. "And then the mozzarella poppers. Let's get to work."

I was elbows deep in fried mozzarella and crispy-edged butternut-squash fritters when my brother and boyfriend finally arrived, wet and bedraggled, at the kitchen door.

"I have dates," Nico said, holding the crate aloft. "Dates and brussels sprouts."

"It's about time," I shot back. "You've been single far too long."

"I'm going to get cleaned up," he said, "and then I can relieve you."

"Take your time," I replied honestly. "I've got everything under control."

And I did. The fritters were done and in the warming oven with a cake pan full of water in the rack below to keep them from drying out. I'd made up the mozzarella poppers by breading the rounds of buffalo-milk mozzarella with batter and panko crumbs before deep-frying them in batches.

It had felt good to work with my hands again, good to do something other than managerial work. I cast a longing eye at Clementine's pavlovas, the baked egg whites topped with quartered figs. There was something soothing about working with egg whites, the frothy pure-white shade they became when whisked.

Nico and Adrian cleaned up before returning to work.

Adrian dropped a kiss on my cheek. "I can take over the fryer," he said. "You can get cleaned up if you like."

I nodded. And it was true — I needed to get the grease out of my pores and repair my makeup. But what I wanted, I realized, was to stay and get the rest of the appetizers out. Logic won out, and I headed upstairs.

Gigi bounced in joy to see me; I washed my face and reapplied my makeup before heading downstairs, which happened to coincide with the arrival of the bridal party and photographer, flushed and laughing under oversized umbrellas.

The guests arrived shortly after; soon enough Sonnet and her fiancé stood at the front of the dining room between the windows, faces glowing, professing their devotion unto death.

And for the second time that day, I thought of Neil.

For a time, I'd wanted this. A wedding, a sense of belonging. That desire had driven me to online dating, to meeting Neil. And for a little while, it looked like just maybe we might have worked.

A hand at the small of my back caused me to turn and look over my shoulder. Adrian looked down at me, smiling warmly. "Hiya," he whispered.

"Hi," I whispered back. "All done in the kitchen?"

"Everything's ready. I missed you."

I smiled up at him, and we looked back to the front of the room in time to see Sonnet and Theo kiss before turning back to face their friends and families.

My eye caught Sonnet's mother, the look of joy on her face, the tears glistening in her eyes.

My heart squeezed and I looked away. "Back to work," I said, placing a kiss on Adrian's stubbled cheek.

I had food to serve and a champagne toast to prepare. Missing my mother so much I couldn't breathe — that would have to wait.

~ Brussels Sprouts with Bacon and Orange Zest ~

4 slices bacon

1 pound brussels sprouts, washed, dried, and halved

2 tablespoons grapeseed oil

1 teaspoon coarse salt

1/4 teaspoon freshly ground black pepper

Zest of one orange

Line a baking sheet with aluminum foil, and preheat oven to 425°F.

In a large sauté pan on medium heat, cook the bacon until almost cooked through, about 2 minutes per side. Remove slices and drain before chopping into 1/4-inch pieces.

Toss the sprouts, grapeseed oil, salt, pepper, and bacon together in a medium-sized bowl. Bake for 5 minutes on lined baking sheet, toss, and bake for another 5–6 minutes, or until sprouts are crisp but not burned.

Return the sprouts to the mixing bowl, and stir in the orange zest.

Serves 4.

3

Give me juicy autumnal fruit ripe and red from the orchard.

— **WALT WHITMAN**

Sunday afternoon smiled upon us; after heavy rainfall Saturday night, the skies had turned unexpectedly clear. I reveled in my morning off, slipping into church a few moments late as a result. I didn't see any of my family members, so I sat by myself near the back.

Adrian and I attended together often, but lately he'd taken to finding an early morning or evening Sunday service, allowing him to run the Sunday brunch and lunch shifts.

For that afternoon, we'd planned a long walk together, in the company of Gigi and steaming hot coffee.

I listened to the sermon and took notes, as usual, but the morning's music selections poked uncomfortably at my already tender heart. The lyrics sang of unyielding faith and unending joy, but the truth was I knew my own faith to be shaky in the wake of my mom's death, and joy in short supply.

My sister Caterina and I had discussed the subject several times.

"It's grief," she said once. "It's real and it's valid, but it's not forever. Don't worry."

But I did worry. I worried I'd spend the rest of my adult life with a heart that felt raw from loss.

I slipped out as quietly as I'd arrived and filled the interior of my car with the soothing sounds of the latest Markéta Irglová album before driving home.

Gigi greeted me upon my return, and I curled up with her in the oversized armchair by the front window until we heard the knock at my door.

Adrian stood on the opposite side, grinning, oilcloth bag in hand.

I smiled into his eyes and stepped back to allow his entry inside. "Hey, you."

"Hi," he said, leaning in for a kiss before bending over and petting Gigi. "I know, it's been a while," he said as she rolled over for a belly rub. He looked up at me. "Nico told me to tell you that we need to increase our order of brussels sprouts."

"No shop talk today — I'm off duty." I

frowned. "When did Nico tell you this, any-way?"

"Just now. He's downstairs."

I ran my hand over my face. This was one of the problems with living ten feet above your place of work. "He needs to take a break."

"He does. We all need a break," he said, standing and wrapping his arms around me to prove his point.

I leaned into his embrace but pulled back as he tipped his head forward. "I don't understand. How could we be out? I picked up those last crates myself, cleaned every one of them with these two hands." I held up said hands, for illustration's sake.

"They're good hands." He caught one and kissed a knuckle. "And you didn't have to do that, babe. That's my job. Or Kenny's job."

I shrugged. "You guys were busy, I had time, I washed the sprouts."

"With these hands," he kissed a second knuckle.

"You're trying to distract me."

"Is it working?" He opened my hand and kissed my fingertips.

It certainly wasn't unpleasant, but still . . . "Who is eating all of these brussels sprouts?"

"The people who pay us for the brussels sprouts. I thought you knew."

My mouth settled into a firm line. "Of course I know. I just didn't know they'd eaten us out of house and sprout."

"You're funny." He tugged on my hand, placing it around his shoulder. "And now you're talking shop."

"I just . . . brussels sprouts."

"Hush. Remember what you just said about Nico taking a break?" He lowered his lips to mine for a kiss.

I didn't know who'd taught Adrian to kiss, and while I didn't particularly want to know, I wondered if I owed her a thank-you note. My muscles relaxed, and my arms loosened before they wrapped around his neck. "Hmm."

Adrian pulled back. "Better?"

"You," I said, tilting my head, "taste like brussels sprouts."

"One. One sprout. Nico's testing a recipe downstairs."

"You ate all of them!"

"You're crazy."

I let a slow smile spread over my face. "Yeah." I placed another peck on his lips. "And you like it."

"You ready for our walk? Lunch is in the bag, and we'll get coffee on the way."

41

"That sounds perfect." I looked over to where Gigi was turning jumps and flips of joy. "Gigi's ready too."

We stopped for coffee around the block and ate the hot panini sandwiches during the drive — my appetite had gotten the best of me. Adrian promised that there was dessert in the bag too but insisted that it wait for our walk.

Every other resident of Portland, it seemed, had the same idea: take advantage of a rare, golden November afternoon by walking by the river. Gigi held her tiny stub of a tail high as she took in the sights and smells.

Adrian and I walked hand in hand, enjoying the brisk river breeze and fresh air.

We'd been dating, casually, since the beginning of August. And maybe *dating* wasn't the right word — we spent time together at work and out. Lately, most of our hours had been logged behind the doors of Two Blue Doors. Now, after spending so many days in a restaurant full of kitchen smells, the riverfront felt like a revelation.

We walked for about half a mile before finding a bench in the sunlight. Gigi hopped up to sit beside me, and Adrian unloaded the bag. "Hand pies," he said. "Apple and ginger."

"Did you make these?"

"Of course I did," he said, looking wounded.

I placed a placating hand on his arm. "Sorry, I didn't have you pegged as a pie man."

"Pastry is food. Food is my thing."

"Fair enough." I unwrapped one of the foil-covered pies. "This looks fantastic."

"Taste it."

I obliged, letting the hot apple-and-ginger filling coat the inside of my mouth, warming me from the inside out. "That's amazing."

He almost succeeded in not smirking. "Thank you," he said, before reaching for a pie of his own.

"I'm looking forward to hiring more staff," Adrian said around mouthfuls of his pie. "It'll be nice to have two days off a week. Kenny's looking ragged around the edges."

"He is," I agreed. "Nico's the one I'm worried about. Someone has to pull him away from the stove."

"He's certainly driven," Adrian agreed.

"It's only been a few months. I hope it's just temporary." The breeze sent hair flying into my face; I shoved it back. "If he were anyone else, I'd suggest he find someone to talk to, a therapist, but . . ."

"I don't see him talking to a shrink."

I sighed. "Maybe a therapist could talk him out of adding new entrées at a moment's notice."

"It's an adventure!"

I raised an eyebrow. "It's murder on the ordering."

"You're in the black, though."

"It's true." And it was, though I wasn't stupid. Our location near the trendy Nob Hill area meant that we were guaranteed plenty of foot traffic from customers who enjoyed what we had to offer. I shook my head. "All right. No more work talk."

"Do you think we could talk Nico back around to adding the bacon-lentil salad?"

I swatted his arm. "Now you're just baiting me."

He grinned at me. "Maybe. What else do you want to talk about?"

"We should go to a movie sometime. Catch a concert." I reclined on the park bench. "See a play."

"You think so?"

"We can get out of the restaurant world from time to time. They'll let us back in, I promise." I reached out and scratched Gigi's ears. "I need to get her out more often

too. Poor thing's not getting enough attention."

"She's practically feral," Adrian drawled.
"What about the holidays? Those are coming up."

I winced, feeling that familiar clench in
my chest as I contemplated holidays without
my mother. "Mmm," I said. "I'm trying not
to think about them."

"Your birthday's coming up too."

"If I could fast-forward to January, I
would." I sighed. "Holidays, birthdays —
just reminders that my mom is . . . that she's
gone. If I could escape Christmas, I would
do that too." I shifted on my seat. "Sandrine
invited us out to the chateau for Epiphany,
though. If we can swing the travel time, I'd
like it." I looked over to Adrian. "You should
come."

His eyebrows furrowed comically. "It's so
weird there's a castle in your family."

"Think of it as a fairly large, fairly old
stone house."

"In France."

"Yes. There are some very grand chateaux
in France, but this one's more of an old
manor house."

"You can talk it down all you want, it's
still a castle in France."

"But it's an inn, now. Basically a bed-and-breakfast."

He shook his head. "Still weird."

"Lots of people own bed-and-breakfasts!"

"Didn't you tell me it has a ballroom?"

"They use it for corporate events now."

He tilted his head as if deep in thought. "Nope. Still weird."

As if she'd tired of the subject, Gigi abandoned her nap and began to sniff in the grass.

"Is she . . ."

I tilted my head as Gigi circled, sniffed, and considered before arranging herself into a ladylike squat. "It appears so, yes," I said, reaching for the roll of biodegradable plastic bags and hand sanitizer I carried in my purse.

"She couldn't have done that farther away?"

I stood, dropping the hand sanitizer into the pocket of my jacket then turning the bag inside out to pick up Gigi's leavings. "If it makes you feel better, I'll give her a stern talking-to while I take this to the garbage can."

Adrian's nose remained wrinkled.

"I'll be back in a minute," I said, laughing. At least there was a can within sight, about three hundred feet away. "You stay here and guard the bench."

We retraced our steps along the river, Gigi and I. Bicyclists raced by, ringing their bells as they passed, while pedestrians smiled at Gigi or ignored us altogether.

I was gazing off into the distance, taking in the river, when a figure caught my eye.

It had to be because Neil had been on my mind recently. Had to be. Because the man standing with his back to us on the grassy riverbank, facing the bridge, looked strikingly like the man I'd met online, the man I'd fallen in love with. The man who'd broken my heart — and whose heart I'd likely crushed at the same time.

Obviously, it couldn't be him, but the stance was the same. The way the sun glinted rose-gold in his hair, his build — lanky but broad enough in the shoulder to appear solid.

I didn't realize I'd been staring until he turned and met my gaze.

My breath caught in my chest; my feet faltered before continuing in their path. It was him.

It was Neil.

He'd shaved his beard, but his face, his eyes — I'd know them anywhere.

Ten feet of muddy grass separated us; I raised my hand in a casual "hello," only to discover that I still held Gigi's bag in my hand.

Oh yes, that was perfect.

I flushed red and veered to the left in order to dispose of the waste once and for all, and squirted a little hand sanitizer into my palms.

He'd begun to walk toward me, and we met halfway. "Juliette," he said.

His voice sounded the same. The same rich tones with shades of his southern upbringing.

"Hi, Neil," I said, breathless. A thousand questions ran through my mind. *What are you doing here, why aren't you in Memphis, how did this happen?*

Why didn't you tell me?

"Gorgeous day," I said, trying to remain calm even as Gigi strained forward to say hello. "I . . . didn't expect to see you."

"I'm working at OHSU," he said, his eyes glued to mine.

"That's great," I said, remembering that we'd met in person the first time because of a guest lecture at Oregon Health and Science University.

"Somewhat last minute, just for the term."

His words sunk in. "Oh. So, you're . . . here."

"I should have called —"

I shook my head. "I could have e-mailed," I said, thinking of the long list of unsent e-mails on my computer.

"How's your mom?"

"She passed away," I said. "September second."

He flinched. "I'm so sorry, Juliette."

"Neil! Hello!" Adrian's voice called out from behind my left shoulder; I jumped at the sound of his greeting, my eyes pulling away from Neil's face for the first time.

"Adrian. Hello," Neil said with a nod, stepping forward to shake the other man's hand.

"Neil's teaching a term at OHSU," I told Adrian, my gaze drifting back to Neil's face.

Adrian placed a gentle hand on my shoulder. "That's great. You can't beat Portland in the fall."

Neil stood up straighter. "Not at all, not at all," he answered, his voice forcibly casual. "Juliette was telling me about her mom's passing."

"Gabrielle was a great lady," Adrian said.

The collection of thoughts and feelings and words written for Neil, but kept to myself, surfaced again. Faced with the man in the flesh, I had too many words to speak.

I'm with Adrian now. I can't imagine not missing my mom. You were right, you were

49

wrong. I miss you, I'm still angry with you. I still don't know what became of my grandfather.

Why didn't you tell me you'd come to Portland?

"She was," Neil agreed. "I only met her the once, but she's a lady who leaves an impression."

I chuckled even as I felt the familiar prick of tears behind my eyes. "True," I said, preparing to change the subject and ask after his friends Callan and Tarissa in my next breath.

Neil spoke first. "You two look like you're out enjoying a day at the river, and I'll let you get back to it."

So that was it, then.

Adrian patted his arm. "It's nice to see you, man. Stop by and see us at the restaurant sometime. It'll be on the house."

Another careful smile from Neil that didn't quite touch his eyes. "I'll have to take you up on that." He nodded at me, stepping away. "Juliette, Adrian."

I raised a hand in farewell. "Good-bye, Neil."

With his arm around my shoulders, Adrian and I turned to walk back to our picnic bench, our stray crumbs having attracted the attention of a rogue seagull, much to

Gigi's delight.

"You're quiet," Adrian said.

"Sorry, it's — that was unexpected."

"He didn't tell you he was in town?"

"We broke up July 26, the night the restaurant opened," I said with a shake of my head. "It's been strict radio silence since then." I looked out at the river and back toward Adrian. "I've come close to writing him several times," I admitted. "Very close. The way we ended — it's not something I'm proud of."

"He told you your mother was going to die," Adrian reminded me, his voice flat.

"I doubt that's something he's proud of either. And" — this was the part I hated most — "he wasn't wrong."

I thought back to that night. It was three months in the past, but felt like three lifetimes. "We were friends," I said softly. "Pen pals, really, before it got romantic. And while breaking up was the right thing, I'm sad it came at the expense of a friendship."

Adrian didn't answer.

I'd come so very close to sending the e-mail I'd written in the middle of the night. How might the afternoon have played out if I'd been brave enough to press Send?

Neil's strangely impassive face as we spoke . . . an e-mail probably wouldn't have changed anything.

Adrian studied my face for a moment as we walked, then squeezed my shoulder. "Sorry, I think we lost our spot."

I looked ahead to where an older couple settled onto our bench and looked out at the river.

I lifted my hand to rest on his. "I'm sure we'll manage. I can eat pie and walk at the same time — Gigi would like that."

"You sure you're okay?"

"Yeah, yeah. I'm fine, just taken aback," I said, smiling up at him.

In the next split second, my gaze traveled over my shoulder, my eyes unexpectedly catching Neil's as he watched Adrian and me walking across the green.

~ APPLE AND GINGER HAND PIES ~

For the Pastry:

1 1/4 cups all-purpose flour
1/4 teaspoon fine sea salt
1/4 cup ice water
1/2 cup unsalted butter, very cold, cut into small cubes

For the Filling:

4 tablespoons butter, melted
2 small apples, one sweet and one tart (Honeycrisp and Granny Smith make a great combination), peeled, cored, and sliced thin
1 teaspoon grated fresh ginger
2 tablespoons brown sugar
1/2 teaspoon vanilla extract
1 1/2 teaspoon cornstarch

To Finish:

1 egg, beaten

In a medium bowl, combine flour and salt. Cut in the butter, using a pastry cutter or two knives, and work the butter into the flour until the mixture resembles lentils. Add the water, 1 tablespoon at a time, until the mixture sticks together just enough to form a disc. Wrap the disc in plastic wrap and refrigerate one hour.

53

Heat the oven to 400°F. Line two baking sheets with parchment paper.

Stir together the apples, melted butter, ginger, brown sugar, and vanilla in a medium-sized bowl. Refrigerate if not using immediately.

To assemble, cut the pastry disc into two pieces, and allow them to reach room temperature. Between sheets of plastic wrap, or using a floured surface, roll each piece of the pie dough into a circle, about 1/8-inch thickness. Cut each circle in half; you should have 4 semicircles.

Using your finger or a pastry brush, rub a thin layer of beaten egg onto the outermost edge of each semicircle. Spoon filling onto one half of each semicircle, about 1/3 cup. Fold the pastry over to cover, and crimp the edges with a fork to seal. Cut three vents into the top of each pie to allow steam to escape. Finish with a light brushing of egg over the outside of each pie, and then place them on the baking sheets.

Bake for 25–30 minutes, or until each pie is golden brown and the pastry has cooked through. Allow to cool at least 5 minutes before serving. To store leftovers, allow to cool before covering.

Makes 4 pies.

Kitchen tip: to keep the butter cold, cut it

into small cubes and then refrigerate the cubes until you're ready to use them.

4

Promises and pie-crust are made to be broken.

— JONATHAN SWIFT

Back at home, after Adrian left, I still couldn't shake the memory of Neil standing by the river, the feeling of seeing such a familiar person in such an unexpected place.

So Gigi and I curled up with my laptop, and I pulled up the draft I hadn't sent, editing it down to hit the key points — that I was sorry we ended the way we did, that I hoped he'd find someone kind and, well, local. But the same thing happened that always happened when I wrote; I found myself processing my own memories, the act of watching my mother die. How she looked like a fading fairy in a hospital gown, her skin translucent and smooth, stretched snug over sharp bones. How she passed a month after the opening, when the leaves just began to turn colors around the edges.

Was that really why I'd written over and over? Not to connect, but as a place to put my feelings?

I spent most of my days trying to outrun my emotions. But when they caught up with me, for some reason I still turned to Neil. Or really, the idea of him.

The real Neil deserved better. So I made the letter sound as sensible as possible, wishing him all the best before pressing Send.

I sat back. For the first time in months, I had sent Neil McLaren an e-mail.

"I heard you ran into Neil," Nico said as I drove him home from family dinner the following night. "He's working in Portland now?"

I rolled my eyes. "Adrian's such a gossip."

"So the guy was just standing there by the river?"

"Just standing by the river. He's working at OHSU for the fall term — but I'm sure Adrian already told you that."

"He did."

We drove in silence for a while.

"How serious are you about Adrian?"

"We're very serious," I said, keeping my eyes fixed on the road. "We watch C-SPAN together every night."

"Juliette —"

"Adrian and I are fine. Nothing's changed." I took a deep breath. "When we started dating, I'd just broken up with Neil and Mom was dying. Adrian's a great guy. We're taking things easy."

"And he knows that's the deal? Because he seems serious about you."

"We've had many conversations about it," I assured him. "He and I are totally on the same page."

"You'll tell me if I have to hire a new sous-chef, though, won't you? Adrian and I have a good thing going, but if I need to hire someone else, I can."

"I . . . We . . . ," I began and failed. His request shocked me, but in fairness, there was precedent. When I'd been young and fresh from culinary school, I'd dated the sous-chef, Éric, from Nico's first restaurant venture. We'd kept it a secret, though I found out later my mother had always known.

Éric had already been thinking about leaving the restaurant and starting a place of his own, but a late-night argument spurred that move sooner than any of us had expected. We argued and Éric quit immediately, leaving for Seattle.

Unbeknownst to me, Nico's restaurant, L'uccello Blu, had been struggling to stay afloat, but without Éric's stabilizing influence the doors closed six months later.

I'd carried the guilt for years, only recently shrugging out of it like a winter coat in June. My brother was many things — adult, for one — and the experience with L'uccello Blu had taught him lessons he'd brought to Two Blue Doors.

"Of course I'd tell you," I said at last. "Why the concern all of a sudden?"

"Adrian said . . ."

I sat up straighter, my hands gripping the wheel. "What? What did he say?"

"He said you looked at Neil like you were still in love with him."

"I'm not," I said. "Neil and I are over. We've been over a long time."

"He came to Portland."

I shook my head. "No. First, he had work connections to OHSU before we met. Second, Neil came to Portland and didn't tell me about it. If he had some kind of agenda, any sort of intention to win me back, then standing around on the riverbank in hopes that I'll finally get outside for the first time in months — well, that shows some poor planning."

Nico shrugged. "The heart wants what the

heart wants."

"Bully for him." I checked my mirrors and changed lanes before responding.

"What the heart wants and what the heart gets can be two different things."

I heard the harshness of my own words but couldn't take any of them back.

Nico's voice softened with caution and concern. "When did you get so cynical, baby sis?"

When Mom died. When Neil broke my heart. When life didn't turn out the way I'd hoped it might.

I didn't answer. I couldn't.

"Look, I'm sorry," Nico said, his voice weighted with regret. "It's been a rough few months."

"It has, hasn't it?" I tried to sound light and knew that I failed. With Nico's complex in sight, I slowed the car and turned into the driveway in front of his building.

"Things will get better," he said. "I have faith. Faith enough for us both, if need be."

I reached out and patted his hand. "I appreciate that."

"You're welcome. And I mean it — a little lead time to find a new sous-chef. Even just twenty-four hours. I can do a lot in twenty-four hours."

"Adrian and I are not breaking up!"

60

"Just saying."

I parked and turned off the car before turning to face my brother. "You're a good chef and a good boss. Two Blue Doors will be fine, no matter what. I doubt lightning will strike twice."

"You've dated two sous-chefs."

"Who else do I see?" I asked with a laugh. "I'm at the restaurant every day all day."

"We have customers!"

"You're right," I answered dryly. "That would be the prudent choice."

Nico laughed out loud, and we said our good-byes before he exited the car and climbed the stairs home.

The week sped by. Adrian didn't mention Neil, and neither did I. I waited for an e-mail response at first, but after a few days I stopped waiting. Neil wasn't going to respond, and that was fine.

We hired new staff. Patrick decided to trade Portland for Williamsburg, so we replaced him with Jade the Artist and added Stan the Cellist.

Nico hired a new line cook, Diego, and trained Kenny to act as sous-chef when either he or Adrian took a night off.

I made Mallory, the young blond server who'd been with us from the beginning, assistant manager. I had her shadow me for a week, but I knew she'd take to the work easily. Half of the manager's job was being the middle person between the kitchen and dining room — if the waiters weren't picking up orders quickly enough, or if the kitchen wasn't getting orders out fast enough, the manager had to step in.

Keeping the customers happy would comprise the rest of her job, but her time as a waitress had already honed those skills.

With her kind yet no-nonsense nature, Mallory was a perfect fit. Her new position meant that I could take an extra day off — two whole days per week, all to myself.

With Sundays and Mondays to myself, I could enjoy not just a leisurely Sabbath but a less leisurely Monday to catch up on everything else. Laundry, exercise, groceries, getting Gigi groomed — all things I now had the ability to be on top of, instead of hopelessly behind on. Adrian and I even went to a movie.

"This is what they call a *theater*," I said in a mock stage whisper as we settled into our seats. "They show *moving pictures* here."

"I don't know," Adrian whispered back. "I'm not sure I believe in such things."

"We live in advanced times."

"It's a good thing we didn't choose a 3-D

movie. We might die of shock."

"Very true."

Adrian grinned. "After this, I'll really have to up my game to make your birthday meaningful."

"Nah," I said, "I don't need much."

"Come on, it's your birthday."

"Eh, it's just a day." I took a deep breath. Yes, my birthday was coming. That didn't mean I wanted to talk about it. I squeezed his hand. "Cat's coming out with her family, Clementine's making me a cake, and you're making me . . ."

"I'm not telling. It's still a surprise."

"And there I was, thinking I could trick you into telling me. I'll get to see the people I care about all in one place — other than that, I could skip it altogether."

The lights dimmed. Adrian leaned close, whispering into my ear before giving the lobe a nibble. "I just want it to be a good day for you."

I turned and kissed him gently, cupping his face. "You're a good guy," I said as the first trailer rolled onto the screen.

He kissed me back. "You make me want to be a great one."

We went to dessert afterward and enjoyed a stroll down the city streets. I relished the feel of our hands entwined together.

■ ■ ■ ■

I sat in my office the next day during the lunch seating, updating the restaurant's social media, printing up the menus for the following week. A glance at the clock told me we'd be closing up shortly, getting ready for the transition between lunch and dinner.

I rose and stretched before heading to the kitchen. The tickets had finished, and the guys were cleaning their stations and washing dishes. I waved; they waved back, and I continued to the dining room.

There were a couple of ladies at a four-top, lingering over their white wine, and two businessmen finishing a work lunch.

And then at the corner window table sat a man I recognized instantly.

He'd come. He wore a striped button-down shirt and chinos, and he sat with a slim tablet device; from where I stood, he looked to be reading a book.

Looking at him hurt, but I couldn't take my eyes off him, either. I checked in with the other diners before stopping at Neil's table. "Hi, stranger." I said, resting my fingers on the tabletop. "Mind if I have a seat?"

Neil looked up, standing immediately. "Juliette," he said, his chair scraping the floor as it moved backwards. "Hi. You're here. Here — have a seat," he said, pulling out the chair opposite his.

"Thanks," I said, willing myself not to blush. "How was your lunch?" I asked, pointing toward his plate, empty now except for a brush of crumbs.

"Very good, very good," he said, reaching for his water glass.

I remained silent while he drank. I could have used a drink myself.

"I got your e-mail," he said after swallowing.

"Oh," I answered. I didn't know what to say. After all, I'd sent it a week ago.

"I'm truly, truly sorry about your mother's passing," he said. "I can't say that enough."

Mallory returned to the dining room with the checks for the four-top; I caught her eye and flicked my fingers discreetly.

"Two mint teas, please," I said when she finished collecting credit cards. "Have you had dessert?" I asked Neil.

"Not yet."

"Two of the pumpkin-custard pies."

Mallory nodded and set off toward the kitchen, carrying, I imagined, the news that I was sitting with a man in the dining room.

65

Eating pie.

I turned back to Neil. "Some conversations are best had over tea and pie."

He nodded. "Can't argue with that." He looked around the dining room. "Nice place. Really, really nice place. I'd tell you you should be proud, but I suspect you already are."

I couldn't hold back my smile. "I am."

"You look really good."

"Ha!" I felt my face flush. "I look tired is what I look like. But I've got yet another eye cream to try, so I have hope. But you, you look . . . rested."

Neil raised an eyebrow. "Am I making you nervous?"

I willed myself to chill out. "You have to admit, this does feel a little . . . well, it's not ideal."

"I should have told you I was going to be at OHSU," he said quietly. "I didn't think you'd want to see me."

"That . . . wasn't untrue, at least for a while. But I should have written sooner."

Neil shook his head. "I wasn't any good at a long-distance relationship, so it's no wonder I couldn't hack a long-distance breakup very well."

"You were fine," I said. "It was my fault."

"No," Neil started, but I held up my hand.

"Look," I said, "we were always going to break up. If it hadn't been that weekend, it would have been some other time."

"You think so?" Neil's face was neutral, his features so carefully arranged they could have been a Dutch still-life painting.

"Of course I do," I said, looking away. I had to look away, because if I looked into his eyes I feared I'd change my mind. "But let's not waste time with all the reasons we already know. Tell me about how you are. Tell me about your fall."

He gave a half smile. "Well, we broke up. I won't lie and pretend that was easy. I missed you, missed your letters. But," he said, sitting up, "I'm good at work, so I worked hard. Hard enough that I started getting offers elsewhere. My research, you may remember, has focused on antibacterial resistance. I've been tapped to teach at OHSU, but in January I'll be moving to Atlanta, to start work with a group that's working on isolating narrow-strain pro- and prebiotics. The idea is that instead of using antibiotics to combat bacteria, we use other strains of bacteria to bring the negative bacteria into balance."

"That's fascinating."

He smiled. "I think so. We'll see where the science takes us. I just know that with the antibacterial resistance we're seeing, not only do we need to back off on the antibiotic use, but we need alternative therapies."

"Makes sense to me. So is Atlanta a temporary or permanent move?"

"I sold my house in Tennessee," he answered. "I don't know how long I'll be in Atlanta, but it's a real move."

"Wow," I said, processing. "I'm sure Callan and Tarissa will miss you."

He nodded. "And I miss them. But they've had some changes as well. Callan took a position in Chicago."

"Good for them! I remember Tarissa talking about the possibility of going back. That's where Callan's from, right?"

"His parents and his brothers are there, yes."

"Which one of you made the jump first?"

Neil tipped his head. "I left for Portland before finalizing the Atlanta job. Callan went job searching immediately after. The timing worked out, though. Callan was ready to leave the South."

"You'll miss working together," I said. "Is Tarissa okay moving? I know she had family in Memphis."

"She's okay. Callan had been talking about it long enough that she'd prepared herself for the possibility. And one of her

sisters already moved away to Columbus."
He sipped his tea. "This is very good. What
kind of tea is it?"

"Moroccan mint. Basically, it's green tea
steeped with mint leaves with lots of sugar."

"Southern sweet tea, just fancier?"

"Exactly." I pointed toward his plate. "Try
the pie. It's my favorite dessert of Clementine's so far."

Neil obliged, nodding as he chewed. "This
is" — he looked up at me — "addicting,"
he finished, his fork already returning for a
second bite. "Your roommate knows what
she's doing."

"You've told me about work," I said, after
taking another bite of pie and a deep breath.
"Have you been seeing anyone?"

5

Food is just something you grow and recipes are just words written in notebooks.

They are nothing until the right person comes along.

And that's when the real magic happens.

— SARAH ADDISON ALLEN

Neil looked down at his pie. "I've been seeing another doctor at the hospital here," he said. "It's casual. She keeps me company."

"That's great," I said.

But no. It did not feel great. I felt like my heart had been slipped into a vise three sizes too small.

"She's originally from Kentucky, so we've got the mid-South background in common."

"I've heard Kentucky is lovely," I said, vaguely aware that he was probably the person to tell me so.

"It is. Her family's in Lexington, which is nice."

"Is she in the immunology department also?" I asked. Each answer squeezed my heart tighter, but I embraced the pain. Embraced it because it was pain I knew I shouldn't be feeling.

We'd broken up.

I'd been dating Adrian for three months.

Both of those decisions were mine; I had no right to begrudge Neil the companionship of a smart, southern lady doctor.

Who was probably pretty. And blond. And without the extra curvature my thighs had developed lately.

I cut another bite of pie, ending the string of insecure thoughts with the finality of my fork against the pastry crust. My thighs were fine, and I wanted Neil to be happy.

"She is," Neil answered, "though our focuses are different. Her work centers on cancer research."

"Good for her. I hate cancer."

"I'm sorry, Juliette."

"No, no, don't be. She works in cancer research. I'm not allergic to the word." Except that I was. The word still had the power to make me short of breath.

I looked up at Neil and knew I wasn't fooling him in the least.

"Tell me about it," he said, his voice soft.

I looked around. We were the only ones in the dining room.

"It was awful," I said. "I won't sugarcoat it. But work is a great distraction, if you can stop crying often enough to talk to customers. Once everything finished — the funeral plans, the memorial — I didn't have the energy for much more than work. Some of the Italian family came out, so someone was crying all of the time. Auguste flew out to be with Sandrine." I shrugged. "It was good to see everybody, but it was a sad time."

"I'm sure."

"But we all worked hard here, and it's paid off. Lots of media coverage, steady reservations, good word of mouth."

"I bet Adrian's been good company."

"He has." It was true. "He's been very kind and very patient."

"I'm glad," Neil said, his face looking both glad and . . . not.

I had to look away from his eyes. It wasn't supposed to be like this. We weren't supposed to see each other again — not ever. That was the one benefit of ending a long-distance relationship: it wasn't as if we lived in each other's neighborhoods.

Not until now. Of all times.

"This is hard," Neil observed.

"Yes. Yes, it is." I rested my head in my hands.

"Can I be honest?"

"Sure," I said, my face still hidden away.

"We live in a social-media age."

"It's true."

"I . . . looked you up."

I sat straight. "You did?"

"I found your Instagram account. And Adrian's. I figured you guys were together."

"Oh."

"And . . . you seemed happy. So I didn't tell you about being in Portland because I didn't want to get in the way of your being happy."

"That's sweet of you."

"Not really." Neil gave a rueful smile. "The truth is — I'm not over you. So I thought it was best to stay away."

"Oh."

"But Portland's a smaller town than I thought." He gave an easy shrug. "I really am glad to see you, Juliette. I'm sorry it's been such a difficult time, but I'm glad you're doing well."

"Thanks," I said, because I had no other words. Not yet.

"And I'm sorry you haven't found the resolution you were hoping your grand-mother's letters would bring."

Letters. Yes — the letters. "I'm still hope-ful," I said. "Sandrine invited us to the chateau for Epiphany."

"Really?" I watched the memories of our time in Provence flash across his eyes, the accompanying emotions flickering over his face. "Are you going to try the key?"

I nodded eagerly. "That's the hope."

"What do you think you might find? What would your grandmother leave behind?"

"Leave behind while taking the key? No idea. And maybe she didn't mean to, maybe it just wound up in the drawer of her prep table and she didn't remember until later."

"But she never returned it," Neil pointed out.

"True. I've been looking for Benjamin," I told him. "Gabriel's brother, my great-uncle."

"Any leads?"

I gave a rueful laugh. "Nope. Not yet, at least. But he's the youngest, so I figure . . . there's a chance, you know?" I glanced at my plate and back at Neil. "I don't have a lot of hope left, in general. It just . . . dried up. But I still believe there's a chance I might find more family. Do you think that's naive?"

"No," he said. "I think it's admirable." He took a deep breath. "When you go back," he said, "give your family there my best. I enjoyed meeting them — they're good people. Kind, even when I didn't speak a word of French."

"Of course," I told him. "Of course I will."

"Neil!"

And there they were. I turned to see Nico and Adrian approach, still in their chef's whites.

"I'm sorry in advance," I whispered to Neil.

"Don't worry about it," he whispered back, before standing to shake hands with my brother and my boyfriend.

My brother, my boyfriend, and my ex-boyfriend, all together in the same dining room.

Peachy.

There were handshakes and greetings, and each man stood more upright than usual.

Adrian stood close to me, his shoulder touching mine.

Neil complimented them on the restaurant, on the deliciousness of his lunch and the success they'd seen.

"Two Blue Doors owes a lot to Juliette," Nico said. "We wouldn't be anywhere without her."

"She's one of a kind," Adrian agreed, clasping my hand in his.

75

"You're both sweet," I said. "And I hate to break up this lovefest, but both of you need to get cleaned up. I'll close up here shortly."

"I need to get back to work too," Neil said. "I've got a class shortly. Thanks for lunch. And dessert," he added, with a nod to me.

"Here, let me get you a box for the rest of the pie," I said, heading toward the kitchen. "It reheats really well."

"Ask her how to reheat it," Nico prodded Neil.

Neil cleared his throat. "How do you suggest I reheat it?"

"The microwave," I called back from the kitchen, grabbing a box from the top of the stack before returning to the men.

Nico and Adrian stood looking at me. Waiting.

"Fine." I boxed the pie and turned to Neil. "Take a paper towel or a cloth napkin, and dampen it," I said, handing him the box. "Place it over the crust and microwave it for forty-five seconds at seventy percent power, which will steam the crust and help the filling to heat through."

Neil nodded. "Makes sense."

"See?" I turned to Nico and Adrian. "He's a scientist. He gets it."

"Physics," Neil said.

I gave him a grateful smile but found once I looked at him, I couldn't look away. Neil held my gaze; I couldn't breathe.

That face. That man. I forgot how much I'd loved him.

How had that happened?

Neil's mouth quirked into a regretful smile. "I need to head back. Thanks for the lunch — and the pie."

With that, he left.

Adrian stepped toward me, pulling me into a hug. "That couldn't have been easy. You okay?"

"I think so," I said, putting my hands on either side of his face and lifting myself onto my tiptoes to give him a quick kiss.

"He seemed like he was lingering," Nico said. "We came to rescue you."

"That's very considerate of you. It was fine — really."

Adrian pressed a kiss to my temple. "I'm glad. I'm going to shower downstairs. Want to take Gigi out afterward? Grab a bite? Find a taco?"

"Sure," I said, wrapping my arm around his waist.

"Careful, there's grease there. Don't want you getting dirty."

"You're sweet," I said, smiling. "I'll see

you when you're cleaned up."

Nico headed home for a nap before the dinner seating. I considered staying in my work clothes but decided three hours in my most broken-in jeans would be three hours well spent.

"What did he say?" Adrian asked as we walked down the street toward our favorite taqueria, Gigi trotting beside us.

I picked through the words available to me, searching for the ones to summarize all that had been shared.

Maybe not all.

"We talked about our breakup," I began. "Regrets about how it happened, that sort of thing. He told me he's seeing someone at the hospital, casually. And he caught me up on his job. He'll be at OHSU through the winter, then be taking a position with a research group in Atlanta. In January."

"Atlanta," Adrian repeated. "That's cool. So he's only around for a couple more months, then."

"It is. In Atlanta he'll be doing further research on probiotic strains."

"Huh. Whatever floats his boat, I guess."

"It's cool research, especially with the antibacterial resistance we're seeing. There's a reason we're careful about the produce we use at Blue Doors."

"And we get the stuff that tastes good."

"That too." I flashed him a smile.

"So is he . . ." Adrian rubbed the back of his neck. "I don't know, I just got a vibe."

"Vibe?"

"I don't think he's over you, babe."

I sighed and threaded my arm through his. "Does it matter?"

"It matters if you're not over him."

"Seeing Neil — it's a lot to process." And it was. It felt like it had been somehow years and seconds since he and I had been together. "I never expected to see him again." I held tighter to Adrian's arm. "But we broke up for good reasons."

"No second thoughts?"

I adjusted my hold on Gigi's leash. "Second thoughts don't matter. It's the next thought after that counts."

"What does that mean, Juliette?"

"It means you're the one I'm walking to get tacos with." I stepped onto my toes to land a kiss on his stubbled jaw. "Neil and I have a history," I said. "But we decided against having a future last summer."

"What do you think about our future?"

"I see tacos in our future," I said. "Tacos and a birthday gathering, if I can't talk you out of it."

"You deserve to be celebrated."

"What if we celebrated just the two of us? Dinner out, somewhere private and romantic?"

"How about we do something after?" he offered. "You'll want to see your family. Caterina will be here." He squeezed my hand. "We'll get everyone together, you don't have to cook, and I'll make sure Nico doesn't try to use trick candles."

"That's very sweet of you," I said, "but the one you really have to watch for is Damian."

"Good to know."

"Usually because he's Caterina's henchman."

Adrian gave a sage nod. "That I can comprehend."

The dinner seating was quiet that night, not unusual for a Tuesday. Nico called out orders and the echoes of "Yes, chef!" called back in an orderly fashion.

By the time the doors closed for the evening, the dishes were already sparkling and the till closed out. Nico and Clementine slipped out the back door together.

Adrian showered in the basement before climbing the stairs to my apartment, where we curled up on the couch together and flipped through the TV channels.

"Hey, *Doctor Who!*" I exclaimed as a TARDIS flew across the screen.

Adrian paused his flipping. "What is it?"

"*Doctor Who,* classic British TV show."

"That looks like one of those old-school phone booths."

"It's close — it's a police call box."

"Fine by me." Adrian leaned back, his hand burrowing into my hair.

"That feels nice."

"You're welcome," he said, continuing to rub my scalp. When he stopped, I glanced over, only to see he'd fallen asleep.

I watched the rest of the episode and didn't move to change the channel when the next episode began.

The next one . . . it seemed familiar.

I'd seen it. I'd seen it with Neil, in Memphis. My heart squeezed with the realization.

A breath in, a breath out. I changed the channel, found an episode of *Parks and Recreation* to watch instead, and rested my hand against Adrian's.

I am exactly where I want to be, I reminded myself as the sound of a saxophone filled the room. I leaned back and closed my eyes, willing myself to remember.

~ PUMPKIN-CUSTARD PIE ~

2 eggs
1/2 cup sugar
1/4 cup molasses
1 1/2 cups canned pumpkin
1 1/2 cups whole milk
1/2 cup cream
1/4 teaspoon salt
1/4 teaspoon ground ginger
1 teaspoon cinnamon
1/8 teaspoon cloves (I use 1/4 teaspoon)
1/2 teaspoon allspice
Scant 1/2 teaspoon lemon juice
1 recipe pastry (see pages 53–55)
1 egg (beaten)
Demerara sugar

In a stand mixer, beat eggs until pale. Add sugar and molasses, and continue to mix for another 2 minutes. Slow to a stir, adding the pumpkin, whole milk, cream, spices, and lemon juice.

Roll pastry dough to 1/6-inch thickness, and arrange inside pie plate. Trim the dough to about 1 inch around the circumference of the plate, and tuck the edges under. Brush the top of the crust — the crust you'll see after the filling is poured in — with the beaten egg, using a pastry brush or your fingers. Sprinkle demerara sugar on top.

Butter the base of the piecrust to prevent the crust from becoming soggy while baking. Fold aluminum foil loosely around the edge, to cover the top of the crust. Pour in the filling.

Bake at 425°F for 15 minutes, then turn the oven down to 350°F for about 30 minutes. Remove the foil, and bake for another 15 minutes, or until the pastry is golden and the pie is set around the edges.

Serves 8.

6

There is nothing better than a friend, unless it is a friend with chocolate.
— LINDA GRAYSON

"Juliette!" my sister Caterina called out the moment she saw me at the Portland International Airport.

"Caterina!" I called back, ignoring the heads that turned.

She approached with open arms. "My darling," she said. "My everything. My all."

"It's been too long!"

"It's been forever!" She wrapped me in a giant hug. The close contact, her perfume — it was the closest thing to a hug from my mom, and I almost dissolved into tears right there by the luggage carousel.

"Hi, Juliette," Damian said, a camera bag and son Luca in one hand, a Thomas the Tank Engine backpack and son Christian in the other, both boys writhing like eels out of water.

"Hi, Damian," I said, not budging from my sister's hug. "Thanks for bringing her."

"You're welcome," he answered cheerfully. "Happy birthday."

"It's not my birthday yet," I said, which only caused the boys to hear the word "birthday" and begin to chant it like a mantra.

Caterina threw a chagrined glance at her flailing, chanting twin boys. "I gave them M&M's during the flight to keep them quiet. They'll be coming down off that high for the next few hours, I'm afraid, and it won't be pretty."

I reached down and picked up four-year-old Luca, hoisting him into the air. "Grandpa's house for you!" I said. "No better place to come down off a sugar high."

Luca squealed and giggled, and I repeated the process a moment later with Christian. And then Luca again. Followed by Christian.

"You're committed," Caterina said. "I hope you know that."

I shifted Christian to my back, where he clung like a monkey. "They'll sleep sometime, right?"

"That," Caterina said, "is a vicious urban legend."

Damian snorted.

"I want to ride on your back!" Luca demanded, tugging my free hand.

"I'll carry you, buddy," Damian offered, reaching for him, but Luca shook his father off.

"I want to be with Auntie Etta!"

Caterina gave a sage nod. "Surely you are blessed among women."

"Christian gets three more minutes," I said, "and then we'll switch."

"And no arguing," Caterina added, "or you're both walking on those big, strong feet of yours."

"The man at the store said they were small for my age," Luca pointed out.

"Small but strong," Caterina answered. "Like a chicken hawk."

Within seconds the boys regaled me with their collected knowledge on the nature of the chicken hawk, which turned to a recitation of every notable bird they'd ever learned about or seen speak in an animated feature.

I loaded the boys into Dad's Volvo, buckling them into the car seats that my parents had kept at their house for Caterina's visits.

"I'll sit in the back with the boys," Damian offered. "You ladies catch up."

"That's very sweet of you." Caterina gave

her husband a peck on the cheek.

"You were about to call shotgun anyway."

She shrugged. "It's true."

He kissed her. "Have fun. We're going to be discussing the finer points of *Despicable Me* versus *Megamind.*"

"Pff. *Megamind,* no contest."

We loaded the rest of the luggage into the trunk before loading ourselves. I'd hardly put the car into reverse before Caterina leaned toward me. "Nico said Neil came to the restaurant."

I finished backing out of my narrow parking space before rolling my eyes. "He did, yes."

"And?"

I gave Cat the highlights — OHSU, Atlanta, his dating relationship with a work colleague.

"Did he say dating?"

"I don't know. 'Seeing'?"

"Hmm."

"It doesn't matter. Neil is an old chapter."

"You guys had a lot of history together, though."

"So do Adrian and I," I answered, hating how defensive I sounded.

Caterina nodded. "That's true. How are things there? He sounded a little squirrelly last time we talked."

"Eh." I shrugged. "He's having a grand old time planning my birthday."

"That's sweet."

"It is."

"But you don't much want a birthday."

I winced. "Not much."

"Tell him to dial back. We can do whatever you want. Dickie Jo's for burgers. Dar Essalam for tagine."

"I do like tagine. He's having a good time, and I hate to get in the way of that."

"Your choice. But you're, like, full-body wincing, and that's not good."

"It'll be fine. It'll make Dad happy."

"I'm bringing him grand-boys. He'll be perfectly contented building train tracks with them."

"That's true. So do you have any hopes and dreams for this trip?" I asked, changing the subject. "Anywhere in Portland you want to visit while you're here?"

"I'd like to go to Powell's. The boys could use some more picture books, and it's cheaper here without the sales tax."

"True."

"And it's a thin yet socially acceptable excuse to go hang out at a bookstore."

"Since when do you need an excuse?"

Cat sighed. "Mom guilt. Pass it on."

"Gotcha. Well, I'm off tomorrow night.

Want to make a trip?"

"Yes!"

"Want to bring the boys?"

"Let's go after they're in bed. Powell's is open late, isn't it? I love my boys very much," Cat said, the sentence punctuated by Christian kicking her seat "like a ninja" and Damian admonishing him to stop, "but I feel at peace leaving them at home to look at books."

"Fair enough," I said, even as Luca caught on and started kicking mine.

Soon enough, we reached our parents' house — *Dad's house,* I corrected myself in my head. I helped unload and carry the luggage while the boys ran up the stairway to the front door and their grandfather's waiting arms.

And trains.

Caterina slung a duffel bag over her shoulder. "Let me know about the birthday stuff. If there's anything I can do to make it easier, you just tell me, 'kay?"

"I will," I promised. "There might not be anything, though. It might just be hard."

"I know," Caterina said softly.

"I'm really glad you're here."

She grinned. "Me too."

"There's something about the smell of

books," Caterina said the following night, taking a deep breath as we stepped through the doors at Eleventh and Burnside.

"Paper and binding agents, printer's ink . . ."

". . . and words," Caterina finished.

"And words," I agreed. "Words are the best." I looked around, taking in the tall shelves. "Where to first? Which floor?"

"I want to look for books for the boys, so maybe do that last? So I'm not carrying picture books up three flights of stairs?"

"Better to carry cookbooks?"

"Exactly."

I looped my arm around her elbow, and we strode toward the aisles of books. That lasted for about fifteen seconds — Caterina wandered down one aisle while I got distracted by another. We worked our way through the store that way, occasionally engaging in a game of Marco Polo, never straying too far from each other.

At least, not until she decided to hit the children's books. I discovered I could entertain myself looking at the vintage copies of *Anne of Green Gables* for a significant period of time, but both of us had underestimated Caterina's capacity for looking at books for the boys.

"Am I a terrible aunt if I'm thinking about

heading upstairs to see if the Rare Book Room is open?"

Caterina laughed and shook her head. "Go in peace. I'll catch up with you in a little bit."

I dashed away with a grateful wave, weaving my way out of the children's department and up the stairs, down the mezzanine, and up the two additional flights of stairs to the Pearl Room.

After jogging up the three flights of stairs, I felt glad for the exercise but a little winded. I turned toward the Rare Book Room, only to be met with a deeply unexpected sight.

Neil McLaren, leaning casually against the information desk. So casual, he might have been in the midst of a James Dean impersonation.

He saw me about a half instant after I spotted him; he straightened, a bemused smile stretching across his face. "Of all the gin joints."

"We seem to keep running into each other," I said, or at least tried to. It sounded more like an asthmatic wheeze to my ears.

"Well, where else is a person going to buy a book in this town?"

"There are, technically, other options."

"But not as spacious — or as confusing

91

— as this one."

I gave a rueful shrug. "It does help to be local. Did you get a map?"

He pulled it from the back pocket of his pants. "I did. Got me here — I've heard the Rare Book Room is really something."

"Is it open? I'd planned to poke my head in if it was."

"I asked. Someone's out looking for the right person with the right key."

"Oh." My face flushed with pleasure. Or maybe it was just the exercise. I couldn't much tell.

"So what are you up to?" He gestured to my pile of cookbooks. "Personal shopping?"

"A little. Cat's here in town; she wanted to make a trip."

"Cat's here?"

"I lost her to the children's section, but yes. You never met Cat, did you?"

"Just Sophie and your brothers. And most of the rest of your family, I think."

I snorted out an awkward chuckle. "You really have met most of my family. Not too many people can say that."

A stereotypically pierced and tattooed employee approached with a kindly smile, and within minutes Neil and I followed her inside the Rare Book Room.

"This is really something," Neil said, with

an appreciative glance over the room's contents.

I turned to my left and pointed to a familiar spine. "This is the one you have to see. Well, you can't see it so much as appreciate the photo rendering. It's the Lewis and Clark book."

"*History of the Expedition Under the Command of Captains Lewis and Clark to the Sources of the Missouri, Thence Across the Rocky Mountains and Down the River Columbia to the Pacific Ocean*," Neil read reverently, his soft southern accent more pronounced. "Oh my."

"It's the most valuable book in the collection. They don't even keep it here. It's in a vault or something. It's listed for $350,000."

Neil nodded. "Fair enough."

"And it's on the website too. I looked once. There was only one review, but I thought it would be a funny one for those crank reviews — you know the ones I'm talking about? Like the Amazon reviews for the banana slicer?"

"And the uranium in a tin? They are funny."

"I feel like someone should leave a funny review, talk about how the plot meandered and the author doesn't seem to have first-hand knowledge, and the romance isn't compelling. Something silly like that."

"No good explosions?"

I gave a soft laugh. "Yeah. Like that."

"Why don't you write it?"

"Me? It'd be the only one. I'd be the strange crank. You never know on any given day whether someone in this town has a sense of humor or not."

Neil gave a rueful chuckle. "I have noticed that. So — tell me about Cat. Is she here for the fun of it or coming out for something specific?"

I sighed and rubbed my neck. "My birthday."

"I feel like I should have known that." He studied me, raising a ginger eyebrow. "I'd wish you happy birthday, but your face is saying no."

"It's . . . not the same without my mom. So really, I'd just as soon skip the whole thing."

"But Cat's here, so you don't get to skip?"

"Cat would pretend it's Halloween and go trick-or-treating with me dressed as the reindeer from *Frozen* if I asked her. Adrian is . . . enthusiastic about throwing a party. What can ya do?"

"You could boycott."

"He's a good guy, and his intentions are in the right place. I'll manage. If the worst I have to deal with are the good intentions of other people, things can't be so bad."

Neil opened his mouth as if to disagree but seemed to think better of it. "Well, I hope you find yourself enjoying the day, somehow."

"That's kind of you. But really, I'd rather just pretend it's not happening."

"Then it's not. I don't mind pretending with you."

"Thanks."

Our gazes caught and held in that moment. It seemed every time we saw each other — three times now — that each encounter led to such a moment. A current of unspoken words flowed between us, enough that I could almost see them, so many I couldn't hope to untangle even a handful.

What I knew most was that I didn't want the moment to end.

In the end, I didn't have much of a choice in the matter.

"Hey, Etta, I finally pulled myself away from the picture books," came my sister's very distinct voice. "I forgot how good the selection is here. I — um, hi."

I tore my gaze away. "Cat. Hi."

"Hi," she answered back. I couldn't read her face.

"This is — this is Neil. Neil, this is Caterina. My sister."

Cat extended a hand toward Neil. "It's nice to meet you. I heard you're in Portland for the short term."

"I am," Neil said. "It's a great city, I've enjoyed my time."

"My husband and I live in Chicago, but in its own way Portland still feels like home." Cat turned back to me. "Well, I'm going to the art-history section —"

"I'll go with you," I said quickly. If I stayed longer, I didn't know what would happen. And I didn't need to know. I was happy as I was, happy with Adrian. Neil would leave Portland eventually, and no amount of mooning at him in a bookstore would change that.

I turned to Neil, carefully schooling my features. "It was good to see you," I said. "I hope you find a good book."

"I hope you have a quiet weekend," Neil answered.

We waved awkward good-byes, and I stepped out with Cat, my hand on her arm for stability.

"Okay — art history," I said, looking around. "Where is that again?"

"No idea. It was the first subject that came to mind — you looked like you were in the middle of something. I was going to give you more time."

"I think more time is the last thing we need."

"So that's Neil. I've seen the pictures you showed me, but wow. He's got a good face. Like, a *Masterpiece Theater* face."

"I don't even know what that means. Shall we check out? If you're not actually interested in nineteenth-century art, and if you're done with the rest of your shopping, I think I'd like to go home."

"We can check out. Are you — wow. I mean, I couldn't tell that you were with someone until I came in." Caterina pulled me into one of the tall, thankfully empty aisles. "Seriously, you looked like you were seconds away from a *From Here to Eternity* moment. Less the beach, I suppose . . . I should probably pick a different movie. But is there something I, ah, need to know?"

"We weren't about to make out, if that's what you're trying to say," I said, pulling away.

She pressed the books in her hands close to her chest. "I'm a married lady, Etta. I know make-out face."

"Is that a thing? And a qualification?"

"I think you're deflecting."

"And you're misconstruing a moment."

Cat sighed. "I'm sorry. You just . . . You looked like you really missed him."

I didn't answer. I couldn't. There were only questions in my head where answers used to be.

7

Bear in mind that you should conduct yourself in life as at a feast.

— **EPICTETUS**

"This is dialed down?" I asked Cat, surveying the birthday scene from the safety of the entryway of my father's restaurant, D'Alisa & Elle. "This is dialed down," she assured me. "You wouldn't believe the things I talked him out of."

I squinted at the sight. "Do I want to know?"

Cat paused. "No . . . ," she said after a moment's reflection. "I don't think so."

I groaned.

"It's cute," she said. "He likes you."

"If you think it's so adorable, I'll send him your way for your birthday."

Cat laughed. "I think it's all for you, darlin'."

I knew she was right, but I couldn't do

99

anything but shake my head. The crowd consisted of my family, Clementine, my friend Linn, and her husband. Surrounding them was enough food to stock all of our freezers for the next three months.

If the dining-room tables hadn't been so stable, they would have sagged from the weight of the food. There were antipasti platters, a butternut-squash *strata* with sage, and a casserole dish of baked ziti. On the sweet side there were pear tartlets, an apple cake, fresh figs with mascarpone and honey. At the end waited a towering croquembouche — a pyramid of cream-filled choux puffs encased in a glamorous tangle of spun sugar.

It was a lovely party, but it didn't matter how much food waited and how many loved ones milled about, half of whom I hadn't seen since the memorial.

It was too fresh. There were too many people. I wasn't ready.

The amount of effort Adrian had gone to — it was sweet. Romantic, from some angles. Many angles. But I also felt a knot of frustration that I'd told him so many times I wanted a quiet day.

I watched as Gigi danced from partygoer to partygoer, enjoying the attention. At least someone was having a grand time. In truth, it looked as though everyone else was. I took a deep breath and pasted a smile on my face. If I could carry on through the last few months, I could certainly carry on through my own birthday party.

I worked from left to right, greeting my guests. I started with my father, using his hug to bolster me through the rest of the room. Before long, I'd exchanged pleasantries with nearly everyone, and I found Sophie in the corner, waving me down.

"Happy birthday!" Sophie, my oldest sister, gave me a warm hug. "This is such a beautiful party."

"I can't at all take credit for it."

"It's your birthday, of course you can."

"Fair point," I said with a smile. Sophie and I had endured our relational ups and downs over the years, owing partly to our age gap — eight years — and partly to the differences in our personalities. Sophie liked certainty, efficiency, and routine with an intensity more typically observed in the military. She'd married her accountant husband, Nelson, at twenty-four and proceeded to live out the suburban dream in a way that felt distinctly foreign to me. But the past months had brought us closer together; we'd gotten better at listening to each other and being gracious about differences in opinion.

Not perfect, but better.

"We need to talk about Thanksgiving," Sophie said. "I'd like us all to make plans before it gets much later."

"Thanksgiving? Already?" Granted it was only a week away, but Thanksgiving meant Christmas, followed by New Year's and Epiphany — all holidays we'd be celebrating without our mother.

Nonetheless, Sophie remained resolute. "It's important for us to be together."

"You're right. We should be together. And it does take scheduling."

"It doesn't have to be elaborate. Speaking of, this is quite the shindig."

"Yes. Yes it is."

"Chloé was looking for you, by the way."

"Oh? I haven't seen her yet — I think Luca and Christian got her first."

"I think there's a boy at school."

I turned and stared at my sister. "Oh?"

Sophie shrugged. "Kid's thirteen. It happens."

"Oh my goodness."

"And I'm the mom — I'm not cool." Sophie shrugged. "Not that I was cool before motherhood, either. But Chloé was very intent on talking to you in person."

"Gotcha."

"Just remind her she can't date until she's sixteen, please? That's the official policy and I'm sticking to it."

"I won't tell her to elope, don't worry."

This time Sophie turned to me. "We do not joke about the *e* word."

"Noted."

"She's getting married in a church. With air-conditioning. None of this hipster barn business."

"I'm sure that by the time she gets married, barns will be out of style."

"Here's hoping."

"I'm sure grain silos will be the next big thing."

Sophie's eyes pressed shut. "You're awful."

"That smooth, modern, cylindrical design. Just wait. So sleek, so modern —"

"So full of corn."

I shrugged. "If they can empty the barn of cows, I'm sure there's an empty silo to be had."

Sophie took a sip of her drink. "You're a monster, I hope you know that."

"It's possible." I winked at my sister. "Don't worry. I've spent enough time in polyester satin to appreciate the advantages of central air." I saw Caterina's boys dashing around and Chloé ducking upstairs. "I think there's a game of hide-and-seek afoot. I'll see if I can catch up with Chloé."

"Tell her to make good choices."

"I'll give you a full report as I'm able."

I followed Chloé up the stairs. There were a number of places to hide on the second floor of the restaurant. Aside from the catering kitchen where Alex worked, there were two private event rooms upstairs that, after the recession, had become storage rooms and never quite transitioned back. As the economy improved, the catering business picked up, but the banquet rooms gathered dust.

I climbed the stairs quietly, though not before Luca caught up with me. I assured him that I hadn't seen Chloé and suggested that possibly he might wish to check the downstairs again.

There was a sturdy old wardrobe that my mother had placed in the upstairs hallway for guests' coats, once upon a time, and we'd found Chloé inside it more than a few times, occasionally asleep while trying to enter Narnia. My mother, a C. S. Lewis fan, had once gone so far as to hang a couple of fur coats inside.

"Knock, knock," I said as I approached. "Chloé, honey, are you in here?"

"I'm hiding from the boys" came a voice

from the wardrobe.

"Room for two in there?"

A slight scuffling noise. "I think so."

I slipped off my sandals and opened the wardrobe door. "Hallo."

My niece grinned up at me. "Hi."

"Are you playing hide-and-seek because you wanted to play, or because you needed to hide?"

Chloé lifted a slight shoulder. "Bit of both."

"How are you?"

A heavy sigh. "High school is crazy."

"Getting around all right?"

"I just feel . . . young." She wrinkled her nose.

"Freshman year's rough."

"Aunt Juliette?"

"Yes?"

A deep breath from Chloé. "How do you know when you're in love?"

"Oh . . . I don't know that I'm the right person to ask," I answered as soon as I could string a sentence together.

"But you love Adrian, don't you?"

"He's very special to me," I hedged.

"So how did you know?"

"The man you love — he's the one you prefer to all others. The one you compare all the others to." I tucked a piece of hair behind my ear. "The one that suits you, whom you can see sharing your life with, making sacrifices for."

"Did you feel that way about Neil?"

"Not enough," I said. "In the end. Why do you ask?"

"He was nice."

"He is." I waited a beat. "Is there . . . a boy at school?"

I didn't need much light in order to see Chloé's flush. "He's very nice."

"Good. He should be."

I could feel her head nod against the back of the wardrobe. "He's nice. He texts me and stuff."

"Cool. Just . . . just remember that having a boy like you — or not — doesn't make you any more or any less special."

Another nod.

"I mean high-school boys think that Axe body spray is cool. So their taste can't always be trusted."

She snorted. "He doesn't."

"I'm relieved." I put a hand on her knee. "Don't worry about falling in love. Those things have a way of working themselves out one way or another."

In my case, it had so often been "another." But I wasn't worse for it — and I didn't want Chloé to feel pressured.

"I should probably head back downstairs," I said, nudging the wardrobe door open with my foot. "If you'd like to come down, I'll protect you. There's some really good food down there."

Chloé climbed out with me. "I think Adrian loves you. He made a lot of food."

"He did. But he is a cook too. It's kind of his thing."

She looked up at me, doubtful eyebrow raised.

I sighed. "You are the spitting image of your mom," I said. "Let's go get plates."

Downstairs, I drank the spiced cider, made small talk, and caught up with Linn, whom I'd seen all too infrequently since the restaurant opened. At the same time, I kept an eye out for Chloé and made sure her cousins weren't pestering her too much. My shoulders were just beginning to loosen when Adrian tapped his fork against his glass.

Everyone quieted — even Nico.

Adrian raised his glass. "Thank you, everyone, for coming and helping me celebrate this amazing woman. Juliette D'Alisa, you're the kindest, strongest, most beautiful woman I've ever known. I'm honored to be in your life, and I'm honored to have gotten to know the people you share it with," he

107

said, acknowledging the other guests. "To Juliette!"

"To Juliette!" everyone echoed back.

Adrian took a long drink from his glass, holding eye contact with me all the while. He lowered it with a sly wink, then set the glass on the table and reached into his pocket.

"And it's because you're so special," he said, his voice only a shade quieter, "and smart and lovely — and one of the best cooks I've ever met."

The hairs on the back of my neck prickled.

"Juliette Carolina D'Alisa," he said, kneeling in front of me and pulling a small box from his pocket. "Would you . . . would you do me the honor of marrying me?"

I froze. A diamond solitaire glinted in the fragile November sun; Adrian's eyes shone with emotion.

Oh. My.

8

I will marry you if you promise not to make me eat eggplant.
— GABRIEL GARCÍA MÁRQUEZ

My gaze flickered from Adrian to Caterina and back, with a side trip to Chloé, whose face echoed an "I told you so" that resembled her mother's.

I didn't know what to say; none of their faces held any answers. Adrian's, at least, hoped for one in particular.

But it was one I didn't know if I could give.

I looked down at the ring again.

It would be so easy. Almost.

I could see our future unspooling, like the longest strand of angel-hair pasta. He and I could marry, could work at the restaurant together during our work days, fall into bed together after hours. We'd have the life my parents had, raise our children amidst the hustle and bustle of restaurant life, teaching them to negotiate life from both sides of the swinging kitchen door.

I saw it; I could understand it.

So why did my mouth feel so very dry?

"That is *so* romantic," Caterina's voice trilled at the edge of the room. "Let's give the lovebirds some privacy, shall we?"

"Juliette?" Adrian asked in a softer voice this time, a voice meant for us and us alone. "Juliette, baby, you're making me nervous here."

"We never" — I cleared my throat but couldn't seem to manage above a whisper — "we never talked about marriage. We never . . . I didn't expect . . ."

Adrian's face paled. "We love each other."

"We — we do." Didn't we?

"I love you, Juliette. And I think we make a great couple. We want the same things out of life. I want to spend my life with you. I thought . . . I thought you wanted the same."

"I don't know what I want," I admitted with a raspy voice.

"What?"

"I —" I cleared my throat again. Adrian reached over to the table and handed me a cup of cider.

"Drink this," he said, his voice soft and

110

controlled. "I think it was Sophie's, so it's very clean."

I would have accepted it if it were Gigi's water dish. I downed the contents, grateful for the tart liquid against my dry mouth.

When I'd emptied it, I set the glass aside. "Stand up," I said. "I feel strange talking down to you."

He stood, snapping the box shut but keeping it in his fist. "This was a mistake."

Perhaps we had both made mistakes. "I thought we were happy as we were."

"You don't want to marry me." It was a statement rather than a question.

"We've only been dating a few months," I said with a shake of my head, bewildered that I had to point it out. "And everything with my mom, and I'm just now *almost* beginning to feel like I'm getting my feet back under me. I'm not ready for . . . for this. And I'm sorry I must have communicated otherwise." I looked into Adrian's stricken face. "Really, I am." My voice hitched, and my eyes welled with tears. "I'm so, so sorry."

"No, I'm sorry. Look at me, making you cry on your birthday." His arms reached for me, and I accepted the embrace.

"Do you ever think you'll want to marry me?" Adrian asked. "I wish I didn't need to know, but . . . I just . . . I have a ring and I need to know what to do with it."

Once again, I envisioned a life with Adrian. There was nothing wrong with it — possibly everything right with it, even. But nothing in my being said yes. No internal cue, no heavenly intervention.

"Is it Neil?" Adrian asked before I could formulate an answer.

"We haven't known each other that long," I repeated. "I don't think Neil factors into this."

"Are you sure?"

And then I saw it, finally. Saw what I should have caught instantly. The insecurity in his eyes. I didn't doubt how he felt about me — I never had, with Adrian. But this moment? It wasn't about his love for me.

It had everything to do with his fear that he'd lose me to Neil. Neil, who'd be leaving for Georgia in a matter of weeks.

"Neil has a different life, I have a different life," I told him. "You know that."

Adrian tucked a strand of hair behind my ear. "I'm not sure it's that simple."

I caught his hand and held it in my own. "Look, my feelings, they're complicated, and don't make me explain why. But the fact of the matter is that Neil and I didn't work and we broke up."

He fingered the ring box. "I don't like feeling like this."

"I don't know what to tell you." My eyes squeezed shut. "I might still love him. I don't know. But it doesn't matter, because *we broke up.* Even if he's not over me either —"

Adrian drew himself up taller. "Did he tell you that?"

"Does it matter?"

"Of course it matters!"

I flinched but stood my ground. "Not enough. And you know why? Because it wasn't ever enough. We didn't choose each other, he and I, when things were difficult. It would never have worked out."

My eyes and nose filled with moisture, my voice sounding impassioned and nasal all at the same time. "There are too many feelings to sort out, so I try to remember the facts. He and I are not in a relationship. You and I like each other. And as far as the future, I'm sorry. I need more time." I sniffed. "I'm sorry."

Adrian stuffed the ring into his pocket. "I need to go for a walk."

There was a time when I would have cringed at the thought of my family witnessing a marriage proposal gone wrong. And while I knew there would be other wince-worthy events in my future, the post-party breakdown wasn't one of them.

Caterina took the lead, yet again, announcing loudly that I wasn't allowed to help with cleanup because it was my birthday, and then promptly bundled me up and loaded me into the car along with Gigi and the boys.

"We're going to the park," she said. "It's dry out, it's not dark yet, and the boys aren't tired enough. I suspect this will be a good evening to aim for an early bedtime."

"I like the way you think," I said, "but what's going on at the house?"

"Sophie's running point. Nico's entertaining the nonfamily guests until they leave. Everybody else is following Sophie's bidding."

"That's impressive."

"We formed a plan inside."

"Everyone was watching?"

"Just focus on the fact that there was a plan."

I shook my head. "Cat, what am I going to do?"

"Do you want to marry Adrian?"

"We've only been dating for three months. I was still trying to figure out what to give him for Christmas."

"I knew I wanted to marry Damian after two weeks."

"I'm not ready — for heaven's sake, there's been too much going on. I haven't even been thinking about marriage."

"Then don't marry him."

"I don't want to hurt him," I said in a small voice.

Caterina's lips twisted into a sympathetic smile. "That may not be possible. You can mitigate the damage, but usually once you decline an offer of marriage . . ."

"I know." I covered my face with my hands. "Sister cone of silence?"

"Sister cone of silence," Caterina affirmed.

"I look at Neil, and all of it comes rushing back. Not all of it, actually. All of a sudden, I can't remember why we broke up. I look at his face, and I don't want to look away."

"I got that. There was some Aragorn and Arwen realness when I walked in. Trust me when I say I think it's mutual."

"We were good at being together and terrible at being long distance. And now that he's here — I don't want to let him go. Which is so, so stupid because he's only here temporarily, and he's *not* mine. What is wrong with me? I can remind myself of every valid reason why we shouldn't be together and still . . ." I waved a hand in frustration. "Why didn't I feel like this when we were actually together?"

"Maybe . . . maybe your mango wasn't ripe."

I squinted at Cat. "I'm not following. You're going to have to take me there."

"There's a part in *You've Got Mail* when Kathleen and Joe have been hanging out together. Joe knows their online identities, but she doesn't. And they go to the farmers' market, and before parting ways she says, 'I hope your mango's ripe,' and he gives her this considering look and tells her that he thinks it is."

"That is a very obscure reference."

"The point is, the mango was a metaphor for their relationship. He'd waited until she'd grown and softened under the sunlight, and once she'd gotten there, he made his move — both before and after revealing his identity."

"It says a lot about Tom Hanks that none of this is creepy."

"True."

"So you're saying that Neil and I weren't ready yet."

"Maybe not. I mean, I just met him for the first time, but maybe you needed the extra time. Maybe you weren't ready yet."

I shook my head. "And I needed to lose Mom and date Adrian to be ready?"

"I didn't say it was a perfect metaphor. Don't blame the mango." She tipped her head. "So, sister cone of silence. Are you thinking of breaking it off with Adrian?"

"No." I shook my head. "It's not his fault."

"You didn't run off and buy a ring."

"He felt insecure. That's my fault."

Caterina exhaled slowly. "Not really. He's still an adult, responsible for his own feelings and actions."

"What am I going to do? This is such a mess. *This,*" I said, my voice rising in volume, "*this* is why I insisted on never dating a sous-chef ever again! And I did it anyway! And look what happened!"

"That really is your superpower, isn't it? You're irresistible to sous-chefs."

"I know it's funny, but it doesn't feel funny."

"Oh, it's funny. Trust."

"You're not helping."

"What do you want to do?"

"I want to get away," I said, not realizing until the words were out how much it was true.

"So get away."

"Thanksgiving is around the corner."

117

"Get away after Thanksgiving."

I toyed with the thought in my head.

I could, really. I could leave. Mallory could run the front of the house, and I could handle any administrative tasks remotely. Gigi could stay with Alex so she'd have a person to hang out with when he wasn't on a catering gig . . .

"You know that if I get away, I'm going to land in your guest bedroom," I said, testing the waters.

Caterina cocked her head. "You say that like it's a bad thing."

"I'm giving you the opportunity to say no."

She snorted. "As if."

"Fine. I'll talk to Nico and Mallory. If Mallory can fill the hours, I will pack a suitcase."

"Yay! When?"

"I'll see if there are seats left on your flight."

Caterina inhaled sharply. "I'm so happy right now."

"You're happy to have an extra set of adult hands to help with the twins."

"That hadn't even occurred to me."

"Liar."

She shrugged. "You're right. It totally did. But can you imagine — I might be able to have a three-second, sentient conversation with Damian during the flight. And if I got to have a three-second conversation with you too, I'd be living the dream!"

"Nico would kill me."

"Nico's a big boy and he owes you."

I grinned. "I'll see what I can do. I'm due for some time away anyway. I've been meaning to get back to trying to find Gabriel's brother Benjamin, or one of his children."

"Still trying to find Mom's secret twin? Alice?"

"My gut says she's out there somewhere. I feel we'd know if it weren't true."

"A lot of things happened during the war that we don't know about, and that generation didn't discuss them," Caterina countered. "It's not good, but it happened."

"I know. I just . . . I just feel like Cécile might have said something — at least, if it were more of an open secret. She was very open about Gabriel, during her good days."

"That's true. Well, come and use my Internet. The boys are in preschool until one, and I teach on Tuesdays and Thursdays. When we're out, the house is very quiet. When we're home . . . less so."

"It sounds perfect."

Caterina gave a beatific smile. "You say that now. Just wait until you find a stray puddle of urine."

"I thought they were doing better with that."

"When they're tired, well — the aim, not so good."

"I'll be on my guard."

"I recommend shower shoes."

"I can wear shower shoes."

Cat reached out and squeezed my hand. "I can't wait."

The plans fell into place with impressive ease that night. Mallory leaped at the chance to take on the extra hours, and Alex happily agreed to let Gigi stay with him. I shelled out a ridiculous amount of money on a one-way ticket, and the boys danced with joy.

I texted Adrian, suggesting we meet in the kitchen before hours.

He showed up looking wonderfully handsome yet frayed around the edges; my heart broke just looking at him. I handed him the extra cup of coffee I'd brewed that morning.

"I'm heading out for a little while, after Thanksgiving," I said. "I need to clear my head, and Caterina's guest room seemed a good place to do it."

He took a sip of the coffee before setting

the cup onto the stainless-steel countertop. "Is this it? Are we done?"

I hated the hurt in his voice. "I didn't say that. I just want to get away for a little while, get my head together."

"It's been a good run, you and me. We're good together."

"I know. I'm just not ready, and I don't have any idea when I might be."

He stepped forward and wrapped his arms around me. "I rushed you. Like a jerk."

"You weren't a jerk."

"Did I embarrass you?"

My silence confirmed it.

"Then I was a jerk," he said. "Can I be honest?"

"Always."

"I was jealous of Neil, when you two were together. He's this smart guy, he knows things about bacteria and stuff." He leaned against the counter. "I'm just a kitchen guy. Seeing him again . . ."

"Ah," I said, feeling stupid, as though I should have pieced it together myself. I *should* have, and I didn't.

"I didn't want you to be the one that got away. I didn't want to lose you to that guy."

I ran my hand over my face. "I don't think whatever happened between Neil and me can be undone. We might be friends in the

121

future, we might not, but . . . that's life, I guess."

"But now you're leaving for Chicago."

"I just need a break to clear my head."

"How long are you planning on being gone?"

"Not sure," I said, looking away. "The one-way ticket was cheaper, and I want to come back feeling . . . feeling like myself again. At least as much as I can."

He considered my words and nodded. "If that's what you need, I want you to have it."

"Thank you for being cool. About this. All of this."

He rubbed the back of his neck. "I've already been rejected in front of twenty people. It's all up from here, right?"

"I — No guilt trips, okay? Nobody forced you to propose in front of twenty people."

"How am I supposed to feel? I throw you an amazing birthday party and then put myself out there —"

I bristled. "I don't owe you my hand in marriage as a *thank-you* for a birthday party. A birthday party I didn't ask for."

"What do you mean you didn't ask for it?"

My calm control snapped. "I told you I wanted to keep the day simple!" I threw my hands up exasperated. "I told you I would rather forget it was happening at all!"

"But it's your birthday!"

"I don't care!" I yelled. "It's my day, I get to decide — Look, now I've gotten myself sucked into an argument over a birthday, like I'm five. But the truth of the matter is that you didn't listen, you carried on with what you wanted me to want. And then you asked me to marry you, without ever discussing it with me first."

"I wanted it to be romantic!" he yelled back.

"You wanted me to pick you," I said, with quiet control. "You wanted me to pick you in front of my family so that you didn't feel insecure anymore."

"That wasn't the only reason," he countered, hoarse. "And I didn't want to spoil the moment by weighing pros and cons first. It was supposed to be perfect."

"If my life were perfect, my mom wouldn't be dead. She wouldn't be dead, and I wouldn't be spending the next chapter of my life knowing that there will be a dozen milestones that I won't get to share with her. *Perfect* isn't anywhere on my radar. What does matter to me is respect, and being heard. I told you I wasn't ready for commitment, I told you I just wanted us to enjoy our time together. And I'm sorry, so very sorry that you're hurting. But you can't will someone into wanting what you want for yourself." I pinched the bridge of my nose. "Look — I don't want to fight. I don't want things to be weirder between us than they have to. I care about you, I care about our relationship. It's just a trip to Chicago, that's all."

Adrian just looked at me, his eyes peering from behind his black curls.

"It hurts," he said after a moment. "It hurts to find out you're the person who cares more."

"Cares differently," I said. "I do care about you, a great deal." I squeezed my eyes shut. "This is such a mess."

Adrian grunted.

"You have every right to feel hurt. After the holiday, I'm going to Chicago, and you don't have to even look at my face for, like, two weeks."

He wouldn't look up. I sighed, said good-bye, and left.

9

If you really want to make a friend, go to someone's house and eat with him. . . . The people who give you their food give you their heart.

— CÉSAR CHÁVEZ

"So," Sophie asked over the phone the following evening. "Can we talk about Thanksgiving?"

I groaned. "You are relentless."

"I get things done. And I need to know if we're disinviting Adrian."

"We're still together."

"Really?"

I could hear the surprise in her voice.

"I'm not questioning you," she said, her voice careful. "I just thought that since you declined his proposal and bought a ticket to Chicago, that you guys were taking a break."

"We're still on. I think. We were and then

we argued and . . . I don't know. It's all weird."

"Okay. Well, we'll have plenty of food, so if he's still coming to Thanksgiving, we won't have to clean out the freezer to feed him."

"I'll . . . I'll ask what his plans are." I realized, in that moment, that I hoped that he might have plans elsewhere.

"So the Monday after Thanksgiving works for you?"

"Yeah, that's still fine," I said. That was the thing about being in the restaurant business — you rarely, if ever, celebrated holidays on the actual day. We got Christmas Day, usually, and Easter — but that was about it.

"Is there anyone else you want to invite? I know it's last minute, but right now it's just family and Adrian. Clementine is with her family, right?"

"That's right. I can ask Linn what they're up to, but they very likely have plans." I exhaled. "Are you sure we can't just skip Thanksgiving? I'm not feeling particularly thankful. I'll feel thankful later, but right now I'm just tired. Tired and sad."

"If you need to stay home, no one would look sideways at you, hon. But I think it's important to stick together, now more than ever."

"You're right, I know you're right." I squeezed my eyes shut. "I love you, Soph."

Sophie paused, as if taken aback. "I love you too, Etta." She cleared her throat. "We're going to make it through. I really believe that."

"I know," I said, even though I didn't. "So, what do you want me to bring for Monday night?"

"Dad's making lamb in honor of Mom, I think, though he won't say as much. Make whatever makes you happy. I don't think anyone's going to leave if the meal doesn't coordinate."

I cracked a half smile. "Okay."

The days ticked by. Adrian barely looked at me, only spoke to me when necessary. I let him be, focusing on work when I was there and thinking about what I'd make for Thanksgiving when I wasn't.

Sophie's words resonated in my head, her admonition to make what made me happy. I thought of her words as we worked through the holiday, serving our prix-fixe menu into the late hours.

On Friday, I pulled out cookbooks, scanned glossy pages full of lovely foods, let my eyes drift over whatever recipe seemed best to get my hands into.

Saturday, I slipped out to the farmers' market. Waiting for me were crates of pears in shades of green, gold, and rose. I fell in love.

I brought home a flat of Comice pears and placed them on my dining-room table. I pulled out a chair so that I could look at them at eye level.

Pears.

Pear cake, pear sauce, caramelized pears, baked pears.

Pear tart. Everybody liked tarts. I could flavor it with vanilla for depth, lemon zest for brightness, and cardamom as a surprise. I could make it as a galette, a free-form tart, and use a buttery puff-pastry crust.

If I wanted to get my hands into food, puff pastry was a good place to do it. The process of making the laminated dough, folding butter into already buttery dough over and over — depending on your mood, it could be hypnotically soothing or mind-numbingly tedious.

It sounded perfect.

Sunday morning after church, I came home, made a quick French-style open-faced sandwich, and set to work while Gigi lounged in her dog bed near the oven.

In the stand mixer, I beat a large quantity of butter until it was pliable and smooth. Just a little flour, more mixing, and then I scraped it all onto a waiting piece of plastic wrap. I used my fingers to shape it into a tidy, flat square, and then wrapped it up and set it aside.

That task done, I made the enrobing dough, stirring the flours into salted water, adding just enough melted butter, and watching the dough take shape. I wrapped up the mixture and put it in the refrigerator to rest before taking Gigi out on a walk.

Within minutes, I felt rain droplets on my hair, my nose, my hand. I squinted at the sky and got a raindrop in the eye for my trouble.

Naturally, I didn't have an umbrella.

If it were just me, I'd keep going and get a cup of coffee while I was at it. But Gigi? She was a white sponge, bless her heart, and I didn't feel like giving her the toweling off — or blow-dry — she'd need if we stayed out much longer.

So Gigi and I turned toward home, and I lengthened my strides to get us there faster.

My phone buzzed halfway there. "Good place for a car repair?" the text read. "The place Yelp most recommended is $$$."

I checked the number.

Neil.

I stopped for a moment, missing the fact that the droplets grew heavier.

It was just a text, a stupid text about car repairs, and I was standing in the rain — so why did my face feel flushed?

"What kind of car repair? Is this your BMW?" I found myself texting back.

"Yep. It's making a weird noise."

"Have you called Boyd's? Across the river but I've heard good things about it from Alex's buddies."

"I have not. I will call. Thx, Jules."

"Anytime," I texted back.

Gigi tugged on her leash, bored — and increasingly wet. I put my phone away and pulled the leash closer. "I'm sorry, hon. Let's go home."

Back at home, I toweled Gigi off just the same and watched as she launched herself in an unending roll across the carpet.

I tucked my jacket away and pulled my phone from my pocket; another text waited.

"How did the birthday party go?"

Too many answers to that question. I settled on vagueness. "Too soon to tell. Hope you had a good Thanksgiving."

I turned my phone to silent after that and returned to the pastry, letting the process of rolling the dough, layering the butter, and folding the layers calm my spirit.

Adrian met me at my front door, late Monday afternoon. "Are you sure you want me to come?" he asked, a restaurant-sized pan of bread pudding in his arms.

"Well, you wouldn't want that to go to waste," I said, pointing at the pan.

"Be serious, Juliette."

"I invited you," I said softly. "And you're my boyfriend. And we care about each other. So yes, I want you there."

He searched my eyes for a moment and then nodded. "Okay."

"Let me get the galette," I said. "And Gigi's leash."

"Gigi's coming?"

I started for the kitchen. "Of course she is. It's not a holiday without her."

"Tell me about this galette," he called after me.

Always with the food, with us. "Pear galette — Comice pears sautéed in butter, in a buttery almond filling spiced with cardamom. Puff-pastry crust."

"Nice. Whose recipe?"

"It's mine. It's just something I dreamed up."

He gave a crooked smile. "Good on you."

I set the galette down on the table and

slid my feet into my ankle boots before attaching Gigi's leash and pulling on my coat. There was no denying the chill by now. I'd skated by for weeks in jackets and sweater coats, but tonight's Gorge winds meant business.

Outside, I tucked my chin into the high collar of my coat. "So you've got bread pudding in there, yeah?"

"Savory bread pudding — acorn squash and sage."

"Alex will like that. Sophie will bemoan her lactose intolerance."

He winked at me. "I made it with coconut milk."

"Did you, now? You're a savvy one."

We rode over in his car, listening to KINK radio and making enough conversation that we almost felt normal.

"So you're flying out to Chicago tomorrow, right?" Adrian asked.

I winced inwardly. "I am," I said, almost teetering toward guilt. Almost. "I'll fly out tomorrow and come back a week or two after, I think."

Adrian nodded, absorbing the information.

"You don't have to go, you know," he said.

"It's Cat. And I haven't been back to Chicago in ages. I'll tell you what the

Chicago chefs are up to, be your intel."

He blew a puff of air. "Like I care what Chicago's doing in food."

I wasn't in the mood to placate him if he wanted to be testy; I looked out the window rather than take the bait. "There are some Christmas lights out already."

"Christmas comes too early, every year. One of these years somebody's going to hang their Christmas lights on the last day of the school year."

"Are you okay?"

"Yeah, why?"

"You just seem . . ." *Unreasonably riled by the Chicago food scene and Christmas-tree lights.* "Tired," I ended lamely. *Tired, tense, unhappy.*

"I'm fine," he said.

We spent the rest of the drive to my father's house in silence.

Sophie greeted us at the door, a cornucopia-printed apron tied around her waist. "Happy Thanksgiving!"

"Happy Thanksgiving!" we chorused back; I could already feel my smile turn plastic.

Sophie and Nelson relieved us of the food, and Adrian followed, giving instructions about what temperature oven would best keep them warm.

133

Caterina wrapped me in a hug. "How's it going?"

"Fine."

"Because it looks awkward."

"That too," I said, my lips settling into a grim line. "He's mad, and he's pretending not to be."

"Well, it is Thanksgiving. Somebody has to have their knickers in a twist."

I lowered my voice. "I told him he didn't have to come. But I think he's embarrassed and out to prove . . . something. That we're fine. That he's fine." I tucked my hair behind my ear.

Caterina and I stood in the foyer together in companionable silence. Because the inalienable truth that neither of us wanted to say out loud was the fact that Adrian and I were not, in fact, fine.

My father broke the moment by rushing forward to hug me, something I chastised myself for not doing first.

"Oh, my Giulietta, so good to see your face."

He smelled of garlic and cedar, rosemary and home. I wanted to curl up in his lap and ask him to fight my dragons for me. I wanted him to tell me I didn't have to be an adult.

But I was, unfortunately, and my father

had dragons of his own. Was that what it meant to be a grownup? To finally realize that your parents weren't invincible, but that they had challenges and struggles of their own?

We sat down to dinner shortly after. My parents had purchased their dining-room table sometime in the eighties; it bore the scars of our childhoods and adolescent years and somehow managed to look more handsome for it. The table fit us all with ease; reaching nine feet when the leaves were in place. We were twelve that night, with Luca and Christian seated between Damian and Caterina.

"I can never tell when to separate them," Cat said, looking at the boys as they poked each other. "Separated, they're bored; together, they're . . . that."

"You might not be able to win," I said. "It may be the Kobayashi Maru of seating arrangements."

Caterina gave a sage nod. "You are very likely right."

We quieted when my father rose from his seat to say a Thanksgiving prayer. He spoke of thankfulness, of the promise of heaven, of seeing our mother again. He asked for a blessing over the food and over the loved ones gathered around it.

Adrian squeezed my hand, and I had hope.

Maybe we'd get through this.

We passed our plates around; gatherings like this were seldom organized. Caterina served the lamb, while Sophie oversaw the brussels sprouts. Other dishes were passed around — it was culinary mayhem, and nobody cared.

Soon enough, the serving ended and the real eating began. Chloé shared about her role in the school play, and Nelson updated us with his job shift from one accounting firm to another.

I couldn't lose sight of the fact that it was the first Thanksgiving without my mother, but the food, easy conversation, and time spent with family soothed my spirit.

That is, until Luca leaned forward and locked eyes with me.

"Are you going to marry Mr. Adrian, Aunt Juliette?"

My mouth dropped open as a dozen potential answers flooded my mind. I could feel Adrian stiffen next to me.

Caterina turned to her son. "That's a very personal question, Luca. Remember how we talked about personal questions?"

"Yes, but it's not personal!" Luca countered emphatically. "Because they were talking about it at the party in front of everyone."

Damian reached for the rolls. "Do you want a roll, buddy?"

Luca shook his head.

"More tartiflette?" Damian tried again.

"I'm full." He wrinkled his nose. "I don't want to be a ring bearer."

"Cole from school was a ring bearer," Christian added. "He threw up."

Chloé leaned forward. "Wait, he threw up during the wedding?"

"This isn't appropriate dinner conversation . . . ," Sophie started.

"No, he threw up in class. He just got really bored as a ring bearer, and his shirt was itchy."

Caterina put her napkin down. "Okay, it's time for a time-out from the table, boys."

"But we didn't throw up!" Christian insisted, his voice raising in fervor. "It was Cole!"

"We don't talk about throw-up *or* personal questions at the dinner table. Come on."

Damian turned to Adrian and me and winced. "I'm sorry, you guys."

"They have futures as investigative journalists," Adrian joked, but I could hear the edge in his voice.

I volunteered to wash dishes after the

meal, mainly to have something to do with my hands. Adrian joined me, and we worked methodically through the dinner plates in silence. "Thanks for coming tonight," I said as I reached for a serving platter.

"What did you tell your family about us?"

"What?"

"What did you tell your family? About us," he repeated.

"I — I told them that I wasn't ready to get married yet, but that we were still together."

"That's all?"

"What else is there?"

He took the washed platter from my hands and set it down hard. "Hardly anyone will look me in the eye, and the ones who do, they look at me like an old dog they feel sorry for."

"I'm sorry. It's just a weird situation."

"Are you serious about us, Juliette? Or are you just passing the time?"

I reached for a towel to dry my hands. "When we first started dating, I was very up front about how I knew I wasn't ready for a serious relationship. I can't tell you how serious I am because I don't know."

"You were serious with Neil, and you two had hardly spent time together."

"And then we broke up," I said flatly. "I

wouldn't use that as a measure."

"But you knew how you felt about him."

"Why are you pushing this? You're not Neil. And I'm not the person he dated, not anymore."

There was a cough behind us; Caterina entered the kitchen, her gaze shifting from me to Adrian. "Don't mind me. Just needed to get some milk for the boys."

Adrian didn't say anything. He just looked at me and raised an eyebrow.

I waited until Caterina left. "What?"

"See? It's weird with your family."

"We're half Italian," I said, picking up an oversized bowl and scrubbing at it. "Arguing is . . . It's a thing. I wouldn't equate it with breathing, but . . . something else common. Sneezing or something. I don't know. It's been a long day."

"So you're telling me that if Neil suddenly showed up and told you he'd moved here, he wanted to marry you, and he wanted to make nerdy science babies with you, you'd tell him what you're telling me?"

"Probably not, because we're not discussing scientifically inclined children, which is a good thing."

"Be serious, Juliette."

I set the bowl down. "I don't know what to tell you, because what you're talking about has no basis in reality. I broke up with Neil, remember? And he might be in town — temporarily — but he's seeing someone else, and he's moving to Atlanta soon. We've parted ways, and our lives are only continuing to move apart."

"You're avoiding my question," he said softly.

"Yes, I would still tell him that I'm not ready to be serious."

Adrian picked the bowl up from the sink and rewashed it before running it under the water to rinse.

"I believe you think so," he said. "I just wish I believed it were true."

"If that's the case," I said, my voice wobbling, "I think we need to break up. Keeping on like this — it's not pleasant for either of us."

He set the bowl down beside the sink. "You may be right."

"I wish I wasn't," I said, my voice thick. Tears welled behind my eyes.

Adrian glanced toward the kitchen door.

I followed his thoughts. "It's okay," I said. "You don't have to stick around. I can get a ride."

He stepped close and wrapped an arm around my waist, his cheek brushing against mine. For a moment I thought he might tell me I was wrong, that we'd be fine, that we'd both overreacted.

"I'll see you around, Juliette," he said instead, and left.

~ Pear Cardamom Galette ~

Juliette likes to make her puff pastry by hand — and you're welcome to — but store-bought dough makes quick work of this free-form tart. If you can locate all-butter puff pastry, so much the better. You can look for puff pastry in the freezer section of most grocery stores, near the frozen pies and dessert toppings.

1 sheet puff-pastry dough (if using frozen, thaw according to package directions)
4 tablespoons butter (preferably salted, but if not, add scant 1/4 teaspoon salt)
1/4 cup maple syrup
1/2 teaspoon cardamom
1 teaspoon vanilla-bean paste
1 1/2 pounds ripe pears, peeled, cored, and sliced thin
Zest of 1 lemon
2 tablespoons cornstarch
1 egg, beaten

Preheat the oven to 400°F. Line an edged baking sheet with parchment paper.

Roll the puff pastry out to 1/6-inch thickness. Using a paring knife, round off the corners to create an oval.

In a large sauté pan, melt butter over medium-low heat. Add maple syrup and stir, allowing to simmer for a moment, before adding the cardamom and vanilla. Add the pears and cook, stirring gently, until pears just begin to soften. Add the lemon zest. Sprinkle the cornstarch over the pear mixture, and stir to combine, being careful not to break the pears. Remove mixture from heat.

Lightly score the inside of the pastry dough about 2–3 inches from the edge. With a fork, gently mark the inside of the circle, avoiding puncturing the pastry. This will prevent the pastry from creating an air bubble in the center.

With a slotted spoon, place the pears into the center of the pastry. Fold the dough over the edge of the filling, using the score mark as a guide. Pleat the dough as necessary to contain the pear mixture neatly.

Brush the exposed top of the dough with the beaten egg, and bake for 25–30 minutes, or until the pastry is golden and the filling has browned. Allow to cool 10 minutes before serving. Serve with whipped cream or vanilla ice cream.

Serves 6.

10

After violent emotion most people and all boys demand food.

— **RUDYARD KIPLING**

I watched Adrian's back as he left, detached, as if I were watching the scene unfold as an audience member, rather than a participant. The front door opened and closed; I heard the car engine turn over.

He was gone.

Sophie stepped into the kitchen. "We were thinking about serving up dessert and coffee soon. How does that sound?"

"Fine. That sounds fine," I heard myself say.

"Did Adrian leave something in his car? I thought I saw him walk outside just now."

"He . . . Adrian left."

Caterina rounded the corner. "Adrian left?"

I nodded. "He, um, left. Can someone

give me a ride home?"

"Now?" Sophie asked.

"No, after dessert. Later. Are we playing a game later?"

Caterina put her hands on my arms. "Juliette, honey, what just happened?"

"Um — we broke up. I think. Yes, we did. Adrian and I broke up."

Nico entered the kitchen from the dining-room doorway. "You and Adrian broke up? Are you okay?"

I squinted. "What is going on? Were all of you . . . Were you all listening in?"

"No!" Sophie protested, her face contorted in horror. "No, we were in the family room, talking about dessert."

"And I heard Sophie talking," Caterina added. "And I thought I heard Adrian leave too."

Nico shrugged. "I was listening in the dining room."

"Nico!" I said, and was surprised to hear my sisters chorusing in.

"What?" He held out his hands. "If they broke up — which they did — I'd probably need a new sous-chef. And I texted a guy tonight who can fill in, just in case. We're booked solid this week."

I frowned. "Who did you get?"

"Tony Cantalano. Who, by the way, is not

interested in women. So he will not want to date you."

Sophie put her hands on her hips. "You're unbelievable."

Caterina covered her face with her hands. "It's not like any of this is Juliette's fault. Adrian was flirting with her the night you hired him — and you hired him anyway."

Nico looked from me to Caterina. "Adrian was flirting with Juliette that night?"

I didn't know whether to laugh or yell. I chose neither. "My feet hurt," I said. "I'm going to go sit down."

And with that, I left the kitchen — and the continuing argument — for the relative quiet of the family room, where I took a seat beside Alex.

"Is Sophie bringing back dessert?" he asked.

"It's anyone's guess," I said. "Can you give me a ride home later?"

"Sure."

I sighed and rested my head against his shoulder. "Thank you. I appreciate that."

Fifteen minutes later, Caterina, Sophie, and a sheepish-looking Nico returned bearing dessert, dessert plates, and silverware. They set everything on the sideboard, and we served ourselves before resettling on the overstuffed furniture.

Damian and Caterina put the boys to bed after dessert, returning from the second floor nearly an hour later.

"Books were read," Caterina said, flopping onto the couch, "songs were sung, water was drunk, and there were two extra trips to the bathroom. All things considered, not bad."

Sophie nodded. "Traveling."

"Yep." She turned to me. "You doing okay? The boys feel bad about asking about a wedding, for what it's worth."

I shook my head. "It's fine. If it wasn't tonight, it would have been a different night."

"It's still sucky. I'm sorry, hon."

"What a mess," I said with a groan.

My father rose from his spot and took a seat next to me. "Do not be worried, Giulietta."

I wrapped my arms around him. "Was it stupid that I dated him so soon after Neil, while Mom was sick?"

"No, you should never regret caring for someone. And you did care for him. I know that, all of us know that. Not every love is meant to last forever."

I looked toward Caterina. "I'm glad I'm leaving with you tomorrow."

Caterina brightened. "Me too! And not

just because I'm excited to have an extra hand during the flights. And I did have a conversation with the boys, so hopefully they'll keep their personal questions to themselves."

"They'll be fine," I said. "They're good kids." I yawned and looked at the clock. "I don't want to go home."

"You could stay here tonight," my father said, his arm around my shoulders tightening in a reassuring squeeze.

"I might do that."

Caterina squealed and clapped her hands together, which would have struck me as funny if it had been any other thirty-something woman.

"I'm glad you're happy. Can I borrow some of your face wash?"

"Of course."

Alex loaned me a phone charger, and I found an old college sweatshirt in the hall closet, which served as a makeshift night-gown.

Gigi curled up and slept by my feet, and I enjoyed a deep, dreamless sleep.

The next morning, I showered, dressed in the previous night's outfit, and raided Cat's makeup bag. We enjoyed leftover galette and pumpkin pie for breakfast, served with coffee so strong I felt I could run a mile while juggling.

Alex drove me home, settling on my couch to read a book while I packed.

I raided my closet for my favorite cold-weather wear, items I seldom wore anymore since work took over my life — cozy sweater coats, soft cotton tees with long sleeves, cardigans with embroidered flowers — all in jewel tones. On top I packed the two cookbooks I'd picked up at Powell's but hadn't had a chance to test.

After I packed up Gigi's necessities, Alex drove me back to Dad's. I left Gigi with Alex, and Dad drove us to the airport.

"Have a good time," Dad told me as we hugged at the departures drop-off. "Sleep. Cook. Meet a man in Chicago, if it brings you joy."

"I couldn't leave Portland," I answered.

"Oh, if you met the right man, I think you could. Be well, Giulietta. And bring me back a bottle of pickles from that shop by Caterina's."

"I will," I promised, and with that, we were off.

At Caterina's, the boys helped me "unpack" by shoving piles of clothes into the half-empty dresser. Caterina chased them into the bathtub, and soon enough the boys were in bed, with Caterina and Damian following shortly after.

My head buzzed with too many questions for sleep. And despite my happiness to be away from home, I found I missed Gigi's presence on my bed.

I pulled out my netbook and opened my web browser. Weeks ago, I'd attempted a search for my biological grandfather's younger brother, Benjamin Roussard, but without any luck. There was a Cajun musician by the name of Ben Roussard, but I was fairly certain he wasn't my great-uncle.

My heartbeat picked up, the way it always did when I set my mind on untangling my grandmother's past. I'd missed this.

Though I hadn't missed the disappointment of dead ends. Once again, the search turned up without any helpful hits. I pressed my palms together and thought, studying the screen.

I knew from Mireille's letters and the wedding ring I'd found that Benjamin had worked for a time with Van Cleef & Arpels. If he and his wife had immigrated to America, would he have continued to work in fine jewelry? I knew plenty of people left professional positions in their home countries and formed entirely different lives afterward.

Would Benjamin have been one of them, or would he have made a name for himself as a jeweler in America?

So I started with the basics: "Benjamin Roussard jeweler" and variations thereof. Nothing, again.

I wrinkled my nose and set the netbook aside. *Enough of that* — I began to reach for a cookbook before another thought distracted me.

After reopening the machine, I opened my e-mail and began to type.

Over the next few days, I let myself be carried away by the chaotic happiness of Caterina's home. Caterina kept the boys busy when they weren't at school. When they were home, I joined in the festivities, making trips to the park and the library. When the boys went to school and Cat went to work, I used the time at the house alone to cook. Caterina's townhouse sat a couple of blocks from a well-stocked grocery store. At about ten each morning, I bundled up, walked down, and purchased whatever ingredients amused me. Back in Caterina's kitchen, I baked chocolate babkas with quinoa flour, tartlets with cream and lychee fruit, roasted vegetables with poached eggs on top.

One morning, I decided on homemade pasta, much to Caterina's delight.

"I haven't had fresh tagliatelle in ages! I'll join you; let me grab an apron."

Together we made wells of flour and cracked eggs inside. Caterina slipped her wedding ring off before we began the mixing process, slowly working the eggs and fine flour together with our fingers.

Slowly but surely, two matching batches of shaggy dough emerged. Caterina set a timer, and we set to work kneading. Folding, pressing, turning, folding, pressing, turning — the regular rhythm quieted my mind.

"I tried looking up Benjamin again," I said as we worked. "I'm just not getting anywhere. Which makes sense, I guess — I mean, he can't be a spring chicken if he's still alive."

Caterina pressed down on her dough. "True. Did you try one of those ancestry sites?"

I shoved my dough down. "I did. I found their immigration to the States during the war — which I already knew about. I guess knowing they didn't change their names is theoretically helpful."

"What's the wife's name?"

"Alice. Same name as Mom's missing sister."

"Right. Have you tried searching for her, specifically? Benjamin's wife?"

I blinked at her. "No, I haven't. I've just been focused on Benjamin. Seriously, I've searched every which way, in hopes that some enterprising journalist decided to profile him as a human-interest story."

Cat shrugged. "It's worth a try."

"You're right." I held up my pasta hands. "I'd check now if it didn't mean washing up first."

She laughed. "It'll just be another . . . seven minutes of kneading."

"I also e-mailed Neil," I confessed.

"You have been busy. What did you say?"

"I told him the birthday was loud, that I followed you to Chicago."

"Did you tell him about Thanksgiving?"

"No. It felt weird, mentioning it over e-mail. I left it out."

"Didn't you say he'd been seeing somebody? I mean, I don't doubt you, but I just remember you mentioning that."

"He said he was, yes."

"But he went to Powell's by himself. Interesting."

"Lots of people do."

"Eh, a visit to the Rare Book Room is a

good date trip. I think it's a sign."

"A sign that he likes books?"

"A sign that he's not seeing anyone any-more, at least not seriously."

"I'm not interested in him that way," I warned her. "At least, I shouldn't be. We're just friends. Seriously, the relationship ship has sailed. It's more than sailed. It has left the harbor."

"Mmm," she replied. I didn't need to ask to know she didn't believe me, and I didn't feel the desire to argue the point. "Has he written back yet?"

"He did," I conceded. "I sent him a few ideas for things to do in Portland — you know, like taking Germantown Road to St. Johns Bridge, that sort of thing. Well" — I cleared my throat and turned my dough yet again before shoving it down — "he did, and had a lovely time. And he liked Tin Shed, which I'd suggested for brunch."

"Smart man."

"He sent some things to do here, though he figured I was busy with you and the boys."

"Like what?"

"Visit Saint Hedwig's, explore Schiller Street, ice cream at Margie's Candies."

Caterina gave an appreciative nod. "Solid ideas, all. Is he from the Chicago area? I thought he was from the South."

"His friend Callan is from Chicago — recently moved back, if I remember correctly."

"Cool. Well, if you're interested in any of those, we can make it happen. And you know you're welcome to borrow one of the cars too."

"I know. I've been enjoying my walks to the grocery store, though."

"I can tell — on my last visit, no less than three employees gushed about you."

"Seriously?"

"Food people like food people. You're an appreciative buyer."

The timer beeped, interrupting our grocery discussions. I picked up my wedge of dough. "How's yours? Mine seems nice and glossy."

"Mine is glorious. Let's set these to rest and see if we can find anything about Great-Aunt Alice."

We washed up and retreated to Caterina's office at the top of the stairs. Caterina hovered over my shoulder as I sat down at her computer.

"Alice Roussard." I entered the name and hit Enter.

Three hits: two random, one obituary.

"Look at that," I said.

"That might be something," Caterina said at the same time.

I clicked the obituary, my heart pounding. " 'Alice Roussard passed away on February 8, 2008. She was 87,' " I read.

Caterina tapped her fingers against the desk. "Bingo."

" 'Alice is survived by her husband Benjamin and three daughters,' " I continued. " 'Lisette Greenfeld of Kansas City, KS; Vi Lipniki of Poughkeepsie, NY; and Rosaline Warner of Saint Louis, MO.' "

"Ha! No wonder you were having trouble getting anywhere with Roussard. Benjamin had three daughters, all of whom changed their names."

"Well, now we've got them."

"Saint Louis is within driving distance, Etta. If we found a number or e-mail for Rosaline . . ."

"It's certainly worth a try," I said, clicking to a new browser window. I typed in Rosaline Warner's name and hit Enter.

"Would you look at that," Cat said when we viewed the results.

I couldn't help but chuckle as well. Link after link featured Rosaline Warner, the James Beard Award–winning pastry chef and proprietress of the Feisty Baguette.

"Genetics," I said. "They'll getcha every time."

400 grams type 00 flour

4 eggs, at room temperature

Water, if the dough feels dry

Cornmeal, to keep pasta separate

Extra flour, for the pasta machine or rolling pin

Clear a space on a flat countertop or table-top. Weigh the flour with a kitchen scale.

Place the flour straight onto your work-space, forming a well with your fingers. Crack the eggs into the well, one at a time — if they run over, don't worry overmuch. Gently work the eggs into the flour, starting with the edges. Blend the eggs and flour together until a shaggy dough forms. If the dough is very wet, add a little extra flour. If it's dry, add a splash of water.

Knead the dough for 10 minutes or until the dough becomes smooth and glossy. Wrap with plastic and allow to rest for 10 minutes.

Once the dough has rested, prepare to cut the noodles. Line two baking sheets with parchment or waxed paper, and sprinkle them with cornmeal.

If you don't have a pasta maker, use a roll-ing pin to roll the dough very thin, flouring the rolling pin to prevent sticking. If the dough breaks, simply put it back together and keep rolling. Pasta dough isn't like pie pastry or cookie dough — it won't become tough if overworked. Instead, the handling simply increases the elasticity of the dough. Roll the dough as thin as possible, and use a sharp paring knife to cut the noodles. Cut about 1-inch width for pappardelle, 1/4 inch for tagliatelle.

If you're using a pasta machine, assemble the machine according to the manufacturer's instructions. Sprinkle some flour over the roller, and then roll a small rectangle of dough through the widest setting. Repeat until the dough can pass without breaking. Adjust the width of the roller by two settings, and roll through again, reflouring as necessary. Once the dough can pass through that setting without breaking, adjust another two settings. Aim to finish at about a 6 — too thin and you'll have problems with the noodles sticking or breaking, unless used immediately. Finally, use the pasta-cutting attachment to cut the pasta to the desired size and shape.

Lay the finished noodles in a round on the baking sheet, sprinkled with cornmeal to prevent sticking — the cornmeal will fall away during the boiling process. Don't let the noodles become too warm, or they'll stick badly and be unusable. Work in as cool an environment as possible. When you've completed a baking sheet's worth, cover with plastic wrap and refrigerate.

Note: The proportions of the dough are very simple — it's one egg to 100 grams flour, and when deciding on serving size, that amount constitutes one generous portion. The above recipe makes enough for 4–5 people. Also, the freshness of the flour matters, so be sure to check the expiration date of the flour. A flour nearing its expiration date will be drier and more difficult to work with.

11

Think in the morning. Act in the noon. Eat
in the evening. Sleep in the night.
— WILLIAM BLAKE

I considered calling the bakery straightaway,
but Caterina needed to pick up the boys. I
elected to join in and wait until she'd be
able to be with me.

We listened to Brandi Carlile during the
drive and discussed picking up canned
tomatoes and a chuck roast for a hearty
pasta dinner.

Once Caterina had gathered the boys and
fastened them into their seats, I half-listened
to their afterschool chatter while pulling out
my phone and opening my text messages.

I couldn't not tell him.

"Found Benjamin's daughter. She's a
pastry chef in Saint Louis," I texted Neil.
"Will attempt to make contact this afternoon."

A moment later my phone buzzed.

"That's incredible! You should hire yourself out as a PI. Hope the call goes well. What are you planning to say?"

I laughed softly to myself.

"I'd be the slowest PI ever. My motto would be 'I'm cheap, and I might have answers in six months. Take a cookie on your way out.' "

Another *buzz.*

"A good cookie should never be underestimated."

I typed out my reply. "True. Also, have not figured out what to say. How do you tell someone that you're their long-lost . . . second cousin once removed? Maybe I should get that straight first."

"You could just say you're working on tracing out your ancestry. People do that all that time. Say you're tracing ancestry and you have some questions about her uncle."

I reread the text. "That's a good idea," I texted back.

"Thanks," he wrote. "You enjoying the Windy City?"

"I am," I typed out. "It's good to get out of town for a while."

"You're texting very quietly," Caterina observed. "You don't have to tell me who it is. I'm just making an observation."

162

"Yes," I said dryly. "Your self-control is much admired."

"I'm just saying. I'm here for you."

I glanced over at her. "That's very sweet of you."

"It's all for you, darling."

My phone buzzed, and I glanced down. "It's Neil. If you must know."

Caterina kept her eyes glued to the road as she turned the corner. "You had Neil-texting energy."

"I'm not even going to try to untangle what on earth that means."

"How is Neil?"

"He's . . ." I read his text: "Did Adrian join you?" I snorted. "He's fishing. Metaphorically."

"Appreciate the clarification."

"He's trying to figure out if Adrian came."

"Of course he is. What are you going to say?"

"Haven't figured that out yet. He did have a good suggestion about how to broach the subject with Rosaline. So that's good."

"You haven't told him you and Adrian broke up?"

"It's not something I'm proud of, so I haven't brought it up for show and tell."

"You mentioned that Neil's a half-decent social-media sleuth. I imagine Adrian's swapped his profile photo of the two of you for something artistic and brooding. Latte art, at the very least."

"Adrian won't brood for long," I said. "It's not in his nature."

"You get what I'm saying. Is Adrian the sort of person who writes cryptic posts about his personal life? I feel like he would be."

I massaged my brow bone. "It's not like I'm trying to be mysterious. I'm not that girl. But I'd very much like the guide that details how long the moratorium should be on communications with other gentlemen after a declined proposal and the end of a relationship."

Caterina thought for a moment. "Which gentleman offered you his handkerchief? Because that makes a difference."

"You know what I mean. It feels a bit weird. I guess it shouldn't, not if we're just friends."

"Honestly?" Caterina steered the car onto her street. "Every relationship and relation-ship dynamic is different. You and Adrian getting together was very . . . organic, I guess, because you'd been working in such close quarters for so long. And you and Neil — there's a history."

"Well, it's the history that we're texting

about. I knew he'd want to hear about finding a relation of Benjamin's. I figured it was . . . I don't know, safe."

"Darling, he's a man," Caterina said as she pulled the car into her garage and slid the transmission into park. "There's no such thing as safe."

We walked to the store together, both to buy beef and tomatoes for the pasta and also to finish wearing the boys out for the day — or at least for an hour. Back at the house, Caterina set the boys up in front of the TV with a bowl of carrot sticks. Their bodies stilled and slackened against the couch cushions as the theme music for *Thomas and Friends* began; Caterina slipped out of the room and followed me into the office.

"I'm going to call now," I said, holding my phone in my hand, my thumb over the Call button. "I've got the number of the bakery plugged in."

"Go for it."

"I do realize that she might not even be in," I said. "But this is a start."

"That's right."

"Right." I nodded. "Right."

I pressed Call and waited, listening through the rings.

"The Feisty Baguette, this is Breena."

165

"Hi! Hi, Breena," I said, vaguely aware that I sounded completely unstable. "Is Rosaline available?"

"Rose? Yeah, she's here. Hang on, 'kay?"

"Okay," I echoed. I could hear Breena calling for Rosaline in the background. "She's getting Rosaline, or Rose. I don't know what to call her."

"Stick with the legal name," Caterina advised. "Unless she identifies herself differently. I don't know either."

I heard the phone change hands. "This is Rose. How can I help you?"

"Rose — hi," I said, before taking a deep breath. "You don't know me. My name is Juliette D'Alisa. I'm doing some genealogical research."

"Oh. Okay. Is this going to take a while? Because I've got some pastry I need to get back to. I can call you back."

"If you need to call me back, that's fine. It's just that I've recently learned that Gabriel Roussard was my grandfather."

"Gabriel?" Her voice changed.

"He was your father's older brother. He died during the war."

"I know who he is. How — You're his and Mireille's granddaughter, you said? Who's your mother?"

"Gabrielle. Gabrielle Roussard Bessette

D'Alisa."

"Oh, my. Where are you? Where do you live?"

"I live in Portland — Oregon, not Maine — but I'm visiting my sister in Chicago at the moment."

"Chicago! You're practically just over the fence!" A pause. "You're really Gabriel's granddaughter, you're not pulling one over on me?"

"No," I said, unable to hold back a chuckle. "I have letters, I have cuff links your dad made, and my brother is the spitting image of Gabriel. I can send you pictures."

"Yes. Oh yes, do. Where is your mom?"

"She — We lost her to cancer three months ago. My grandmother — Mireille — she passed last winter."

"Oh." Rose's voice turned somber. "I'm very sorry to hear that. It sounds like you've had a rough couple years."

"Yeah," I said, and that was all I could say. I could already feel the tears in the back of my throat.

We exchanged contact information, and Rose promised to get in touch with her sisters. "Dad lives in Kansas City near my sister, Lisette. He'll want to meet you. I'm just telling you that now."

"We can drive to Saint Louis," Cat reminded me in a stage whisper.

"My sister just reminded me that we can
drive to Saint Louis," I told Rose.

"How many of you are there?"

I laughed. "I'm the youngest — two older
sisters, two older brothers."

"Five children?"

"It's true."

"Goodness. Well, I wasn't lying about that
pastry; I have to get back to it before it gets
too warm. But I will be in touch with you
— don't doubt it."

I rolled out the pasta dough in a daze. The
repeated action of pressing out a square and
rolling it through the pasta machine gave
my fingers something to do as I processed
my conversation with Rose.

Caterina worked on her second machine,
our actions mirrored. The hand-pressed
square went through the machine at the
widest setting, twice, to help the dough
adjust to the idea of being stretched. Two
clicks on the dial, some extra flour, and we
pressed the sheets just a little thinner as the
dough became more elastic. Two more
clicks, and this time we passed them
through, cranking by hand, as the dough
became fine and thin. A second pass, more

flour, and then a trip through the pasta cutter, which shaped the sheets into tagliatelle.

The finished pasta rested on a chilled metal baking sheet, with cornmeal sprinkled over the top to prevent sticking.

"I think what gets me about all of this," I said as I folded a broken pasta sheet and ran it through the press, "is that Mom's gone. I finally find Rose, and Mom's gone. And I wish I'd found her sooner."

"Juliette —"

"I had those letters before Mom died. I could have put the pieces together, searched for Aunt Alice before. Mom might have been able to meet her cousins."

"She was fighting for her life. And she told you that it didn't much change her world — she loved her family; she was content."

"I know that, on one hand. But on the other, I feel like I . . . I failed her."

Caterina put her arm around my shoulders. "Oh, honey, no. I don't think she felt that way at all, and if you asked her now, she'd tell you the same. And truly — she read the letters as well. If she'd wanted to, she could have asked you to look for Benjamin's family, or hired someone who specializes in those kinds of things. She could have sent you to the chateau, to see if

169

that key works after all. But she wanted to spend her time with us, with Dad. If she'd wanted to do otherwise, we both know she would have moved heaven and earth to make it happen."

Suddenly, my eyes and nose began to run. I sniffed, setting the pasta sheet down in order to blow my nose. "Sorry," I said, wiping my eyes and taking a breath. "I just feel so frustrated sometimes. Like somehow we stumbled into the wrong story. Mom dying of cancer — it feels so truly, deeply wrong."

"I know, honey."

"And yet I know it happens. We met the other families in the waiting room. I know it wasn't just us. Sure, we have huge advances in medicine but people die from cancer every day. I just didn't want *people* to mean *my mom.* And now that it has —" I shook my head. "And the more I find out about her family's past, the more my heart breaks that she couldn't be a part of it."

Caterina reached for another disc of dough and began to work it with her fingers. "You know," she said thoughtfully, "there are a few ways to look at it. They're Mom's family and Mom's history — but it's your history too."

"But I —," I started to protest.

"Hear me out. Just for a moment. You're

the one who found the photo in the cook-book, went searching through Grand-mère's effects to find her mementos of Gabriel, and found the letters in Provence. They didn't mean a whole lot to Mom; she had other priorities at the time. But they meant — and continue to mean — a lot to you. And maybe that's enough."

Caterina gave an uncharacteristically quiet smile. "Maybe," she said, "these stories are for you."

To: Me, jdalisa@twobluedoors.com
From: Rose Warner,
rose@thefeistybaguette.com

First off, I can't tell you how thrilled to the depths of my bones I am that you found us. My parents spoke very little of the war; my father has mentioned a few things about his life before the war since our mom died.

I spoke with my dad over the phone, and he's extremely excited to meet you and learn more about your family and your grandmother.

If you're willing to come visit, my father and sisters would like to meet you as well (and your sister, and whichever family members would like to come along for the ride). I could try having my sister take him to you, but at his age he doesn't travel distances well (and Chicago is a distance for him).

Rose

To: Rose, rose@thefeistybaguette.com
From: Me, jdalisa@twobluedoors.com

Dear Rose,

Caterina and I would be delighted to come to you! The five of us can come Monday — if you're running a bakery, I figure that's the most convenient day for you as well. It'll be me and my older sister Caterina, as well as her husband and twin four-year-old boys.

How does lunch on Monday sound? Caterina is fond of reminding me that anything worth doing should be done over food.

Juliette

To: Me, jdalisa@twobluedoors.com
From: Rose, rose@thefeistybaguette.com

Juliette —

Your sister and I will get along. Lunch Monday, make it 1 p.m., at my house — 1482 Whistlewoods Way, St. Louis, MO. My sister Lisette will join us, and she'll bring Dad. Vi will join us if she can. Call me at the bakery if anything comes up.

Rose

To: Nico, ndalisa@twobluedoors.com
From: Me, jdalisa@twobluedoors.com

Nico —

Longish story, but we found Gabriel's brother Benjamin, and we're visiting his daughter (our cousin — once removed? Or something?) Rose (who's a James Beard Award–winning pastry chef, naturally), who's invited us to visit and meet all of them on Monday. We're all going, Damian isn't catering those days, and Cat's pulling the boys out of school — road trip!

!!!!!!!!!!!!!!

Could you mail a few things to me? I'd like the photo of Gabriel (the one from the cookbook), the cuff links, and the letters. All of them are in Grand-mère's trunk in my room, behind the secret panel in the lid (not because they're secret, it just seemed logical). Please pack them VERY carefully and FedEx them overnight to Caterina's (just tell me how much it is and I'll reimburse you).

Thankyouthankyouthankyou, you're the best!

J

To: Me, jdalisa@twobluedoors.com
From: Nico, ndalisa@twobluedoors.com

What the what? You found Benjamin? And his kids? And we have a JB Award–winner in the family?

I thought you were just going to Chicago to chill out for a while. That's some effective work.

How much am I keeping on the hush? Why don't you just call Dad and tell him so that I don't blurt out to Sophie that I just mailed stuff to you in Chicago so you can show it to our long-lost relatives? She'll have a panic attack about the expansion of her Christmas gift list less than a month before Christmas.

Which would be kinda funny. Not gonna lie.

Also, we have to talk about the Christmas Eve menu. I can't decide between Cornish game hens or prime rib. We could do turkey again, but man, I hate plating turkey. It's like plating sawdust. I don't understand America and turkey. Turkey is the protein for people who hate themselves.

I hate turkey.

Nico

To: Nico, ndalisa@twobluedoors.com
From: Me, jdalisa@twobluedoors.com

I like the idea of Cornish game hens, wondering if we should save them for New Year's? I mean, the turkey was a big moneymaker. Maybe do the turkey the way you'd do duck? Prime rib makes me feel cringey. Lamb?

Thanks for mailing stuff! You're right, I'll call Dad. And Sophie. I'll have Caterina call Alex.

Also, I'm not great at this relaxing thing.

What do you think about turkey wrapped in turkey bacon?

Etta

To: Me, jdalisa@twobluedoors.com
From: Nico, ndalisa@twobluedoors.com

I think that's the worst idea.

Ever.

But I do like the idea of Cornish game hens for Christmas. They're ready for a comeback, I think. If cupcakes can be a thing, game hens can be a thing. Same concept. Maybe we'll call them cupchickens. Cupchicks. Chicken pops.

I'm still working on it.

Nico

To: Nico, ndalisa@twobluedoors.com
From: Me, jdalisa@twobluedoors.com

Follow your heart. Do the Cornish game hens. May they be your Christmas miracle.

J

~ TAGLIATELLE WITH BEEF RAGU ~

1 pound fresh tagliatelle

1 tablespoon sea salt plus 1 teaspoon, divided

2 tablespoons olive oil

2 pounds chuck roast, cut into large cubes and trimmed of excess fat

2 tablespoons olive oil

1 celery stick, minced

1 onion, minced

1 large carrot, minced

3 cloves garlic, minced

1 28-ounce can Italian diced tomatoes

1 cup dry red wine

4 sprigs fresh thyme

1/2 tsp dried whole fennel

8 ounces cremini mushrooms, halved

Salt and pepper

Grated parmesan cheese

Preheat oven to 325 degrees.

Dry the beef with paper towels, and salt and pepper the pieces. Heat the oil in a dutch oven, and brown the pieces on all sides in batches. Once browned, remove the beef and add the celery, onion, carrot, and garlic, and give them a stir. After a minute, return the beef to the pot, followed by the tomatoes, wine, thyme, and fennel.

Cover and place in the oven. After 2 1/2

hours, add the mushrooms and stir. Cook for an additional one hour. Remove from oven, and use two forks to gently shred the beef. Taste and adjust seasoning as necessary.

For the pasta, fill a large pot with water, add 1 tablespoon sea salt, and heat to a boil. Add fresh pasta, cook for 3–4 minutes, or until al dente. Gently drain and rinse the pasta. Serve immediately with heaping quantities of the sauce and plenty of parmesan cheese. Leftover sauce may also be frozen.

Serves 4.

12

Cookery is not chemistry. It is an art. It requires instinct and taste rather than exact measurements.

— **MARCEL BOULESTIN**

Four and a half hours in a car with two four-year-olds will really mine a person's collection of road-trip games. We played I Spy, looked for letters on signs and license plates, and sang along enthusiastically with *Abbey Road.*

After a while, we turned off the freeway onto a thoroughfare, winding our way onto progressively smaller streets until we reached Rose's neighborhood, ultimately pulling up beside a house largely obscured by the front garden.

"Is that it?" Caterina asked. "That looks like the right number."

"Fourteen eighty-two," Damian said. "That's it."

"It looks scary," said Christian, casting a critical eye upon the untamed arrangement of plants covered in snow and ice.

"It looks like a witch's house," Luca observed.

Caterina rolled her eyes and turned around to face her boys in their booster seats. "Boys. We are about to meet cousins we've never met before. Remember how Chloé is your cousin?"

They nodded.

"Well, these nice ladies are cousins too, but they're even better. They're like grandma-cousins."

Christian scrunched his mouth to the side. "I miss Grandma."

Caterina's voice softened. "Me too, honey. But we get to meet the grandma-cousins, and that's exciting. So we're going to be very nice to them. Can each of you think of a nice compliment to give to Cousin Rose?"

"Cousin Rose is a grandma-cousin?"

"Yes. And it would be very rude to be unkind about her garden."

Christian looked out the window. "I like that some of the plants have red on them."

Caterina nodded. "That is a good compliment. Luca? Did you think of one?"

Luca shook his head.

"That's okay," she said, unbuckling her

seat belt. "Just keep thinking."

We piled out of the car, a puff of snow landing in our faces as we disembarked.

Caterina, Damian, and I herded the boys past the gate and through the yard, which featured raised beds waiting for a new year of produce after the snows subsided.

We tromped onto the porch, likely sounding like a team of Clydesdales; I knocked on the door and waited, my heart thudding.

A wiry woman with steel-gray curls, skinny jeans, and a blanket cardigan threw open the door. "Hello! I'm Rose. I'm so glad you all made it."

"Hi, Rose, I'm Juliette. This is my sister Caterina, my brother-in-law Damian, and my nephews Luca and Christian."

"Yes, yes, come in — all of you. That's a long drive for you boys," she said, looking down at Luca and Christian once everyone had shuffled in. "Are you two ready for lunch?"

"Your red plants are pretty," Christian said.

"The holly? Thank you," Rose answered with a pleased nod.

Luca scrunched up his nose. "Can you do magic?"

Damian groaned.

Rose knelt down to look Luca in the eye.

182

"Young man, I make dough from flour, oil, yeast, and water, and I put it in the oven and out comes bread. If that's not magic, I don't know what is."

Luca considered this. "I like bread with butter and jam."

"That's good," Rose said. "There's bread inside. Follow me, you're family. And not in an Olive Garden way, you're all actually family. Come in, don't worry about your shoes, everyone's inside."

Caterina grinned at her. "Thanks for having us today."

"What are you talking about? It's my pleasure! Thank you for driving," she said, leading us deeper into the house. "Everyone's here. We're so excited. Dad! Look who's here!"

We followed her down the hallway, which was — appropriately enough — covered in photos and paintings of breads and pastries. Soon enough, we were surrounded by more relations, women who looked like variations on a theme and what I assumed were husbands and children.

In swift succession we met the other sisters. Vi, the oldest of the three, had very dark hair and a love for bright lipstick. She pulled each of us into an enthusiastic embrace, waving away any comments about the fact that she'd flown in from New York.

Lisette, the youngest, was softer than her sisters — more petite, a little rounder around the edges, her hair falling in gentle blond curls. Christian in particular warmed up to her instantly.

And finally, the sea of people parted, and Rose introduced us to Benjamin.

I could see some resemblance between the man in front of me and the photo of Gabriel I'd found so many months ago. The resemblance to Nico remained strong — in some ways, it seemed as though I were seeing into the future. I suspected that Benjamin's face and features were longer than his brother's, and I harbored hopes that he might have pictures of himself as a younger man.

Benjamin looked up at us, his eyes welling with tears as he clasped my hand. "Gabriel's granddaughters — and great-grandchildren. I — I never thought. I never thought we'd be so blessed as to find each other."

Instant tears flowed down my face. "I'm so, so very glad to meet you," I said. I felt as though I hadn't said anything else for the last fifteen minutes, but the sentiment remained deeply true.

Benjamin embraced Caterina as well and exchanged handshakes with Damian before leaning down to meet the boys. He coaxed a smile out of Luca and a laugh from Christian before Rose announced lunch.

"I've been told that anything worth doing should be done over food —" she started.

"Amen!" Caterina interrupted gleefully.

"— so let's take the party to the sunroom and get some grub," Rose finished, before reaching to unfold a walker for Benjamin.

We made a slow parade to the sunroom where a long table waited, piled high with food. Rose handed plates to everyone and herded us to the buffet while explaining the offerings.

"There's a baked ziti that will warm you right up — not too spicy, just a kick, I promise — some roasted sweet potatoes, brussels sprouts, and a green-bean salad. There are some carrot sticks for the boys too, and if you need something else, we can raid my fridge together."

"This looks great. The boys should be fine," Caterina said, "though it can change with the phases of the moon."

Once everyone had a plate full of food, we settled in at the long farmhouse table to eat and share stories. I sat next to Benjamin and Vi, with Rose close by and the other family members tucked in around the table.

"Tell us all about yourselves, Juliette,

Caterina," Rose prompted. "We want to hear everything about you and your family."

Caterina took the lead, which I appreciated. My gut told me that what Rose really wanted to know was how I'd found her, and that would require a longer explanation, as well as a dive into a deeply unpleasant chapter of her father's life.

History could wait for lunch. For the time being, we focused on Caterina's family in Chicago: Damian's catering business, Caterina's language and cuisine courses, and the boys.

Shortly after, the conversation shifted to the Portland family. I explained about our mother's passing but focused mainly on my siblings and their lives.

Rose and Benjamin, in particular, were delighted to hear how many of us were trained chefs and worked in the food industry.

"Gabriel was such a master of pastry," Benjamin said. "When Rose began to bake, at a young age, I recognized it instantly."

"I was lucky," Rose admitted. "So many other parents would have seen me and simply said I'd make a good wife and homemaker someday. My father pushed me to go to culinary school and open a *boulangerie.*"

Benjamin shrugged. "I knew she would not be happy unless she spent at least half of her life covered in flour up to her elbows."

Lisette shared about teaching kindergarten for thirty years, and raising her son and daughter. Vi talked about her years as a high-school French teacher, as well as her daughter who now lived in New York City, a cellist for the New York Philharmonic.

Both Lisette and Vi's husbands had tagged along, but seemed content enough letting the women do the talking.

Once we'd finished lunch, Rose served coffee and sent us into the living room.

"Tell us how you found us, Juliette," Rose prompted me as she handed me a slice of chocolate cake. "You explained a little on the phone, but I'm sure it's a longer story."

"It is," I said, taking a bite before sharing the story — how I'd inherited the prep table after Grand-mère's death and found her favorite cookbook, with the photo of Gabriel pasted inside the dust jacket.

I reached into my skirt pocket, where the small drawstring bag rested. "I found these in Grand-mère's trunk. Tracing them led me to the name Roussard." I opened the bag and poured the contents into my hand carefully — the ring and cuff links that Benjamin had made.

"Oh. Oh my," Benjamin said, holding them close to his eyes with hands that shook with age.

Rose leaned closer. "What is it, Dad?"

He cleared his throat. "I made these, when I worked for Van Cleef & Arpels. The ring I made for Mireille when I worked at Van Cleef & Arpels. The cuff links were commissioned by Mireille to give to Gabriel."

"Every Van Cleef piece has a number," I said. "I discovered that the ring was purchased by a G. Roussard. And the cuff links were purchased by Madame Roussard, which told me that they were married."

Vi cackled at that. "I'll bet you were relieved! Until then, he could have been anyone! Didn't she remarry?"

I nodded. "She did; she married Gilles Bessette. He was the grandfather I knew." This was the part I didn't know how to explain. "My grandmother had her reasons for keeping her secrets. I don't know what happened during the war."

I went on to explain about the letters I'd found at the chateau the summer before, how they'd detailed Mireille's school days, romance with Gabriel, and marriage. How I'd discovered that Benjamin had been the one to make the rings, and all about Mireille and Gabriel's life with the twins. And then how, suddenly, there was the cryptic letter to Tante Joséphine about Gabriel's death.

"I don't know what happened, and I don't know how the letter wound up in the collection. Truly, I don't know how the letters became such a complete collection."

Benjamin shook his head. "I only know what my parents told me. Alice and I left France before the worst of the trouble started. We were in New York when I had a letter from my parents. They told me that Gabriel had been shot in Paris, during the Vel' d'Hiv Roundup."

"I'd wondered," I said. "At least about the roundup. The dates lined up."

Benjamin turned to the other family members. "The Vel' d'Hiv Roundup was a collaboration between the Parisian police and the Nazis to remove Jews from the city. There had been previous arrests, but the Vel' d'Hiv took women and children, as well as the men. They were held in the velodrome on the outskirts of the city for weeks. Later, they were taken to labor camps. Concentration camps.

"My older brothers . . . Nathan had left a professorship in Warsaw. He had trouble finding work in Paris, but it was still safer for him to be in Paris than Warsaw — at least for a while. He bought a cart, and Gabriel got him delivery work with restaurants he had connections with.

"It was more than that, though. And I wasn't supposed to know, but I overheard one night. Gabriel and Nathan were using Nathan's cart to deliver leftover food from Gabriel's restaurant to the *Oeuvre de Secours aux Enfants* — OSE, or the Children's Relief Committee — one of the charitable organizations within the city that protected and cared for Jewish orphans.

"Alice and I left for America two weeks before Gabriel died. I don't know what happened, exactly — my parents received a note through a messenger telling them to leave Paris the night that Gabriel was killed. The note was in my brother Nathan's handwriting, but unsigned.

"My parents fled their home, and friends hid them in an abandoned flat. But the conditions were poor, and they died soon after the liberation. Nathan wrote me from Spain, once, but I wrote back and never received a reply." Benjamin took a deep, ragged breath. "I never saw my parents again. I lost both my brothers."

The silence that followed wrung my heart.

We watched as Benjamin's chest rose and fell in a deep breath. Vi reached for her father's hand; he gave it an absent pat.

"Alice and I built a new life for ourselves. I found a job with Tiffany's in New York. Violette was born, Rosie and Lisette shortly after. We made a new family of our own. We were happy. But — I always missed my brothers."

"I'm so sorry," I said, hating the pain I saw in his face, hating that my questions had brought that pain to the surface. I glanced toward my newfound cousins. "We can be done with the questions."

Benjamin gave me a warm smile. "Those were difficult days. But there were happier days too. Not that one makes up for the other, but," he continued, "neither do the difficult days make the happy ones matter less."

In the end, Rose ordered her father to take a nap, and Lisette and I did the dishes. Damian chatted with the husbands, and the boys ran wild in Rose's spacious backyard. Vi and Caterina got to talking about teaching languages — as it turned out, Vi taught French during her graduate-school days.

Rose came and helped Lisette and me set the dishes out to dry before asking about our travel plans — and offering another slice of chocolate cake.

"What is in this, anyway? It's so moist,

but I'm also getting a faint earthiness."

Rose's eyes twinkled. "Beets. My sainted husband's mother's recipe."

"How long has he been gone?"

"Oh, it's been ten years now. Cancer." She shook her head. "It's nasty, there's no getting around it. But we had twenty-three good years, and more recipes than that cake for me to remember him by."

"I admire you," I told her plainly. "Your bakery, the way you've carried on after losing your husband . . ."

Rose held up a hand. "Never underestimate the benefit of a licensed therapist. The bakery, my therapist, and my women's Bible study kept me from going completely to pieces. I still miss Stephen, don't get me wrong. But I have family, loved ones, and a business that keeps me going. Enough about me. Tell me about your travel plans."

I took another bite of cake first. "We'll stay the night tonight, head back tomorrow. The boys will miss another day of school, but Caterina didn't blink over it."

"Well, I should have asked sooner, but I have a friend — who's in the Bible study I mentioned — who runs a nice little inn nearby. The building is on the historical register. I know she'll have rooms available, this part of the week, and she'll give you a

very nice rate. Under normal circumstances," she added, "I'd put you up here.
But with the family here, I'm out of beds
and air mattresses."

"The inn sounds lovely," I said. "I'm sure
we can adjust our reservations."

"I'll call Martha. A fair warning" —
Rose's voice turned serious — "she'll try to
spoil the boys rotten."

"There are worse things," I said, as if I
hadn't already caught her sneaking cookies
to Christian and Luca, who'd overcome
their initial shyness with their new cousin.

I walked outside to find Caterina and relay
the message. Within the space of ten minutes, we'd rearranged our accommodations
and booked rooms with Martha, who offered a shockingly low rate for our two
rooms.

We enjoyed the rest of the day with our
newfound family. I refrained from asking
any more about the past and instead focused
on getting to know everyone better. By the
time we finally left and checked into the
inn, both boys were punch-drunk tired.

We settled in quickly at Martha's inn,
thanks to a glass of wine for the adults and
cookies for the boys.

I curled up in bed, feeling the exhaustion
deep in my bones, but my brain kept ping-

ing. I couldn't stop thinking about Gabriel, about Benjamin, and how he'd lost his birth family to the war.

Before I could think better of it, I texted Neil. "Met Benjamin today. And his daughters. Learned more about Gabriel, but still missing pieces."

A moment later, my phone rang.

13

This is my invariable advice to people: Learn how to cook — try new recipes, learn from your mistakes, be fearless, and above all have fun!

— **JULIA CHILD**

"This is a change of pace," Neil said when I picked up. "You in central time, me on Pacific."

"True," I said with a chuckle. "How does it feel?"

"Nice. I'm sitting on my patio, enjoying the evening. Tell me about Benjamin."

I shared what I'd learned at lunch, about Gabriel's involvement with the OSE, about how he'd been shot, about how Nathan had disappeared in Spain.

"What amazes me about your family," he said afterward, "is how every answer creates new questions."

"Right." I rolled onto my back and drew

my knees up. "So many questions."

"Did you ask about baby Alice?"

"I didn't. He seemed worn out after talking about losing his family, and I don't want to wear out our welcome. But he and his wife — also an Alice — left Paris before the Vel' d'Hiv. So I doubt he can tell me much. The only thing might be if his parents knew."

"What are your cousins like?"

"They're amazing. Lisette is the sweetest; Vi is like the New York version of Caterina. They got along like a house on fire."

"Genetics, man."

"And Rose — she's incredible. She's what I want to be when I'm a grownup."

A soft laugh. "You are a grownup."

I pressed the back of my hand to my brow bone. "I mean, a real grownup. One with her act together, who knows what she's doing. I mean, Rose — she's a force of nature." I exhaled. "She kinda reminds me of Sandrine."

"Yeah?"

"Just her nature. And she had a friend with an inn, set us up in a great place, low rate for the night. Sandrine did the same when I flew into Paris, sent me to a friend. Anyway, Rose is a James Beard winner too. And she has a whole program about train-

ing at-risk kids in her kitchens. She's —
she's fearless."

"You've got your own adventurous streak."

"You're sweet. I'm pathologically cautious: I know that to be true about myself."

"You dated a guy you met on the Internet."

"Aww, come on — have you met you?
Give yourself some credit. If I'm pathologically cautious, you're pathologically trust-
worthy." I took a deep breath and plunged
forward. "Speaking of dating," I said,
"Adrian and I broke up. I'm just, um, yeah.
That happened," I ended awkwardly.

A pause. "How do you feel about that?"

"Oh . . . all kinds of mixed up. Just a lot
happening at once. Let's be honest. Two
breakups in four months, plus losing my
mom in the middle? I think I need to hole
up in a nunnery for a while."

He chuckled. "I'm not sure I can see you
as a nun."

"I'd just be a temp or something. A
novice? You'd think with an Italian father,
I'd know more about such things." I pinched
the bridge of my nose. "I just . . . I feel like
I need to get my head on straight."

"What makes you think it's not?"

I gave a bitter laugh. "I'm running from
my problems, for one thing."

197

"Chalk it up as an excuse to get out of town and see your sister. You and Caterina are close, aren't you?"

"She's my best friend," I answered simply.

"When are you flying back?"

"I haven't purchased my return ticket, but I told Nico I'd be here a week or two. Christmas is coming, so I can't hide away too long. Christmas in Portland is pretty great."

"If you need new places to go, just ask me."

"Thanks, and back atcha. Trying to decide — I can't say if you should wait in line at Salt & Straw or Voodoo Doughnuts. Do you have a preference?"

"Not waiting in line? Portlanders are surprisingly willing to wait for their food."

"They're willing to wait when the food is worth their time. I think Salt & Straw. And really, they've got a smart setup to keep your wait as short as possible, and they give out samples while you're in line. At least, they did when I was there."

"And this is . . . artisanal salt? And straw?"

"It's ice cream," I said with a laugh. "Really good ice cream, with fun, inventive flavors. And even if you don't want inventive, the basics are worth the wait."

"Well, if you're sending me to ice cream,

198

then you have to get Cat to take you to Black Dog Gelato. Once you're back in Chicago, at least."

"That shouldn't prove too hard," I said, though the last word got swallowed by a yawn. "Sorry."

"When are you leaving for France?"

"January. But I haven't bought tickets yet — waiting to see how my work schedule shakes out."

"So you might not go?"

"If I don't in the winter, I'll go in the spring."

"And if not spring, summer?"

I laughed. "Not sure I can make it *that* long. I just feel like we're so close to finding something. It's anyone's guess what that something is, but I just . . ." I yawned again. "There's something. I'm trying to be practical about work, though."

"I should let you sleep."

"I probably should. It'll be another big day."

"Tell me how it goes with Benjamin tomorrow. Enjoy your new family."

"It's nice having new family," I said. "A new family with new family recipes."

"Of course you'd think of it this way."

"Family recipes got me into this — looking through Grand-mère's cookbook."

"And look what happened."

"Look what happened," I echoed, trying and failing to stifle a third yawn.

Neil chuckled. "Sleep well, Juliette. Dream of chocolate cake."

I didn't dream of chocolate cake, but I did dream of Neil. Once again, we were walking through the lavender field outside of Chateau de l'Abeille. Our hands were intertwined, the sun was on our faces, the wind teased the ends of our hair. On waking, I stayed in bed with my eyes closed as long as possible, then felt guilty once I woke.

Nostalgia about that relationship — it wouldn't lead to anything good.

I'd only just tied my hair back into a ponytail when the boys knocked on my door. I slapped on enough blush and lipstick to look convincingly alive before following the boys back out and finding Caterina in the breakfast room below.

"There you are!" Caterina smiled broadly when she saw me. "I'm fairly certain Rose is planning on feeding us again, but I woke up hungry. Coffee?"

"Yes to coffee."

"Let me get some for you. Boys? Sit down, feet off the seat. We're just having a snack and then going to Miss Rose's." Caterina used a tray to fix plates for me and the boys before filling a mug with hot black coffee. She gave me a once-over as she set my plate before me. "Are you all right?"

I reached for the coffee and held it tight. "Strange dreams. Again. I'm fine."

Caterina arched an eyebrow. "Pining?"

"Nope. No pining. None at all."

"I'd believe you more if you didn't say it three times over."

I sipped my coffee and didn't answer for a moment. "Nico's working out the Christmas Eve menu," I said, evading the topic. "We need to look ahead to New Year's too."

Whether Caterina noticed I was holding her off or not, she let it go. "You're planning on going to Provence with us for Epiphany, right?"

"I was just talking about that with Neil," I said. "As long as I can get away, I hope to make the trip."

"And if you can't?"

I cringed at the thought. "I'd go later, but I'd hate to wait. Too many mysteries."

"There are mysteries, that's for sure." Caterina waited until the boys were wholly occupied with their food before posing her next question. "So, how much are you pining?"

I rolled my eyes. "And here I thought I'd

201

distracted you."

She snorted. "As if."

"Well, I'm not going to waste away in a Parisian garret, if that's what you're worrying about." I shrugged. "I need a break from men for a while. Neil and I are just talking. As far as a relationship goes, that door has closed."

"I saw him. That door looked . . . ajar, from where I was standing."

"But he's not going to stay in Portland."

"So, what would it take, hypothetically, for you to leave?"

I shook my head. "I couldn't."

"Not at all?"

"With everything that's happened, with the restaurant, with Dad . . . I couldn't leave."

Caterina leaned forward. "If you were in love — truly, madly in love — Dad would tell you to leave. You know that, right?"

"I do. He told me to find a man in Chicago. But I've got responsibilities in Portland. Roots."

"Whether you want to stay at the restaurant forever is your decision. But I really think Nico could learn to carry on if you left."

"My . . . my memories of Mom are there."

Caterina covered my hand with hers. "I know."

"And at any rate, the issues between Neil and me weren't just geographical. I didn't fit into his world."

"Was that really the problem? Like, an insurmountable problem?"

I remembered what I'd told Adrian: Neil and I hadn't chosen each other. We were too scared, too selfish, too distracted. "It feels like a lifetime ago," I said. "Don't worry about me. I'm not pining. And maybe I'll meet someone in Chicago, like Dad told me to."

Damian entered the room, making an immediate beeline for the coffee. "I need caffeine," he said. "When are you guys planning on going to Rose's?"

"Soon," I said. "Not until after you're done with your coffee."

He raised his mug in a salute. "Glad to hear it."

As I anticipated, Rose provided a beautiful spread. The house was so full of delicious scents that I enjoyed a second breakfast like a respectable hobbit. After helping with the breakfast dishes, I sat down on the love seat next to Benjamin.

My great-uncle Benjamin. I still couldn't

get over it.

"I still have questions," I said, "if you're up for them. I know it was a difficult time for you."

"But you forget," he said. "I knew your grandfather. He was a very curious man. Both of us would have been disappointed if his granddaughter had no curiosity."

I grinned. "Fair enough. Well, I want to know more about him, about Gabriel. And the other piece of the puzzle is my mother's twin, Alice. You see, we didn't know about her until I found the letters."

Benjamin's eyes rounded in alarm. "You did not know about Alice? How do you mean?"

"We didn't know she existed, and I don't know what happened. Mireille got to safety at the chateau," I explained, "after Gabriel's death. I really don't know how; it wasn't easy after Paris fell. But she did, somehow, and she had both girls with her. After that, though, we don't know what happened. I had hoped — I'd hoped you might have an answer."

He shook his head. "I do not. I know that my parents tried to find Mireille, and that there were letters to the chateau, as well as a phone call. The letters were returned, and the gentleman who answered said that there was no Mireille Roussard at the house."

"She did remarry," I said. "And shortly after, I think. The house never left the family — my cousin runs it now. Someone didn't want Mireille to be found, and it could have been Mireille herself." I sat back. "I'm sorry your parents were turned away."

"Difficult times. And the residents may have had good reasons."

"I know that Mireille married Gilles at some point, and shared the chateau with Richard and Cécile until Gilles's death."

Caterina approached and put a hand on my shoulder. "Would you like another cup of coffee? Rose has a fresh pot on."

"Oh, sure. Uncle Benjamin?"

"Coffee? Oh yes. Always," he replied with a sly smile.

Caterina returned with the coffee, and I gestured for her to join us. "Uncle Benjamin, we were really hoping you could tell us more about our grandfather."

"Of course," Benjamin answered with a broad smile. "And thank you." He paused for a moment to stir his coffee. "He was a good man, my brother. I idolized both brothers, but I knew Gabriel best. Nathan left for Warsaw and married and lived a separate life. Gabriel and I shared a garret in the city together. He was a serious boy, very earnest. Also stubborn, which was difficult when we couldn't agree, but good when I needed an advocate. And the stubbornness paid off — he worked very hard to be a master pastry chef. And it took patience. He used that same patience when he courted Mireille."

"What were they like together?"

"Like springtime in Paris. Flowers and smiles and a love you could see. They were easy together. He worshiped the ground she walked on." He folded his hands. "I remember when he first came home from class and told me there was a young female student."

"Really?" I asked.

"I asked if she was any good, and he said he didn't know yet. He hated the way the other students treated her but loved how she fought back. And he always had a story, always paid attention. I thought he might harbor an affection for her. One day I asked if she was pretty, and he became flustered."

I hugged my arms to myself. "Did he?"

Caterina grinned. "This is better than a romance novel."

"He was a gentleman, my brother. And while he was respected throughout the city for his pastry, he was also shy with women. So he waited until the end of the class, you know, to approach her. The day they went to Ladurée, I don't think his feet touched the ground. And when she left for home? He didn't smile for a week, not until her first letter arrived. I think it was a relief to us all when they married."

Caterina set her empty coffee cup down. "How did your parents feel about it?"

"Uncertain, I think. Mireille came from a very old, privileged family, and they married without her parents' approval. It wasn't what they had wanted for Gabriel. But Mireille was very respectful and kind to our parents, and after time I think it became easier. They were so happy together."

"I'm glad," I said, wrapping my hands around my coffee cup.

"I hope she was happy with her second husband," Benjamin said. "I hope she had a good life."

"I always thought so," I said. "I wish I knew more."

"He died in '76," Caterina offered. "Sophie remembers him a little bit. She doesn't remember him saying much but said he had candy in his pockets."

"Grand-mère spoke well of him," I added. "I think she respected him a great deal. They had a son together."

"Ah, yes?"

"He's . . . a little difficult. Protested us

opening a restaurant in Grand-mère's bakery, among other things."

"It happens. Violette gave Alice and me fits for years."

"What's that, Dad?" Violette called from across the room.

"Nothing, dearest," he called back with a secret smile.

"I know the rest of my family will want to come and visit," Caterina said.

Benjamin patted her hand. "I look forward to that. What a Christmas present! I am a fortunate old man."

The rest of the afternoon passed too quickly. We talked, ate, and talked more, trying to absorb as much of each other's stories and histories as possible.

When it came time to leave — the boys needed to be in school the next day — Rose sent us home with bags and bags of bread.

"Eat it, freeze it — try a bread pudding with that cinnamon loaf," she said, before giving each of us a tight, fierce hug. "Merry Christmas," she said. "And I look forward to seeing you all soon."

"Be well," Benjamin said, holding tight to his walker as he bade us good-bye. "And welcome to the family."

14

Proust had his madeleines; I am devastated by the scent of yeast bread rising.
— **BERT GREENE**

I vaguely heard Caterina leave for the school run the next morning. Around ten thirty, it occurred to me that I ought to get out of bed. I reached to pat Gigi but found pillow instead.

Right.

I was in Chicago, at Cat's, because Adrian and I had broken up, and yesterday we'd been in Saint Louis with Gabriel's younger brother, Benjamin, and we'd met his daughters, our cousins, and come home with misty eyes, full hearts — and even fuller stomachs.

As if on cue, mine rumbled.

I rose to find Caterina sacked out on the sofa; she lifted her head when I entered.

"There's French toast in the fridge that

Damian made this morning, bless his heart. And coffee. There's coffee in there." A pause. "I should drink more coffee. I don't think I drank enough."

I made myself a breakfast plate and poured coffee for myself and a second cup for Caterina, wafting it under her nose when I returned to the living room.

"The giver of life," she said. "I smell it."

"If you sit up, you can drink it."

"I shouldn't be this tired," she said, slowly righting herself.

I pressed a hand to her forehead. "Are you coming down with something?"

She winced. "I sure hope not. But my chest feels leaden — not a good sign, at least."

"Well, maybe drink your coffee and chase it with some herbal tea and a fistful of vitamins."

Caterina leaned against me. "You take good care of me."

I patted her head and sipped my coffee. "You're welcome. What's your agenda today?"

"No classes until tomorrow, so that's nice." She lifted the coffee to her lips and gulped it down as if it were a flagon of ale. "Oh, that's good. Anyway, the boys were chattering this morning about putting the

Christmas tree up, and I'm inclined to go along with it."

"I still think it's a tragedy, you and your fake Christmas tree."

"I know it rankles your Oregonian sensibilities, but trees are pricey out here, and we're usually traveling for Christmas anyway. I like to think of our tree as vegan: no Christmas trees were harmed in its manufacture. And this way we can put up a tree, travel anywhere we like for as long as we like, and it still looks as fresh as ever after Epiphany."

"There is a lot to be said for that."

"No, this is a good week to do it, before the parties start, and it'll get the boys excited for making crafts to put on the tree. I try to encourage creation over destruction, when possible."

"All of these are good reasons."

My phone buzzed several times in my pocket; Caterina cut a glance at it. "Nico misses you. He is also the only chef I've ever heard of who asks his GM about the menu."

I shrugged. "He likes the creative feedback, I think," I said, as I reached for my phone. Sure enough, I had two e-mails from Nico and a text from an unfamiliar number.

"Hi, Juliette," the text read. "This is Neil's friend Tarissa. He mentioned to Callan that you're visiting your sister here in Chicago, and your sister is in Bucktown. We're in Bucktown! Don't want to interrupt your visit, but would love to grab lunch or have you to dinner if you've got time. :-)"

I read the text twice over before handing my phone to Caterina.

She stared at the screen for several moments. "Oh."

"Is that normal?"

"Did you guys really hit it off when you met in Memphis?"

"I thought so. I stayed at their home; they were very welcoming. I just didn't think that after we broke up . . ."

Caterina handed the phone back. "Well, either she's feeling you out because Neil's interested — or she thinks he should be — or she just thinks you're great and wants to say hello while you're quite literally in the neighborhood. You can make an argument for either one."

"I feel like she just passed me a note in study hall to meet in the cafeteria."

"Pretty much, yes. You should do it and then tell me all about it."

"You could come too. I'm sure she'd like you."

"Mmm, you get to do this bit of recon on your own this time. How's Nico?"

"Haven't read his e-mails yet."
I returned my attention to the screen.

To: Me, jdalisa@twobluedoors.com
From: Nico, ndalisa@twobluedoors.com

I talked to my supplier, and we are go for
Christmas Miracle Cornish Game Hens.
That's what we're going to list them as on
the menu. I'll have Kenny carve little "presents" out of radishes to put on top.

(I'm 90% kidding about that.)

Also, Adrian has decided he's cool to stay
on as sous. You've got final say, because
you're the sister and you come first. If it's
weird for you, I can send him packing.

To: Me, jdalisa@twobluedoors.com
From: Nico, ndalisa@twobluedoors.com

I've been thinking about New Year's. I'm
so tired of poultry (with the exception of
Cornish game hens), I want to light it on
fire. And then I thought, why not?

What do you think about doing Duck
Flambé? Festive, huh?

Nico

"He wants to light ducks on fire," I told Caterina. "I should call him."

She shook her head. "It's always something. Okay, I'm going to shower and take the vitamins and come out feeling like a human being." She stood and stretched her back, hands on hips. "If I don't see you before lunch — if I disappear into the shower and don't come out — there's leftover tagliatelle with lamb in the fridge. If you were anyone else, I'd give you reheating instructions, but I know that you are strong in the ways of the Force."

I put an arm around her shoulders. "I appreciate you."

"I know. Call Nico."

He picked up after the second ring. "Hey, sis. So do you want me to fire Adrian?"

"No, you don't have to fire Adrian," I said, rubbing the bridge of my nose. "He's a good cook and an important part of the restaurant. If he chooses to leave or stops doing his job, that's one thing, but the fact that we're no longer romantically involved isn't a reason."

"I love working with the guy, but you're my baby sister. And I know you're also a professional and very good at your job, but still. You come first."

"You're a softy. And thanks."

"Did you get my e-mail about the duck?"

"I did. Why don't you work up a few duck dishes and decide which one you like best from there?"

"I could."

"You just want to set fire to it."

"Maybe."

"I might have to talk to our insurance guy first."

"What are you afraid of? You know it burns out fast."

"What would you serve with it?"

"Carrots."

I laughed. "Make it up, wait until I get back if you can, and we'll give it a taste. Have you talked to Steve? Does he think he can get us good oysters? I don't want to bother with them unless they're very good."

"I will. I do like oysters for New Year's."

"We'll do a complimentary champagne toast as well."

"Always classy."

"Everything is good there?"

"Like a machine. We've got a great staff. You made a great system. Enjoy your time with Cat."

I exhaled in relief. "Thanks, Nico."

"Just don't stay away too long. We might not need you, but that doesn't mean you're not missed."

215

We said our good-byes, and I opened my texts to reply to Tarissa. I told her that I'd love to see her and which days I knew I'd be free.

A short moment later, my phone buzzed in reply: "How about brunch?? We can be ladies who brunch."

I agreed, and we set plans for Saturday, three days away.

With Benjamin's family found, I felt more at loose ends than ever. It had been so long since I didn't have twenty things to do that when I had a chance to relax, I didn't know what to do with myself.

And I didn't have Gigi or a man to distract me.

So I cooked. I made a root-vegetable galette, chanterelle soup, and bread pudding from Rose's gifted bread.

When Caterina brought the boys home, we made gingerbread cookies, decorating them with piped peanut butter and dried cranberries, things that, as Caterina said, "let us pretend it's healthy."

And then we got to work on the tree, assembling it from top to bottom, fluffing the boughs as we went. Caterina lit a candle "to remind us what a forest smells like."

When I opened my mouth to tease her, she threatened to open a window "to remind us that it's cold in forests."

We ate my day's labor for dinner, which both Caterina and Damian appreciated. Damian had been busy with clients, and Caterina still wasn't feeling like herself yet — I still suspected she was coming down with something.

Those suspicions were confirmed the next day when Caterina woke up without a voice.

"I don't know what I'm going to do," she confessed in a whisper over tea in the morning. "I'm teaching tonight! Damian's going to try to get out of an event early, but he's catering for a group that tends to start late and run long."

"Um, there is another option," I said, raising an eyebrow. "I could teach it for you."

"Could you? Do you still have your Italian?"

"Certo che parlo ancora Italiano," I said. *"Sara' nel mio cuore per sempre."*

"And you were in Italy just recently. How did I forget that? Of course you could teach it. What's wrong with me?"

I patted her arm. "You've got a virus; it happens. You can't be superhuman all the time."

"Okay, well, if you're teaching tonight, I'm going back to bed."

"Good plan. Where's your curriculum?"

"If you go to my computer, the curriculum is in my Docs folder, and it's listed by date." She sneezed. "Okay. I'm serious."

"Yes, you are. Go to bed."

That evening, I dressed in my favorite jeans and red wrap top, borrowing Caterina's gray pinstripe apron. As the students filed in, I felt my nerves grow and my mouth dry.

"Good evening, everyone," I began. "I am Juliette D'Alisa, and I'm Caterina DeSanto's sister. Caterina has lost her voice." I paused while people clucked in sympathy. "Fortunately, I have been in town to visit, and I offered to substitute tonight. Like Caterina, I also graduated from culinary school. I worked as a food writer for several years, and I now manage my brother's restaurant."

With that out of the way, I dove into the evening's lesson. Caterina taught largely in Italian. Tonight's lesson was a breadcrumb cake, and the idea that so many Italian desserts were less about being impressive — as so many French recipes were — than about being resourceful. "After all," I said, "tiramisu is just cookies dipped in coffee and liqueur, layered with custard."

For the breadcrumb cake, I walked them through how to make the breadcrumbs.

"There's no sense in buying breadcrumbs, not in that quantity."

We sliced the crusts off of the bread together, toasted the slices lightly, and ran the bread through the food processor.

Afterward, we grated the dark chocolate, peeled and sliced pears, cracked eggs, and measured cream. The thick batter came together quickly, and we placed them into the ovens.

While the cakes baked, I walked them through the *pasta fritta alla Siracusa,* the angel-hair pasta twirls fried in a shallow amount of oil. We boiled up the pasta, then stirred together honey and candied orange before chopping pistachios and adding some cinnamon.

One by one, they dropped the knotted pasta into the oil and cooked them on both sides. After draining them, we drizzled the honey mixture over the top, followed by a sprinkle of the pistachios and cinnamon.

The process of frying the pasta bundles, one by one, kept everyone busy until the breadcrumb cakes finished baking.

They asked questions, some adventurously in Italian, others timidly in English. I answered in the language they were asked. It wasn't a college course; I was more concerned with everyone having a good time. In between instructions, I shared about my summer's trip to Montalcino and the food we'd enjoyed at Nonno's party.

After the cakes came out of the ovens, I showed them how to drizzle the Nutella across a cake and sprinkle the hazelnuts on top. I offered them the cake I'd made previously, which had set, so they knew what to expect once they reached home with their own creations.

When the class was through, my face was flushed and I felt a deep sense of pride.

I returned to Caterina's to find her in pajamas on her couch, watching *The Bachelor* and drinking tea.

"How did it go?" she whispered.

I untangled my scarf and joined her on the couch. "Well! I loved it. Want some cake?"

"You ask such useless questions."

I plated two slices and brought them back to the living room.

"You're such a lifesaver," she said as she took her plate. "Damian's still at the event."

"I'm happy to help," I said, cutting a bite of cake for myself with a fork. "I wish we weren't so far apart."

"Me too. Is that your way of telling me you're going to book your flight home soon?"

I pointed at the tree. "Christmas is coming."

"Technically, Christmas is always ahead of us."

"True."

"But you're right. I have to share you." She flopped back, heaved a sigh, and took a bite of cake. "This really is good."

"One of your students asked me out after class."

"Which one?"

"He introduced himself as Nate. Short hair. Goatee."

"Oh yeah. Nate, huh? Bless his heart, I think he's on the hunt for a wife. Did you break his heart?"

"I told him to try the redhead. Emily?"

"He's tried already."

"Maybe he needs to try harder."

She laughed. "It's possible. Shaving off the goatee might help." Another bite. "So when are you thinking of flying out?"

"Monday or Tuesday — I'm meeting Tarissa on Saturday."

She squeezed my hand. "I'm going to miss you."

"I'll see you for Christmas?"

"Wouldn't miss it."

~ BREADCRUMB CAKE WITH CHOCOLATE AND PEARS ~

7 ounces dark chocolate, grated or chopped fine
3/4 cup brown sugar
1 1/2 teaspoons baking powder
3 eggs plus 1 egg white
7 tablespoons butter, melted and cooled
3/4 cup heavy cream
3/4 cup whole milk
2 teaspoons vanilla extract
1 1/2 ripe pears, peeled, cored, and sliced
2/3 cup Nutella or other hazelnut spread
1/2 cup hazelnuts, very finely chopped
Whipped cream for serving (optional)

Lower the oven rack to the bottom third of the oven before heating it to 350°F. Butter and flour a 9-inch springform pan.

Stir the breadcrumbs, chocolate, brown sugar, and baking powder together in a medium-sized bowl. In a larger bowl, stir the eggs, butter, cream, and milk together. Add the dry ingredients to the wet, and stir — batter will be very thick.

Spread half the batter in the springform pan, and arrange the pears in a circle. Add the second half, smoothing the top. Bake 50–60 minutes, or until browned and the sides have pulled away.

Allow the cake to set, at least 20 minutes. Once the cake is cooled and removed from the pan, spoon the Nutella into a resealable bag and snip off one corner. Drizzle Nutella over the top, then sprinkle with hazelnuts. Serve warm with whipped cream.

Serves 8.

15

First we eat, then we do everything else.
— M. F. K. FISHER

Tarissa waved at me when she spotted my entrance to Mindy's Hot Chocolate. I waved back and weaved my way to the table she'd snagged along the wall.

"So good to see you!" she said, wrapping me in a hug. "I can't believe Callan and I moved to the same neighborhood as your sister!"

"Me either," I said, taking in the sight of her. She wore a tailored ivory wool coat and pale-gray trousers that contrasted beautifully with her umber complexion. "You look fabulous, as always."

"So do you! I love that scarf."

I untwirled the soft knit garment from my neck. "Thanks — it's such a relief to get to wear *color*. I'm in black every day for work, and after a while, it gets to me." I looked around the restaurant, with its painted brick walls and wood beams. "This place feels like home — what do you like here?"

"Well, the hot chocolate is what they're famous for, obviously. I thought it's something a foodie like you would enjoy. The cups are huge, and they put their homemade marshmallows on top. And the brunch is good too — Callan likes the breakfast biscuit, and I go for the French toast. I've had the quiche too."

The waiter came and took our orders, and I asked Tarissa about their move to Chicago.

"I miss being close to my family, of course, but Callan is very happy with his new job. I'm in the process of getting my small-business license so I can start building a new interior-décor clientele."

"Is that hard? Starting from scratch?"

"It is," she said without prevarication. "But it was the right move."

"Did your Germantown house sell easily?"

"It did." She allowed herself a smirk. "Side benefit of being a decorator. We listed the house and had our pick of offers within twenty-four hours."

"I'm sure it showed beautifully."

"We're still settling into our new place, which is good for the blog. You know how it is. Lots of pictures, lots of social media. I've got a few people waiting for consults — it's positive." She took a sip of her water. "Enough about me. How are you? Neil mentioned that your mother passed away recently. Callan and I were very sad to hear that."

My throat closed up, the way it so often did when my mother came up. "Yes. September second."

"Bless your heart." She shook her head. "But the restaurant is good?"

"It is," I said, regaining my composure. "Strong opening, reviews have been good, and we've been able to hire some more staff. That's what allowed me to come out."

"Did you come out for Thanksgiving?"

"No, Caterina came to Portland for Thanksgiving and I followed her back."

"Just some sister time, or . . ."

I recognized fishing when I heard it. "It just seemed like a good time for a break."

Tarissa gave me a level glance. "During the busiest time of year for restaurants?"

She was good. I had to give that to her.

The waiter arrived with our hot chocolates at that moment, but I knew that no amount of stirring and marshmallow dunking would put her off.

"After Neil and I broke up," I began, "I

started dating Adrian, who's also the sous-chef at the restaurant."

Tarissa nodded, waiting.

"We dated — casually — through the fall. He was very kind; it was a difficult time." I took a sip of cocoa. "This really is very good. The chai spices are coming through nicely." I stirred the cocoa before continuing. "Adrian and I had a . . . miscommunication about the nature of our relationship. And when Neil showed up in town, it set off some insecurities. So on my birthday, he proposed."

Tarissa's eyes opened wide. "He pulled out a ring? After three months?"

"Three months and a few weeks, yes."

"You're not engaged, obviously," she said, eying my unadorned left hand. "So what happened?"

"I said I wasn't ready — which I wasn't. And then he came to Thanksgiving dinner with my family, and one thing led to another, and we started arguing while washing the dishes. He wouldn't believe that Neil and I were done." I shrugged. "I couldn't change his mind. So . . . we broke up. And I'd already booked the ticket to come here, to get away. So that worked out, at least."

"This is going to sound cliché coming from a black woman," Tarissa said, patting my hand, "but, girl, that is a lot of drama."

"Yes. Yes it is." I released an awkward laugh. "You are not wrong."

"Does Neil know about any of this?"

"I told him that we broke up at Thanksgiving," I said. "I left out the rest."

"He doesn't know that fool proposed to you?"

I pulled out my phone and started scrolling through pictures. "Okay, before you think very badly of me, you have to see him." I flipped until I found the photo of Adrian in my kitchen, grinning as he fed Gigi a bit of apple. "And he's very sweet."

Tarissa took the phone in hand. "Look at those curls! You're right. I'm not judging. I can see how he would be *very* comforting in a time of need."

"But . . . also insecure in a way that I didn't see coming and couldn't dissuade him from."

She shook her head. "Nothing you can do with a jealous man."

"This is between us," I told her. "Neil and I are . . . well, we're talking. As friends. But we've both moved on. He doesn't need to be in the middle of my drama any more than he has been."

"He hasn't moved on," she stated, point blank.

"He has," I said. "He told me about the woman he's been seeing at the hospital. It's fine. I'm fine. And really — I hope we can continue being friends. But as far as a relationship goes . . . at the first real tests, we pulled away from each other, rather than toward. That's not sustainable in life, not in a partnership. No." I looked down at the table. "We're better as friends."

"Those are good observations," Tarissa said. "The two of you encountered more challenges than most people do in relationships. Now, I'm not going to meddle too much — Callan would have my head — but you should know two things. When you two broke up in July, it caused him to do some thinking. Oh sure, he was angry and hurt at first. But I'm not sure he's the same man he was before. And I'm sure you're not the woman you were before your mother passed."

"No," I said. "That's certainly true."

"And secondly, Neil's not seeing anyone."

I frowned. "He said he was, when he came to the restaurant last month."

"I think he mentioned someone to Callan, Ginny or Jenny or something like that. But it wasn't serious, and I don't think he's mentioned her for a while."

"I see," I said.

Tarissa raised her eyebrow.

"I'm not in the market for a relationship," I insisted. "Like I said, Neil and I are better as friends."

"Does he know that? I was serious before. Neil hasn't moved on."

My heart clenched in my chest; I made myself breathe through it.

I thought back to the fight we'd had in Memphis, the breakup over the phone before the restaurant opening. I'd been in the hospital with my mother all night; he'd been planning to fly out before work intervened. Our argument had been fueled by grief, exhaustion, frustration, and disappointment, a potent combination of emotions that burned our relationship to the ground within minutes. My breath caught just remembering the way my heart had shattered.

Tarissa put a friendly hand on my arm. "Look, maybe you're right and you're better as friends. But every relationship has its heartbreak, and you learn how to fix it and move on. Callan and I have spent our time with a marriage therapist, but I don't see that as failure or a sign that we're a bad match. I see it as being two people who love each other enough to be flawed and fight for each other at the same time. But," she continued, "only you and Neil can decide if you have enough love between **you** to fight. I'm done meddling."

"Callan would be proud," I teased.

Our plates arrived then, and we welcomed the subject change.

A long while later, we parted ways with hugs and clasped hands. "I'll have Caterina give you a call," I told her as the chill wind whipped around us. "And I'll try not to be too jealous of how close the two of you are."

"I'd enjoy that. And you stay in touch, Juliette — I mean that. No matter what happens with you and Neil, we're friends, you understand?"

"I do," I said with a wide smile. "And I'm glad to hear it."

We waved good-bye, and I left with a heart that felt full — but also a little conflicted.

Was she right? Was Neil even remotely interested in starting again? I couldn't comprehend such a thing, but neither could I forget the way we'd looked at each other when we'd met by accident at Powell's.

I shook my head as I walked down the street toward David's Tea.

We'd broken up twice; trying to make a third go would be ludicrous. It'd be Jim Carrey and Kate Winslet's characters in *Eternal Sunshine of the Spotless Mind,* without the erased memories.

Why had we broken up, anyway?

The thing about this time away was that I had an uncharacteristic amount of time to think.

The first time we'd broken up, I'd said that I couldn't handle a long-distance relationship. The stress of being apart with no real end in sight had been too much. Shortly after, we'd talked it over and decided to try again, and Neil had flown out to France to join me in my Continental adventure.

The second time ended in an awful argument but in truth began with a thousand tiny fractures. His parents in Memphis, my mother's worsening health — these were factors.

But always, it was the distance that made the difficult things insurmountable.

For a moment, I allowed my mind to wonder about the possibilities, if he and I tried just one more time. I remembered the ease of his company, the way his touch warmed me clear through. There was so much that was so *good* — and so much to fall apart when our worlds shook and we couldn't be in the same room.

Tarissa did have a point. I wasn't the person I'd been before my mom passed. But rather than make me somehow wiser, softer, or better, I felt more like a table missing a leg.

No.

Neil and I could be friends. But anything more than that?

He deserved better.

I picked up five ounces of the Cold 911 tea for Caterina, who was on the mend, though not as quickly as she would have chosen, and a bag of the cinnamon rooibos chai for myself.

Back at Caterina's townhouse, I made dinner for Cat and the boys, while Damian worked late. We took bowls of popcorn — plain for the boys, tossed with coconut oil and sea salt for the grownups — to the living room and watched *Arthur Christmas* by the light of the Christmas tree, so comfortably curled on the couch that both boys fell asleep.

Cat watched them for a while, giving them fifteen minutes to drift all the way off, then hit the Pause button. "So are you going to tell me about brunch with Tarissa?"

"Feeling the cabin fever? Have to pump me for tales from the outside world?"

"You have no idea."

I chuckled and reached for the popcorn

233

before sharing the highlights of the conversation.

"Well, of course she wants the two of you back together. You're a catch."

"I'm a disaster," I said dryly. "But thanks."

"You're not a disaster."

"I've been thrown a lot of curve balls that I've promptly fumbled. And I think I'm mixing my sports metaphors. But how many romances for the ages have started with two breakups and managed to overcome the odds? I'm too jumpy."

"Who did the breaking up with Adrian, again?"

"He did, I suppose. So maybe less jumpy there."

"But you didn't care about him the way you did Neil. And maybe the way you did about Éric."

"Are you suggesting that I panic and bail because of how Éric and I broke up?"

"Maybe, maybe not. You can tell me if I'm full of squash."

I chuckled. "Squash?"

"I have young children. I have to get creative."

My gaze shifted to the Christmas tree's multicolored lights while I considered her words. "I was really into Éric. And I was very young."

"Éric was a very good-looking man. I remember that much. Like Alexander Siddig, with longer hair and a beard."

"It's still good hair. Or it was when I saw him in Seattle." I watched the lights for another moment. "He'd already been married and divorced when I saw him. There was still — there was chemistry between us, even though we hadn't seen each other for years."

"I think you left that out of the sister retelling."

"He flirted some, made noises about me moving up there. We both knew he wouldn't leave the restaurant, even to open another in a new city."

"One of these days," Caterina said slowly, carefully, "a man is going to love you so much that you'll know he's all in. No need to feel jumpy."

I wiped the beginnings of a tear from the corner of my eye. "Is that going to be enough? Would I even be able to trust it, recognize it if it were in front of me?"

"I think so. I really do."

"I spent so much time trying to keep Mom out of certain aspects of my life." My eyes filled with tears. "And now that she's gone, all I want is to ask for her opinion, hear her thoughts, hear her tell me everything is going to be okay."

Caterina grasped my hand with her own. "Now, don't cry," she said, her voice shaky. "Because you'll make me cry, and if I cry I won't be able to breathe."

I snorted. "Emotional blackmail?"

"Is it working?"

"Enough," I said with a soft laugh. "I'm going to miss you when I go home."

"I'm going to miss you too. But I'll see you soon, and we'll watch *White Christmas* to our hearts' content."

We grinned at each other, and Caterina turned the movie back on. We laughed as the elf managed to wrap a bicycle using three pieces of sticky tape, fulfilling the wish of a little girl's Christmas letter.

"Do you think there are more letters at the chateau?" I asked Caterina as the screen filled with the image of Santa's mailroom.

"Could be," Caterina answered. "But who would she be writing? Weren't the letters mostly between her and her sister and her sweetheart?"

"And her aunt," I added. "But if Tante Joséphine remained in Paris, mail between the Vichy side and the south would have been heavily scrutinized." I took a handful of popcorn. "And it's not like she'd be writing her sister if they lived together."

"Did she write to Gilles, do you think?"

"They were practically neighbors." I shook my head. "I suppose there's only one way to find out."

"You'll have to make the trip," Caterina agreed. "Pass the popcorn."

~ STOVETOP POPCORN WITH
COCONUT OIL AND SEA SALT ~

3 tablespoons plus 1 1/2 tablespoons unrefined coconut oil, divided
1/3 cup popcorn kernels
Sea salt, to taste

In a 4-quart saucepan with a well-fitting lid, heat 3 tablespoons of coconut oil over medium-high heat.

Place 3 of the popcorn kernels in the pot, and cover. Wait for those kernels to pop, then add the remaining kernels. Cover, and remove the pan from the heat for 30 seconds. Do not turn off burner.

Return the covered pot to the burner. Once the kernels begin to pop again, shake the pot a little bit over the burner to keep them moving. You can tilt the lid a bit to release some of the steam.

Once the popping slows to 4 or 5 seconds between pops, quickly transfer popped corn into a separate bowl.

Add the remaining 1 1/2 tablespoons of coconut oil to the hot pan, and pour it over the popcorn. Add salt to taste, and toss well. Enjoy while warm.

Serves 2–3.

16

Well, never mind. This day's done and there's a new one coming tomorrow, with no mistakes in it yet, as you used to say yourself. Just come downstairs and have your supper. You'll see if a good cup of tea and those plum puffs I made today won't hearten you up.

— L. M. MONTGOMERY

I read Neil's text seconds after my plane touched down on Oregonian soil; I had turned my phone's connectivity back on to find a smattering of e-mails, texts, and other notifications.

Neil's I read first. "You coming back from Chicago anytime soon?"

I read through the rest of my e-mails — mainly confirmations from suppliers, and a stray missive extolling the virtues of celery root from Nico — before answering Neil.

"Just landed at PDX. Will somehow manage to forgo the pleasure of photographing my feet on the carpet."

"I noticed that's a thing," he texted back. "Did you leave your car there?"

"Alex is picking me up," I wrote. "At least that's the plan. It's been known to change."

The other passengers began to gather their belongings and jostle toward the exit doors. I pocketed the phone and retrieved my carry-on before disembarking and walking down the long corridor toward the gate.

Home.

Home, home, home. What would be in store for me this time?

I took the escalators down to the baggage claim and waited for my suitcase to glide up to me on the carousel.

I pulled my phone back out, finding messages from both Alex and Neil.

Alex told me he was at the cell-phone lot; I messaged back to say I was waiting on my suitcase.

"I hope it's a quick journey home," Neil's message read. "Want to join me for lunch this week? I need to get off campus."

"Sure," I wrote back.

Because we were friends. And because we were better in person than over the phone.

By the time we set a date two days out, I saw my suitcase sail past and pocketed my phone in time to catch it.

Alex brought Gigi along in his car, buckled up in her car harness. We enjoyed a happy reunion, made happier by a trip through the Burgerville drive-through for chicken strips and a milkshake just before they closed.

Traffic cooperated, and we made it home shortly before midnight.

Nico saw us from the kitchen window and met us in the back. "You've returned to us!" he said, his arms open wide. "You've got the color back in your cheeks. It's good to see you."

"It's good to be back," I said, hugging him back. "Place hasn't burned down, always good to see."

"Of course not. I'm pretty much done down here. I'll help you with your stuff."

Nico hauled my suitcase and Alex took my carry-on, leaving me with my purse and Gigi's leash, feeling a little silly to be doing so little of the heavy lifting. We turned toward the restaurant, where a familiar figure stood in the doorway.

"Hello, Adrian," I said.

I waited, looking at him standing there in his chef's whites, hair tied back with his favorite red bandanna.

He gave a crooked smile, an expression of resignation — but no antipathy. "Hey, Juliette. Good trip?"

I nodded. "Very. Good to be home."

Seeing him again, I felt the uncomfortable stirrings of sadness with a touch of regret. Uncomfortable — but by no means unmanageable.

I hadn't missed him, I realized with a start. Having returned, I was glad to see him well, but the sight of him didn't fill me with longing.

"Doesn't look like you need a hand," he said, pulling me from my thoughts.

"I'm fine," I said, glancing back at my brothers. "You could carry my purse, but I think that's taking chivalry a bit far."

He tipped an imaginary hat. "Have a good night, then. Glad you've made it back."

I gave him a real smile then, and started for the stairs.

On paper, we should have worked. Were we unsuited, or had the loss of my mother simply reduced my capacity for affection?

I wouldn't ever know, I thought as I reached for my key. Men like Adrian were seldom without female companionship. Better to let him move on to someone who better knew what she was about. I'd miss his company, but the idea of him dating someone else didn't cause my breath to stutter the way it had to find out that Neil was seeing someone from the hospital.

That was something to be grateful for, at least. I had enough to do, coming back from being away. I needed all the breath I could get.

The lights were off inside, and I figured Clementine had turned in hours ago. Nico pulled my suitcase to my room, and Alex placed my bag on the armchair by the window.

"Thank you, guys," I said softly. I hugged them both and saw them to the door before peeling off my clothes and showering off the day of travel.

I fell asleep, happy to be back in my own bed with Gigi at my side.

I woke the next morning, my throat swollen and raw and aching. Caterina's cold. I groaned with the realization and rolled over, which only made it hurt worse.

I texted Nico with the news. As a person with a communicable disease, I was persona non grata downstairs.

He texted back his sympathies, along with a plea to stay away, and perhaps Clementine should stay with a friend for a few days?

I couldn't argue; instead, I belted myself

into my bathrobe and embraced my Patient Zero status with a pot of tea and soft scrambled eggs before returning to bed with my laptop. Gigi didn't begrudge the cuddle time, and I whittled down my inbox and to-do list between catnaps.

Caterina called shortly after my soup-from-the-freezer lunch. "Nico texted and said you were sick! Say it's not so!"

"It's not bad," I said, my raspy voice betraying me.

"You sound like Eartha Kitt."

"Thanks?"

She sighed over the phone. "I'm so sorry. I'm sending you the best care package."

"You don't have to do that. I'm fine, I've got a pantry full of tea and a freezer full of soup. All I lack is human company, but you're providing that for me as we speak."

"It's not enough. My guilt remains. Do you have ginger? I swear by ginger."

"I think I can get Nico to slip some through the mail slot, as long as he wears gloves and washes his hands after."

"That sounds promising. Also disturbing, but I get it. Well, you don't worry — I'll send you some ginger concentrate."

"I'm really okay —"

"I'm already putting on my shoes, so stop arguing with me."

"Fine. Hug your children for me."

"Pet your dog, and make sure you rest, okay? Rest and watch Eurovision videos on YouTube."

Nico texted me minutes later. "Bringing you ginger," he wrote. "Per instructions."

By Tuesday, my throat felt fine but my head was thoroughly congested. I showered well past the prune stage, breathing the steam and willing my nasal passageways to reopen.

Afterward, I bundled into my coziest sweatpants and hoodie and curled up on my couch with Gigi, a box of Kleenex, and the latest Sophie Kinsella book.

Gigi slept, snoring occasionally, but woke at the sound of footfalls on the stairs.

I wasn't expecting anyone. Had Clementine left something behind?

A knock sounded at the door; Gigi leaped from the couch and jumped in glee at the prospect of visitors. I rose quietly and peered through the eyehole.

Neil stood on the other side, somehow looking handsome even distorted by the bend of the glass.

I scooped Gigi into my arms and opened the door. "I'm so, so sorry," I said, my face flushing in embarrassment. He looked sharp and I looked . . . not sharp. "We made plans and I completely forgot."

"Don't be sorry," he said, an easy smile on his face. I'd forgotten how easy that smile was. "Your brother told me you were under the weather when I asked after you." He lifted a handled grocery bag. "I thought you might need some supplies."

"You didn't have to do that," I said, but I found myself stepping back to let him inside. "Really, I'm fine. There is a restaurant conveniently located downstairs."

He strode inside, walking to the kitchen. "So you've eaten?"

I chewed on my lip. "I think I forgot about lunch."

"A restaurant downstairs and you've forgotten to eat?" He raised an eyebrow. "I'm just teasing you. I thought you might like some soup. And these —" He reached into the bag and pulled out a bouquet of daisies. "I looked for tulips, but apparently they're out of season."

"I like daisies," I said, fingering a petal. "They're friendly." I took a deep breath and looked up at him. "This is very, very nice of you."

He reached back into the bag. "I discovered something my first month here — Thai soup is great for colds. I got sick and the Thai place around the corner from me had soup, and they delivered right to my door."

"Smart."

He found the cupboard with my oversized mugs and pulled down two. "And then I realized that I'd hit the jackpot, because I could actually taste it. I didn't know what you liked best, so I brought you Tom Kha Gai with chicken and Tom Yum with prawns, in case you're tired of chicken."

I tried and failed to fight the feeling of warmth that spread through my bones. "That sounds perfect."

He poured the Tom Kha into the first mug, putting a spoon into it before handing it to me. "There you go. Drink up."

I wanted to tell him it was too much, that *he* was too much, that I worried that my feelings would start to get jumbled up again.

Was that all it took? Flowers and soup?

I thanked him and tasted the Tom Kha; my eyes closed in happiness. "It feels so good to taste something again. Yesterday I had butternut-squash soup and had to let my imagination fill in the gaps." I nodded toward the soup container. "Make a bowl for yourself if you haven't eaten. I hate to eat alone."

He followed suit; we carried our mugs to the living room and made ourselves comfortable, Neil in the chair and myself on the sofa.

"Tell me more about Benjamin's family," Neil said. "Did you learn anything else about Gabriel?"

"Actually, yes." I told him about Benjamin's observations about Gabriel and Mireille's marriage. "What he didn't know, though, was that something happened to baby Alice. That came as a surprise to him."

"So Alice is still in the wind."

"She is."

"What about the oldest brother? Nathan?"

"Disappeared in Spain, along with his family. His parents survived, but Benjamin lost both brothers."

Neil shook his head. "I can't imagine. But thinking about Alice — we know that she made it to the chateau, or we're assuming the chateau. Mireille said she was in a safe place in that last letter, and the letter made its way to the chateau garret." He thought for a moment. "You said Nathan made it to Spain?"

"Benjamin said he had a letter from Nathan, from Spain. When he replied, he never heard back."

"I was just wondering if there was any reason for Nathan's family to take Alice and she disappeared with them." He shrugged his shoulders. "Occam's razor, you know? The simplest solution is often the best. So if you've got a missing child and a missing brother, maybe they were missing together."

I winced. "How awful."

"I'm sorry. Maybe they made it, just under different names. Your mother certainly did. Just because families were broken up doesn't mean those lives were necessarily lost."

"I suppose that's true."

"When are you seeing Benjamin's family next?" he asked.

I felt myself relax into the happier topic. "We're talking. I hear from Rose pretty regularly. Benjamin is too frail to fly, but we're thinking of seeing them either on the way to or from France after Christmas."

"That sounds nice," Neil said. "Tarissa's trying to get me to come to Chicago to have Christmas with them."

"She's the best," I said. "I don't know if she mentioned it, but she and I had brunch when I was back there."

"I was going to ask you about that," he said, his face looking a little rosier than it had a moment before. "I hope it wasn't awkward for you. I had mentioned in passing to Callan that you were headed out that way."

I wasn't too congested to tease him. "You were talking about me to Callan?"

"I was," he said, his voice almost flirtatious.

"Well, we had a good time," I said, when he didn't elaborate. "We decided that no matter what, we were going to be friends."

"That sounds like Tarissa."

I tipped my head. "She's good at girl talk, that one." A little soup for courage, and I continued. "I know I told you Adrian and I broke up. I don't think I mentioned it was the night we celebrated Thanksgiving."

Neil lowered his mug. "I wondered."

"How did you wonder?"

He shrugged. "I don't know. Intuition? Holidays? I have a theory that Thanksgiving brings out the worst in people."

"Do you?" I asked, before a set of sneezes overtook me.

Neil handed me a tissue from the side table. "It's just a theory. Don't let me interrupt."

I blew my nose, making a honking noise that could never be construed as delicate. "Adrian and I broke up because he proposed," I said, taking a second tissue to wipe my nose. "And I said no."

"He proposed on Thanksgiving?"

"My birthday, actually."

250

Neil stilled. "Wait a minute — you told me you were worried about your birthday. That he was throwing a large party and you wanted to pretend it didn't exist."

"That is true."

Neil raised an eyebrow. "And you told him all that?"

"Of course I did."

"And then he asked you to marry him?"

I flopped back onto the couch. "Yes."

He stirred his soup and looked out the window. "I'm not a guy inclined to violence. But I kinda want to deck him."

"Please don't. I can assure you he's suffered enough."

"Juliette, your mother passed away. You're grieving. And you told him what you wanted, and he did the opposite."

I shrugged. "It was a miscommunication. Which . . . granted, led to a mistake, but it is what it is."

Neil shook his head. "I'm sorry."

"Oh, I'll carry on, and so will he. We're all fine." I reached for my mug. "Please tell me you're having more romantic success than I am."

He gave a smile I couldn't decipher. "I'm not sure yet."

I thought about the woman he'd mentioned, the one that Tarissa said he wasn't seeing anymore. Same woman, or a different one? "That's a pity."

"Agreed." He clasped his hands together. "But there's time."

"Remind me: when are you scheduled to return to the South?"

I asked because I needed to be reminded. I needed to be reminded before I found myself falling for him all over again.

"Fall term ends on the nineteenth, and I'm assisting in a study for a couple weeks before Atlanta. My sublet is up on the eighth of January, and then I'll drive to Atlanta."

"Sounds dreary." I set my empty mug back down and rubbed my arms. "I'm cold. Are you cold?"

"I'm fine." He leaned forward and pressed the back of his hand to my forehead. "You're feverish, though."

I yawned and rested my head against the couch. "Look at you being all doctor-y."

He gave that easy, southern smile again. "Where are your fever reducers?"

"Bathroom cabinet," I said, planting my feet on the floor to stand. "I'll get them."

Neil opened his mouth to protest, but his upbringing must have taught him not to insist on digging through a lady's medicine cabinet.

I found the bottle with ease and popped two, stopping on the way back for a pair of extra socks.

When I got back, I found Neil in the living room, where I'd left him, and Gigi standing by the door looking very much like she needed to go out.

"I can take her," Neil said when I started looking around for my shoes. "It's not raining. Why don't I take her for a walk, give her some exercise?"

Don't, I wanted to tell him. *Don't be nice and make me want to get used to you.*

But the fact of the matter was that Gigi needed exercise and I had a very kind, very male volunteer. I wasn't an idiot.

So I hooked up her leash and thanked him before curling up on the couch beneath a blanket, waiting for the meds to work.

And then the book in my hand started to feel heavy, but not as heavy as my eyelids. So I lowered both, the overstuffed couch claiming me as a victim yet again.

I woke when the blanket moved, or maybe it bounced. Gigi jumped up, then settled on the sofa above my head. Someone pulled the blanket up over my shoulder.

My eyes opened, just enough to see Neil's shoulder.

"Get some rest," he said.

I opened my mouth to protest, but Neil silenced me with the motion of his hand against my hair. "I'll call you tomorrow," he said.

And because of the virus, the softness of the sofa, and the warmth of his voice, I fell back to sleep.

17

Only the pure in heart can make a good soup.

— LUDWIG VAN BEETHOVEN

By Friday my sinuses cleared, my cough quieted, and I was allowed to rejoin society. I noticed that the waitstaff weren't running quite as efficiently as they had before I'd left. With a little encouragement, they picked up their pace.

I caught up on the accounting when I wasn't in the dining room, smiling and greeting customers, delivering plates, making drinks. My muscles got back into the rhythm of the work and the nightly cleanup that followed.

Adrian and I found our own rhythm as well. He laughed and joked with Nico in the kitchen, and if he quieted when I approached, that was fine, but he no longer looked at me like I'd removed his heart with a melon baller. As for myself, I didn't resent him for making my birthday *and* Thanksgiving more emotionally complex than planned. At least, not overmuch.

In between the work, I thought about Neil.

His hand smoothing my hair, his face over mine before he'd left the apartment. My psyche clung to those moments, even as I told myself not to be foolish.

After work, I pulled out my Christmas decorations and listened to Joni Mitchell and Brandi Carlile, missing my mom so badly that sometimes I couldn't breathe. I didn't have many decorations, but the ones I had, my mom had given me. For a woman who tended to embrace an elegant minimalism the other eleven months out of the year, she had a surprising love for kitschy Christmas decorations. Vintage bubble lights, elves, and miniature trees — she loved them all. I had a box of items she'd passed to me over the years, as well as a set of felted poinsettia toss pillows, decoupage deer, and hanging Moravian stars in a variety of sizes. Gigi thought it was great fun, but when I came close to weeping over a porcelain elf, I gathered her in my arms and stroked her ears.

What would Christmas without my mother be like? I knew she'd want us to carry on. I knew she wouldn't want me weeping over elves.

But it was a holiday for which I was supposed to feel happy. Instead, I felt several tidings short of comfort or joy.

I lay down on my back, stretching out on the rug with Gigi beside me, and tried to picture my mother in heaven. Was she happy? Did they decorate for Christmas? Did she see me, or was she too busy doing heavenly things to look?

I wished I had more time with her. I wished I had used our time better.

Gigi snuggled against me, and I rubbed her belly as fresh, salty tears slid sideways down my face and onto the woolen rug.

Whether I liked it or not, the holidays would come. Life would carry on.

I just wished I knew how to carry on too.

Footsteps sounded on the exterior stairs; Gigi leaped for the door. I sat up and swiped at my eyes.

The door opened, and my brother stepped through without knocking. "Hey, Juliette, I —" Nico stopped and took in the piles of decorations around me and my tear-stained face. "Rough afternoon?"

I sniffed and nodded.

He closed the door after himself, lowered his tall frame, and took a seat next to me, taking in the holiday detritus.

"Remember how we served the seven-hour leg of lamb last month?" Nico asked after a quiet moment. "I adapted it from Mom's recipe. I didn't realize how much of *her* it was." He ran a hand over his hair. "I kept having to slip away to the walk-in. I hid a box of tissues behind the butter. And don't worry — I washed in constantly. No health-code violations. But every time I smelled that lamb . . ."

I nodded. "I get it. Obviously." I pulled my knees up to my torso and clasped my hands around them. "We need to think of something to do. I don't know. Something — something to take our minds off . . . things."

"Good old-fashioned distraction?"

"It's Christmas. There ought to be something. Something to look forward to."

"We'll think of something," Nico said. "I promise."

"I got a role," Braeden the operatic server told me, his face flushed with excitement and anxiety the next morning.

"Did you?" I answered cautiously.

"It's for *A Christmas Carol* — I'm the second understudy for Scrooge. The lead was deported and the first understudy has mono. I'm so lucky!"

"I'm pleased for you," I said, and I really did mean it. "So tell me what your theater schedule means for us at the restaurant."

He winced. It was the kind of perfectly executed wince that gave me the impression that he'd worked on it with his acting group. "I'll have performances every weekend," he said. "From now until Christmas. So I'll need to change my hours."

I nodded and thought fast. With younger waitstaff, I knew that there would be a certain amount of unreliability — few servers chose to stay in the position forever. Braeden was good at his job, so I'd try to keep him as long as I could.

During the days to come, though, I'd need all the help I could get, and without Braeden . . . "Ask around," I told him. "I can switch Jade or Stan to cover your shifts, but that means moving someone off lunch and onto dinner, which means I need another server. So if any of your friends who can carry a tray are looking for a job, let me know."

Braeden promised to ask around, saying he'd texted a couple friends and hadn't heard back.

He left my office, and I immediately pulled up my calendar to examine the existing schedule.

Well, I'd wanted a distraction from the holidays, and here I had it.

By Sunday, two of Braeden's contacts called me about the position. No doubt he'd told them our customers tipped well, on average, making the position an attractive one.

I had them in for interviews, working the lunch and dinner shifts, running orders while still making sure that food and communication flowed well between the front and back of the house.

The first interviewee was . . . not great. He knew Braeden from the acting community, but his lank posture and lack of eye contact told me that he wouldn't make it as an actor *or* a waiter.

The second held more promise. Hannah told me she was new to the area, had a serving job at a trattoria downtown, but needed more hours. I hired her on the spot, pulling a W-9 form from my desk for her to fill out while I scanned her ID into the computer.

After work that evening I pulled out my phone to text Neil. We'd exchanged a few short texts since I'd gotten back on my feet, but I knew I owed him more.

He'd brought me soup, walked Gigi — I still couldn't get that moment before he'd left out of my head. Before I could lose myself in those memories, I typed out a quick text inviting him to lunch at the restaurant.

Five minutes later, my phone dinged.

"Glad you're feeling better. Tuesday for lunch?"

"Tuesday, 1 p.m.?" I texted back.

"I'll be there," he replied.

I knew he meant lunch. I knew it. But that was the trick — my silly, sentimental brain read his message as a promise.

Tuesday arrived in a snap of a ginger cookie. I dressed with care that day, wearing one of my nicer black dresses with a black wrap cardigan that made my waist look particularly petite. I chose my makeup carefully as well, choosing a shimmery and sheer berry lipstick that made my skin glow and my eyes pop.

I considered eyeliner but decided against it. We weren't dating, after all. There were limits.

There were already a few diners waiting when we opened for lunch. I seated them right away. Mallory had arrived and tied on her work apron, but Hannah was already twenty minutes late.

After Mallory and I took the drink orders, I stepped away to try Hannah's cell.

No answer, and no time to stew about it — more guests arrived at the front. The hairs on the back of my neck lifted.

This wasn't going to be an easy lunch shift.

I sent texts to Jade and Stan, to see if they could come in at the last minute. Stan replied that he was teaching lessons; Jade didn't respond.

Our ordinary lunch shifts were well handled by two servers. Sitting it out with Neil wouldn't have been difficult at all. But today? It was as if everyone had woken up that morning craving our butternut-squash soup.

Not that I blamed them. I woke up craving that soup myself.

I clipped my hair back and knotted an apron around my waist before washing in and grabbing one of the mini-tablets we used for orders.

For the next hour and a half, I poured drinks, carried plates, fixed mistaken orders, and talked guests into boxing a slice of pie to go. I carried bowl after bowl of butternut-squash soup without sloshing it over the edge of the bowl.

By the time Neil arrived, I didn't have to look into a mirror to know that my face was flushed with activity and that strands of hair

had escaped from my clip. I finished helping a guest choose a glass of wine to go with
the cassoulet before meeting him at the
front.

"My newest hire didn't show up. And I
thought that things might slow down, but
—" I looked around. The only open table
was the one I'd reserved in the corner for
the two of us once it became clear that seating would be at a premium. "I'm so sorry. I
should have called you to reschedule."

He glanced around the room and gave a
half smile that made my heart skip. "Call
me with what free moment?"

"Are you hungry? I set aside a table, and I
can bring you food at least. Company I can
provide another time. Please?" I cringed at
the thought of sending him away on an
empty stomach.

"I'd never turn down lunch, you know
that."

"Oh good," I said, exhaling the breath I
realized I'd been holding. "The table's right
over here. Can I bring you something hot
to drink? Coffee?"

"Coffee," he answered, shrugging out of
his overcoat to reveal dark-brown chinos
paired with a chunky fisherman's sweater
knit in an ivory yarn. It was a good look for
him, but I had to stay focused.

"Coffee," I repeated. "I'll be right back."

"I feel silly making you fetch and carry for me."

"Don't!" I answered with a laugh. "I'm the one who knows where the industrial-sized coffeemaker is."

He leaned back against his chair, but I could tell that the thought of being waited on — by me, at least — bothered him.

At the beverage station, I set up a coffee tray with one of our oversized mugs, a hearty pour of coffee, and a small pitcher of cream next to one of the crystallized sugar stirrers we supplied to our guests.

Neil the Scientist enjoyed examining the sugar-crystal formation on the wooden stir stick, and I left him to look over the menu while I dropped checks at two tables.

I checked in on the kitchen, Nico in particular. "You holding up?"

"Like champs," Nico answered, his face flushed and triumphant. "Is it as full out there as I think it is, or is everyone extra hungry?"

"Both."

"Hannah never showed?"

"Nope."

"That might be the end of that one."

"It might," I agreed. I'd gotten lucky — I hadn't had to fire anyone so far. But staying employed meant showing up. Hannah had broken rule number one.

I grabbed my orders from the bar the moment Nico set them down: two of our panini and soup combos for the two-top by the window, delivering them to the waiting diners while the food was fresh and hot. We had pull-down heat lamps to keep food hot on the bar, but not for much longer than a few minutes, and only for plates that needed to be uniformly warm.

After delivering those plates, I stopped back to check on Neil. "Anything look good?"

He looked up at me, his expression guilty. "This still feels weird."

"Didn't you ever visit friends in school who waited tables?"

"Not really," he said, and I remembered that he'd kept to himself after the death of his best friend. "This is new territory for me."

"Well, what sounds good?"

He pointed at the menu. "Your spiced macaroni and cheese — it's not very spicy?"

"It's got a kick, but kids like it. It's what Chloé asks to eat for her birthday dinner every year."

He smiled. "I'll do that, then. And the — *insalata mista*? That's pretty much just a green salad, right?"

"Italian for 'mixed greens,' " I said with a smile. "We just make it tasty with a good balsamic dressing, blue-cheese crumbles, pine nuts, and some delicious cherry tomatoes."

A sheepish grin. "I trust you."

I grinned back. "You'll like it. And if you don't, I'll bring you something else. And it looks like it's slowing down a touch," I added, looking around, "so I might be able to join you."

I put the order in and stepped back into the dining room, only to find a party of . . . one, two, three, four, five, six, seven?

We certainly wouldn't have to worry about the day's take, that was for sure. I looked over my shoulder at Neil with regret — our lunch today really, really wasn't going to happen.

I let the party know I'd be right with them, and with Mallory's help, cleared and then pushed together our two four-top tables to create enough seating. The dining room really wasn't designed for large parties. Even Yelp proclaimed that we were not "Good for Groups." But I wasn't going to turn away hungry people looking for a place to lunch.

With the table ready, I seated the party,

set out the water carafes, and handed out our menus — single pages printed front and back onto cardstock. I took drink orders and left to pour a glass of Chardonnay, a taste of the Pinot Gris, two iced teas, and three coffees.

I carried those back, nearly knocking into Mallory in the process.

Two other tables held up hands, asking for their checks. I left the seven-top to peruse the menu before ringing the other tables up and then swinging by the kitchen to find Neil's meal on the bar.

"Just in time," Nico said. "I was about to take this one out myself."

"Party of seven walked in," I said. "What a zoo."

And really, if Nico stayed put and didn't quite figure out who sat at table five, I was okay with that. Not that it was the deepest secret — I'd invited Neil to the restaurant, after all — but if it escaped Nico's notice, I wouldn't have minded.

I returned to Neil's table to find Neil . . . elsewhere. I set the plate down and looked around.

He leaned over the table that had just emptied, stacking plates and gathering discarded napkins and placing them into a bus bin.

I crossed the small dining room. "Let me give you a hand with that."

"You looked busy. I wanted to help," he said.

"Your food's ready," I said, pointing toward his table. "Where did you get the bin?"

"Mallory. I suppose a tray is nicer, but I didn't trust myself."

The urge to kiss him hit hard. I resisted, of course. Because we were in the dining room, and I was working, and he had a bin full of dishes in his hands, and seven people needed their orders taken.

I wanted to tell him to stop being helpful. But I knew that he was simply being himself — a guy that took care of people, who felt more comfortable diving in with a bus bin than watching everyone take care of things without him.

"Thanks," I said. "Don't forget to eat, 'kay?"

He looked at me, his gaze flickering from my eyes to my lips and back. " 'Kay," he echoed.

"I should go take orders," I said, more to myself than to him.

"Do your thing, Juliette," he answered with a nod to his table. "I'll be over there." A shy smile. "When I'm done with the

268

tables, at least."

I nodded and walked toward the seven-top with unstable legs.

In the end, Neil had to leave for campus before my shift finished.

"I'm so, so sorry," I said as he slipped his arms into his overcoat. "I'm firing Hannah. Of all days . . ."

He shook his head. "Don't worry about it. Gives us an excuse to do this again, right?"

I nodded, breathless.

He smiled that warm smile of his. "Next time, my treat."

There were so many reasons we'd broken up, reasons I'd recited to myself over and over to remind myself why Neil and I had no future.

As I watched Neil leave Two Blue Doors, I wondered about those reasons.

I wondered if they were real or if they were simply a list of facts that I'd used as a fence around my heart.

~ BUTTERNUT-SQUASH SOUP ~

1 tablespoon grapeseed oil

1 large butternut squash, cut in half, seeds removed

2 tablespoons olive oil

1 large onion, diced

2 carrots, diced

2 stalks celery, diced

1 teaspoon salt

Cracked black pepper to taste

2 Granny Smith apples, peeled, cored, and diced

2 cups chicken stock

1/4 cup maple syrup

1 cup cream

Parmesan cheese, grated, for serving

Line a baking sheet with foil, and heat the oven to 400°F. Pour a little grapeseed oil onto the lined baking sheet, and place the squash cut-side down. Roast for 25–40 minutes, or until a fork pierces through with ease. Allow the squash to cool enough to handle; remove and discard the skin before cubing.

In a large soup pot, heat the olive oil over medium heat. Add the onion and sauté, stirring occasionally, until the onion becomes translucent. Add the carrots, celery, salt, and several cracks of fresh ground pepper, and cook until the veggies are soft. Add the apple, and continue to cook until the pieces break down and lose some of their moisture, about 2 minutes.

Add the roasted squash and chicken stock, and bring to a boil. Lower to a simmer, and allow to cook for 30 minutes before removing from heat.

Purée the soup in batches in a blender, or right in the pot with an immersion blender. Purée until very smooth. Add the maple syrup and cream. Taste, and adjust seasonings as needed.

Serve hot, with a drizzle of cream and a sprinkle of parmesan cheese across the top.

Serves 6.

18

If the home is a body, the table is the heart, the beating center, the sustainer of life and health.

— SHAUNA NIEQUIST

The call came in while we were seated around the table together, during an informal family dinner.

Dad rose to look at the incoming number on the house phone. "It's Sandrine's number at the chateau," he said. "I should take this."

"*Bonjour,* Sandrine," he said in his Italian-accented French. *"Ça va?"* A pause. "Oh . . . *c'est triste, c'est triste . . . Ah . . . oui, Juliette est ici. Un moment, s'il te plait.*"

My heart clenched within my chest. I took the phone and raised it to my ear. "Bonjour, Sandrine," I said.

"My dear Juliette," she said. "I am sorry to tell you that my *maman,* she has passed away in her sleep."

"Oh," I said. "Oh, Sandrine, I'm so sorry." I could hear my father explain it to the others softly beside me.

"She didn't suffer, I don't believe," Sandrine said. "I'm sorry. I know you were hoping she'd be able to tell you more about your grandmother."

"It wasn't meant to be," I said. "Don't even think about me. I'm so sorry for your loss." I ran a hand through my hair.

"Thank you," she said. "She had a good life, I think. She married a good man, had children who visited."

"A daughter who took care of her while running an inn. That means a lot."

"I did what I could," Sandrine said. "I will let you get back to your dinner. Auguste sends his love."

"I know we're quite far," I said, "but if there's anything I can do, from here, let me know, *d'accord*?"

"*Merci,* Juliette."

"If it were easier for you, we can reschedule the Epiphany trip," I began, but Sandrine interrupted me.

"*Non, non, jamais.* Please come, if you can. Your sisters are coming and I know you are hoping to come with the others — it gives me something to look forward to after my daughters leave."

"I'll talk to Nico," I promised, looking up at my brother as I said the words. "We'll figure something out so I can be there."

We said our good-byes, and I passed the phone back to my dad before recounting the conversation to Nico.

He nodded. "We'll make it happen."

My father continued on the phone for another few minutes with Sandrine, then hung up.

Silence hung over the table.

Another loss, that's what it felt like. Another loss heading into the holidays, another memorial — one I wouldn't be able to attend — another sense of missed opportunities.

Maybe learning more from Cécile wasn't meant to be, but that didn't make it easier.

I excused myself from the table and walked outside to the back deck.

The rain had stopped sometime in the last hour or so. I pulled my wool sweater close, ignoring the bite of the December air against my hands and face.

When I'd found that photo of Gabriel, so many months ago, it had seemed as though I had all the time in the world.

But I didn't. At least, not enough to discover what I wanted to discover and share it with my mother, to find out what I could about her true father.

Losing Cécile felt like another failure, and I felt immediately guilty. Because I was supposed to be sad — sad without complications. Sandrine had lost her mother, after all, and her daughters their grandmother.

Standing outside let me clear my head, because right now my thoughts were a tangle of sadness and guilt.

But maybe that was the nature of loss.

I heard one of the French doors opening behind me, and a moment later Alex stood beside me with a cup of coffee. "You look cold. Gigi was looking for you."

I accepted the coffee and gave him a kiss on the cheek as Gigi trotted toward me. "Don't worry about me," I said. "Sometimes a girl just needs a touch of fresh air."

"Don't stay out too long," he said. "Dad's on the phone with Oncle Henri, now. Henri's talking about coming down next weekend."

Henri. Their sibling relationship hadn't always been easy, but Henri made several trips from Seattle after Mom's illness worsened. She'd told him about the letters during one of his visits when she was sick; he hadn't said much, only nodding and thanking her for telling him.

"It'll be nice to see him," I said, rubbing my arm with my free hand. "Are he and Tante Margueritte coming to Provence, did he say?"

"He mentioned it, but that they already have plans in Palm Springs."

"Fair enough."

"What's Clementine up to tonight?" Alex asked.

"She's working with her caterer friend. They're doing a wedding."

"Dinners are quieter since, ah . . ."

"Since Adrian and I broke up? You're not wrong." I shot him a rueful glance. "I told him he's welcome to join us, but . . ."

"But it's not the same. Especially since you were his reason for wanting to be there in the first place."

I shrugged. "Me and Mom's cooking."

We were silent a moment. "It's cold," I said. "Let's go in."

Gigi and I drove home, Gigi buckled into the front passenger seat, her face resting against the inside of her fleece-lined car harness.

I saw flashing lights in my rearview mirror and pulled over as two fire trucks rushed by with lights flaring and sirens cutting through the Darlingside track playing over my car speakers. Another glance in my mirror showed an ambulance. I petted Gigi's head while we waited. She rested her head on the edge of the seat and sighed.

When the road cleared, I pulled back out and continued down Glisan toward home.

I turned one corner, then another.

What I expected to see was my street after dark — quiet, gently lit by streetlights and the occasional porch light.

But I could hardly process the scene in front of me. The quiet replaced by shouting, the gentle lights replaced by the harsh lights of the emergency vehicles.

And at the center of it: my home. My home, my grandmother's home. The space where she opened her bakery, La Petite Chouquette.

Two Blue Doors, the restaurant Nico and I had created together. A single building with so much history, and now flames licked up the sides.

I parked in the middle of the street, leaving all of my things inside, and strode forward as if drawn.

A strange hand on my shoulder. "Ma'am? Ma'am, you can't enter that building."

"It's my family's — I live here, I manage the restaurant." I shrugged away, staring transfixed at the stream of water coming from the fire hose. "What happened?"

"I don't know, ma'am."

Another stranger in a uniform. "Was there anybody inside?"

"I . . . I don't think so," I said, reaching for my phone. Clementine said she'd be working late. "My roommate's out, I think," I answered even while I dialed. "The restaurant was closed today, the stoves weren't even on."

The line connected, and I held my breath while pressing the phone to one ear and covering the other with my hand.

"Juliette — hey. I'm on my way back," Clementine said, sounding tired but fine. Alive. "I hope you like stuffed mushrooms. I've got a ton of leftovers."

"Hi," I said, my breath releasing in a whoosh. "There was a fire at the restaurant. I just needed to know where you were."

"A fire? How bad?"

"I have no idea."

"I'll be there soon."

I confirmed and hung up. "The place was empty," I told the uniform to my right. "Can someone please tell me what happened?"

"The fire marshal will be able to tell you more," he said, "but it looks like a fire originated in the kitchen."

"With the kitchen closed, there shouldn't have been anything to ignite. And our sprinkler system was up to code."

"I don't know what to tell you, ma'am. It still caught on fire, and it looks pretty bad."

"How bad?"

"There were second-story flames when we arrived."

I put a hand to my forehead.

It could have been bad. It could have been really bad, but instead it was just terrible — property damage, but Clementine and Gigi were safe.

Who knew about my computer, my clothes — *the letters.*

I swayed on my feet, and the two uniformed men — men who likely had names and families and lives, but at this moment remained faceless — kept me from tilting onto the pavement.

"Ma'am? Is there someone you can call? You can't stay here tonight."

I tossed the words around in my head for a few moments before a response began to formulate. "Call? Yes. I should make calls. I need to call my brother — he's the chef. And my dad." I raised my phone, not sure where to begin.

My head didn't, but my fingers dialed of their own accord.

My fingers dialed Neil.

"Juliette?" he answered. I must have woken him. "Juliette, what's going on?"

"There was a fire at the restaurant. I'm fine, Clementine and Gigi are fine, but, but I —"

"Are you there?"

"I'm outside, yes."

"I'll be right there."

"Okay."

"Don't go anywhere."

I gave a short laugh. "I don't know that I can."

I hung up and realized that I was shivering — which made sense, because it was nearing midnight in December.

The firefighters had turned off the hoses, and I knew that whatever wasn't burned inside had to be waterlogged.

My computer, in all likelihood, was toast. But the ordering records didn't much matter, because I had a feeling that my dining room stood in two inches of water. The kitchen equipment was probably fine, once it dried off.

Unless it rusted, I supposed. Did kitchen equipment rust? I felt like I should know, but I didn't. At least, I didn't at this moment in the middle of the street in front of my ruined home.

Nico would know.

I dialed Nico's number.

Nico wouldn't know about the upstairs, though, I thought as his phone rang. My clothes — Grand-mère's clothes.

Grand-mère's prep table. The letters — they'd gone back into the antique chest, the one at the foot of my bed. Maybe they'd survived — but the chest was wooden, and wood burned.

As I looked at the building, grotesque in the flashing lights, my heart clenched within my chest. I'd failed Grand-mère.

"Juliette?"

Nico's voice snapped me out of my mental recitation of regrets.

"Nico. There was a fire at the restaurant."

"What? How bad? Was Clementine there?"

"No, she was still on the catering job."

"I'll be there in ten. You hold down the fort, I'll call the family, okay?"

"Okay." I paused. "I called Neil."

Nico processed that information. "Good. I'll see you soon."

I hung up; with the water off, I could hear Gigi barking in the car.

"Ma'am," another one of the uniforms said, "my crew is still checking that the fire is fully out. The fire reached the roof on the south side."

I nodded, wrapping my arms tighter around myself. "Juliette," I said. "My name's Juliette D'Alisa."

He offered his gloved hand. "I'm Lt. Kerning."

"How — how bad is it?"

"Too early to say. The bulk of the damage seems to be on the first floor."

Hope flared. "Really?"

"Like I said, it's too early to say. Old houses, fire can spread fast." He put his hands on his hips. "The origin of the fire looks to be the wall behind the stove. My guess is that the wiring caught, smoldered until it flamed, and reached enough grease to become a problem. After that, the fire went up the wall to the outside, away from the sprinklers." He shook his head. "Bad luck is what it is."

The slam of a car door, the sound of my name being called.

I turned to see Neil striding toward us, already slipping off his overcoat. "You look like you're freezing."

Neil introduced himself to the officer while I took in his appearance. His hair was disheveled, his eyes creased with worry. He wore a sweatshirt and rumpled jeans; the overcoat was now draped over my shoulders.

One of the firefighters called out to the

282

officer with us, and with a nod to let us know he'd return, he strode away, leaving Neil and me to ourselves.

"Your coat is warm," I said. "Thank you."

"Are you okay? Were you inside?"

"I'm okay. And no, I was driving home from a family dinner, and I came home to this." I shook my head in disbelief. "I pulled over for the emergency vehicles. I had no idea they were going to my home."

"They don't know about the damage yet?"

"They don't want us going in tonight." I hugged my arms tighter. "Neil — the letters, the physical letters were in there. The letters, and my computer, and . . . and the Christmas decorations my mom gave me . . ."

Neil folded me into his arms as I began, finally, to cry.

"I know they're just things," I said against the soft fabric of his sweatshirt. "But they were my mom's, and my grandmother's, and I *know*," I repeated, "that they're just things. But without the people, I was fond of having the things. Now all I have are the memories."

"Never discount your memories."

"My memories feel threadbare after a while. I need the reminders."

His hold tightened. "As far as I'm concerned, I'm just glad you're okay."

"Thank you for coming."

"Of course," he said, leaning back far enough to look down into my eyes. "Always. I . . . I'm glad you're okay."

"Nico's on his way," I told him. "But — you were my first call."

Neil slipped his hand into my hair, cradling my head.

I lifted my face to his. "I'm not over you, Neil. It's important that you know that."

A smile flickered over his face, but my eyes slid shut before I could fully appreciate it. His kiss began tenderly, carefully, but deepened as we remembered each other. The familiarity of his scent, the feel of his nearness. I raised my hands to his face, needing the feel of his skin beneath my fingers.

Neil's embrace turned fierce, and I could taste the fear, the anxiety that had driven him here. I met every new caress with one of my own, a reminder that I was there, we were together, we were safe. We created our own haven in each other's arms, shutting out the melee outside.

Shutting most of it out.

A car door slammed, footsteps approached. "Hey, Juliette!" my brother's voice called out. "Glad to see something good's come of this."

19

Cooking is one failure after another, and that's how you finally learn.

— JULIA CHILD

Another car pulled up, and Clementine emerged. "Sweet Julia Child," she said, taking in the scene. "What happened?"

Nico tipped his head to the side. "Romance can be incendiary. Look at the end of *Like Water for Chocolate.*"

Clementine's focus shifted from the burned restaurant to Neil and me. "Oh. *Oh.*"

I looked up at Neil. "Will you forgive my family and friends?"

"Will you forgive mine?"

I gave him a quick peck at the corner of his mouth before stepping back, but I didn't let go of his hand. "Hi, Nico," I said, giving my brother a one-armed hug.

"Hi," he said, rubbing my back.

"Our restaurant caught on fire."

"It's just a building," he answered. "Nobody's hurt. That's what's important."

The fireman I'd been talking to earlier returned; I introduced my brother and let Nico get caught up.

Like me, he couldn't believe that such a fire had happened.

"It's old wiring," Lt. Kerning explained. "The fire marshal will come and investigate and write up the report. A crew will remain on site to prevent anyone from trying to enter."

"Do you know when the fire marshal will arrive?" I asked.

Lt. Kerning shook his head. "Depends on his caseload. We'll contact you when he does. You don't have to stay."

"Oh." We could go.

We could go, but I hated to leave. But Gigi was still in the car, panicking, and Clementine looked cold, and staying to keep the house company wasn't exactly practical.

Never mind that we needed to sleep sometime, because the morning would bring a whole new set of challenges.

"Want me to drive you back to your dad's place?" Neil offered.

I thought it over. "I wish you could, but I don't want to leave my car here. Do you want to come over with us, though? I can promise hot chocolate."

Neil gave a wry smile. "You don't have to feed me, Jules. I'd come just for you."

The four of us drove our separate cars to my dad's place: Neil, Nico, Clementine, and me.

My dad and Alex greeted us with relieved hugs, celebrating our safety. My father held me close, his hug even more rib crushing than usual.

My dad offered food, of course. I asked for tea — after the evening's events, my appetite was nowhere to be seen.

If he and Alex were surprised to see Neil, they didn't say. My dad made him a sandwich.

Nico left when he felt we were safely settled. Clementine headed to bed in the guest room, the one that Alex and Nico had shared as boys. In the years since, my mother had replaced the carpet, painted it violet, and decorated in French toile prints.

Dad and Alex returned to bed shortly as well, leaving Neil and me alone together downstairs.

I looked down at Gigi, curled into my lap, and back up at Neil. "We kissed tonight."

A slow smile spread across his face. "We did."

"We should probably talk about it."

"We could. But there was also a fire at your home *and* place of work."

I nodded. "There was."

"So you might want to get some sleep."

"I won't be able to sleep. I'll need to figure out what we're going to do, how long repairs will take — if it's even reparable. At the very least I need to look up our OpenTable account to look at our reservations so I can cancel them. And then there's our vendors, and I'm feeling way in over my head." I exhaled. "And Frank. I have to call Frank."

"Frank's your investor, right?"

"Correct. And aside from all of that — which is a lot," I added, "there's you." I looked into his eyes, those eyes that I loved. "And that alone would keep me up all night."

"So what are you going to do?"

I chewed on the edge of my lip. "I don't know yet."

"Want me to stay with you?"

"You've got work tomorrow."

"So do you."

Gigi groaned, stretched, and decamped from my lap to the empty space beneath the armchair. "Your students deserve better," I said with a rueful chuckle.

He shrugged. "I drink coffee."

I leaned forward and kissed him.

Kissed him, as if it were the easiest thing. As if we hadn't been apart for too long.

I tilted my head back, my eyes focusing on his with effort. "You should go home and sleep," I said. "Can I see you tomorrow?"

We walked to the door. I put a hand on the latch but stopped when Neil's hands settled around my waist.

"That day at the river?" Neil pulled me toward him, and I didn't consider resisting. "I thought I was hallucinating. You were the most beautiful thing I'd ever seen. Beautiful but so far out of reach." His hand stroked my hair in small, gentle gestures, like he was trying to reassure himself that I stood in front of him. "Juliette, I love you. And if we start this again, I want us to make it forever."

I inhaled sharply as I processed his words, but Neil shook his head. "Don't answer. Not tonight. But if you want to know my intentions, there they are." He pressed a kiss to my forehead. "I'll see you tomorrow."

"I'll see you tomorrow," I echoed, raising myself on my tiptoes for a goodnight kiss. "Whatever it may bring."

Sophie arrived before I rose from bed the next morning, bags in hand. "I brought underwear for you," she said. "I got it from Target first thing this morning, then took it home and washed it. I promise it's as fresh as a May daisy."

"We're sisters," I said, sitting up. "I'd wear your clean underwear."

"That's sweet," she said. "But I need more underwear myself. I can't afford to share."

"You could have bought yourself more underwear at Target."

"I may have."

I raised a hand in the air. "High five. Here's to new panties."

Sophie gave my hand an awkward almost-slap. "Something a wise woman told me once: 'There comes a time in a woman's life when she takes stock of her underwear drawer and decides she deserves better.' "

"That was totally Cat, wasn't it?"

"You guessed it. Did you get any sleep?"

"Umm . . . well, I woke up, so I'm guessing yes? No idea how much, though." I picked up my phone. No calls from the fire department, but there was a text from Neil wishing me a good morning.

I set the phone back down.

"Neil and I are back together. I think." I replayed the events of the previous evening through my head. "No, we are. If I'll have him, we are."

Sophie sat down on the bed near my feet. "And will you?"

I thought for a moment. "Yes."

"Nice to have that settled, then."

"Yes, settled." I wrapped my arms around my knees. "Thing is, that's the only bit that's settled."

"You've got the most important part figured out," she said. "Everything else is gravy."

"Chunky gravy."

"I shouldn't have woken you up," she said dryly, patting my legs.

"No, it's fine," I said, swinging my legs around and planting my feet on the floor. "I've got quite a lot to do today."

Sophie pointed at the second bag. "I pulled a couple pieces from my closet for you, and some toiletries. That wraparound plaid skirt you like, and a couple sweaters. I didn't think you'd want to wear last night's clothes today."

"You're a good sister."

Sophie stilled. "You think so?"

"Of course," I said, resting my head on

her shoulder. "And not just because you brought me underwear."

In the shower, I thought over our options as I massaged shampoo into my scalp. We were short a restaurant. More specifically — we were short a restaurant building. What if we found a building?

We had a financial cushion, but it wouldn't last us for long. We still needed to bounce back from this, and fast, before people found their next new favorite spot.

I dressed in my new underwear and the clothes that Sophie brought in her bag. My clothes from the night before smelled of smoke.

I massaged her tinted moisturizer into my skin and used her cream blush to bring some life back to my complexion. But there was no mistaking the circles under my eyes, and I found I didn't have the energy to fight them. I decided instead they were a badge of honor.

Another text, this one from Adrian. "Heard about the fire," he said. "Glad you and C are okay."

I texted him back, thanking him. He really was a good guy, just not the guy for me.

As I dried out my hair, a rough plan formed in my head.

I found Dad in the kitchen, stirring. "What are you making?" I asked.

He looked up at me and smiled. "Hot chocolate. I thought you might want some for breakfast."

I grinned at him. "You really are the best."

He shrugged. *"Sì, lo so."* He knew. He gave me a peck on my cheek. "Have a *cornetto* — they're fresh."

"Thank you."

I took a bite, chewing thoughtfully as he ladled cocoa into a cup and set it in front of me with a gentle *clink.*

"I have a question for you," I began after swallowing. "And I want you to know you can turn me down."

"Ah yes?"

"Would you mind sitting down?"

He sat.

I pulled my chair closer. "Here's the thing. Two Blue Doors has near solid reservations every weekend through New Year's. I hate giving that up, and who knows how long the repairs are going to take. We've got everything we need, everything but a restaurant." I leaned forward. "D'Alisa & Elle has the upstairs banquet rooms."

My father gave me a shrewd nod. "That would be interesting."

"And if we could use the catering kitchen

294

— with Alex's cooperation, of course."

He crossed his arms and leaned back in his chair. "Haven't I always said you were the smartest of all my children?"

"Haven't you always said that about each of us?"

He shrugged. "True enough."

"You think it might work?"

"What do you think it would take to bring it about?"

"A lot of kitchen cooperation, that's for sure — the upstairs walk-in is much smaller. We'd want to streamline the menu, or offer a combination of menu options between the two restaurants. That's probably the better idea." I thought for a moment. "I'd want to contact an event supplier, maybe look for some room dividers, screens of some sort. Potted orchids for the tables."

I tried not to think of the beautiful leather chairs we'd had in the dining room at Two Blue Doors. "I think a blend of menus would be intriguing, and a promise of free champagne . . ."

"You are a restaurateur through and through."

"We'll find out, won't we?" I looked down at my hands. "What do you think would happen, *Papa*? If I left Two Blue Doors?"

"I do not know," he said, rising to take my

empty plate and cup. "No one knows, not for sure. But you may have new adventures before you, yes?"

I felt my face turn pink. "Yes. I just . . . I don't want it to hurt Nico, and I don't want it to hurt the restaurant. I worked hard to help turn it into what it's become. You know," I said, taking a deep breath, "before it caught fire."

"You should feel very proud."

"I never thought I would be that girl."

"Which girl?"

I wrinkled my nose. "The girl who gives up her job for a man."

He snorted. "Wherever you might go, I am certain there are restaurants, or places to start them. But dreams change, my Giulietta. Even if it's not a restaurant," he said, patting my shoulder, "whatever you choose to do will be grand."

"Thanks." I squeezed his hand. "So the double restaurant — you think we could pull it off?"

"Pay attention!" he admonished. "I think you can do anything."

After my talk with Dad, I called Nico to tell him my idea. "I was just about to call you," he said. "The fire marshal is ready to walk

296

us through the building. Want to come down?"

"Already putting on my shoes."

"What were you calling about?"

I shared my plan as I drove, down to the menu.

"If Dad's game," he said, "I say we go for it."

"Good." A smile stretched across my face. "How about this? You call your people, I'll call mine."

"Get the band back together?"

"Something like that. But I need seventy-two hours to make it happen."

"You think we could get it going by Christmas Eve?"

I thought about it and nodded. "I'm good at what I do — and so are you. If you can make the kitchen come together, I can get the dining room set up and do my best to transfer our reservations."

"Then let's do it," he said. "What else have we got?"

~ ITALIAN HOT CHOCOLATE ~

1 cup plus 1 1/2 cups whole milk, divided
4 tablespoons cocoa powder
2 tablespoons sugar
3 tablespoons potato starch
Pinch sea salt
Whipped cream and chocolate shavings, for
   serving

In a medium saucepan, heat 1 cup of the milk over medium heat until just simmering. Add the cocoa powder, sugar, potato starch, and salt, whisking until smooth.

Add remaining 1 1/2 cups of milk, stirring constantly until the mixture begins to simmer and thicken. Remove the pan from heat, and pour it into serving cups or mugs. Top as desired.

Serves 4.

20

A recipe has no soul. You, as the cook, must bring soul to the recipe.
— THOMAS KELLER

The outside of the restaurant still smelled of smoke. I could hear the fire marshal talking over specs to Nico, but I couldn't stop thinking about the acrid scent.

If we cleaned and rebuilt, how long would that smell take to dissipate?

The first glimpse of the downstairs took my breath away. I heard Clementine's gasp behind me.

Water puddles still covered the tables and floor, which had begun to warp. Black smoke stained the walls, especially near the ceilings.

The major kitchen appliances looked fine, but anything wood handled was definitely the worse for wear.

We walked up the exterior stairs, which

299

were on the opposite side of the burn, and untouched. I held my breath as I opened the door, not knowing what was inside.

The smell of smoke hung heavily in the air, and I wrapped my scarf firmly around my mouth and nose.

Nico placed a reassuring hand on my arm. "The insurance policy covers burn restoration. We'll get things cleaned and taken care of, Etta."

I nodded, taking it in.

The dining room and kitchen had been taped off. "There's burn damage below," the marshal said. "It looks like there's a kitchen island of some sort in there — not sure how that hasn't fallen through the floor, to be honest."

The prep table.

The table Gabriel made.

"That table is an heirloom," I told the marshal. "If there's any way to move it safely as soon as possible, I would appreciate it."

"I'll see what I can do."

I wanted to say more but refrained. "Thanks."

The lieutenant's prediction had proved accurate. Most of the damage occurred in the kitchen — the broken window, the charred, sooty wall, the residential appliances half-melted, grotesque. Bits of the floor had burned through, others looked like they'd crumble without more than a sneeze.

At any moment, I expected the prep table to simply fall through the floor. Parts of the carpet in the living room squished beneath my feet. The papier-mâché Moravian stars were long gone; the heat from the blaze had caused the vintage bubble lights to shatter. I touched one of the porcelain elves on the mantel, rubbing some of the ash off.

I turned away and peered down the hallway. "Is — is it safe to look at the bedrooms?"

The marshal nodded, and Clementine and I proceeded down the hallway.

Clementine's room was fine — sooty, but fine.

The wall connecting my room to the kitchen was blackened, the window broken. Powerful hoses had stopped the fire from burning through the wall, but it had left my belongings soaked in a mess of water and ash.

I had no hope for the computer on my desk.

With shaking hands, I lifted the lid of the trunk and slid open the storage compartment in the lid.

The letters were inside, just as I'd left

them, perfectly dry.

I realized, as I took them out, that the finish on the trunk had protected them from the water.

The letters. I had the letters, and they were fine.

Carefully, I placed them into a gallon-sized Ziploc bag and tucked the bag into my purse.

My clothes — at least the ones in the closet — were none the worse for wear, other than smelling of smoke and melted microwave. I sent Sophie a quick text, asking if she could help me move the contents shortly. Between the two of us and her family vehicle, I figured we could make quick work of it.

In the meantime, I filled a duffel bag with clothing to launder and threw two of my work dresses over my arm.

Clementine followed with Nico shortly after, a bag of her own packed up.

"It wasn't bad," she said as she got into the car. "I expected much worse."

"Good," I said absently. "I'm glad to hear that."

Back at my dad's house, I started a load of clothes in the washer, then sat down in the office and stared out the window.

Nico knocked on the doorway. "Etta?"

I swiveled around. "Hi. I'm fine. I was just . . . There's a lot to do for this hybrid-restaurant concept."

"Etta . . . take a day off. Please."

"There's a lot to do. I, um, got a call from two of the news stations. They want interviews in front of the restaurant this afternoon. We need to have a plan that I can talk about on camera."

"One day. Or do the interview, and take the rest of the day."

"I need this."

Nico sighed. "If it's what you need — if it's really what you need, fine. But Grand-tante Cécile just passed away and the restaurant caught fire and turned into a lot of personal-property damage and you got back together with the guy you've been pining over."

I lifted my chin. "I have not been pining."

"Shut up. You've been pining and everyone knows it. I'm just saying, if you take a day off, the sky's not going to fall down."

"I'll do the interview. And then I'll take a day."

"Good."

"And by take a day, I mean that Sophie and I will try to get my things out of the apartment and work on getting them cleaned up."

"Whatever you need to do."

I needed to fix things, that's what I needed to do. It's what I was good at. But at that moment I felt so truly and deeply over-whelmed.

"Want to go over the menu?" I asked. "If we get the menu nailed down, I can talk to our suppliers."

Nico heard the pleading note in my voice, his shoulders lowering in resignation. "Sure."

I dressed with care for the news interview, wearing a pale-pink peacoat from Sophie's collection.

The TV crew met me there, and I steeled myself. Historically, live TV was not my thing. The last time I was on camera, I'd lost my breakfast afterward. If that turned out to be the case today, well, I'd already scoped out a likely spot behind the build-ing, behind the boxwood.

The initial interview proceeded in a blur. I explained that there had been a fire, that it had been dealt with effectively by the city's emergency services.

I knew that my interview would likely be chopped into bite-sized sound clips, but I forged ahead. This was free publicity, if they'd air any of it. "It's important that our employees remain employed through the holidays," I said. "We'll be opening a temporary pop-up on the second level of D'Alisa & Elle until we can return to this building." I looked over my shoulder to the once stately building, my grandmother's pride and joy. "This building belonged to my grandmother," I continued. "It's an important part of Portland's history, and we'll work to make her beautiful once again."

The reporter wrapped up the segment and gave the signal for the cameraman to cut.

A thin layer of sweat coated my forehead, despite the cold, and I could feel my hands shake.

Nico gave me a huge hug once the van had disappeared. "You were great!" he said. "I hope they use all of that." He put his hands on my shoulders and looked me over. "Are you going to hurl?"

"I don't think so," I answered after taking stock of my stomach's stability. "I think the boxwood may come out scot free."

He gave me a quizzical expression. "I don't know, don't think I wanna. Let's get you back to Dad's place."

I shook my head. "Sophie's going to meet me here," I said. "We're going to move stuff."

"Aren't you going to get dirty?"

"I'm borrowing Nelson's gardening jacket. Sophie's bringing it."

"Comes through in a pinch, that one."

I looked at the restaurant. "I think this qualifies as more than a pinch, but yes."

Nico raised an eyebrow. "So you'll move some things and then relax?"

"That's the plan," I told him. "Don't worry about me."

I tried relaxing. Really, I did. But once Sophie and I finished gathering up my clothes and bedding, I felt restless.

"Do you have other plans today?" I asked her.

"Chloé is going over to Grace's house to 'study' this afternoon, so I've got the rest of the day."

"Want to go look at the banquet rooms? See what I've gotten us into?"

Sophie nodded. "Let's do it. I'm in."

I reached across the center console of the car and grabbed her hand. "You're the best."

We were practical first, starting a load of wash and dropping several items off at the dry cleaners, but soon enough we found ourselves at the restaurant where we'd both grown up.

We greeted the servers on the way in, several of whom we'd known for ages. We climbed the stairs and used our copies of the restaurant master key to open up the double doors that led to the first banquet room.

Sophie and I surveyed the room together.

"This is going to take work," she said.

"You are not wrong," I answered.

Old tables and chairs were stacked on one side, with the catering plates and glassware stacked on the other. Décor from past eras cluttered up the in-between spaces. Black blinds blocked out the streetlights.

Unlike the downstairs, the light fixtures up here were semiflush rather than pendants. The lights were fine, at least. The art glass had proved, so far, to be ageless. But because they were higher, the space felt less intimate.

Looking back down at the tables, some of my hair fell in front of my face, and a wave of irritation — fueled by lack of sleep — struck hard. I batted the offending hair away. "I need a haircut."

"Unless I'm mistaken," Sophie said, reaching with a motherly hand to help smooth it back, "you haven't had time for a cut."

"That's true. I should have gotten one in Chicago. There was a painfully hip-looking salon two blocks from Caterina's place."

"There are painfully hip salons near your place."

"Yes, but I'm feeling rather short of time now." I took a deep breath. "Sorry, I'm just a little nutters, don't mind me. Do you have an elastic, by any chance?"

Sophie dug through her purse. "I have a ribbon — it's left over from some project of Chloé's."

"I'm desperate. I'll take it." I took the ribbon from her outstretched hand and used it to tie my hair back. "There."

"Feel better?"

"Much better." I shot her a grateful smile. "Occam's razor — the simplest solution is the best solution." I looked back out at the scene in front of us. "And I think I know what to do in here."

Over the next hour, I took measurements and made plans before getting on the phone.

There was too much clutter for us to handle on our own, but before we even began to move things, there had to be a place to move them to.

Nico and I had already had a discussion about renting a storage unit for the furniture and equipment at Two Blue Doors while the repairs were underway, so within a short period of time I located a storage facility with two units large enough to hold the items from Two Blue Doors and the D'Alisa & Elle banquet rooms.

The second step involved Post-it notes. Sophie and I went through the tables, chairs, screens, and other decorative items that we wanted to keep, and marked them with notes.

She left to pick up Chloé from Grace's house, and I called Nico, who called the rest of the restaurant staff.

I gave Mario, the chef that night, a heads-up, and ordered a platter of crostini, polenta rounds with tomatoes, and a bottle of wine, charging it to the family account. By the time everyone arrived, I had a picnic set up in the center of the room.

There were hugs all around, even between Adrian and myself. He held my hands in his for a moment. "I'm glad you're all right," he said.

"Thanks," I said, smiling. It was good to see him. There was still affection between us, I could feel it.

But it was different than what Neil and I had. With Adrian, it was a spark, a connection. With Neil?

A full-on tractor beam.

The moment with Adrian didn't last long, not with the full staff and a selection of ap-

309

petizers. Soon enough we were all seated on the floor, talking with our mouths full — and I was the worst offender.

"The segment about the restaurant will air on the news tonight," I explained. "Who knows what they'll cut, but all of you need to know that Nico and I are committed to keeping the restaurant open and making sure you all have work."

The air was already relaxed, but I swear I heard several exhalations of relief.

"The holidays are hard enough without looking for temporary work. Yes, we will be closed for a few days, but the plan is to open back up in these rooms for the Christmas Eve dinner seating."

"What about lunch?" Mallory asked.

"We'll do lunch for a week or two and monitor the numbers. What we don't want to do is hurt the D'Alisa daily takes. What the D'Alisa doesn't do is brunch, and we'll give it a try on the weekends. The menu," I continued, "will be a little bit different. We'll have a limited number of the D'Alisa's most popular menu items available."

"And desserts?" Clementine asked.

"Desserts are going to synergize the other way. Clementine, you'll make larger batches and we'll make your desserts available downstairs as well. In the end, both restaurants benefit."

Clementine nodded. "I can do that."

"You'll have access to the pastry station of the downstairs kitchen," I told her. "The rest of the kitchen crew will use the upstairs catering kitchen."

Nico clasped his hands together. "The food storage is smaller but we should be fine."

"The biggest task," I said, "is putting half of this stuff in storage and setting up the rest."

"It's a challenge," Adrian said with a grin. "Whadya say we get started?"

～ POLENTA ROUNDS WITH CHERRY TOMATOES AND ROASTED GARLIC ～

Grapeseed or olive oil
2 18-ounce logs of polenta
Coarse salt and pepper to taste
1 dry pint cherry tomatoes
1 1/2 tablespoons jarred roasted, chopped garlic
2 tablespoons fresh basil, chopped fine
1 teaspoon balsamic vinegar
4 ounces shredded parmesan cheese

Preheat your oven broiler to high. Line a baking sheet with foil, and spray lightly with oil. Slice the polenta logs into 1/4-inch-thick rounds. Place the rounds onto the baking sheet, spray the tops lightly with the oil, and sprinkle with salt and pepper.

Place under the broiler, about 5 minutes, flip gently, and broil another 5 minutes. Allow rounds to drain on paper towels and cool. If not using immediately, refrigerate and reheat later in a 375°F oven for about 5 minutes, or until the rounds are just sizzling.

In a food processor, lightly pulse the tomatoes. Move tomatoes to a mixing bowl, and stir together with the garlic, basil, and vinegar. Salt and pepper to taste. Refrigerate until ready to serve.

To assemble, use a slotted spoon to place a small amount of the tomato mixture onto each polenta round (you may want to drain some of the liquid ahead of time). Top with parmesan cheese and serve.

Makes about 26 rounds.

21

It seems to me that our three basic needs, for food and security and love, are so mixed and mingled and entwined that we cannot straightly think of one without the others.

— **M. F. K. FISHER**

In the end, we pushed the tables around the outside and sprinkled a couple in the middle. We found a room divider shoved into a corner and unfolded it to create a narrower entryway. It felt more intimate that way, walking in, as if you were walking into a cozy room rather than a space at the top of some stairs.

Having everyone together made quick work of it. After the loss we'd experienced in the past twenty-four hours, being able to have a plan kept everyone in high spirits.

Still, it was far from a full workday, and

everyone but me and Nico headed out by nine.

Once again, the work reverted to Nico and me. Nico would be drawing up the hybrid menu, keeping the ingredients streamlined. He and the kitchen staff would do a practice run Tuesday, making sure that everyone had the flow worked out. The last thing we needed was to have a successful reopening thwarted by a slow, clumsy kitchen. They'd need to be able to execute each dish as quickly as if they were in their home kitchen, and be able to throw in the new-to-them D'Alisa & Elle dishes as well.

As for me, I'd be running the marketing and PR, as well as having the new menus printed and training the servers. Since I'd fired Hannah, we were still down one. But my dad had a lunch server, Tory, who'd recently asked to switch to the dinner seating.

"Everything go well with the insurance guy?" I asked Nico at the end of the day, leaning against the wall and surveying the room.

"As well as it could, I guess. Dad was there. We'll get the old girl back together, but it'll take time. This" — he nodded toward the room — "this is a good idea." He slung an arm around my shoulders.

"And by 'good idea,' I mean 'this will keep us in business, and thank you.' "

I put my head on his shoulder. "You're welcome."

"What would I do without you?"

"You'd think of something. I did have another idea, about the repairs."

"Yeah?"

"Since it's all being repaired, it's a good time to update. And I think you should consider converting the second floor."

He turned to face me, eyes wide. "What?"

"The second floor. Look, we've been squeezing diners in as full as good taste and the fire marshal will allow."

"We've met him."

"Yes, lovely man. It's been tight, is what I'm saying. So if we're doing the repairs, we might as well expand the seating."

"Where will you live?"

"I . . . don't know."

"What about Clementine?"

"I haven't talked to her about it yet. But she's got steady work now, so she'll be fine."

"Does this have to do with you and Neil being back together?"

"He and I haven't discussed it, if that's what you're asking."

"It's not."

"We're back together, but we haven't

spent as much as two hours together. But you're getting distracted," I told him. "Think of the seating!"

"Where's he living? After his gig at OHSU?"

"Atlanta."

"Direct flight, at least." He looked at me. "It's a good idea."

"I haven't run it by Dad yet."

"He'll like it," Nico conceded. "I'll miss you."

"There aren't any plans, you big lug."

"Not yet there aren't. Are you going to go see him?"

"That was my plan," I said.

"Then I won't get in the way of true love."

I gave him a cheeky smile. "You're the best."

A couple texts, and I got into my car to drive to Neil's place. I parked on the street and walked to the front doors of his apartment building, my heart thudding hard. A man walked out just then. Coincidence? Providence? I didn't ask but simply slipped through the open door, looking like I knew exactly where I was going.

An elevator ride later, I found myself on Neil's doorstep.

Now or never. I rapped on the door before

my courage failed altogether.

Footsteps, and the door swung open.

"Juliette!" Neil said, surprise and happiness coloring his voice. "How did you —"

"Tarissa," I said, still breathless. He looked wonderful, standing there dressed in moss-colored corduroy pants and that ivory knit fisherman's sweater with a high collar. He looked wonderful, and I stood there with a flushed face, sounding as though I'd climbed the stairs. "I asked Tarissa."

"Come in," he said, swinging the door wider. "Do you want to take your coat off?"

"I — I want to go with you."

Neil closed the door behind me, his face intense. "What?"

"When you leave Portland. When you move to Atlanta — I want to go with you."

He said nothing, just stared at me.

"I mean, if you want me to," I said, panic rising. "But I love you, and I think you might love me, and if we want a chance, just a chance for this to work out —"

Neil pulled me into his arms and silenced me with a kiss.

"Yes," he said some time later, sounding as breathless as I had. "I don't want us to let go of each other again."

"Never," I said, tears stinging my eyes. "Never ever."

The tears fell, but Neil kissed them away. And then we were lost again, our kisses becoming assurances of love, relief, and joy.

"We should probably talk details," I said, threading my hands into Neil's thick, gingery hair.

His hands tightened on my waist. "That sounds like the adult thing to do."

"I'm serious!" I said, though my eyes closed again as Neil pressed a kiss high on my cheekbone.

A brush of lips against mine, and he stepped back. "Hi."

I looked up at him, my grin stretching stupidly across my face. "Hi."

"I'll have to thank Tarissa for sharing my address. Though I would have given it to you if I knew you'd wanted it."

"I didn't know if I'd lose my nerve on the way."

I felt his smile against my cheek. "I'm glad you didn't."

"I've just never told a guy that I wanted to, you know, move with him."

Another kiss from Neil. I kissed him back before stepping away. "You'll distract me again."

He gave a rueful chuckle. "I'll distract you? I find you extremely distracting." He caressed my shoulders with care. "What if we take this to the patio?" he suggested. "Can I offer you some coffee? I just started a pot of decaf before you knocked."

"No wonder this place smells so good." I turned to take in his apartment for the first time. "That view!" I walked toward his patio, pressing my hands to the glass. "The bridge, the river — it's amazing!" Soft rain fell just past the covered patio. "Are you sure about sitting outside, though?"

"I have a system," he said. He poured coffee for the two of us before tipping his head toward the patio.

I stepped outside, and he followed me out, blankets in hand. I watched in fascination as he took one and plugged it into the outdoor outlet.

"Electric blanket. You're a genius."

He winked at me. "You're welcome."

We sat together on the rattan settee. It felt cold at first, but the wiring of the electric blanket began to warm and stay trapped beneath the second fleece blanket. I wrapped my hands around the coffee and snuggled closer to Neil. "This is nice."

He looked at me. "Better than nice, I'd say." His arm stretched across my shoulders. "Fall term ends tomorrow," he said. "The position at Biogen starts next month, on the nineteenth."

I nodded, thinking. "Okay."

"I'm not questioning you," he said, fingering the ends of my hair, "but are you sure you can leave Two Blue Doors?"

"Two Blue Doors is going to be in the midst of repairs for a while," I began, before explaining our plans at D'Alisa & Elle.

"Impressive," Neil said, lifting his mug to clink with mine. He drained the rest in a few gulps and set it aside.

"I think it'll work. And if not, we gave it our royal best." I took a sip of my coffee. "I told Nico to convert the apartment to seating. It just seemed . . . time." I set my cup down. "I'm not here because I'm homeless. I'm here because I finally figured out that you're my home. Wherever you are, that's where I want to be."

"There's just one of Two Blue Doors."

I sighed. "I . . . I think they were the doors I needed to walk through to get here. It was a place to figure out that I really am good at what I do. I got my confidence back, and I'm grateful for that." I rested my head on his shoulder. "But now that I've done that, I want to find you too."

"I love you."

I smiled into his sweater. "I love you back. There is one other thing: the post-Christmas trip to the chateau we were planning before the fire, before Grand-tante Cécile passed away."

"Cécile? I didn't know."

"I'm sorry — Sandrine called during family dinner, the night of the fire."

Neil rubbed his thumb against my head in a soothing gesture. "You've had a time of it."

"That I have."

"You've got to be exhausted."

"Somewhere between exhausted and wired. Probably something you experienced in medical school."

Neil gave a soft laugh. "Something I see in class most days."

"The trip is from the fourth to the twelfth. After the holidays, the restaurant load lightens. I've trained Mallory to manage the front of the house, and she's good. Adrian's capable of running the kitchen, and Mario will probably enjoy having my dad away. With my mom gone, we need something happy. And now Sandrine needs it too."

"I want to go with you," Neil said.

"Are you sure? Can you spare the time?"

"It's between classes and the start of my job. Absolutely. Especially if I'm packed before the trip."

"We could go from Montagnac to Atlanta together. We wouldn't have to part ways at the airport again."

Words hung in the air alongside the misty fractions of raindrops.

"What if . . . ," I began, but my mouth dried out too much to continue.

Neil reached for my hand, cradling it within his own. "Marry me, Juliette? Provence, Atlanta — let's get married and face those adventures together. Always, together."

I caught my breath. "You mean that?"

Neil rose from the settee, and I froze as I watched him kneel. "I love you, Juliette. I love you with everything I am." His voice wavered, but I didn't question that he meant every word, every letter. "We can get married here. We can get married in Provence. We can elope to Vegas."

I suppressed a smile.

He chuckled. "We can elope to somewhere else."

"It's not that — it's Sophie. She's terrified Chloé will elope on her. Calls it the *e* word."

I tossed the idea around in my mind. For the longest time, I'd envisioned my wedding a certain way. My father walking me down the aisle, my mother seated at the front. Months of planning, a giant dress.

But my mother was gone, and instinct told me that my father valued my happiness over sentimentality. I spent all my time planning events. What I wanted now was Neil and the promise of a life together.

I cleared my throat. "Are you teaching tomorrow?"

"Classes in the morning, then I'm all done for the term — with classes, at least. There will be grading after."

"Want to drive to the coast? Get married?"

He reached for my face, cupping it in his hands. "Sure," he said. "I've always wanted to get married on a weekday."

22

There's a lot of cheer in a cake.
— **MARY BERRY**

Friday morning I woke up early and took Gigi for a brisk walk. I packed an overnight bag and drove to D'Alisa & Elle.

My dad sat in his office; I rapped gently on the door. He beamed when he saw me.

"Giulietta! Come in! Do you want to sit down?"

"For just a moment," I answered, seating myself in the opposite chair and folding my hands in my lap. I looked down at my hands and then back at my father.

"Neil and I are going to drive to the coast today," I said. "We're going to elope."

His eyes widened. "Oh."

"We'll be back Sunday. Neil has office hours Monday. I know it's sudden —"

My father lifted a hand. "No, my Giulietta, you do not have to explain. I met your mother on the plane, coming to America. We argued for . . . most of the flight. At the end I knew that she was the one I wanted to marry, that we would have a beautiful life together. And we did. It was beautiful. I wish . . . I wish we'd had just a little more time, but I am being selfish. We had more good years than most. If you want to marry Neil, and you want to marry him today, go marry him." He thought for a moment. "You left Gigi at the house?"

"Yes —"

"Good. I will make sure Alex takes her out."

"You don't mind that we're running away together?"

He crossed his arms. "This is not the old country. If you think he is worthy, that is all that I need."

"He is. Neil is" — I searched for words — "wonderful."

"And he is coming to Provence then, yes?"

"Yes. I thought we could have a family ceremony at the chateau."

"Oh, yes, yes, that will be very nice." He looked me over. "Is that what you're wearing?"

"I have a dress I'll pick up at the cleaner's," I answered. "I won't get married in jeans. Promise."

"Come," he said, beckoning me to the back room.

I followed.

He opened the door to reveal a table full of flower arrangements for the evening's tables. He pulled a white rose from a vase, dried the stem with a towel, and tucked it behind my ear.

"There you go. Be happy, *cara.*"

I picked clothes up from the dry cleaner on my way to Neil's apartment. He met me downstairs, dressed in a charcoal-gray suit and overcoat, then kissed me before insisting on carrying my bag upstairs.

I shared about my conversation with my father while we rode the elevator. "He gives his blessing," I said. "But reminded me I didn't need it."

Neil chuckled. "I look forward to getting to know him better. He sounds like a good man to know."

"He is."

Neil opened his apartment door for me, and I followed with my dry cleaning over my shoulder. The door closed, and he leaned in for a kiss. "Nervous? Second thoughts? We can just go out to lunch if you want to change plans."

"Nope," I said, weaving my fingers

through his. "I'm good."

"I e-mailed three churches and two chapels, and I found an officiant willing to marry us this afternoon, on the beach if we'd like. Unless you'd rather stick with the courthouse."

"Nah, I can deal with the beach. You're amazing." I looked around the apartment, toward the kitchen. "Sorry to break the mood here — you got any food? Eloping makes me hungry."

"I picked up some food from Elephants Deli," he answered. "Someone told me it was good."

"Someone?"

"Someone," he echoed, and my heart flipped.

We ate together at his kitchen countertop, laughing and making plans. Butterflies filled my stomach, but not enough to dampen my appetite. After polishing off a slice of chocolate cake, Neil tidied the kitchen while I changed into my dress in the bedroom.

Made of soft ivory cashmere, it was easily one of the most luxurious items in my closet, as well as being the least worn. With its long sleeves and pencil skirt, it could have been conservative to the point of plain. But the neckline dipped in a becoming V, and it fit me like a glove.

Because it was December and cold, I wore a cardigan sweater over it in a muted, leaf-green wool. Brown boots kept my legs warm.

I felt pretty.

I thought back to the plans I'd had when I was younger, plans for a giant dress and a church full of people. But as I heard the *clink* of dishes being washed and put away by the man I loved, I knew that the list of things I wanted had shrunk.

The big wedding? Didn't even make the cut. But the man in the kitchen? I'd go anywhere for him.

Neil stilled when I reentered the living room, taking in the sight of me. "I don't care that it's bad luck to see the bride before the wedding," he said. "You look beautiful. I hope you don't mind if I did a little shopping this morning." He reached into the pocket of his blazer, pulling out a velvet ring box.

He opened it with a smooth motion, lifting it as he did so.

The ring inside glistened in the winter light. "I don't know if it fits," he said. "And if it doesn't, we'll have it sized correctly. And if you don't like it —"

"I love it," I said. "Of course I love it. It's beautiful."

Neil slipped it from the box and reached for my hand. The platinum band slid past my knuckles with just enough ease, the filigree work setting off the center diamond.

I beamed up at him. "It's perfect. I have to be honest: I don't have a ring for you."

"I picked one up for myself. Promise you like it?"

"Promise," I said, tugging on the lapels of his jacket as I gave him yet another kiss. "Now let's go get married."

The sky poured buckets during the drive to Astoria — the coastal town home to the Clatsop County clerk's office, though best known for being the film location for the '80s classic *The Goonies.* We ran, laughing, into the courthouse, navigating the halls until we found the marriage-licensing department.

The clerk handed us the paperwork and reminded us about the three-day waiting period.

Neil and I exchanged glances.

"There *is* a waiting period," the clerk repeated dryly. "Something has to set us apart from Nevada."

"Other than sales tax?" I quipped.

"What does it take to waive the waiting period?" Neil asked.

"Fifteen dollars and approval from a judge or the clerk."

Neil fished an extra fifteen dollars from his wallet. "We've got an appointment with an officiant at three," he said.

"Can you verify that?"

Neil pulled out his phone and showed the clerk the e-mail.

She gave us a once-over. "Well, you both look sober."

We nodded.

She reached for the form and scrawled a signature on the bottom. "There you go, you two crazy kids. Go get married."

Neil and I married on the beach, under a giant umbrella that threatened to turn inside out at any moment. Our witnesses included the chapel secretary, Delores, and the janitor, Sam.

Delores held my bouquet, calla lilies I'd spotted in a vase outside of the florist's shop on the way to the chapel. Sam snapped pictures with my phone. Neil and I stood, our hands clasped together, our noses — rather cold noses — nearly touching as we repeated the vows.

Under the umbrella, which protected us from a fine, misting rain, it felt like a private world. Just Neil and me together, on the beach, making vows.

We slipped the rings onto our fingers, and Reverend Tavish declared us man and wife.

That was it. We belonged to each other.

And then Neil kissed me, and all I knew was him.

Afterward, we trudged back through the damp sand to the chapel, thanking Reverend Tavish, Delores, and Sam heartily. I promised them each a free meal at Two Blue Doors when they next came through Portland.

We climbed back into Neil's car; Neil turned to me. "What next?"

My cheeks burned. "I think — I think we should find cake."

"Let's find cake," he said, starting the engine. "Cake and coffee."

We warmed up at a cozy café, snuggling on a couch together with cups of coffee and cupcakes on saucers.

"We can look up hotels on our phones," Neil suggested. "Unless you'd rather go back to Portland."

"We ran off to the beach," I said, threading my arm around his. "Let's stay a little longer. We'll have to go back to the real world soon enough — let's take today for ourselves."

So we did.

~ WEDDING CUPCAKES FOR TWO ~

For the Cupcakes:

1 egg white
2 tablespoons sugar
1 teaspoon vanilla
2 drops orange oil
2 tablespoons butter, melted and cooled
1/4 cup flour
1/4 teaspoon baking powder
Pinch salt
1 1/2 tablespoons milk

For the Frosting:

2 tablespoons butter, softened
1/2 cup powdered sugar
1–2 teaspoons milk
1/4 teaspoon vanilla
1/2 teaspoon orange-blossom water
Edible flowers, for garnish

Preheat oven to 350°F. Line a six-cup muffin tin with two liners, and fill the remaining cups with water.

In a medium bowl, whisk together the egg white and sugar. Stir in vanilla, orange oil, and melted butter. Add the flour, baking powder, and salt, whisking until smooth. Pour in milk, and mix until just incorporated.

Carefully pour the batter into the cupcake

liners. Bake the cakes for 12–15 minutes, or until the cakes have risen and turned gently golden. Cool on a wire rack.

In a small bowl, stir together all of the frosting ingredients. Add more milk if it feels too thick. Spoon into a plastic bag — a pastry bag or sandwich bag, both will do the job — and cut 1/2 inch off one corner. Pipe the buttercream onto the cooled cupcakes, and top with the edible flowers. If edible flowers aren't your thing, try candied orange peel or candied ginger.

23

We should look for someone to eat and drink with before looking for something to eat and drink.

— **EPICURUS**

I woke up Saturday morning to find a man staring at me.

"Hi," I rasped, my mouth dry. Dry, because I'd been drooling on the hotel pillow. "How long have you been looking at me?"

Neil's eyes twinkled. "A while."

I wrinkled my nose. "My mouth tastes disgusting." I sat up. "You know, I always thought I'd wake up on my honeymoon and jump out of bed and brush my teeth and my husband would never notice, and *apparently* those dreams are for nothing because . . . I think I married a morning person."

Neil laughed and pressed a kiss to my lips. "Good morning, wife."

I climbed out of bed. "I'm brushing my teeth and drinking a glass of water before I kiss you back." I used the bathroom and loaded up my toothbrush, scrubbing my mouth thoroughly before returning to the warmth of the bed. I returned Neil's kiss and leaned back, studying his face. "So," I said. "We're married."

"We are. Any regrets?"

I thought for a moment. "Nope. I'm good," I answered, before flopping back on the pillow. "It's the 'going back home' I'm not quite sure about."

"No?"

"Because right now, it's just us, and I like that. Pretty soon it's going to be more than us. And the pop-up is opening . . ."

"Come on, you're excited about that."

"I am." I leveled a steady gaze at my husband. "We rather hit the ground running, didn't we?"

"We did. Do you wish we'd waited? Gotten married and taken a private honeymoon?"

I didn't even have to think it over. "I'm with you right now," I said. "That's all I need."

I considered phone calls, considered e-mails — briefly mulled the merits of a skywriter

— but in the end decided to tell each of my siblings in the order of their birth.

Alex hugged me, told me he'd wondered if something was up when I'd left Gigi behind on a mysterious trip.

Sophie attempted to give me her version of "the talk."

Caterina squealed over the phone before she started laughing and crying at the same time; Damian joined her on the phone when she started choking on happy sobs.

Nico nodded in approval. "Good for you," he said as we stood together in the quiet dining room that would host Two Blue Doors. "I'm glad. Really. I just hate to lose you." He took a deep breath. "Brother me is happy. Coworker me is sad to see you go."

"I get it," I said, hugging him even as my phone buzzed.

He nodded toward the phone. "Did you tell Caterina?"

"Yes," I answered before explaining my birth-order rollout of information. Another *buzz.* "She's still texting me about it, though."

"Call her back soon," he said. "The boys have been sick, so the wedding's a nice break from that."

"That's true. How are things here?" I asked, my gaze drifting from the dining

338

room to the kitchen.

"Good. We've got our ingredients, the D'Alisa dishes are coming out quickly and tasting, if I might say so, better than they do downstairs. We're ready to open. Again."

I nodded. "We're going to pull this off, aren't we?"

"Looks like it. How's the retention rate for the reservations?"

"About eighty percent. I invited Linn and Marti from the newspaper, and Frank is bringing guests. The second seating looks like we're at seventy percent, so really I think we're in good shape."

He put his hands on his hips. "When are you and Neil leaving?"

"After Montagnac," I answered. "It'll be a wedding trip of sorts and then Atlanta from there."

"Atlanta."

"Atlanta," I repeated, drawing out the syllables. "For better or for worse. We're road-testing that part of the vows first."

"You know I'll miss you, right? Both brother me and coworker me will miss you."

I gave him a soft jab with my elbow. "You old softie."

My phone buzzed again.

"Call Caterina back," Nico said. "It's the humane thing to do."

■ ■ ■ ■

The last *buzz* turned out to be an e-mail from Sandrine, rather than Caterina. I dialed Sandrine back, gazing out the window while the phone dialed.

"*Allô?*" Sandrine's voice came through the speaker.

"*Allô! C'est moi,* Juliette," I said.

"Ah, Juliette!" She switched to English. "Did you see my e-mail?"

"I did, that's partly why I called. I wanted to tell you that we're absolutely planning on coming to Montagnac, and also that Neil will be coming too. We eloped yesterday, Neil and I."

"*Merveilleux!* That is wonderful news. I could cry, that is so happy! And so romantic."

I could hear her husband Auguste in the background, asking what the commotion was all about, and listened as she explained and Auguste gave a *whoop* of joy.

"So the trip," I explained when she returned, "it'll be something of a wedding trip."

"You'll have a wedding here?"

"No, it's more like a honeymoon."

"But you eloped, you had no ceremony.

You should have a ceremony here at the chateau, Juliette. We will find you a dress and bring the *prêtre* and it will be beautiful."

"Oh yes, that would be very beautiful. I will talk to Neil about it."

"*Oui,* you talk and I shall plan."

"Okay," I said. Yes, there was a lot being lost in translation. But Sandrine had nursed my mother for a month. If she wanted me to spend the trip walking on my hands, I'd do my best to accommodate her.

We said our good-byes and I called Caterina next.

"I think I'm having a wedding ceremony in Provence," I said.

"What?"

"Wedding ceremony. Me. Neil. Chateau. And a French-speaking priest that Neil won't understand."

"Sweet mother of dragons, that sounds amazing. I love it. You eloped and a ceremony is loping after you."

"That is a terrible joke," I said dryly.

"I laughed. But seriously, so pretty. The boys will be ring bearers. And a good excuse to get everyone together, that's the whole point of a wedding, anyway. We can see if the Italy family could come. I'd love to see Nonno."

"And it's Sandrine," I said. "I'd have to be a monster to tell her no, I won't have a wedding ceremony in a pretty dress at her gorgeous chateau."

"There are first-world problems," Caterina said, "and there are 'just get ahold of yourself' problems. I'm thinking that's the latter."

I laughed. "You're right, per usual."

"You're so sweet." She took a breath. "I just can't believe the two of you eloped. That's just crazy and perfect, all at the same time."

"It is," I agreed. "I'm moving some things into his place later today."

"You are only going to be one hour's time difference from me." She gave a happy sigh. "I can't wait."

"It'll be nice," I said.

If I were honest with myself, I was glad to have her closer in some way. Atlanta felt very far away, I wouldn't have a job immediately, and Neil would be away at work.

I took a bracing breath and straightened my back.

"I should get back to things. We'll talk more later," I promised. "I'll let you know how the opening goes Wednesday."

"You've got this," she said. "You're a pro."

"Thanks," I said with a grin. I hung up

and started down the stairs, but my foot stilled on the stair when I saw Adrian.

"Hi," I said.

"I hear congratulations are in order. Sorry — nix that. Best wishes. That's what you say to the bride, right?"

"Yeah," I said, still frozen in place.

What was I supposed to say? Adrian asked me to marry him and I fled for Chicago. Neil? I married the man within twenty-four hours.

Awkward, to say the least.

"It's — Neil and I are right together," I tried again. "I hope you find that."

"Is he going to put you first?" Adrian asked without blinking. "You're leaving for, what, Atlanta, aren't you?"

My heart raced. "He puts us first," I said. "I was the one who insisted on going with him to Atlanta."

"That's what you want?"

"He's what I want," I said, as gently as I could.

Adrian winced anyway.

"I don't want to hurt you," I told him, "though we have enough history that I'll probably succeed without trying. I just — I just wanted to say that I want you to have good things."

A muscle in his jaw twitched, and I knew

he was physically holding words back.

"I want you to have good things too," he said finally. "I just thought we were one of them."

There wasn't anything I could say to make it better. No amount of platitudes or kind words.

So I gave him a kind smile. "You're a good guy, Adrian. See you at the opening?"

He ran a hand through his thick curls. "Yeah. Yeah, I'll see you then."

I said good-bye and left, wishing that his words hadn't found a sensitive place in my heart.

At my dad's place, Gigi and I snuggled up on the couch along with my laptop, and I caught up on work. I shared pictures of the new dining room on social media, followed up with guests who promised to come to the opening.

And then I opened up a new document and began writing notes. I wrote about accounting, our social-media management, and the restaurant policy for handling guest complaints, both in person and in online reviews.

Because in just a few weeks, I'd be handing off my job. I'd need to start interviewing. While Mallory made a great assistant manager, she wasn't ready for the accounting and paperwork part of my job. Nico would need someone who could do it all.

I'd be passing my job off to a stranger, and the thought threw me; I distracted myself by e-mailing Caterina.

To: Caterina, cdesanto@beneculinary.com
From: Me, jdalisa@twobluedoors.com

Adrian did not take the news particularly well. Don't know who told him, but my gut says to blame Kenny.

J

To: Me, jdalisa@twobluedoors.com
From: Caterina, cdesanto@beneculinary
.com

Poor Adrian. Poor Kenny.

Are you doing a color scheme for your chateau wedding? And cake? And a dress?

(You're having ring bearers, so I thought I'd check about the rest. It's a slippery slope.)

Love, C

To: Caterina, cdesanto@beneculinary.com
From: Me, jdalisa@twobluedoors.com

Colors are . . . um . . . butternut squash and pear.

Cake: same.

Dress: TBD

Sorry. I'm . . . nervous about the reopening. And Adrian's words got to me in a way that I'm embarrassed about.

J

To: Me, jdalisa@twobluedoors.com
From: Caterina, cdesanto@beneculinary .com

Aww! Sending love and hugs from Chicago. You've got this. And while you have, of course, forgiven Adrian, don't forget he's also the guy who didn't listen to you and threw you the birthday party you never asked for and never wanted. He's a nice guy but doesn't know everything. Even if he does have good hair.

(I will probably never get over those curls. BUT Neil's hair is kinda gingery, right?

Gingers are super en vogue right now.)

Are you moving into Neil's tonight??

Love, C

To: Caterina, cdesanto@beneculinary.com
From: Me, jdalisa@twobluedoors.com

Moving in tonight! Moving from my dad's place to my husband's, like we're in the old country (at least he doesn't live with his parents). Most of my stuff is going into storage, his is already there — it's a furnished apartment. We'll make our Atlanta place a bit more "us" when we get there.

The following days flew by. I moved my clothes and toiletries into Neil's. We enjoyed a late family dinner at D'Alisa to welcome Neil to the family. Neil charmed them all with his easy southern manners and exuberant love for every dish that came out of the kitchen. At the end of the night, we drove back to his place together, hands entwined.

Christmas Eve morning, I found myself awake well before dawn, my stomach already in knots. Before I knew it, I was back in my favorite work dress and ballet flats, giving the servers last-minute tips before our first diners arrived.

Soon enough, a steady stream of guests arrived, and I bounced from table to table, greeting people, explaining specials, accepting praise for our creative reopening. I brought out platters of our cranberry-and-pistachio-crusted goat cheese to thank diners for visiting us at our new location. Though the evening had barely begun, things were moving even more smoothly than I could have hoped.

Still, I kept an eye on the front for Neil, who'd promised to come after a meeting with colleagues.

The more I watched the front entrance, the more I realized why I'd been extra jittery.

The last time we'd opened, Neil and I had broken up.

My rational mind knew that this time was different. We were married. We lived in the same city — the same apartment.

But my irrational mind? My irrational mind wanted to see him in the entryway. My irrational mind hadn't yet wrapped around the fact that just a week ago, Neil and I hadn't been together, much less married.

I stepped into the kitchen to the drinks station, pouring a drink order for a two-top in the window, my thoughts whirling.

Mallory touched my arm, interrupting the flow. "Last-minute reservation. I know we don't normally take them, but I made an exception."

"Oh?"

"Six-top."

"Six?"

"They asked for the seven o'clock slot. We'll have a full house!"

"That's good," I said. "We don't usually take last-minute reservations," I added.

"The caller offered a credit-card number," Mallory said. "To hold it. Said to charge it if they were late."

I shrugged. "We'll see how it goes. Change the policy if it works out, but if they don't show or it doesn't, no last-minute reservations after, m'kay?"

I delivered the drinks and carried on. At 6:15, my phone buzzed with a text. A text from Neil. "On my way," he said. "I love you."

He loved me. He was coming.

I needed to get a grip. Phone in hand, I stepped out to the fire escape and pressed the button to call him back.

"Hi, love," he answered.

"I just want you to know," I said, "that I love you. And I trust that you love me. And if you don't come, or can't come, I trust that you still love me."

"I'm going to come," he said, sounding baffled. "You got my text, right?"

"I did."

"Is this . . . ? We've had our bumps, Jules. And some of them have been ugly. But we're good. And I'm going to see you soon."

"I trust you."

Neil chuckled. "That's good. Hang tight, Juliette, I'm on my way."

I smiled despite myself. "Okay. You're very charming, you know."

"It's the accent. I'll see you soon."

I was in the kitchen picking up the food for a four-top when Mallory found me again. "The party of six arrived," she said. "I'll run these if you want to seat them. They look like VIPs, so you should probably handle them."

"Thanks for the heads-up." I gave her a rundown on which dish went to each diner before walking back out to the front of the house.

Neil stood by the maître d's station, grinning from ear to ear, flanked by one, two, three — five people in work attire.

It was him all along. He was the mystery caller.

I tipped my head and walked toward him. "Hi there. Table for six, I presume?"

He grasped my hands and planted a kiss on my cheek. "Juliette, there are some people I'd like you to meet. These are my colleagues. And this" — he gestured to me — "is my talented wife, who's responsible for this place."

He introduced me around, and I shook hands and learned names before walking them to the long grouping of tables we'd set up especially for the six of them. I gestured to the menus at each place setting and took drink orders. I bent to kiss Neil on the cheek before returning to the kitchen. "Thank you," I whispered in his ear.

"I'm so proud of you," he answered softly, his eyes crinkling at the corners. "I'm proud of you and I'm proud to be here."

I had no words left; I pressed a kiss onto the corner of his mouth and left to make the drinks, my heart overflowing.

He hadn't just shown up; he'd brought new patrons. That was the guy I'd married. And with that, the shadow in my thoughts melted away.

Everything would be fine. The restaurant would survive. And Neil and I?

On our way to Provence, in the blink of an eye.

~ GOAT CHEESE WITH PISTACHIOS AND CRANBERRIES ~

1/4 cup unsalted, hulled pistachios, rough chopped
1/4 cup dried cranberries, rough chopped
4 ounces soft goat cheese, such as chèvre

Allow cheese to warm on the countertop, about 30–60 minutes. Mix the pistachios and cranberries together in a wide, shallow bowl. Roll the cheese into the mixture, pressing gently to help the mixture stick to the soft cheese.

Wrap in a square of waxed paper, and refrigerate until set. Serve with crackers, baguette slices, apples, or pears.

Makes about 6 servings.

■ ■ ■ ■

PART II

■ ■ ■ ■

24

Winter is the time for comfort, for good food and warmth, for the touch of a friendly hand and for a talk beside the fire: it is the time for home.

— EDITH SITWELL

"It looks completely different in the winter," Neil commented from behind the wheel. "Still pretty, just different."

I gazed out the window at Chateau de l'Abeille, where my grandmother had grown up. "It looks like something from a Victorian novel." I looked over my shoulder. "We're here, you guys!"

We'd rented two Citroen Grand C4 Picassos after our flight. There had been much debate, previously, about taking the train versus driving, but Alex and Neil wanted to drive, and Caterina didn't trust the boys' ability to remain civil for a train ride in public after a transatlantic flight.

As it was, they'd had a number of squabbles because Christian had leaned on Luca, and Christian's hair on Luca's arm had caused Luca's arm to itch, and so on, until they'd fallen asleep for lack of better options.

Alex's van, carrying my dad, Nico, Sophie, Nelson, and Chloé, pulled up beside us as we parked in the circular driveway in front of the chateau.

Caterina sighed. "They've probably been discussing politics and current affairs, like the Kennedys at the dinner table." She turned around to the boys in the third row of seating. "Wake up! We're here!"

We poured out of the vans just as Sandrine and Auguste emerged to greet us, coats pulled tight to protect them from the wind. There were hugs to be had all around, double kisses on cheeks — for Neil in particular. We carried the luggage inside, following Sandrine through the halls as she assigned rooms. Sandrine gave Neil and me the room she'd given him the summer before, all dark woods and drapery.

Accommodations settled, we drifted to the kitchen, where Sandrine presented a spread of fruits, vegetables, and cheeses. Auguste took the boys to the barn to run off energy, promising a stack of hay to jump into.

A thread of daylight remained, but Sandrine had the place surprisingly well lit — lights we hadn't needed over the summer were switched on and casting their rays with the help of antique mirrors. The chateau should have been dreary but instead felt snug and cozy — as cozy as possible for 4,500 square feet.

The adults caught up, the conversation bouncing with alacrity. In short order, we covered Cécile's passing and memorial, the birth of Sandrine's second grandchild in Toronto, and Christmas Day at the chateau.

And with an *"Et toi?"* the conversation topic flipped back to the American contingent.

As usual, our Christmas was simple. I'd never known the kind of extravagant celebrations my classmates' families often enjoyed. Instead, our family took advantage of the postholiday quiet to celebrate on the Twelfth Day of Christmas, Epiphany.

Neil and I had exchanged simple gifts in front of his table-top tree, but in truth I'd been dead tired after our hectic Christmas Eve. We'd Skyped with his parents, who made overtures of joy and guilt about not witnessing our marriage or our Christmas.

There were plans for us to visit North Carolina, once we got back to the States.

"We'll stay with my sister," Neil had promised. "And we'll go skiing. Nothing distracts my parents like skiing."

I kissed him and told him I'd be fine. My own family could be a handful; it would be shortsighted of me to resent his relations.

Auguste returned two tired and hay-dusted boys to the kitchen, where Caterina made sandwiches with peanut butter she'd brought in her suitcase. She'd just set the plates in front of them as the headlights of a taxi flashed in the driveway outside.

We rushed outside — all of us but Caterina and the boys, who would not be parted from their taste of home — to greet the Italians spilling from the oversized taxi. Letizia, her husband, Riccardo, Nonno, *Zio* Alessio, and *Zia* Matilde.

There were even more kisses and exclamations of joy than before. Nonno took my face in his hands as he kissed my cheeks, and repeated with Neil, exclaiming all the while about his happiness over our marriage and his hopes for our future.

Once inside, we laughed and caught up in a mix of languages, learning quickly that we all spoke food fluently. Within the space of twenty minutes, we had a fresh feast to enjoy around the kitchen's oversized farm table.

Once the boys had been bathed and put to bed with a baby monitor, yet another item Caterina had wisely schlepped across the Atlantic, the adults and Chloé retired to the great room where a fire blazed behind the grate. Auguste served coffee and Sandrine brought the cheese plate, and we talked about the Epiphany plans for the following evening and what to do during the day.

Neil gave me a gentle nudge.

I nudged him back before standing and finding a place next to Sandrine.

"I have the key," I said. "The key that might fit into the third-floor closet."

"Yes!" Sandrine brightened. "First thing tomorrow. Unless you would like to look tonight?"

"Really?" My gaze bounced from Sandrine to Neil and back.

"We are here," Sandrine pointed out. "The key is here."

I laughed. "I don't see why not."

We made quite the procession to the third floor; Sandrine led the way, followed by Auguste, myself, Neil, and the rest of my immediate family.

"It sounds like fun," Letizia said, eying the hallways, "but I think we will go to sleep. It was a long day, you know. Tell us about the mystery in the morning, *tutto bene?*"

We climbed the stairs to the third floor while Sandrine narrated, turning on lights as we ascended and entered new rooms. "Someone — very likely my grandmother — facilitated a remodel during the twenties or thirties. Some of the servant rooms were turned into storage closets, once they started using a smaller house staff. She worked to modernize the house, you see. She could be very practical." We came to the end of the hallway. "This closet has resisted my efforts to open the door. Perhaps your key works, perhaps not. It's for the house to decide if she would like to give up her secrets. There are pipes nearby. I thought to add a bathroom up here, for guests, but I would have to access the wall behind this closet, and the house said *non.*" She shrugged. *"C'est la vie."*

Neil placed a hand at the small of my back. "Want to do the honors?"

I took a deep breath and reached into my cardigan pocket for the key.

Throughout the journey, I'd been so afraid of losing the key, fearing it might become misplaced somehow. But we were finally here — the closet lock and the key separated by a span of inches.

I straightened my shoulders; I could either

look at the door all night, or find out if the key actually worked or not. So I placed the key inside the lock, releasing my breath as the key fit smoothly inside, finding myself without breath as it turned, the bolt sliding away.

Sandrine crossed herself. "So it is. It is the key."

I placed the key back within the woolen confines of my pocket before trying the handle.

However, many decades had caused the door to shrink and warp several times. I pulled hard, feeling a little give, and harder a second time, this time with both hands on the handle.

The door gave way, opening with complaint but without catastrophe. We stepped forward together, as if choreographed.

The closet's contents were covered in dust, not surprisingly, and more spider webs than I found strictly comforting. Shelves lined the space, with boxes and clutter filling each one, with additional boxes and a trunk on the floor.

Over the space of the next two hours, we removed each item, dusting when necessary, and giving the contents a cursory check in case of rodent nests or insect infestations.

Only one box looked to have fallen prey to pests, but the pests were nowhere to be seen and were likely several decades departed.

My eyes fell on a faded carpetbag on a center shelf. I lifted it carefully, but clouds of dust filled the air anyway.

I set it on the floor and sat down next to it, my legs crossed.

"What did you find?" Caterina asked, putting down a lamp to look at the bag.

"Not sure yet," I said, carefully working it open. The hinges gave way, and the opening folded away from the center.

"It's — clothes?" I said, opening the bag wider. I worked my fingers around the textile, being careful not to damage the fabric — or disturb any critters.

After a moment I lifted the top item from the bag, and everyone stopped to look.

"What a lovely jacket," Caterina exclaimed, looking closer, fingering the fabric. "That's definitely silk."

I held it up, the pale ivory silk glowing in the light; it felt alive in my hands. And then recognition struck.

"This is from her wedding suit. Remember the wedding photo? With *Grand-père* Gilles? The cut of the lapel — I remember this." I handed it off to Sophie and looked in the bag again. Sure enough, the skirt lay below.

Sophie examined the pieces carefully. "I have several of her old pieces," she said. "These look like they fit a little larger."

"She'd had twins," Caterina noted. "It takes a body a little while to bounce back from that."

Sandrine peered into the bag's depths. "What else is in there? It looks like there is more inside, *non*?"

The next layer was white lace; my breath caught. With reverent care, I lifted the next garment, standing to allow the full length to hang.

Nobody said a word, only looked.

It was a long, white, lace dress. The sleeves were long and unlined, the neckline edged in pearls and landing in a sweet V over a satin base with a sweetheart curve. The pearls continued down the front, all the way to the floor, edging the long sleeves as well.

The dress she wore to marry Gabriel. It couldn't possibly be anything else, not in this bag with her wedding suit.

The two dresses, hidden away together for all these years.

One last item waited: a fingertip-length veil with silk orange blossoms on the comb.

Sophie ran her hand over her face. "It's

killing me that these have been in a *carpet-bag*."

I tipped my head, looking closer. "None of it seems the worse for wear, just wrinkled."

Sandrine fingered the lace. "You'll want to steam it out and look at it closely. Folded like this, the fabric could have become old and brittle."

"If only," Caterina said, eying the dress and eying me.

I shook my head, following her thoughts. "There's no way. She was too tiny. Most of them were, back then." I passed the dress to Sophie. "I bet Chloé could fit into it, though," I said softly. "If she wanted pictures taken in her great-grandmother's dress."

Sophie nodded. "We'll do that. If she's interested."

"If I'm what?" Chloé asked, her teen ears perking up at the possibility of being discussed.

"We were saying that the dress is so small, it won't fit any of us. Juliette thought you might want to try it on — carefully — and have pictures taken in it."

Chloé's eyes widened and she nodded, speechless.

Caterina crossed her arms. "That jacket,

though —"

"Yes, try on the jacket," Sandrine instructed.

I tugged off my boiled-wool cardigan and slipped my arms into the sleeves of the jacket with care.

Sophie's hands went to her face. "Oh my word."

Caterina examined the fit like a *Project Runway* judge. "The seams hit you perfectly, though it's a little snug in the shoulder."

"And short in the arm," I pointed out.

Caterina gave a dismissive wave of her hand. "It's bracelet length. It doesn't look bad."

"So that's it?" Nico asked from his position on a window bench. "Just clothes?"

Sophie rounded on him. "It's your grandmother's wedding dresses!"

"Yeah!" Caterina crossed her arms. "Respect, dude!"

Nico's eyes cut to Damian. "Your wife called me 'dude.'"

Damian shrugged. "The '90s were a big decade for her. I don't know what to tell you."

"You look beautiful, my Giulietta," my father said, ignoring the bickering. "You should wear it for your wedding ceremony."

Neil stood and pressed a kiss beside my

ear. "You look pretty, no matter what."

Caterina held the veil in her hands. "I can't bear to put this down. Let's go look for some hangers and maybe some kind of batting."

I slipped an arm out of the jacket. "Good idea."

"And after that," she added with a wince, "I've got to go to bed."

"I'm with you," Sophie said, standing. "I'm fading here."

The others agreed, one by one saying good night to me in order to say hello to their beds.

I remained in the hallway, in the middle of the closet's contents, strewn around the floor. "If you want to go to bed, love, that's okay," I told Neil.

He slipped his hand into the small of my back. "What are your plans?"

"I just . . . I feel like there's something else. She took that key back with her. Would she do it just for the wedding dresses?"

"You think it was intentional?"

"She was in the kitchen every day. She had to know it was there. Keeping the key — it feels intentional."

"Would she have thought Cécile had a copy?"

"Maybe once, but Sandrine has no memory of it ever being accessible." I shrugged. "I don't know. I can't explain it, but my gut tells me that there's something else."

Neil nodded and rolled up the sleeves of his cabled knit sweater. "Okay. Let's keep looking."

So we did. We went shelf by shelf, working our way from the ceiling to the floor.

One box contained a smaller box of love notes between Mireille's parents in their youth, but after going through the contents we were no closer to finding what I'd hoped for.

After an age, I set the final box aside. "What if I'm wrong? What if it's not here?"

Silence.

"Neil?"

Neil's head lifted from where it had been resting against the wall. "Yes. What?"

I pressed my lips together in an attempt to control a smile. "You fell asleep."

"No, I didn't."

"No? What was I talking about a moment ago?"

"You said . . . I don't remember." He ran a hand through his hair. "I was asleep."

"You're funny." I leaned forward and rested my elbows on my knees. "I'm worried that what I want to be here isn't."

"Let's go to bed, wife." Neil stood with

effort and reached down to offer me a hand.

I considered attempting to pull him down, but after our travel day I didn't trust his ability to defy gravity. So I took his proffered hand and stood up, dusting off my hands.

"I'm going to look more tomorrow," I said, scanning the interior of the closet.

"I know."

I wrinkled my nose. "We've left a mess."

"You can worry about that tomorrow too."

My nose didn't unwrinkle, but I allowed Neil to lead me by the hand, back to our room.

25

Why, sometimes I've believed as many as six impossible things before breakfast.

— LEWIS CARROLL

I woke the next morning with a head full of worries and a nose full of sweet scent. "Caterina's been in the kitchen," I said, sitting up. "I can smell it."

When we made it to the kitchen, I discovered I'd been right. Caterina had prepared French toast that she'd topped with sweetened, orange-scented ricotta cheese, marmalade, and wedges of tangerine.

I piled a large serving onto my plate and cleared it with speed. "That was amazing," I told my sister, wrapping my arms over hers in a sisterly hug. "Don't mind me. The closet calls."

Worry flickered over her face so quickly I wondered if I'd imagined it. "Go look," she said, squeezing my arms. "I hope you find what you're looking for."

Once again, I climbed the stairs to the third floor. This time, light streamed in through the windows.

Neil followed me up with a plate full of second servings. "We should get this recipe from your sister," he said. "I could eat this all day."

"You can try to eat it all day, but you'll have to fight Nico off."

Now at the top of the stairs, I surveyed the mess. "I didn't make it through all the boxes, I suppose. Everything will have to be put away, of course, but looking at this, I don't know how it all fit in the first place."

Neil's nose twitched. "It's bigger on the inside."

"Don't joke. I wouldn't be surprised. I mean," I said, walking inside and turning around to face him. "It's not that much . . ."

My words trailed off as my eyes spotted something unexpected.

A box.

There was a box on the second-to-lowest shelf, shoved in the back in such a way that I would have had trouble seeing it from the doorway, at night.

It was a hinged and wooden, roughly the size of a loaf of bread. The hairs on the back of my neck stood up. I knew the box well —

the wood inlay on the top, and hasp in front; a matching box rested on Grand-mère's dresser in my room.

"I think," I said, reaching for it, "that I found it."

I carried it to the window seat.

Neil sat down beside me. "Well? Are you going to open it?"

"I— It might be nothing. It might be just a box with nothing inside."

"Allons-y," he said. "You won't know until you look."

I lifted the lid and looked inside, barely able to breathe.

Inside lay a worn book, bound in blue leather, and a stack of photographs, tied with ribbon. I reached for the photos first, untying the ribbon with unsteady fingers.

"Look," I said, "it's Mireille." I pointed at the figures. "And Gabriel — and the girls. Both of them."

At that moment, we heard footfalls on the stairs.

"We're here!" Caterina called out. "We're here for round two."

Sophie and Sandrine rounded the corner to the landing, taking in the sight of Neil and me huddled over the pictures. "What's that?" Sandrine asked. "What did you find?"

"Photos," I breathed, holding the photo

higher. "And this one shows all of them — Mireille and Gabriel and the twins."

Sophie, Caterina, and Sandrine peered over my shoulder as my father and brothers followed.

"Oh, la," Sandrine said. "Look how little they are!"

"I can't believe how much Nico looks like Gabriel. Nico, come look at this." Caterina motioned for Nico to join us.

Nico looked over Cat's shoulder to see. "That — that's weird."

I passed the photo to Sandrine, who passed it to Sophie, and looked at the next photo. A wedding photo, Mireille and Gabriel attempting a serious wedding portrait, the sheer joy in their eyes belying their somber pose.

"There's the dress!" Caterina exclaimed. "Look at her — she's so young."

There was an infant photo, one of a tiny scrunched-up infant in a striped blanket, another photo of an infant in a dotted blanket. Their names were scrawled on the back — stripes for Alice, dots for Gabrielle.

Another photo showed Gabriel in his chef's whites, standing in a kitchen. The last one showed Mireille and Gabriel together at the beach, just looking at each other with a kind of happy calm.

I looked up at Neil. "I'm glad you're here," I said quietly.

He squeezed my hand. "I wouldn't have it any other way."

While my family passed them around, I reached for the book.

The leather warmed in my hand as I cracked it open, the spine creaking from disuse.

My eyes fell onto the text inside — handwritten, in letters I knew well.

Dear Gabriel,
I hardly know where to begin.

"It's her journal," I said. "You guys — it's Mireille's journal."

My eyes fell on the next lines of text.

Tante Joséphine sent this journal to write in now that you are gone, so that I don't, I suppose, spread sadness and misery in my wake.

I write in English, for these words are private. One of my family members might find it, but the staff cannot read it, so in that way I have just a little privacy.

Only a little — I have no illusion of ever having more.

Oh, my darling. One day we were living our lives, holding our children, making love, making bread, and the next I'm
a widow.

"This is it. Maybe there *aren't* letters,
because she was writing here, in her journal." I paged gently through the pages. "And
it's in English, all of it."

"English?" Sandrine echoed.

I wanted to skim the text for immediate
answers, but I closed the book instead. "We
have to read it together."

"*Mais oui,* that would be lovely," Sandrine
said. "But surely you would like to read it
yourself first."

"*Non,*" I answered firmly. "Not this time.
This time, we read together."

Our Epiphany dinner was a feast to end all
feasts. At the end, I decided I probably
wouldn't eat for the rest of the trip — or
until breakfast the next morning.

"What will you do when you move?" Zia
Matilde asked me during a brief lull in the
conversation. "Will you look for another
restaurant to manage?"

Neil and I exchanged glances. "I've
learned I have a talent for restaurant management over the last few months."

Nico raised his glass in agreement.

"But I've missed having an opportunity to cook," I continued. "The pop-up that we started for Two Blue Doors — that was fun. So I might look for a management position, but I'm also excited by the idea of trying my hand at pop-ups."

"My students raved about you," Caterina added. "You could add cooking classes to your vision, if that interests you."

I grinned. "Lots of adventures ahead," I said, catching Neil's eye. "I can't wait."

"When do you move?" Letizia asked.

"We're taking a long wedding tour," I replied. "We're visiting my great-uncle Benjamin and our cousins in Missouri — well, the rest of the family's going to be there with us." In a few sentences, I summed up for the Italian relatives how I'd found our extended family members. "They wanted to be here, of course, and they were invited, but Benjamin is too fragile for such a long journey, and with the cousins' work schedules . . ."

"Another time," Sandrine assured me.

"After that," I continued, "Neil and I will fly to North Carolina to see his parents."

"My parents are hosting a reception for us," Neil added. "Only a couple hundred of their closest friends."

"We'll have a reception and ski, apparently. And from there, we'll go to Portland, pack up the last of my things — and Gigi — and drive cross country."

"That is a lot," Caterina noted, shaking her head. "I mean, I get it, but that's a lot."

"The way I see it" — Neil squeezed my hand — "is that we're simply going home the long way around."

Sandrine passed the cake plates around the table after dinner. "Those who would like to enjoy the fireplace in the study may take their cake with them, of course. And there is some very nice Cognac there as well."

Riccardo volunteered to take the children to the study but promised to keep them from the Cognac. Damian joined him, giving Caterina a kiss on the cheek and extracting a promise from her to catch him up afterward.

The rest of us scooted closer around the table.

I took a bite of Sandrine's King's cake — the same recipe as my grand-mère's — before reopening the journal and diving into Mireille's words.

Dear Gabriel,
    I hardly know where to begin.

Tante Joséphine sent this journal to write in now that you are gone, so that I don't, I suppose, spread sadness and misery in my wake.

I write in English, for these words are private. One of my family members might find it, but the staff cannot read it, so in that way I have just a little privacy.

Only a little — I have no illusion of ever having more.

Oh my darling. One day we were living our lives, holding our children, making love, making bread, and the next I'm a widow.

You were helping the Jewish families get food. The Children's Relief Committee needed help, I'm sure. It was noble, foolish, honorable, and stupid. I'm angry with you, I'm proud of you.

I wish you'd told me. I wish you hadn't died with secrets between us. I understand why. I know you were trying to protect us. I wish you'd been able to protect yourself.

Your brother, Nathan, escaped to Marseilles, where his wife's family resides. I wish them well. He used your contacts to get out of Paris, the way he told me you'd planned to take us out.

Gabrielle and I now reside at my parents' estate in Provence. Alice is as well, but she is staying with our family's cook, Françoise. I shall explain that shortly.

I wish you'd seen the chateau, just once. The lavender fields scent the air, and the hum of bees creates its own music. When I last went to the symphony, the wind section, the oboes — they reminded me of the bees at home.

But back to the explanations. You should know, first, that I've married Gilles.

Nathan, Gilles, and my father cooked up the idea. They reasoned that since Gilles had been away in Toulouse on business long enough, they could marry me off to him quickly, pretend Gabrielle was our daughter. Gabrielle, because, you know, she's the fair one. Alice looked as much like you that day as ever, all dark curls and round eyes.

But I am not the only one starting an unexpected marriage. My dearest sister, Cécile, has married her sweetheart, Richard.

For the next four weeks, Alice resides with Cook. She is to be Cook's granddaughter, the child of her son the pilot who has recently died in action.

In a month, Richard and Cécile will adopt her. They will tell the villagers that they believed it their duty to care for the orphans of our French heroes.

We will raise the girls together, Cécile and I, but Nathan insists that there are informants who would happily tell the Germans that two Jewish children and their mother reside at Chateau de l'Abeille.

For that reason, we've used contacts of Nathan's to make new records for the girls. Alice has a new first name; Gabrielle has taken Gilles's surname.

I don't know who these contacts are, or how Nathan came to know them. I only know that their identities have been changed and the papers look just as official as the old ones.

It makes my heart sick, but what I want most is for both of them to be safe.

Until the day I die, Gabriel, you must believe I will regret marrying Gilles. I ended my engagement to him all those years ago because he loved the idea of the estate, the idea of being my father's heir, more than he loved me.

And, also, I was very young and bored with life in the country. I moved to the city to study pastry, and it led me straight to you, straight to us.

Sometimes I wonder what would have happened if I'd enrolled sooner, or later, if I would have missed your pastry class altogether, if we wouldn't have found each other, made the girls. But the more I think about it, the more I think I would have seen you in the halls, met you at the market — I think I would have found you, you would have found me.

I miss you.

Caterina dabbed at her eyes. "That is awful."

"*C'est étrange,*" Sandrine exclaimed. "My mother adopting Alice . . . I thought I would know if I had an adopted sister."

"If it's anything like the letters, we'll have just as many questions in the end as answers," Sophie commented dryly.

"At least we will know more," my father said, patting her hand. "And who knows? How much writing is in the volume, Juliette?"

I flipped through to the back. "Nearly to the end."

"*Sì, sì,* many answers to be had. Keep reading, Giulietta."

So I read on.

Dear Gabriel,

Gilles is kind to me and I hate him for it. I know it's not strictly rational behavior, but there it is. I see him, and I am angry that it's him and not you.

It's not fair, because having him at the chateau has been beneficial for my father. They spend their days talking over the lavender crop, the honey, and the horses. Richard joins in, but he is a carpenter, whereas Gilles's first love is the land and the outdoors.

Age has not been kind to my father — I see it more now that I've returned. His walk has slowed; his shoulders are more stooped. He still looks fine, but I worry for his health. Cécile told me that the doctor worries for his heart.

But I'm angry with Gilles because I'm now his wife, and I know what it's like to be a wife — and I won't, can't be a wife to him. I don't know what he expects, and I'm not going to ask in order to find out.

Does he intend for us to remain married, or divorce after the war? Making my way in the world with Gabrielle wouldn't be easy, but I could make it.

Does he intend for us to, one day, have a real marriage? There's no way I could ever, ever love him even a little the way I loved you. We were engaged once, but I was young, and I didn't know what it was like to really, truly love a person from the depths of the heart.

And now that I know, how could I ever go back?

I must be grateful, though, for he provides Gabrielle and me with protection, with a new name.

Tante Joséphine believes that I should try to make a new life with Gilles. How can I, though, when I still look for you from the corner of my eye, reach for you in bed, dream of you every night?

How can I move on, while Alice yet sleeps in Cook's cottage?

Each morning, I wake expecting to be in our Paris apartment, the girls in the next room.

I miss you. You would know what to do, what to say.

Dear Gabriel,

Tante Joséphine has arrived. I felt such relief at her presence, that surely she will bring good sense to the house.

And while she has requested that my mother stop hovering, an understandable sentiment, she had troubling words of advice.

She drew me to the garden, along with Gabrielle — I won't be parted from her — and asked after the four of us: myself and Gilles, Gabrielle and Alice (I can't write their new names here, it hurts too much).

She told me I must be strong, and I must be a wife to Gilles. That our survival and Gabrielle's happiness depend on my being extraordinary. That I must not allow ghosts and regrets to rule my life.

I told her that trying to have a life with Gilles made me feel as though the last three years hadn't happened.

And she replied that I had Gabrielle as my reminder, but that in these times, maybe setting aside those three years wasn't a bad thing. That as hard as I fought for Gabriel and me to be together, that I had to work even harder to build a life with Gilles.

"It won't be easy," she said, "and it's certainly not fair. But Gabrielle needs a future, even more than you or I. You must put aside your old life and create her a new one."

I gave my very best arguments, which weren't really arguments at all but a recitation of my distaste for every aspect of the situation.

She let me argue as long as I wished and then turned a shrewd old eye at me. "You're right, of course. But then you know I am too."

I told her that I can't even look at Gilles. She told me to see him differently.

I think she'd be very happy as a wise old woman living atop a mountain, dispensing advice to travelers whether they like it or not.

I will hide you close in my heart, dearest. You may be hidden away, but I carry you close.

~ FRENCH TOAST WITH RICOTTA AND TANGERINES ~

1 loaf challah or brioche, cut into 1-inch slices
5 large eggs
1 1/2 cups whole milk
15 ounces part-skim ricotta cheese
1/3 cup honey
1/3 cup orange juice
Pinch salt
Zest and fruit segments of 6 mandarin oranges
3/4 cup orange marmalade

In a shallow bowl, whisk the eggs and milk together.

In a medium-sized bowl, stir together the ricotta cheese, honey, orange juice, salt, and zest.

Dredge challah slices in the egg mixture, cook on a heated griddle until browned, then flip. Repeat until all slices have been cooked. Serve with a generous dollop of the ricotta mixture on top, followed by a spoonful of the marmalade and a sprinkling of the mandarin wedges.

Makes about 8 servings.

26

Eating and reading are two pleasures that combine admirably.

— C. S. LEWIS

Caterina, Nico, and I made breakfast for everyone early the next morning, despite Sandrine's protests. Neil ducked into the kitchen, heard Caterina and Nico bickering, and pulled me aside.

"You need me?"

I looked over my shoulder at my siblings and back at Neil. "You can go find somewhere quiet."

"Are you sure?"

I gave him a peck on the cheek. "I am. I'll see you at breakfast."

Nico made a quiche, while Caterina made a fruit-filled crumb cake. I made breakfast biscotti for the Italian family to eat with their coffee, and once it was in the oven, set to work on the espresso.

Alex joined us in the kitchen at the last minute, prepping fresh fruit and plating it on three platters to place down the table.

Damian helped carry the food to the table, and my father served the coffee. Caterina's boys placed napkins around the table, while Sophie and Chloé set out the plates and flatware. Nelson poured water.

We laughed and talked, Nico and Caterina ribbing each other while also admitting the other's food was delicious.

Damian leaned over to Neil. "I'm a chef too, you know. But even *I* don't go into the kitchen with those two."

After breakfast, Letizia joined Sandrine and the rest of us around the table for the next foray into Mireille's diary.

Caterina grabbed a piece of biscotti first. "Here. I've armed myself for another round of sadness."

Dear Gabriel,

I dream of you often. I wish they were happy dreams, variations on memories of our life in Paris, but instead they are nightmares about your death.

My mind pulled together the elements of the story I'd been told, piecing them together until it became a terrible film reel in my mind played over and over.

You unaware, the officers, the gun, the shot — and repeat.

And Alice was there, and crying. There was nothing I could do.

I awoke to Gabrielle crying, and realized that when I'd heard Alice in my dream, it had been Gabrielle startled awake by my weeping.

After a moment or two of rocking and humming she drifted back to sleep again. Myself, I was not so lucky: I feared going back to sleep and returning to the dream.

Perhaps I should have Gabrielle sleep in the next room, if I'm going to disturb her. I hate the thought of having her so far, and yet nothing good can come from a sleep-deprived toddler.

We woke Gilles. Did I tell you about our sleeping arrangements?

Maman insists that we must do our best to make the servants believe that we are married, that we have been married. Only the housekeeper saw us all walk in, Gilles and I and the girls arriving first, followed by Nathan and his family in his truck. Papa kept the rest of the servants away from us, with the exception of Cook — for there are never any secrets from those who feed us.

And Cook was as a second mother to me, teaching me how to find my way around the kitchen when I was a young girl. So she consented easily to being a part of the deception, taking Alice to her sister's with the story that she was her son's love child, recently delivered by a mother determined to make a life for herself in Toulouse. As for Gabrielle and me, the story going into the village remains that Gilles and I married quietly in Toulouse and had a child.

These stories are all predicated on Toulouse being a good place to make secret children.

I don't know why Gilles and I would have kept such a thing secret, but it's not a lie I'm interested in telling in the first place, at least not enough to create a believable story. People will probably decide that Gabrielle is a love child and that I had difficulty getting Gilles to agree to marry me, or some similar sort of nonsense.

Gilles and I now occupy a suite of rooms at the chateau. There's a bedroom and a sitting room, and a door connecting the sitting room to the nursery. The first night, after we married, I worried he would want to join me in my bed. If he had, Gabriel, I would have fought him like a fury.

I suppose that is me flattering myself. Few men desire a weepy woman with a short temper and several kilos of pregnancy weight still clinging to her body.

Instead, without conversation, Gilles made a bed for himself on the settee, with the footstool giving his giant feet a place to rest.

Dearest Gabriel,

I think Tante Joséphine talked to Gilles. Because this afternoon he asked me if I would teach him to cook.

I asked him why, and he looked away before saying that he thought it might be practical. And also, that it was something important to me, and so it could be important to him.

Obviously, it was Tante Joséphine's idea. No man would think of such a thing himself. I considered dismissing him out of hand. But I knew if I did, I'd hear from Tante Joséphine about it.

So I agreed. But I couldn't manage to be particularly polite about it.

"Poor Grandpa Gilles!" Caterina exclaimed. "He's trying! He wants to cook!"

"I think it's sweet," Sophie said.

"He sounds like a very smart man," said Letizia.

Damian shook his head. "I feel bad for him."

"How much is left in the book?" my father asked.

I flipped through the pages. "Seems like a lot."

"We will stop interrupting you, or you shall never finish. And have others take turns — no need to go hoarse for history."

I grinned at him. "Okay, Papa. Here's the next letter. 'Dearest Gabriel,' " I began.

Truly. Nothing good comes of a toddler with too little sleep. Gabrielle has been fussy and petulant all day, despite an afternoon nap so long I checked to see the rise and fall of her chest as she breathed.

Tonight she'll be in the nursery. I dread it, though Anouk seems to be relishing the chance to have me to herself.

I know that Cécile, likewise, would like more . . . time. For reassurance of a sisterly connection. She's so careful, I can see it in her eyes. She doesn't know what to do with me, and unfortunately it's mutual. I love my sister so much. She is so happy with Richard, but I know the impending adoption of Alice weighs heavily on them. Neither wishes to feel as if they are depriving me of my daughter.

She has so much joy. I worry that if she spends too much time with me, my vinegar will overtake her sweetness.

Cécile visits Alice, where she resides with Cook's sister. In two weeks, Cécile will declare herself so smitten that she will bring Alice back to the chateau.

My beautiful Alice, who wears your face in her own sweet, feminine way. I anxiously await and dread having her back. It is safer for her not to be yours; no one would believe her to belong to Gilles. Cook's son had a dark complexion, which helps to further the veracity of the story.

But what if she doesn't remember me?

And what if she does?

How much more can my heart take without breaking in two?

Dearest Gabriel,

Tante Joséphine suggested that we make a gravesite for you on the property. We wouldn't have your body, of course

— I don't know if the police returned it to your parents, or . . . no, I cannot think of it. The important part is that you do not now inhabit your physical body.

She suggested we could bury a memento or two, and if we could not part with anything, a lock of hair from Gabrielle, Alice, and myself.

She meant a lock, likely a small one at that, but I asked Maman's maid to cut my hair into a short, serviceable bob.

It's much more practical short, and I have no desire to coax my longer hair into any other, more fashionable styles. You liked my curls, and without you I have no use for them.

I placed my hair, which had become too long anyway, into a box, along with a curl of Gabrielle's and a curl from Alice — procured by Françoise. Maman was quite shocked by my short hair, as you would expect. Cécile charitably said it made me look like Myrna Loy, the American film star, which . . . I suspect not. But it was kind of her to say.

Papa spoke to a mason for a length of stone, which will remain unmarked for now. We trooped outside, all of us, to bury the box of hair.

Tante Joséphine said a few kind words

when she saw that I could not speak, not without weeping again and frightening Gabrielle.

I set the box in the ground, in a hole that Tante Joséphine asked Gilles to dig. We took turns throwing earth over the top. I took the shovel, at the end, and buried the box the rest of the way.

When I turned around, I saw that Gilles remained with Gabrielle, Anouk sitting at his feet, but the rest of the family had returned to the house.

"We can plant flowers there, if you like," Gilles said.

Gabrielle seemed so at home in his arms that it nearly broke my heart anew. But my heart was too broken to respond as it would otherwise, and I told him that some flowers would be nice. I carried daisies when we married, do you remember? I told Gilles I'd like some daisies near your headstone, and he felt they'd have plenty of sun there. So that's settled.

Dearest Gabriel,

I had a terrible nightmare again, this time watching you die from afar, too far away to be able to do anything. And I saw Alice; her cries pierced my heart, and I woke sobbing to find Gilles sitting on the bed, having taken Gabrielle to comfort her before trying to wake me. I must have cried out in my sleep, startling Gabrielle. Anouk was curled into a ball on my pillow, as close to my head as she could get.

I asked what he was doing, and he said our cries had woken him, that he was only trying to help.

I considered snapping at him but thought better of it — I was sensible enough to know he was trying to do a good thing. I sat up and took Gabrielle into my arms, and she pulled at my nightdress to feed. Gilles blushed — I could not see it, but I knew it was there. I fed her discreetly with a pillowcase draped over myself (not that I cared at all, but Gilles is certainly rather delicate). As Gabrielle's cries subsided, my own breathing began to even out.

"I should put her in the nursery, shouldn't I?" I asked Gilles, hoping he might disagree with me.

"She might sleep better," he said instead.

I thought about it, mulling in my head the idea of having her so far away. In truth, it would be the farthest she'd ever slept — in our Paris apartment, of course, she was never more than six meters from me at any time. But the distance from my bed to hers in the nursery had to be nine meters. A short distance for many, but too far for my comfort.

But as I held her close, I knew that my comfort must matter less than hers. She'd already begun to drift off. When she finished eating, I drew my nightdress back over my shoulder and stood to carry her to her own bed, to finish out the remainder of the night. Gilles steadied me with a gentle hand on my elbow, and the three of us — four, with Anouk — walked to the nursery.

The room was snug and warm enough, and when I placed Gabrielle in the crib, she simply curled up on her side and continued to sleep.

I didn't want to leave, but I'd already begun to sway where I stood.

Gilles helped me back to bed, and nodded at me before returning to his settee.

The next morning, Gabrielle was bright eyed and cheery. It's the right thing, Gabriel, but that doesn't mean I must enjoy it.

Dearest Gabriel,

Maman has hired a nursemaid for Gabrielle. Marise is young, a year younger than Cécile, but she comes from a large family and has a canny way with Gabrielle. When Alice arrives, she will care for them both. She can sleep in the nursery with Gabrielle, so she will not be alone. This brings me some comfort, for if I cannot be with her, at least she will have company.

My dreams have not ceased, but at least I am not disturbing Gabrielle.

They disturb Gilles, though. I have suggested he take a room farther away, but he shakes his head and offers me a glass of water, waiting until I have quieted to go back to his settee.

There is gray at his temples that was not there before, when we were young. I suppose it was only a few years ago, but it feels more like a lifetime ago. I remember him differently. Is it possible he has changed? It seems uncharitable to think it impossible, for I know I'm not the girl who left the chateau to study pastry in Paris.

Tante Joséphine has been a comfort to me, but she and Maman have begun to argue over the menus and the gardens, and the best place for the sideboard in the drawing room. For my sake, I hope they find peace. I don't yet know what I would do without her. Poor Gilles. I still hate what has become of our lives, and I remain unhappy that we're married, and yet with the combination of sleeping on the settee and being woken up by my nightmares, even I have noticed the dark circles beneath his eyes, the way he moves as if in pain each morning.

I overheard one of the hands teasing him about it, assuming that our nightly amour had taken its toll on him.

I suppose it's a good thing that the hands believe we're a married couple in all ways, and yet I felt my face flush with embarrassment.

That morning, after breakfast, I asked if he would take a walk in the garden with Gabrielle and me. Once we were well away from the house, I asked if he wanted to move to a different room, and when he declined, I told him that if he meant to stay in the room, he may as well sleep in the same bed.

Gilles flushed red, which I pretended not to notice.

It's a large bed. And Anouk will be there.

I wish life wasn't as it is, but the fact of the matter is that this man is my husband and he's suffering on my account.

I wish it were otherwise, Gabriel, but you left us in this precarious position. If you hadn't died, you know, Gilles would be sleeping in his own bed at his parents' home . . . though perhaps it is better to be on a settee at the chateau than under the same roof as Madame Bessette.

As this is my private journal, I can write here that I would rather sleep in a barn than share a home with that woman.

At any rate, he accepted my invitation (which sounds so much more salacious than it actually is), and gave one of his own — for the three of us to drive into the village market to purchase grocery goods with which to teach him to cook.

I considered rescinding my offer. Just because I don't want him to sleep miserably on the settee doesn't mean he and I are friends, or that I want to teach him to cook.

Is that ungrateful of me? It's true that he's given up the chance to marry some nice, simple girl in the village and married me instead, giving Gabrielle and me the protection of his name. Yes, it is ungrateful, but I miss you so terribly I can't manage to feel bad about it.

But Gilles looked so tired that I agreed to the trip to the village. The man's been waking me from nightmares and bringing me water, and I'm not the cold hag that I try to convince everyone that I am.

I dressed for town and made an effort, since I knew that this would be the first time the two of us would be seen — and discussed — as a couple.

If only it could have been us. I would have introduced you to Remy, who runs the café, and to Marcel, who stocks the best produce at his stand.

I would have taken you to the bakery, where the bread is good, and the patisserie, where the pastries are not. Everyone would have admired what a charming couple we made, how well spoken you were. You might have suggested to the pastry chef how to chill the butter longer, how to create a flakier croissant, and the entire village would have celebrated the day you arrived.

But instead Gilles and I walked through town, and the town was not as I left it. The rations had taken their toll on the villagers. I carried Gabrielle, who looked fetching in a white sundress that would remain white for about fifteen minutes.

I helped Gilles choose fruit, telling him what to look for in peaches, aubergines, heirloom tomatoes, and blackberries. These were terribly expensive — the shortages, you know — but I paid extra just the same, knowing it would help the families with less than mine.

Rather than scoff at how selective I was being, he listened carefully and asked a few questions.

But we didn't shop unnoticed. Everyone who knew us stopped to say hello, to meet Gabrielle, to marvel at the news of our marriage, to swoon over the romance of it all.

That was the hardest, the ladies who were convinced it was romantic, how we'd married quietly in Toulouse and returned with our beautiful child. There were winks from those who, of course, believed Gabrielle was our love child.

I forced a smile until my head ached with the strain. When the strain began to show, Gilles apologized and said I'd been recovering from a recent illness.

Gilles apologized once we returned to

the car. "I didn't realize it would be like that," he said.

I held Gabrielle close as the car bounced over the road. "I was a curiosity enough before I left," I told him. "Returning home with a husband and child — people were bound to be interested."

He nodded and studied the road as he drove, which I appreciated. And then he said he thought I was brave, and that Gabrielle charmed everyone, and that he could go to town next time and spare us the trip.

I told him that while the trip had been difficult, it hadn't been the most difficult.

It feels strange to be riding together with Gilles. We used to drive together before, that lifetime ago when we courted and became engaged. To think that here we were again, accompanied by my daughter — such strange times.

27

Nobody says anything at any meal, to anybody. All the passengers are very dismal, and seem to have tremendous secrets weighing on their minds.

— CHARLES DICKENS

We were quiet after the reading. I tucked the bookmark in place, feeling guilty. Would it be better to read alone? I shoved the idea away quickly.

My family had suffered losses, yes. But we were resilient. And we knew that the owner of the diary, Mireille, had been a woman of great strength. As I placed the book on the table, I reminded myself that while the story felt sad and difficult now, we had more than a glimpse at the ending. We had to hang on, as readers, to let Mireille tell her story in its entirety — the hard parts that we knew had to fold into the better days.

Still, there was a time for balance.

"Let's make ravioli today," I said.

Letizia cheered, Caterina clapped, and I felt a relief in their response.

We cleared the breakfast plates and cleaned the kitchen first.

Nelson, Damian, and Riccardo took the children outside while the rest of us piled into the kitchen. We cleaned the farmhouse table thoroughly before weighing out the flour and cracking eggs. I showed Neil how to work the eggs into the fine flour, and we laughed as all of us began to knead at the same time. My father began singing his favorite song, *"Io Che Non Vivo,"* and my zio, zia, Letizia, and Caterina all joined in. I sang along, singing the lyrics to Neil.

He leaned close and pressed a kiss to my lips. *"Ti amo,"* he said, before returning to his dough.

My heart felt so full, I thought it might burst.

We let our balls of dough rest for an hour. Some of the family members returned, others sought out a quiet place to read or gathered for a raucous game of cards.

Because there were two pasta makers, I showed Neil how to use one, Sophie used the other, and Letizia, Caterina, and Nico all competed for who could roll the best ravioli dough by hand.

Letizia won.

Meanwhile, Sandrine and Chloé made the filling with ricotta, spinach, and parmesan, seasoning it with salt, pepper, and a little nutmeg.

We made long strips of dough and plopped teaspoons of the filling on top before placing a top strip of dough, cutting the squares, and crimping the edges.

"I had a roommate in college whose aunts spent a weekend in December making tamales," Neil said as we prepared another row of raviolis. "This reminds me of that."

"And they freeze," I said. "Like tamales. Though with a group this size, it still won't last long."

We paused for lunch, enjoying leftovers from the previous night, before pressing to finish the ravioli. By the end, Neil felt proficient in using the pasta maker and even tried his hand at rolling out the dough.

After a dinner of ravioli in a butter and sage sauce, served with roasted carrots and broccolini, I reached to the sideboard for the diary.

"Let me read," Sophie said. "I'll take a turn."

I handed the diary to her and watched as she found her place. " 'My dearest Gabriel,' " she began. " 'Our sweet Alice is now at the chateau.' "

I closed my eyes and let the words wash over me, picturing Mireille at her writing desk, processing the twists her life had taken.

I've not seen her for seven weeks. Her adoption by Cécile is quite legal, or as legal as it could be with her forged papers.

She prefers Cécile. I have not held her; she has not reached for me.

The household made a celebration of her arrival, and I celebrated along with them. She is here. She is safe. She is under the protection of Richard and Cécile, as well as Françoise's son Luc's reputation as a French hero.

She is safe. That is all that matters.

My dearest Gabriel,

While Alice may not feel at ease with me, she has not forgotten her sister. Is it the fact that they shared my womb, a little over a year ago? Gabrielle is over the moon to have her sister back. They clap and make nonsense conversation and scuffle over toys.

Cécile is genuinely good with her. They sit together, Richard and Cécile and Alice: the very image of a young family.

Alice is safe. That is all that matters.

My dearest Gabriel,

I ache for my daughters, the feeling of having them both safe in my arms. I ache, and I don't know what to do about it.

But Alice is safe. Gabrielle is safe. That is the only thing that matters.

My dearest Gabriel,

I could not sleep for weeping, tonight. I ache for my Alice.

Gilles eventually began to stroke my hair, from the crown of my head to the nape of my neck. I closed my eyes and pretended it was you, Gabriel. I imagined it was your hand, and fell asleep.

I miss you.

Dearest Gabriel,

Perhaps the most upsetting thing about having a husband — whom you do not love — be kind to you is the feeling of obligation to be kind back. It's deeply inconvenient.

(And yes, I am aware that Gabrielle and I are protected and safe because of him. I ought to be thankful rather than resentful, but the fact that he is not you places him at a very distinct disadvantage.)

Anyway, so as not to be an ungrateful cow, I asked Gilles if he wanted to join me in the kitchen for the afternoon. Marise watched over Gabrielle, and Françoise let me take over a section of the kitchen.

I told Gilles we were going to practice knife skills. I borrowed two chef's knives, showing him how to hold the knife in order to make it an extension of his hand, how to curl the fingers of his opposite hand to avoid slicing a fingertip.

He watched me very carefully before imitating my actions. We stood there together, not talking, slicing carrots. Carrot after carrot. (Thankfully, we had a significant carrot crop.) I sped up my pace, slicing perfect, even rounds, and his sped up as well.

We didn't speak, but after a while it began to feel . . . easier. I asked after the fields, and he told me which sections they were having irrigation troubles with, and his concern about the crops, and how he and Richard had been discussing a way to distill the lavender oil themselves. He spoke well of Richard, which spoke well of him to me.

Once we'd amassed a great pile of carrots — probably a kilo? I announced that we needed to continue with the rest of the meal. Richard had checked the snares in the woods earlier and found a nice brace of hares, which Françoise had skinned and quartered.

I would have browned them with some lardons, if we weren't saving the pigs for later, but made a nice mirepoix base of leeks, shallots, and carrots just the same, before returning the rabbit and adding some white wine (this is Chateau de l'Abeille — I suspect there's white wine beneath the floorboards) and a little flour, to thicken, as well as a little more salt and some fresh thyme.

Obviously, this didn't make more than a dent in the carrots, as you can imagine. So I set a stack of carrot slices in front of him and gave myself a matching stack, and we set to work chopping them as finely as possible for a carrot cake.

You know that it's best to grate the carrots, of course, but I reasoned that a very fine mince would come out just as well.

I am grateful for the farm at the chateau, for while we do not have large quantities of butter, we have enough — more than most, to be sure. I sautéed the carrots in butter first to soften them before making the rest of the batter. The resulting cake had the deliciously nutty taste of browned butter.

After we placed it into the oven, Gilles thanked me very sincerely for showing him how to slice carrots — so sincerely I almost giggled, but it would have ruined a moment of generosity on his behalf.

And then he asked if Gabrielle and I would join him on a picnic the following day, and I nearly panicked right there in the kitchen. What did he mean by such a thing? What did he want from me, and would I be prepared to give it?

But he'd been very kind, and very patient, and I know Gabrielle could use the time in the sunshine.

So I said yes.

My dearest Gabriel,

Cécile caught me after breakfast this morning, while both girls were with Marise.

I shall confess to you: I have been avoiding her. My dearest sister, my sister who is caring for our Alice — I have avoided her.

I have not known what to say, or how to be her friend, much less a sister. She is no less dear, of course, but I am filled with such grief that a night of sleep is a rare thing.

But she sought after me, much as she did when we were young and had argued over something silly: a doll, a book, a ribbon. She chased after me the same way as she did in those days, seeking a renewed assurance of affection. We sat in the window seat in the garret, our old hiding place. She clasped my hand and asked me if I could continue to bear the plan that had been laid out for Alice, or if we had to find some other way.

I held her hand and reassured her that this was still the best plan — here we were all home, we were far from the war zones. While we might have been safer outside of France, there were no assurances, and the travels held perils of their own.

Even if the soldiers who had sought you out traveled this far south, we all had new names, new papers.

I realized I had to be stronger. And that, to give our brunette daughter the safest future, I had to accept her new identity in my heart. She was no longer mine, but Cécile's.

I told Cécile so, and — Cécile being Cécile — she welled up into tears and reached for me. We hugged each other tight, weeping together. I thanked her for her care of Alice, for being willing to step into such difficult shoes, and for marrying so lovely a man as Richard. She laughed and wiped her tears, saying that marrying Richard was certainly no hardship. But she also looked self-conscious, and asked after Gilles and myself, how I was managing.

I'd made no secret, in the past, of my distaste for Gilles and relief that he and I did not marry. But I had to admit that my opinion of him had changed. Perhaps not a great deal, but I no longer viewed him as wanting me for my inheritance of the land. I knew he loved the land for its own sake. He loved the lavender farm for the same reason that I loved pastry.

Gilles and I — we're a little older now. The things I wanted when I was younger, adventure, independence, well, I think I've had plenty of adventure. And as far as independence, in this time of war I believe survival depends on depending on others. On being interconnected.

I almost laugh sometimes, because my life is exactly what I was trying to escape so long ago — marriage to Gilles, motherhood.

And yet I arrived at that place so differently than anticipated. And no matter what happens, I will always have you in my heart, you — my best and favorite rebellion.

I regret nothing. And I told Cécile so. We're all doing the very best we can. We hear of arrests and rumors of arrests, of women and children being sent to labor camps. I know there are families in hiding, which is not so very different from us. We hide in the open.

And she hugged me and told me she loved me, and that she missed me and that she was so very sorry for the strife that had plagued my family.

In turn, I told her that we were managing, Gilles, Gabrielle, and I, and that I was fine, and that I hoped Alice was not interrupting her honeymoon with Richard too much. She colored and said that they'd managed.

And then she had questions of a lady-like nature (I am far too ladylike to recount them to you, dearest, as they were posed in confidence), and I answered her with a forwardness that both shocked and delighted her. We had a good marriage, you and I, and I want the same for Cécile — and knowing Richard, I believe she will have it.

Caterina hooted at the last few lines. "We would have had quite the reading experience had Grand-mère not been so ladylike."

Nico looked down at his empty plate. "I'm not sure I'm old enough for this."

Letizia swatted his shoulder. "You Americans. You are so sensitive about people and sex. How do you think you are here on this earth, really?"

Nico looked back at her, his face stoic. "The stork."

~ Spinach and Ricotta Ravioli with Browned Butter ~

This simple ravioli filling is tasty with a variety of sauces, but a basic browned butter won't compete with the gentle flavors of the spinach and ricotta. If you'd like to add a protein, leftover roasted chicken or sautéed prawns would be tasty. Just add a little extra butter so you'll have enough sauce.

For the Ravioli:
1 8-ounce package frozen spinach
1 cup ricotta
1/2 cup parmesan
1/8 teaspoon nutmeg, freshly grated
Salt and pepper to taste

For the Pasta:
1 recipe Homemade Pasta (see pages 158– 160)
1 tablespoon salt

For the Sauce:
1/4 cup salted butter
1/3 cup shredded parmesan
Fresh ground pepper

In a medium-sized saucepan, boil the frozen spinach until the spinach is entirely thawed and just cooked, about three to five minutes.

Pour spinach into a strainer, pressing several times to remove as much moisture as possible.

Add the spinach and cheeses to a large mixing bowl and stir thoroughly, seasoning with the nutmeg, salt, and pepper. For best results while assembling, chill.

To make the ravioli, line a baking sheet with parchment or waxed paper, and sprinkle with cornmeal.

With your pasta maker, roll out a sheet of pasta to about a 5-level of thickness, making sure to keep the sheet as wide as possible. Place the sheet on your work surface. Starting at the top, place 1/2 teaspoon-sized scoops of the spinach mixture down half of the length of the sheet, about 3/4 inch apart. If you have a 16-inch length of pasta, aim to fit about 8 scoops onto one side, in four rows of two.

Brush the areas around the filling with water, and fold the dough over the filling to close. Form the individual packets with your fingers first, pressing in between the mounds of filling, then use a knife or ravioli cutting wheel to cut them apart. Crimp the edges with a fork, and set the completed ravioli onto the lined baking sheet. If not cooking immediately, cover the baking sheet with plastic wrap and refrigerate until use. Ravioli may also be frozen.

Set a large pot of water to boil with a tablespoon of salt. In a large saucepan, melt the butter over low heat. Add the ravioli to the boiling water, turning the heat down to simmer gently (about medium-high). Keep an eye on the water — a rolling boil can cause the ravioli to burst. Meanwhile, stir the melted butter occasionally. Allow the butter to simmer until it turns a light golden brown, about 6–8 minutes. Remove from heat.

Cook the ravioli for 3–4 minutes; cooked ravioli will float to the top. Drain them gently and return to the pot, tossing gently to cook off any remaining moisture. Pour the butter into the pasta pot (or vice versa, it doesn't much matter), and lightly toss the ravioli in the browned butter to coat. Spoon the ravioli into bowls, and top with the shredded parmesan and cracked black pepper.

Serves 4.

28

Once you start cooking, one thing leads to another. A new recipe is as exciting as a blind date. A new *ingredient,* heaven help me, is an intoxicating affair.

— **Barbara Kingsolver**

"I have a bad feeling about Alice," Sandrine confessed to me as we washed dishes. "A part of me wants to read the diary to the end, find out what became of her."

"Then do," I said, rinsing off the pasta pot.

She shook her head. "No, I don't want to walk around knowing secrets. What is it you call them? Spoilers? No, I prefer having us share the story."

"If you change your mind," I said, "you know where it is."

"I have questions for my mother, now. Questions I never knew to ask — and I'm sure you feel that way about your grandmother."

"I do. Sometimes it makes the missing worse. I feel I miss the person *and* the opportunities to ask questions about such things."

"Oui," Sandrine agreed. "I thought I knew everything. My mother was very open. But she never told me about an adopted sister or secret cousin. And so I fear the worst befell little Alice. Otherwise, it would be a story that we knew a version of."

I nodded. I knew there was no functional use in worrying over a toddler who hadn't been a toddler for seventy years, but I knew I'd feel uneasy until we knew something. I knew too that there was no guarantee that the end of the diary would bring the answers we looked for. It wouldn't have been the first time history had swallowed its secrets whole.

There were many wonderful things about the chateau, and one of them was the sheer number of rooms. Neil and I found a sitting room on the second floor that quickly became our quiet place.

The room faced south, with large paned windows and a long window seat beneath them. A cushion and toss pillows made the seat inviting, but there were also three restored sofas, so you could always sit and face the light.

It was quiet and private, but not so far from the guest rooms and gathering rooms that we were isolating ourselves.

I took a book with me and curled up on the sofa directly facing the windows; a short time later, Neil knocked on the open door. "Do you mind company?"

"You're funny. Come and sit with me."

He sat, and I leaned into his chest, sighing as he stroked the top of my head.

"Are you sure about Atlanta?" Neil asked as we looked out the window at the night sky.

"I have a Pinterest board dedicated to places to eat and visit in Atlanta," I answered. "Don't worry about me."

He chuckled. "I can't argue with a Pinterest board." He pressed a kiss to my hair. "I just want you to be happy."

"I do too. That's why I'm going with you."

Neil didn't respond, but I could hear him arguing in his head.

I patted his hand. "You're just going to have to trust me," I said. "I'm not going to change my mind."

Silence.

"And I'll have Gigi," I continued.

He wrapped his arms around mine. "I'm

glad for that."

But as we gazed out at the Provençal evening, I couldn't shake the knowledge that Neil had a point. I'd certainly traveled in my lifetime, but I hadn't moved. I knew enough about Georgia to know I'd be in for some very real cultural shifts.

I could do it. I was a grownup — I had to leave home sometime. But I'd be kidding myself if I believed it would be an easy transition.

"We'll be together, and I'll make new friends, and I'll teach cooking classes," I said. "Don't worry about me. I'll stay busy."

"Let's take our coffee into the parlor," Caterina suggested Thursday morning. "And I'll take the reading shift."

"I'll take notes," Sophie offered. "So if someone needs or wants to be elsewhere, it'll be easy to loop back to the salient points."

"Bonne idée," Sandrine agreed.

Letizia offered to bring the platter of *cornetti,* just in case the edge of hunger returned so far from the kitchen.

We settled together in the parlor, making the most of the winter morning's light, and reentered Mireille's world.

Dearest Gabriel,

The house feels easier, of late. Cécile and I spend a good deal of our days together. The girls play together, running naked in the garden when Maman isn't around.

In my mind, Alice isn't my Alice anymore. She is called a different name, has grown taller, lost some of her infant roundness. Do not misunderstand me — she is and always will be our daughter, especially since she is the very image of you. But when I look at her, I see her — she's made your features her own, in her sweet girlish way. She is called a different name, looks different, sounds different. She reaches for Cécile, and Cécile holds her close, her eyes glowing with love.

My Alice — she is tucked away in my heart, and we cannot be parted. This child — I love her, but it is different, non? She is not mine to love, and she does not suffer for it.

Gabrielle is likewise growing, and that one I rarely allow to stray from my side. She does not much mind. We spend a good time outside, walking through the forest, letting Anouk sniff about the ferns.

I've been gardening more. Françoise keeps a lovely kitchen garden, and I do what I can. Namely, I dig and water and pull weeds, and while I'm usually filthy at the end — Gabrielle too, for that matter — it's satisfying work. At the end, I can see that I've done something productive. I do have to be quick, though — twice, Gabrielle found the slugs before I did, and it took me hours to stop cringing (almost as long to clean her up — I can't even think about it now).

Gilles joins me in the garden as he is able. If it were not for the aspirations of Mme. Bessette, I believe he would have been the happiest gentleman farmer, for he dearly loves a chance to roll his sleeves past his elbows and work his fingers into the earth. He knows the amounts of water that various plants should receive, which ones do better with more acidic soil.

He has told me he will have to return to Toulouse day after next. The poor man: we have disrupted his life ever since he found us by the side of the road on our way to the chateau, that sad and fateful night.

I asked what he planned; for all I knew,

he would simply decide to return to Toulouse, where he keeps a quiet pied-à-terre and a manservant. No messy widows or children there, and I could not blame him if he decided to spend the rest of the war there.

Instead he answered that he would be back in a week, sooner if he was able. He had to look in at the factories that he'd invested in two years prior, but that his presence wasn't needed on a daily basis.

He looked out onto the lavender field and then back at me, and said again that he'd be back as soon as he was able.

I'm not quite certain how I feel on the subject. If I felt about Gilles the way that I used to feel about him, I would feel relief at the distance.

But the feeling in my chest — it does not feel very much like relief.

Dearest Gabriel,

Gilles left two days ago, in his roadster, the same one that brought us to the chateau after the truck broke down.

After all this time, it feels strange to be at the chateau without him. Gabrielle has gone looking for him, particularly in the garden when she's found a handful of dirt she's particularly proud of.

Anouk is grateful for the extra space on the bed, but after growing accustomed to a person beside me, his absence is that much more noticeable.

It has only been two days. I will go to the garden and be useful. There are some lovely aubergines, and I think they will make a very nice vegetable tart.

On another subject altogether, I believe Cécile to be enceinte. She's very sensitive to kitchen smells, and weeps along with Alice when Alice bumps or bruises along the course of the day. She hasn't mentioned anything to me, and neither has Maman or Tante Joséphine, though Tante Joséphine shot me a significant look the other day when Cécile teared up about spilling her tea on her skirt.

A baby for Cécile and Richard — I am delighted for them. But a part of me also twinges in my heart.

My pregnancy with Gabrielle and Alice — it certainly wasn't easy. Only now does my body seem to begin to return to its former self. But I would have loved another child with you, in time. A son. Or perhaps more girls — we would have loved any combination of children, I am sure.

So at times, watching Cécile's life carry forward reminds me of the ways that ours won't. Our little family is done, and not only done, but divided.

And life carries on.

I really must go to the vegetable garden. If I sit and write any longer, I'm simply going to stay at my desk and cry.

Dearest Gabriel,

Gilles left five days ago. No word, as yet. I had wondered if he might call, but I imagine he's been quite busy. We've listened to the radio, and there have been no reports of military action in that area.

I'm sure he's fine. I wish I could sleep at night, but Anouk does her best to be a fine companion.

Cécile came and told me that she suspected she was expecting, and I told her I had suspected as much also. She blushed prettily, saying she had missed her last two flows. I told her that she should see the physician in town, or have Maman insist he come to the chateau, but that in all likelihood she and Richard would have a child by late spring.

Cécile and I have not spoken about what is to come at the end of the war. It is too uncertain to know. Can one trade a child back and forth like a pair of gloves? I know the Londoners have sent all of their children to the countryside, where they are out of the path of the shellings.

We worry less about shells, here. We worry about the whispers of neighbors and those we would call friends. So often I feel worry is a heavy, wet, wool blanket we wear about our shoulders.

If only it was not already raining.

Dearest Gabriel,

Gilles left one week ago. No word, but I do expect him today. In preparation, I have harvested some lovely squash and roasted it, then folded it into croissant dough. I made two options: one sweet with sugar and cinnamon, the other savory with sage. We shall see which one the family prefers.

Both girls are cutting teeth — we may be pretending they are cousins, one adopted at that, but they do like to do things at the same time. Despite the despair created by sore gums, the household hums in anticipation of Gilles's return.

Remember when you traveled to Lyons

for a week? When you returned, I'd made you almond croissants and chocolate mousse, and then you built a fire, and we, ah, reacquainted ourselves with each other? Your kisses tasted of chocolate mousse with a hint of almond. Writing this, years later, my heart flutters in remembrance.

I do not believe that will be the homecoming Gilles will receive, but I confess that the news has me wondering what the future might hold.

When we married, we believed it to be for the rest of our lives, even though my parents would have liked very much if I'd decided to annul the union and come home. But we chose each other. Marriage, as an institution, meant a great deal to me.

And now that I am married to Gilles — granted, under wholly different circumstances — how does that change my stance on the state?

We have not, of course, consummated our vows, so ending our attachment would simply be a matter of paperwork, and the church would have no cause to consider raising its hackles. But even though we haven't shared that particular intimacy, I do feel Gilles and I have shared others.

We both know that there are many kinds of intimacy in a marriage. All that to say — I don't know what he wants from me. Are we to part ways after the war, and I will live out my life as a rather scandalous widow? Or have Gilles and I collected enough intimacies, built enough trust, to grow a real marriage? And if so, is that something that I want?

It does seem strange sharing this here, dearest, but I feel you'd want to know, and that you'd have an interest. If the situation were reversed, I'd want you to have a companion, if only to reassure me that you'd eat at least two meals per day and wear the occasional clean garment.

(Please do not feel insulted, dearest. But it's true that you got tied up at work quite often and forgot about social niceties.)

I wish you could answer me. Tante Joséphine believes Gilles and I ought to have a real marriage. I cannot decide if that's wisdom or wishful thinking.

He's good to Gabrielle, though. No matter what else one might say, he's very kind to her.

She's waking from her nap, speaking

of our daughter. And it's for the best, or I'd sit here all day writing myself in circles.

Dearest Gabriel,

Gilles has been away for nine days. I am not certain what to do. He has not called. There have been no telegrams.

I feel on edge and I am not hiding it well; Tante Joséphine patted me on the hand and told me that he would return soon.

I tried to call his flat, but the operator could not find his listing. I would have asked his mother — but I would have had to ask his whereabouts of Mme. Bessette. I don't want to ask my mother-in-law where my husband is, even if we're just barely husband and wife.

If Gilles and I were truly husband and wife, I would know his whereabouts.

And yet I can't decide if I'm angry, hurt, or very, very frightened.

Dearest Gabriel,

Telegram from Gilles. He has been held up at the factory, and apologizes for his delay, as well as the lack of word. Expects to return next week.

Dearest Gabriel,

Gilles returned very late last night, having worked, eaten a bite, and then begun the journey.

I had retired about an hour earlier, and didn't know he'd returned until he knocked softly on the door of our suite.

He entered the bedroom, apologizing for the late hour and telling me not to get up. But I sat up anyway, and asked about his journey.

He sat down next to me and said that the factory had required much more of his time than he'd expected, and he apologized for not sending the telegram sooner.

And then he put his hand on my knee and said he'd missed me, but that he knew it was very late and that he wanted to take a bath before going to bed.

I lay there, trying to sleep, listening to the sound of the water rushing through the pipes, of Gilles lowering himself into the bath.

After a fashion, I heard a different noise — snoring.

He'd gone and fallen asleep in the tub.

I stifled a laugh. He'd likely wake up at some point, but the idea of him asleep — well, I worried it could end badly, and the last thing I needed was a husband who'd accidentally drowned in the bath.

So I rose, slipped into my bathrobe, and knocked softly on the washroom door.

The adage that children are peaceful when they're sleeping? It's also true about grown men. The worry and concern in Gilles's face had eased in sleep, his head resting against a folded towel at the apex of the tub.

I studied his face because I dared not look elsewhere. Another stack of towels rested on the stool near the tub, and I reached for one before touching his shoulder.

"Gilles," I said, and I touched his shoulder again.

His eyes flew open, and he looked at me in confused alarm.

"You fell asleep. Come, dry off and come to bed."

"I'm naked," he said.

Again, I dared not look away from his face. "Yes, it's better to bathe that way. I have a towel for you. Let's get you dried off before you dissolve."

I held out the towel, looking away, my arms outstretched.

"I didn't know I was so weary," he

said, standing slowly from behind the towel. He turned and took the towel; I could see the blush on his face before I turned around altogether.

I reminded him that it had been a long drive, and a long week, and then I went back to bed.

He slipped into his pajamas and joined me a moment later.

For the first time since he'd left, I slept soundly through the night.

29

Love is a bicycle with two pancakes for wheels. You may see love as more of an exercise in hard work, but I see it as more of a breakfast on the go.

— **JAROD KINTZ**

"I can't stop there," Caterina said, after recounting Gilles's bathtub nap. "I'll keep reading, if you like."

Letizia waved a hand. "But of course."

"Chloé and I have plans to drive into town today," Sophie said. "The rest of you are welcome to join us, if you like."

Caterina placed her elbows on the table and rested her chin in her hands. "Town. Any good boutiques in town?" she asked Sandrine, her gaze cutting toward me. "Dress boutiques?"

"Ah, Montagnac is small, the real shopping is in Toulouse or Bordeaux, but there are a couple shops."

"Might be worth looking," Caterina said lightly, turning to me. "Are you game?"

"Yes," Letizia chimed in. "Because you need a dress, Juliette."

"No bridal boutiques," Sandrine cautioned. "The local girls travel for their wedding dresses."

I looked down at the diary and back up. "I'd be into a trip to town, see the sights. Are you okay reading just a little bit longer?"

"Can I wash my hair first?" Chloé asked. "Before we leave?"

Sophie nodded. "Of course."

Chloé bit her lip. "Can you help me with the faucet?"

Sandrine explained the nuances of French plumbing, and mother and daughter exited with promises to join us when we were ready to explore town.

"Not much more this morning," Caterina said as she picked the blue diary back up. "I should give Damian a hand with the boys today, so I shouldn't linger too long before we leave." She turned pages, finding where she'd left off.

"Mireille sounds happier," Sandrine observed.

"There are so many terrible jokes I could make," Caterina said. "But yes," she added dryly. "I'll get back to the diary."

Dearest Gabriel,

I woke this morning to find a steaming cup of chamomile (coffee is too dear, you know) and toast with jam on my nightstand. I ate and enjoyed the luxury before dressing and readying for the day.

Gilles sat at the desk in the sitting room, and when I entered, he gestured for me to join him at the settee.

I sat and tucked my ankles beneath myself.

He looked at his hands, and then at me. "I am very sorry," he said.

I shook my head and told him not to trouble himself — I knew he'd been very tired.

He reached out and took my hand. "I should have sent word sooner. I was thoughtless. I'm not a bachelor any-more."

"No?" I asked. And I meant the question, because I didn't know, exactly, what we were.

Gilles searched my face, so I searched his. I hadn't really looked at him since I left home. I didn't look that night beside the road. I'd looked everywhere else since Paris, since we rewrote our own histories because an army of madmen decided that we mattered.

He'd changed; lines emphasized the shape of his eyes — he'd inherited the Bessette eyes. Large, almond shaped, and the same gray-green as lavender leaves, framed by low, thoughtful brows. An indelicate person would call his nose strong, but it suited the sharp cheekbones and cleft chin. His was a face of angles and shadows, eyes designed to study the clouds to divine the weather.

I don't know if he saw clouds or fair skies in my face, but he spoke after several long moments.

"No, I'm not a bachelor anymore. I have you and Gabrielle to think of, and I should have told you sooner. I hope I didn't cause you worry."

"Not much," I said, aiming for lightness.

I don't think he believed me.

"The Germans have taken more of my factory workers and shipped them to the German factories. The existing factories are working on a third of the employees. I worked with the foremen to arrange it so that the remaining workers work for a week each per location — the output is only a little higher, but the accidents are fewer. If we lose any more, though . . ."
He gave a shrug.

"That's clever," I said. "Are you sure you can afford to be here? Do you need to return to Toulouse?"

"I believe I'm needed here," he said. "As I said, I'm not a bachelor anymore. Additionally, it is a miracle this place hasn't been visited by soldiers yet."

I mentioned that being in the woods had its advantages.

"The woods will keep them out only for so long. Your father, Richard, and I need to have a discussion about how to protect the family's assets."

"Maman hid the Dutch masters the instant the Nazis marched across the border," I reminded him.

"The Dutch masters are important, but so are the food stores and the live-stock. And the longer the war goes on, the more the neighbors may become a problem."

I widened my eyes. "You believe your mother will sneak into the garden to steal carrots?"

"Not my mother, I don't think. But the villagers on rations may feel desperate enough to see what they can take."

"Do you intend to build a wall? Like China to keep the Mongols out?"

"I thought to use a rainwater cistern

to irrigate a rooftop garden, and pipes from the well water to supplement."

That surprised me a good deal, though it sounded like it might work. I asked if he thought to keep the livestock up there as well. He shook his head, and said he was still thinking of ideas, though too many were predicated on the animals not making the sounds that animals do.

And then he said that there may come a time when the animals were simply going to be appropriated, and that we might be better off butchering, drying, and preserving what we could, and then storing it somewhere hidden.

In another time, I would have dismissed such talk as being paranoid and cynical. But I had heard enough to know that he was entirely right — we were at the mercy of enemy soldiers.

Dearest Gabriel,

Richard and Gilles are in agreement. They have informed my parents that they think it wisest to stop keeping household staff, with the exception of Françoise and Marise. They conceded that they could hire a housekeeper to clean once a week, but that economies must be taken, and if we are to have secret food stores, they must be a secret.

Gilles laid out a plan involving the removal of items of value, the closing of unused rooms, and the building of false walls.

At this point, my father's eyes grew shifty. He explained that the chateau had been built and then added on to, over the centuries, and that the very oldest parts had a few "architectural surprises."

First, there was a tunnel from the kitchen cellar to a door hidden in the forest, and another near the stables.

Second, there was a passageway leading from the master suite — my parents' rooms, built during the second phase — running the full height of the building. They could go to the roof or the main floor. The builder of the first passageway must not have known about the other passageway, my father concluded, or else the two would have connected usefully. He supposed that the second was included with the political tensions of the Revolution in mind, should the titled landowner need to flee without detection. Or, he added, sneak into his mistress's chambers.

Maman was horrified that he'd said the word "mistress," but Papa just shrugged. Cécile and I had to work very hard not to laugh.

Maman couldn't conceive of the idea of not having a house full of staff, but when she protested, Gilles pointed out that fewer people in the house meant fewer people who could inform.

And that made Gabrielle and Alice just a little bit safer.

Maman couldn't disagree with that.

Cécile and I promised that we would do our part. Cécile was excited — she has always longed to be useful — and I used to keep our Paris apartment, you know. So with a maid coming for the necessary scrubbing, I'm sure we will get by.

Our job next week is to take into account the household valuables, and that will be difficult.

It's only been in the family for four generations; my ancestor bought it for a song and restored it to life.

However, it's four generations enough, especially considering that my great-grandmother had an obsession with period furniture and bric-a-brac. There are Louis XIV chairs and a great many sideboards and highboys and other pieces of furniture that I cannot identify other than by saying "it has drawers."

We will assume, out here, that German soldiers will have no wish to cart the larger pieces out. Maman has already hidden the Dutch masters, but intends to set aside the best of the silver for storage.

Little has been done yet, but there is a plan.

I confess, my heart is warmed hearing Gilles's desire for the safety of both girls.

Dearest Gabriel,

Richard suggested that neither Cécile nor I stray too far from the grounds, in case we find soldiers or desperate persons who might do us harm, reminding us that wars can make enemies of friends.

I wished to visit the orchards, which are at the edge of the property and near to the forest. I'm still saddened, dearest, that you were never able to see the chateau for yourself.

So because I wished to go to the orchards, I asked Gilles to join me. I carried a basket with my right hand, but as we walked, his hand slipped around my left hand, taking hold, encasing it. We walked that way, companionably, until we reached the orchards.

There are pear trees and apple trees. The apples weren't quite ready for picking yet, but the pears needed to come off.

I explained to Gilles what I'd learned in school about pears — that they must be picked early and chilled, and then given time at a warmer temperature for them to ripen evenly.

He asked why not simply allow the pear to remain on the tree, and I explained how it would make the fruit too soft at the center, sickly sweet or even rotted.

I showed him how the pears came off if I tipped the pear horizontally. We picked pears, making a game that we tossed the pears to the person closest to the basket. I found myself relaxing, even laughing.

Our fingers brushed when we reached for the same pear a few times.

We smiled at each other when we finished; before he reached for the basket, he reached out and brushed the hair that had escaped from my coiffure away from my face. His touch was tender, sweet.

It felt strange and welcome, all at once.

I do not know what to do, dearest.

Caterina closed the diary with a sigh. "I feel confident she'll figure it out."

By the time we were ready to leave, the day's sunlight had already begun to fade. I returned to our room to find Neil at the desk, speaking on his cell phone. I brushed my teeth and straightened my hair before removing my coat and scarf from the armoire.

"Going to town," I mouthed.

He held the phone away from his ear. "It's Callan," he said. "You're leaving for town?"

"Caterina thinks she's finding me a wedding dress."

"Have fun," he said, reaching out to caress my waist, albeit through the wool of my coat. We exchanged parting kisses, and I left, ready for an adventure.

As it turned out, just getting everyone into the van turned into an adventure. Sandrine joined us, and Sophie convinced her to drive. Letizia played copilot, while my sisters, niece, and I piled into the back of the Citroen.

We drove down the long, bumpy road to town; Sandrine parked the van at the edge of town, and we toppled out onto the

444

cobblestones, laughing.

The streets were lit, the lights glowing against the soft twilight. We took care of Sandrine's grocery needs first, returning those items to the van before exploring the *chocolaterie.* Sophie opened her handbag, telling everyone to pick out the confection of their choice, her treat.

Chloé, being savvy, negotiated for two.

We walked the streets, taking in the decorated shop windows.

Chloé rubbed her hands together. "I'm cold. How long are we going to stay?"

Sophie frowned at her daughter's hands. "Where are your gloves?"

"I left them at home."

"At your room, or at *home* home?"

"At our house," Chloé clarified.

"Why didn't you bring them? It's winter here too," Sophie exclaimed, her face distorted in exasperation.

I opened my mouth to make a suggestion when something caught my eye. "Wait," I said, stopping midstride.

Sophie, Chloé, Caterina, Letizia, and Sandrine clustered around me as I turned, pointing at the shop window.

"Oh," Sandrine said. "This shop is new. I haven't been in yet."

I peered through the window. Beneath

lights and displayed on a dress form was a hunter-green dress.

While the color was subdued, the style wasn't. With its lace bodice, cap sleeves, and full tulle skirt, it made the perfect, festive holiday dress.

Holiday dress, or . . .

"You have to try it on," Caterina said, taking my hand. "Are they open? They have to be open."

Sandrine took the lead, stepping forward to try the door and, when that worked, ushering us inside. Once we were inside, she explained to the clerk in rapid-fire French that I wanted very much to try on the dress in the window.

Within minutes, I found myself in front of a three-way mirror, the other women looking on.

"It's perfect," Caterina breathed.

"The color suits you," Sophie agreed.

"Très belle," Sandrine said, fingering the tulle.

I turned to examine the back. It fit a little loose in the waist, nothing that a few stitches couldn't fix. A row of green beads twinkled at the waist.

"The jacket," I said, turning to my family. "I could wear Mireille's jacket over this."

Caterina covered her mouth. "That would

be perfect. Oh, Etta —"

"You can keep looking," Sophie said. "If you want to, we can go to one of the larger cities, find a bridal boutique."

"I want to wear the jacket," I said, realizing it to be true as I said it. "Well, I'd love to wear the dress, but it's just too tiny. And matching the jacket to a white or ivory dress wouldn't be easy. But this —" I nodded. "This is the dress."

Sophie reached for her handbag. "Dad sent me with his card. He told me that if you found a dress, he wanted to buy it for you."

"He what?"

"I think he meant to tell you himself, but he got distracted helping Auguste in the kitchen." Sophie tilted her head. "They would have paid for your wedding, you know, Mom and Dad. And not because you couldn't," she said, holding up a hand before I could argue. "But because they wanted to."

"And for heaven's sake, they paid for mine and Sophie's," Caterina pointed out.

"I haven't even looked at the price tag."

Sophie shook her head. "It doesn't matter."

Caterina reached for the tag herself. "It's marked down, sis. Consider it a sign."

I lifted an eyebrow. "A sign? A sale is a sign?"

Sophie nodded toward the mirror. "Do you like it?"

I couldn't help but look at myself again. "I do." My gaze took in the movement of the fabric. "It swishes."

"Two wedding dresses," Caterina said, wrapping her arm around my shoulders before planting a sisterly kiss on my cheek. "Lucky duck."

We drove back, singing along to the Christmas songs on Chloé's iPod. At the chateau, Letizia insisted on making dinner along with her parents and Nonno. I found Neil with Nelson, Damian, and the boys, and stole him away until dinner.

I resumed the reading that evening.

Dearest Gabriel,

The staff has been dismissed, with the exception of Françoise and Marise, and Maman has taken to her rooms in despair. She fears she will receive guests only to be perceived as having come down in the world, as requiring economies.

You didn't know my mother well, but surely you can imagine that this is all very trying for her.

Cécile and I are doing our best to keep up with the house, which largely means tidying up after the girls. And really, with Cécile expecting, she tries hard but must rest often. Cécile tells me that after being a bachelor for so long, Richard is quite adept at keeping his own things. Gilles is . . . less so. But I know he tries.

We left the girls with Marise and went, just the adults, to explore the secret passageways. Cécile and Richard flirted with each other; Gilles and I, of course, did not. He did keep his hand at the small of my back, though, which I admit felt nice considering the damp stone and occasional cobweb. I didn't think I was claustrophobic, but after five minutes I began to wonder otherwise.

To Gilles's delight, the passageway did, in fact, lead to the rooftop greenhouse. "It didn't used to be a greenhouse, of course," my father explained. "But my great-aunt had a wish to garden with a view."

Tante Joséphine, who was there, of course, smirked and said that clearly great-aunts could never be trusted.

Maman wrung her hands over the idea of having to move her prize-winning roses, but agreed that the ability to maintain a food garden had merit.

Myself, I have enjoyed being able to dig in the dirt, and have mourned the imminent end of that season as the months have passed.

Even though winter comes, I'll still have a bit of earth, and the thought brings me pleasure.

Dearest Gabriel,
Gilles kissed me today.

Chloé and Caterina squealed; Sophie shushed them.

We were in the kitchen; he had asked if I could teach him to make bread.

Now, more than ever, he has significant responsibilities, but he asked to bake with me that morning and I could not tell him no. Not when he's building a false wall in the cellar to hide goods in, not when he's falling into bed already asleep each night, having worked with the animals or tended seedlings in the greenhouse.

He still leaves his effects strewn about the room, but has begun to look sheepish about it as he realizes that no one's going to tidy up after him.

So when he asked to join me in my efforts to bake a morning loaf of bread, as I've done to lighten Françoise's load, I could not refuse.

I showed him how to mix the dough by hand, and how to knead the dough, over and over, folding and pressing to increase the elasticity and improve the crumb.

When we set aside our respective balls of dough to rise near the oven, he looked at his floury hands, shirt, and pants, and laughed. In comparison, I wore an apron and had very little flour go wild. I laughed with him.

He reached for my face, running a tender finger from my cheekbone to my chin.

Forgive me, dearest, for it felt somehow comforting and discomforting all at once. When he stepped closer I did not move away, when his lips lowered to mine, I did not turn away.

We'd kissed before, when we were engaged all those years ago. When I had never lived anywhere but our little village, when I still thought the world made sense. When Gilles hadn't yet become a man who so clearly put the interests of others before his own.

Those earlier kisses were the kisses of youths, and lackluster ones at that. These?

Someone taught him to kiss in the intermediate years. And that, truly, was my first thought.

It wasn't a kiss of possession or persuasion; rather, his lips on mine felt like a greeting, a reintroduction.

It was the kiss version of a strong handshake.

What's interesting, I say as a woman who married and was well loved, is that kissing back becomes a reflex. Like saying "thank you" after a compliment.

So I kissed him back without thinking. Would I have kissed him back if I'd stepped back and thought it over first? I do not know.

But I did kiss him, is the point I'm trying and have oversucceeded at making. He paused, surprised, I think. The kiss changed — the difference between a handshake greeting and being clasped in the arms of a dear friend.

He ended the kiss with a final brush of the lips, before caressing my face a final time.

I finally stepped back, dazed.

We did not speak of it.

We returned to the bread after the rising and kneaded some more, without any other amorous advances. Such considerations have not stopped me from wondering. Has that kiss changed nothing — or everything? Will he expect further intimacies? I do not know and I'm ashamed to be too cowardly to simply ask.

Oh, dearest, I miss you. I miss our kisses, your uncomplicated love.

Are you angry? Resigned? I cannot know.

Dearest Gabriel,

I am very angry with you today. Forgive me.

I am angry at you for risking your safety, for being in the wrong place at the wrong time, for dying and leaving our family in such upheaval.

I am angry at the fact that your family found themselves on the police's lists. I'm angry at the police for following along with the plans of madmen.

I am angry with you for leaving me behind.

Because now I must sort out a future — and yes, I do recognize that the middle of a war is very poor timing to make any plans.

But I'm married to a man who is not you, a man who kissed me yesterday, who was gentlemanly enough not to continue that conversation in our bed last night.

(This is partially because I went to bed early and feigned sleep. No need to remind me I'm a coward; I'm already painfully aware.)

I'm angry that I know what real, true love is like, and I'm afraid of settling for less, but I'm also practical enough to know that security counts for a lot in these times.

And . . . I'm afraid I might grow to love him. What would that mean?

If it were not for you, I would not have to find out.

"I did not expect," Nico said, "for this to become a kissing book."

"It's more complicated than that," Sandrine pointed out. "She's falling in love with the husband who's present in her life, but feeling disloyal to the husband she lost just months before. Moving on is always hard, but Mireille had to move on more quickly than most, *non*?"

"And when it got easier," I said, "is when she felt guiltier."

Chloé leaned toward me. "Was she talking about having a conversation," she asked in a whisper, "or about . . . sex?"

Sophie's eyes widened, and she watched me like a hawk as I searched for an appropriate answer.

"Difficult to say," I said at last. "But I think she and Gilles are still working on their communication skills, don't you?"

30

Cooking is at once child's play and adult joy. And cooking done with care is an act of love.

— CRAIG CLAIBORNE

Caterina, Letizia, Sophie, and I stayed up late in the sitting room, nursing our decaf coffees. The men had long since begged off, but the four of us enjoyed rare time together.

"You know," Sophie said, her head resting against the settee, "I wasn't expecting for my grandmother's diary to be the catalyst for questions about sex from my daughter."

"I'm not looking forward to that," Caterina said. "I'm hoping to be an embarrassing enough parent that they'll take their questions to Damian."

Sophie nodded. "Not a bad plan."

Letizia propped her feet up on the ottoman. "When I was a girl, my grandmother

— my father's mother — told me that she'd almost had an affair with a professor. He propositioned her after an academic event. She declined, and eventually he married someone else." She shook her head. "Anyway, she asked me — me! when I was sixteen if I thought she should have gone through with the affair. But," she added, "we should not be surprised. After all, *we* came from somewhere, no?"

"Unless you subscribe to Nico's stork theory," I said dryly.

Caterina laughed. "Poor Nico. Is he dating Clementine yet?"

"Not yet. But he threw himself into work pretty deeply after Mom died. He'll come up for air eventually."

Sophie put her hand to her forehead. "I feel like I should read ahead in the diary to make sure it's appropriate for Chloé. But on the other hand . . ."

"Married people have sex," Letizia finished for her. "Who knows what's in the diary, but your mother had a brother, yes? Better to have her hearing from a woman working through her marriage than whatever nonsense comes up on your American television. What's in the diary — that is real."

Sophie nodded. "You're right. It was just

easier when she thought that babies came from ice cream."

I chuckled. "Those were the days."

"You just wait," Sophie warned.

Caterina cleared her throat. "Yes, but Juliette can live her own life path, no matter what it brings — if it's children or a passel of puppies. It all has worth." She raised her coffee cup. "Infertile woman soapbox. Not even sorry."

"Nor should you be," Sophie said, patting her sister on the leg. "You're right. I'm sorry."

"Juliette can live whatever life she would like," Letizia agreed, "but we want to know more about it. This elopement, it sounds very romantic. Neil has the face of a man in love. And you are moving, yes?"

"To Atlanta, yes."

Letizia shook her head. "You must go on a proper holiday. You're newlyweds, you need to get away to do newlywed things."

I flushed. Caterina hooted and patted Letizia's hand. "Letizia, I wish we lived closer."

"No, you must simply come to Rome more often," Letizia insisted before taking a sip of her coffee.

Caterina turned to me. "How do you think the diary ended up in the closet, anyway?"

"As far as I can tell," I said slowly, "everything in the closet more or less belonged to Mireille. I think everything she left behind — they weren't things she was ready to take with her. But I don't know that she meant for anyone else to have them."

"So she took the key," Sophie finished.

I nodded. "She took the key. I only hope that by the end, we might know why."

When the hour turned very late, I wished my sisters and cousin a good night.

Walking down the halls, I turned a corner and found the familiar figure of my second-oldest brother, a phone pressed to his ear. Something made me pause; a moment later, he murmured a good-bye before hanging up.

I continued on my path, and Nico turned to see me.

"Hi," he said, his cheeks coloring in the dim light.

I glanced at the phone and the expression on his face. If my guess were correct, he'd been talking to Clementine.

"Is she well?" I asked.

He hesitated before nodding. "Yes."

I pressed a sisterly kiss to his cheek. "Don't wait too long," I said, before continuing down the hallway.

The table for the morning reading ran decidedly female the next day.

"I think the men have been frightened off," Sandrine commented dryly.

We shared a laugh before Sandrine began to read.

Dearest, dearest Gabriel,

Forgive me for yesterday's anger. One thing I have learned as a widow is that each new change spurs a fresh wave of grief. It's as if I stand in the ocean during high tide, holding still as each wave threatens to knock me off my feet.

Yesterday I felt angry; today I feel sad and tired. The skies are gray; I have taken Gabrielle with me to the greenhouse. She is delighted to be reunited with dirt, and we enjoy the privacy. We play clapping games and watch for the rare intrepid autumn bird.

Marise offered to take Gabrielle to put her down for a nap, but I joined her instead, curling up with her and enjoying the closeness of her small body against mine.

I am so grateful for Marise. She has her hands full, as Cécile's pregnancy has her napping almost as often as the girls.

I awoke from my own nap to find an extra blanket over us both, and Gilles at his desk in the next room. Gabrielle toddled over to greet him, but he looked at me soberly, with an expression I had difficulty reading.

He asked if he'd upset me, the other day, in the kitchen.

And I didn't know what to say. Because I had become upset, but for a whole host of reasons that, to be honest, had nothing to do with him.

I told him simply that there had been a great deal of change lately, and that I was very tired, and probably a few other excuses that sounded weak to my ears. So I told him that I was sorry, and that it wasn't him, not really.

He didn't much believe me, I don't think.

Since then, he has been outside, in the cellar, or everywhere else but where I am.

Dearest Gabriel,

Gilles is still avoiding me. For the last week, he's come to bed after I've retired, risen before I wake. Richard and Cécile speak of how busy he is, how busy he is building the secret cellar.

I don't know what to do. I want to tell him everything is fine, that I want to return to the way things were.

But everything isn't fine. I have stayed busy in the kitchen, canning the pears that have ripened, slicing the apples to dry.

Maman is beside herself. Word in the village is that Papa's business prospects have failed, which is why the family buys few provisions in the village and fired most of the staff. We have told her that this may protect us, if the villagers believe we have come down in the world.

But she believes she will never be able to play bridge again.

Cécile and I have had trouble being able to be as sympathetic as Maman has desired.

Some things in our little world have not changed.

Dearest Gabriel,

Two days ago, German soldiers arrived at our door. I could not write in this diary yesterday, for my hands had not yet stopped shaking.

A carload of soldiers arrived, laughing, as if they were simply out on a jaunt in the countryside. And perhaps they were.

They arrived at the door and asked for a meal and a place to stay for the night.

Françoise prepared four extra servings for dinner. She is a savvy one, that Françoise. The food was generous and tasty by wartime standards, but by no means ostentatious. She made a wintertime variation on ratatouille, with generous helpings of noodles.

Maman showed the "guests" to their rooms, and we retired for the night.

I slept not at all, with chairs wedged beneath the door to our suite and the door to the bedroom. Gabrielle slept in our bed, her sweet little feet kicking and prodding me at intervals. Cécile slipped me a note after dinner, saying "She will not leave our sight," and I knew she meant Alice.

Gilles and I have spoken little in the past two weeks, and we spoke little that night, but when he wrapped his arm around me I felt grateful for it. He is a good man, though we seem to have difficulty finding our way.

We made very pretty good-byes to the soldiers the next day, saying nothing when they relieved us of household goods and various decorative objects.

Several chickens are also missing, and we shall miss their eggs. Gilles assured me that he has been reading about how to brood chicks in the winter months — and that the soldiers had taken a few of the lazier layers.

We shall carry on. I know there are many with far fewer resources. I worry for Gabrielle and Alice, though, and for Cécile's child. We do not know how long this war will last, and the countryside has already suffered greatly. We would not do so well if it weren't for Gilles and Richard.

Dearest Gabriel,

Christmas is around the corner. Maman suggested going to Marseilles to shop for presents, but Cécile and I suggested staying home and making gifts for each other. We suggested purchasing simple supplies in the village, which would help support our neighbors. Maman seemed pleased at the idea of once again being a benefactress, and settled on that.

I haven't knitted in ages — not since I was pregnant with the girls — but Tante Joséphine decided it was time that I start again. In truth, I found the repeated motion comforting. There was a knitted blanket in one of the bedrooms made of good wool. Tante Joséphine showed me how to pull it apart, loop it into skeins, and soak them until the fibers relaxed. We let the skeins dry near the furnaces, then wound them into yarn balls, ready to be used.

Anouk found the process fascinating. She loves the smell of wet wool and nesting on the dry wool.

Tante Joséphine's old housekeeper, she said, would make the cleverest shawls from old blankets and remembered what the woman had told her about the process. We haven't told Maman, of course, but woolen mills are just another industry that has come to a halt during the war. We are happy to make do.

Gabrielle shall have a smart knit jacket and matching hat. Gilles is much out of doors; I shall make him a hat and try my hand at gloves. Tante Joséphine feels certain that between the two of us and Françoise that we should be able to figure it out.

Dearest Gabriel,
   Thinking about Christmas has me thinking about how I and my family have

465

always celebrated the birth of Christ, and how your family — your mother's family, in particular — have another set of much older, more esoteric celebrations.

I wouldn't even know where to begin with them. I know they were something your mother observed but your father did not.

Tante Joséphine and I unraveled another blanket; I will be knitting another sweater — this time in forest green — for Alice.

I have decided to place a pocket on the left side of each sweater, and embroider your initials on the inside. No one would know it was there, but I will, and now you as well. They'll carry a bit of you close to their hearts.

Dearest Gabriel,

The papers are full of the news that Marseilles Jews have been arrested and deported. I worry for your brother and his family; I did not receive word that they went elsewhere, though I hope they perhaps might have been able to reach another destination in time.

On the heels of those arrests, I have heard that the one Jewish family in the village, the Bernheims, has disappeared. I hope that they found a place of safety, but I fear they have been arrested and deported as well, though they were French citizens.

My father, Nico, and Alex returned for the evening reading, along with Auguste and Riccardo.

"We heard there's a war on," Alex said before sipping his coffee.

"You just wait," I warned. "Romance might be around the corner."

Dearest Gabriel,

I cannot stop thinking about the Marseilles arrests. Those arrests remind me of the Paris arrests, and my amazement that we were able to make it out of the city. How is it that we were so lucky and so many were not? I do not understand.

Do you remember when we walked the streets of Paris, stopping to taste chocolates and pastries? Those bright days feel so far away. I hold those memories close, though they came before the girls, before we discovered how very deeply we loved each other.

Do you remember when we took the girls to the riverbank? Alice wanted so badly to eat the grass, and squawked when we removed each blade from her chubby fingers. The poor dear, so thwarted. Those were lovely days, but already I felt your troubles, your burden for the children left behind.

But your burden didn't mean you loved us any less. I must cling to that. And I don't believe you ever thought your actions would place us in danger, would send officers to our door.

Dearest Gabriel,

I am not the only one troubled by the arrests. Yesterday Gilles took me into the passageway, to one of the more spacious landings. He'd stacked pallet mattresses, blankets, and pillows in a corner, and placed a small table with an oil lamp nearby.

"When they come again, you and Cécile and the girls will hide here. I will place extra pantry goods if you don't want to go to the cellar. But you must hide here until Richard or I come get you. And if we do not return, Richard and I have built and hidden bicycles at the end of the tunnels. Bundle the girls to you and ride to the next village. Armand in the green cottage will be able to help you."

I protested, but he wouldn't listen to a single argument. "I must know that if the worst comes, you will be safe."

I didn't know what else to do, after the long weeks of silence and distance. I reached a hand to cup his face, and lifted my lips to his. He started in surprise, but responded swiftly, gathering me into his arms and kissing me with a passion that startled us both.

When I was younger, I did not believe Gilles to be capable of such passion. I believed the fields to be his first love.

And perhaps that was true. The poets write often of the power and purity of first loves. But I wonder at the power in a second love, a love that follows experience, loss, or disappointment.

For a moment in the passageway I wondered if, perhaps, our marriage might become more than a legal union.

But Gilles pulled away, though not without three more kisses — like an ellipsis, promising more but ending just the same.

He said something — I barely remember what, my sense had not yet returned — and led me back to the central doorway to the west drawing room. He deposited me there before disappearing back down the stairs.

I still feel jumpy, as if he will appear in a doorway and we will discover what lies on the other end of the ellipsis. For shame. There is a war on, after all.

I believe I shall find Gabrielle and tidy up the greenhouse garden.

If my thoughts are to be distracted, I might as well do something useful with my hands.

"Even the cool parts like the secret tunnels get turned into kissing parts," Nico said mournfully.

I leveled a stern gaze at my brother. "This is your grandmother's diary. If you want secret tunnels and explosions, go read Dan Brown."

"You know I'm teasing. And I'm a Pérez-Reverte man."

"Where are the tunnels?" Chloé asked.

"I take guests to them with tours," Sandrine answered. "It's part of our marketing — a chateau with secret passageways! Everyone loves them. But I keep them locked up so that no one goes wandering."

I winced. "That could end badly."

Chloé leaned forward. "Could you show them to us?"

"*Mais oui,* but of course."

So we left our places at the table and followed Sandrine. She led us to a small door near the kitchen and unbolted it. "This is the old cellar," she said. "I don't take people through the tunnel to the forest anymore. One of these days I'll have a contractor come and make sure it's stable enough. Until then, it's best not to risk it."

We followed her down the steps into the cellar, and I immediately wished for a warmer sweater and gloves. "We don't use this for food storage so often, unless we run out of room." She walked toward a section of floor and bent down to pull on a metal ring. "This was added later. Papa said that they used a wooden shim to open the door from this side."

She lifted the ring, and up came the door in the floor. Sophie gasped.

Auguste grinned. "After you?"

Sophie peered down. "Is there — is there a light?"

Sandrine gave her husband a swat on the arm. "No, there is no light. It is not wired for electricity in there. We give our guests headlamps instead." She reached toward a box on a shelf. "Who wants to go?"

Sophie took one, as did most of the others.

471

Caterina hung back. "I'm good," she said.

Damian put an arm around her. "Small dark spaces are not your thing."

"Nope." She looked over at her boys, both vibrating in excitement. "You can take them. I'll wait here. Just bring them back, okay?"

He pressed a kiss to her temple. "You're very brave in other ways."

"I know." She kissed him back, and the rest of us took turns descending the ladder and into the space.

"It feels like *Raiders of the Lost Ark,*" Neil said, resting his hands on his hips as he looked around, the light on his lamp moving with him.

The floor beneath the ladder was about four feet by four feet, with stairs directly opposite. "This is one of the original passageways," Sandrine explained. "Some of the ones that my father and uncle constructed by hastily walling off rooms are only connected, floor to floor, by ladders."

We followed her up — Chloé with a gaping mouth, Caterina's boys wide eyed and holding tight to their father's hands.

We continued up, the stairs spiraling, until we found the landing that Mireille described in the letter. The bedrolls and tinned foods were long gone, but it still felt, oddly, more recently lived in than the rest of the passageways.

Auguste led us to the greenhouse on the roof, or what was left of it. "We can garden on the ground now," he said. "There is too much work with the fields and house to keep it up, but perhaps one day we shall replant. I have fixed the glass, though; it's been broken by hailstorms a couple times. Several of the panes are now Plexiglas."

I looked out the windows. Somehow, these spaces made Mireille's text even more real — even though I'd been walking the halls of her home.

The rooftop garden had enough room for everyone, but only just. We looked out onto the fields, brown for winter, and the forest that still bordered the chateau.

After several minutes, we made our way back through, our eyes having to readjust to the light of the kitchen after emerging.

Caterina sat at the farmhouse table, cake plate in hand. "Lovely time?"

I gave her a sisterly hug. "Let's go find a fire to sit near. I think that's what Mireille would have us do."

31

Food is symbolic of love when words are inadequate.

— **ALAN D. WOLFELT**

"Did your mom ever talk about the war years?" I asked Sandrine after Caterina and the others left to turn in for the night.

"A little. Different parts of Provence were hit harder than others. In many places, crops rotted in the ground, she said, because there weren't enough laborers to harvest them. But the family fared better than most at the chateau because of the efforts of my father and Oncle Gilles. Gilles could not fight because of his eyesight, and my father had served in the army for two years before returning to Provence." Sandrine set her coffee cup down. "He wasn't a soldier and he knew it — he considered it his duty to stay out of battle. My father and Gilles managed much of the labor of the farm. So there was food, and as we have read, they were very careful to preserve it. The rest is all information I have gathered for myself. She spoke of it very little."

"It was a difficult time. I can understand not wanting to relive it." I hugged my arms to myself as questions ran through my head. One question poked at my mind, but I kept it to myself and finished the rest of my coffee.

Caterina offered to read the next morning as we sat in the sunny front room. "We just have a couple more days. I think we need to blaze through some, don't you?"

I sighed. Neil squeezed my hand.

I wanted to leave and didn't, all at the same time. I hated to leave the coziness of Provence in the winter — but home?

Home meant new adventures with Neil, new projects, new challenges — and I couldn't wait.

I leaned against Neil as Caterina began to read.

Dearest Gabriel,

When I began this diary over the summer, I had recently learned of your death, watched the invasion of our home by soldiers, fled the city, married a man

475

I did not love, and saved a daughter by letting her go.

I miss you.

But you're gone. I can't think about it much. I can only hope that you received a proper burial somehow. I have to remind myself that your spirit, your beautiful soul, is far from that place. And I like to think that a part of you remains with me, with our girls.

Maybe it's the war, maybe it's the routine of the chateau having so little to do with our life in Paris. But our life — mine and Gabrielle's — feels so separate.

So perhaps that's why. Because my life and Gabrielle's is now so deeply entwined with Gilles's, I feel as though my initial perceptions of him have changed.

To begin: I no longer hate or resent him.

For a long while, I believed him to have insinuated himself into my family, into my life, for the sake of the land. I don't believe that anymore. He loves the land, but he loves people more. That love is simply expressed differently. Quietly, but no less real.

He's sacrificed a great deal to be here, to be working the land, to be caring for me and Gabrielle.

My feelings for him have changed. Is it love? Is it gratitude?

I don't know — and I'm not sure that it matters.

I joined Tante Joséphine in the drawing room this morning. We sat and knitted together, speaking of this and that.

And then she asked about Gilles, and about our marriage.

I didn't know what to say.

She asked if we intended to stay married, and I told her I believed so, but I wasn't sure exactly.

And then she lifted her eyebrow, and said rather dryly, "You probably ought to figure that out."

I don't think she's wrong. And then I confessed that there had been some showings of affection, which had not been unpleasant, but that it had caused me to grieve the loss of you all the more. And to worry that it was too soon for me to love another husband.

There were also the words I couldn't voice. My worries that my heart might be softening for Gilles only because I have been so long without your touch. That I might be feeling affection only to rationalize a chance to be held in a man's arms again.

Tante Joséphine put her knitting down and took my hand.

She said that she knew that I loved you very much, and that I had honored you during our time together, and honored you after your death.

She told me about how she felt when she and her husband were trying — and failing — to have children. For years they didn't travel, and she avoided buying new dresses because she thought she'd outgrow them with a pregnancy soon enough.

But after the years passed, she realized they couldn't live like that forever. They didn't give up, not yet, but they traveled to Spain, Portugal, Egypt, and America. She bought beautiful clothes that she liked.

"We never had a child, as you know," she said. "But we lived our life and we had a happy marriage. We found a way to enjoy the life we had. So I believe the same may be true of you. You don't have the life you'd wish. But you have a daughter who needs a father, and a husband — a living husband — who loves you."

When I protested, she raised an eyebrow and silenced me rather effectively

478

before continuing.

"You have a husband who loves you. There is no sin, no shame in living a life with him."

I have carried those words with me these last several hours.

My dearest, I miss you. But it may be time for me to love another.

Dearest Gabriel,

I waited up for Gilles last night. After I put Gabrielle to bed, I took a bath and slipped into my coziest nightgown. I lit my lamp and read a book until I heard Gilles's footsteps and he opened the door.

He nodded when he saw me. Whatever he'd been doing, he'd been hard at work — his hair curled with sweat, his shirt clung to his shoulders and torso.

He took a bath, and I thought back to the night he'd returned from Toulouse, when he'd fallen asleep in the tub. Tonight, however, I could hear movement, splashes of water, and then the chug of the water down the drain.

Shortly after, he returned to the bedroom, this time dressed in pajamas and smelling of lavender and lemon.

I set my book aside and waited as he

climbed into bed.

I asked if he meant for us to stay married after the war, and he met my gaze and held it.

We have been so skittish around each other for weeks that I drank in the sight of his eyes.

He took my hand and said that he loved me, that he has always loved me. His thumb caressed the inside of my palm as he said that he wished we might have married under different circumstances, but that he had not wished to end our union. He admitted that he had not expressed his love well when he was young, before I left.

As sweet as his words were, I had difficulty focusing on them, for the feel of his thumb stroking my hand had me dizzy.

He repeated that he loved me, and that he loved Gabrielle, and he would have us be married always, if I would have him.

Gilles isn't you, Gabriel. His face, his scent, the calluses on his hands. Until that moment, I think I'd been afraid that if I loved Gilles, really loved him, there would be no room left for you in my heart.

But in that moment, I wondered if maybe love creates space, rather than taking it away. Because I felt love for Gilles, but that love didn't crowd you out. It simply made my heart larger.

I leaned forward and kissed him then — he might have talked all night if I hadn't.

This kiss was different from the other two we'd shared.

The first was a kiss of reintroduction; the other tangled in feelings of fear, relief, and gratitude.

This one: gentle, accepting. Gilles reached for my face, brushing my hair away and cupping my cheek.

It was the gentle kiss a groom might give a young bride.

But I was no blushing bride, and Gilles had waited a long time.

I awoke a little disoriented in the morning light, unused to the feel of waking in a man's arms. I rolled over to see Gilles, sound asleep, his arm still draped across my body. The memories flooded back, and for a moment I began to panic.

But just as my mind began to whir, fearing I'd made a mistake, had acted foolishly, Gilles opened his eyes and gave me a sleepy smile. That smile reminded me that he was Gilles Bessette, the boy I'd grown up with, the man I'd grown to trust.

So I smiled back and curled deeper into his arms. It felt like a revelation, being close to someone again.

We missed breakfast. Gilles has gone to the kitchen for a tray.

Caterina paused. The room remained dead quiet; Caterina resumed reading without comment.

Dearest Gabriel,

I'm tempted to hide in the greenhouse until the rest of the household retires for the night.

Tante Joséphine has looked all day like the cat who ate the canary.

Cécile pulled me aside at the first opportunity for the sort of frank discussion that passes between sisters.

Apparently, Gilles has had an air of je ne sais quoi that spoke of pleasing marital relations. I tried to get Cécile to describe it, but she shrugged in a knowing way that is particularly infuriating, coming from a younger sister. I was the one who was supposed to know everything. And then she said my cheeks were glowing, and I glared at her.

You'd think there wasn't a war on and there was nothing else to think of — I miss the privacy of our Paris garret.

But I suppose in its own way, seeing love unfold is its own kind of hope. That if something good and pleasant can happen, maybe goodness can happen in the world as well.

You'd be pleased to know the girls are well, everyone is healthy. Alice has taken to hugging Cécile's growing belly.

We've become friends, Alice and I, though I confess I maintain my distance out of self-protection. She prefers Cécile and Marise, but is glad to have me near, especially if I'm willing to play games.

Her dark curls have grown longer, reminding me of your hair before a haircut.

But she is safe and loved.

And Gabrielle is safe and loved. In these days, we are foolish to wish for more.

My dearest Gabriel,

Our days have been happy. Gilles and I work side by side many days, tending the greenhouse together, and if we are apart — if I am canning apples in the kitchen, or baking bread, or pickling beets — he will find me every few hours, place a hand on my waist, a short kiss on my lips, sweep the hair from my brow.

Just a short moment, and then we return to our responsibilities.

He is a good partner. He is good to me.

His Christmas hat is completed, as well as one glove, with Tante Joséphine's help. The second glove . . . that one may come after the holiday. Or perhaps I shall save it for Epiphany.

My dearest Gabriel,

Christmas brought shepherds to our kitchen door — Armand and his son Jean-Luc. They came with a woman and two children, and begged to come inside.

One look at their faces and I knew them to be Jews. Forgive me, dearest, I thought to turn them away. I wanted nothing more than the safety of Gabrielle and Alice, and feared that might be compromised if we brought Jews into our home.

I'm so ashamed, and grateful that it was not a question left to me, for I would have failed so, so very deeply.

Instead, they were met first by Françoise, whose soul is better than mine, and then by Gilles.

Gilles spoke with Armand for a moment before taking the small family to the wing we have closed off. He nodded to me, in a gesture that told me to trust him, that everything would be fine.

I was ready to turn away refugees at Christmastime. My soul is wretched.

Dearest Gabriel,

I have not seen the refugees since their arrival; Gilles squirreled them away in the east wing. But I have spent extra time in the kitchen, cooking extra food to send to them. I didn't see much of them when they arrived, but they did look skinny, and we have more food than most.

I'm trying.

I'm also having nightmares again, dreaming of soldiers arriving at the door to take the girls away before pointing a gun at me, soldiers finding us at the neighbor's apartment, more guns. The guns fire and I wake up, terrified.

Gilles pulls me close and strokes my hair and holds me until I stop sobbing and fall back asleep. It is nice having a husband again, in that way, but I do feel guilty about how much I'm interrupting his sleep.

Not to mention how guilty I feel about being afraid that the refugees will bring more trouble to my door. So I chop, and bake, and make excellent food for Gilles to take upstairs to them.

I'm trying.

Dearest Gabriel,

My worst fears came true. Soldiers came in search of the woman and her children. I heard them in the foyer, the sharp sounds of commands barked in German, the clack of their boots in the hall echoing off of the tall ceilings.

I was in the drawing room with Cécile, Gabrielle, and Alice. When Cécile and I heard the clatter from downstairs, we exchanged a look.

I nodded to Cécile, and she scooped up each girl, setting one on each hip, and murmured in a singsong voice as she walked toward the second-floor entrance to the passageway. Amazingly, both girls seemed to think it great fun, rather than an unwanted interruption in their play.

Gilles's voice echoed off of the ceilings; there was too much of an echo for me to understand what he said, but I knew he was down there. So it was left to me.

First I ducked into my suite and retrieved my diary, which I would not want to be found by soldiers.

With the diary secure, I continued to our visitors.

I made my way to the second floor of the east wing on quiet feet, planning a route in my head. I knew which room Gilles had taken the woman and her children to, so I made my way there. When I stepped through the door, though, I could see no one.

So I spoke up, saying that I was the daughter of the house, that there were soldiers, and that they needed to come with me to safety.

The wardrobe cracked open, and a hand emerged, followed by the full form of the woman. She pulled her daughters out; I picked the youngest up and led them to the servants' staircase that ran the vertical length of the house. We moved swiftly up the stairs, and then I led them to the entrance to the secret passageway on that floor.

Cécile waited with the girls; her eyes widened for a moment when she saw that I'd brought the woman and her two children.

The children, I should probably mention, were about three and six, the older one a girl and the younger a boy. Though they might have been older; they were nearly skin and bones.

Cécile passed Gabrielle to me; her eyes were red, her face damp, and she'd clearly changed her mind about how much fun she found the entire escapade. I held her close until I felt her body relax, and a moment later shifted her sleeping form in my arms.

Alice, on the other hand, had enjoyed the company of her mother all along, and now felt content to unwind thread from a bobbin.

I tried to lay Gabrielle down on a mattress roll, but she clung to me in her sleep, so I made a comfortable place for myself with one of the mattress rolls and attempted to make conversation with our guests.

The mother's name is Tovah, her daughter's name Adina, and her son's Samuel. They spoke an Alsatian dialect I could only partly understand, but we managed enough to exchange names and for me to tell her that we were as safely hidden away in the chateau as possible.

Hours have passed. Gilles has yet to come.

Dearest Gabriel,

It has been a day, and neither Gilles nor Richard nor my father has come for any of us. The children are restless; Cécile and I have tried to invent simple games — hide-and-seek with the blankets, watching tops spin, simply running from one side of the landing to the other with our hands in the air.

Yes, I feel quite ridiculous, but the alternative — wailing children — is unacceptable. The nights have been cold enough that we are only just warm enough if we huddle together, though Cécile declares it the ideal temperature.

I peered out of the greenhouse windows very carefully. There are two military vehicles parked outside the door, with enough frost on the hood, I believe, for me to think they've been there since their arrival.

I fear for Gilles. I fear that I have not told him that I love him. The feelings have been there, but the words have not come. Je t'aime.

Gilles, je t'aime.

I will say the words. I must say them, when I see him.

Dearest Gabriel,

Two days. Today is cold to the point that the children have simply decided to stay together under the blankets.

Dearest Gabriel,

Third day, morning. Cécile and I left the children with Tovah and discussed how long to wait before going to Armand's cottage.

It's possible it might no longer be safe to go to Armand's. We don't know if they came looking for Tovah here because they've already found Armand. So if we didn't go to his cottage, we wouldn't know where to go.

And it is winter, and the girls are young.

So for now we stay.

Dearest,

Late last night, Gilles and Richard came through the third-floor entryway after the children were asleep.

They called out quickly so that we would know it was them.

Cécile and Richard embraced, and carried a sleeping Alice to bed.

Gilles placed a kiss on my forehead before taking Tovah, Adina, and Samuel back to the east wing, though he did so with Gabrielle's arms looped around his neck, her head pressed against his collarbone.

She would not be parted from him until I put her down to bed. Once she was in bed and settled, Gilles and I returned to our room. I could wait no longer — I held him in my arms and kissed him, and said the words I feared I might never be able to say.

He held me close and told me that he knew, but that he appreciated hearing the words. And then he kissed me back, reminding me that we had been apart for far too long.

Dearest,

Germans arrived at the door again. This time, Tante Joséphine rose from her seat in the drawing room. Did you know she speaks fluent German? She does.

The soldiers were on our doorstep with plans to use the chateau for their own purposes. Joséphine marched past Gilles and Father and proceeded to tell the soldiers to leave the property and the chateau in peace. And she continued in such a fashion for several minutes.

I felt certain that she would be arrested or executed on sight. But instead the strangest thing happened: they left.

Richard went to town a week later. According to the locals, the Germans believe that Tante Joséphine must be very well connected in order to speak so forcefully.

She may have connections, but not to any that count. No, it was simply Tante Joséphine being imperious.

But it's been two weeks, and there have been no new visits from soldiers or attempts to take over the chateau.

32

To feel safe and warm on a cold wet night, all you really need is soup.

— **LAURIE COLWIN**

"How much is left?" Sandrine asked Caterina. Caterina flipped a few pages. "Not much."

Sandrine reached out her hand. "Let us continue. I will read. Your voice sounds tired."

Dearest,

The days have been busy; I have not written here in quite some time. Gabrielle is growing. The greenhouse garden is struggling at the moment, but our stores still have enough, and it will be April in two months.

I tried to help with breakfast this morning, but the scent of food cooking turned my stomach. It turned my stomach in such a specific way that I sat down and thought back to the last time I'd had my courses.

I believe I'm expecting. And I never expected to be expecting. For some reason, these past few months with Gilles, it never occurred to me that in this time of war, so many new things might grow — a love for Gilles, and a child.

A child with Gilles.

I love Gilles. Am I ready for a child with him? We haven't been married for long, and truly married for less. I feel as though I'm turning the pages of my life faster than I can read.

I haven't told him yet. I haven't told anyone yet.

That's probably something I should do.

Dearest,

I told Gilles. A giant, foolish smile spread across his face before he remembered to worry, but I saw it. He's delighted.

He asked if I knew how far along I was, and I thought about it. The last time I remembered having my time was during the Christmas holidays (of course). Which meant that it's very likely that we made this child together after I told Gilles I loved him for the first time.

There's a rightness about that, I think. Perhaps Gilles and I have somehow managed to stumble onto the correct page together.

June 1943

Dearest Gabriel,
    Cécile had her baby early this morning, a tiny ruddy little girl. The baby is Suzette —

Sandrine abruptly stopped reading, lifting the diary closer to her face, her eyes running over the text again.

Caterina gasped; Sophie sat up straight.

"What is it?" Letizia asked.

I glanced at Sandrine before answering. "Suzette. She is Sandrine's younger sister."

Sandrine couldn't look away from the diary. "I don't understand. The rest of the sentence reads, 'She and Alice, Cécile, and Richard make a lovely family tableau.'"

I nodded; the pieces had been clacking together in my mind for days. "In the beginning, she wrote that they changed Alice's name."

Sandrine closed the book and set it down as though she'd been burned. "That is not possible. How would that be possible? How could — I don't understand."

Letizia looked from me to Sandrine, eyes wide. "Sandrine — She is Alice?"

"No," Sandrine said, her voice sharp. "My parents were Richard and Cécile Caron. There must be . . . This cannot be."

My father took the book gently, his hand resting on the cover. "Your parents were Richard and Cécile, of course. But it is possible that they were not your biological parents."

"People always said how much I looked like my mother — Auguste, you heard them!"

"Oui," he said. "But your mother and your aunt looked very much alike. And the book does say that Gabriel had darker coloring."

"Non," she said, shaking her head with vehemence. "My mother would have told me. She would not have hidden such a thing."

But we knew that Mireille had hidden as much and more. Was it any stretch to imagine that Cécile might have done the same?

Sandrine stood up. "It is late. I have chores to do. You must excuse me."

Auguste followed her out of the room with an apologetic wave toward the rest of us. Mireille's diary remained on the sofa.

None of us dared touch it.

Auguste and Sandrine left the chateau for the day, leaving the rest of us behind, feeling bewildered.

"Is she mad at us?" Chloé asked her mother.

"No, honey," Sophie answered, smoothing Chloé's fair blond hair. "She just received a shock — or the possibility of one. She needs some time, but she's still our Sandrine."

I wished for Sophie's confidence. It didn't help that the weather turned, sending storm clouds in our direction. Rain pummeled the windows and winds whipped around the chateau.

So I retreated to the kitchen, opening cans of San Marzano tomatoes and methodically seeding them before roasting them with brown sugar.

I felt a hand at the small of my back, then heard Neil's voice near my ear. "What are you making?"

"It's raining," I said, "and awful outside. And everyone is stressed. I'm making tomato soup and grilled cheese."

"If I hadn't already married you," he said,

sweeping my hair from my face, "I would propose just for that."

"You could propose again," I told him, my eyes creasing.

"Juliette," he said, "would you do me the honor of becoming my wife and eating tomato soup and grilled cheese with me?"

I lifted myself up on my toes to kiss him. "Done."

"Can I help?"

I passed him some shallots to sauté in butter, and within moments the kitchen began to smell truly wonderful. The shallots cooked on the stove while the tomatoes roasted in the oven, and soon enough they were simmering away together.

While the soup cooked, I sliced provolone cheese and white bread, buttering the bread in preparation. Rather than ask who'd be joining us, I planned on feeding everyone. I baked the sandwiches in the oven, flipping them over once to brown on the other side.

The family gathered around the farmhouse table, but the lack of Sandrine and Auguste's presence created an uncomfortable tension. Still, the soup warmed us through, and I chuckled to watch Caterina instruct Letizia on the essential points of dipping her triangle of sandwich into her soup.

Alex and Nico began work on the evening meal, with Damian and me helping with the prep work, and my father alternately giving directions and singing Dean Martin while he stirred a pot of béchamel on the stove.

That was the scene Sandrine and Auguste found upon their return.

I raised a hand in greeting and gave her my easiest smile.

She raised a hand in greeting as well, uncoiling her scarf from her neck before going first to my father. *"Je regrette,"* she said, holding him in a hug. "I do not know if you were married to my cousin or my sister, but that shouldn't matter, not really."

There were hugs all around, followed by gratitude that we had supper well in hand and assurances on our part that we were more than happy to pitch in. There were, after all, six trained chefs among us.

We ate lasagna that night, made from the last of the pasta dough. As the meal wound down, the table grew increasingly quiet.

"Auguste and I brought cake back from town. If I'm going to find out about my biological origins," she said, "I would like to have cake."

~ ROASTED TOMATO-BASIL SOUP ~

2 28-ounce cans whole tomatoes
3 tablespoons dark brown sugar
4 tablespoons butter
4 large shallots, chopped fine
1 tablespoon tomato paste
Pinch ground allspice
1 3/4 cups chicken stock
1/2 cup cream
1/4 teaspoon hot sauce
1/2 cup fresh basil, chopped fine, plus more
  for garnish
Salt and cracked black pepper to taste
Grated parmesan, to serve

Line a large rimmed baking sheet with two layers of aluminum foil (one heavy-duty layer is fine).

Place a fine-mesh strainer over a large bowl. Pour contents of the first tomato can over the strainer and into a bowl carefully, holding back tomatoes with a spoon or spatula. Press juices through with the back of a spoon, if necessary. Reserve the tomato liquids.

With your hands, carefully open each tomato and push the seeds out and into the strainer. Alternately, you can use a tomato corer/strawberry huller tool to scrape the seeds out. Place each seeded tomato onto the baking sheet in a single layer. Discard the seeds.

Place oven rack in the second to topmost position, and preheat to 450°F before repeating the process with the second can of tomatoes. Sprinkle the brown sugar over the tomatoes. Bake until the tomatoes have grown dark red in color, about 20–30 minutes. Allow them to cool a bit, and then scrape them from the foil into a bowl.

Melt butter over medium heat in a large saucepan or soup pot. Add the minced shallots, tomato paste, and allspice. Sprinkle a bit of salt over the top, and reduce the heat to low. Cover and cook, stirring occasionally, for 8–10 minutes.

Whisk in chicken stock, followed by the tomato juices and roasted tomatoes. Increase heat to medium and bring to a simmer, then simmer on low for about 10 minutes.

Remove soup from heat. Purée soup in batches, or use an immersion blender, until soup is smooth. Add the cream, hot sauce, and basil, taste, and adjust seasonings. Rewarm if necessary. Serve with lots of parmesan cheese.

Kitchen tip: Low-acidity tomatoes make a lower-acidity soup. If the soup seems acidic,

temper it with a little extra brown sugar.
  Serves 4–6.

33

My love is pizza shaped. Won't you have a slice? It's circular, so there's enough to go around.

— DORA J. AROD

"I can read," my father said, once everyone had a slice of chocolate cake in hand. "Let me take a turn." He pulled his reading glasses from his shirt pocket and arranged them on the bridge of his nose. A clearing of the throat, and he began to read.

Our own baby is growing; I've been terribly ill much of the time. But the springtime is returning, and Gabrielle seems ever taller.

There are days when my only worry is the war, and when I'm not contemplating the fact that in fields across France, men die and crops rot in the ground — in the moments when Gabrielle laughs and Gilles smiles and I can feel the baby turn — I feel happy again. I used to think I might not feel happy again. Sometimes those moments are short, but for now I cherish them.

So much has changed, but it feels like a moment ago; something will happen, Gabrielle will say something (yes, she has things to say), and I'll want to tell you. Or I'll make something in the kitchen and want you to taste it (this was, admittedly, well before the pregnancy), and the fact that I can't share something with you takes my breath away.

July 1943

My father paused in his reading. "There is another date here, but it seems significant."

Dearest Gabriel,

One year ago, you were killed by soldiers in an alleyway.

I sat by your grave today, cross legged on the ground. For several moments, I felt like the most disloyal widow, sitting there carrying another man's baby in my womb, one of our own daughters settled in a new family.

My heart feels split in two. I feel disloyal to you if I feel happy, and disloyal to Gilles if I feel sad. There are days when I wish life hadn't happened so swiftly.

And then I tick back over the last year . . . and I wouldn't have done anything differently. The decisions I made, we made — they protected the girls. And then I fell in love with the man who stepped forward to protect them, and protect me. This baby nestled inside of me is the natural product of that.

It happened quickly, but I don't know how it could have happened differently, not in this time of war.

One year. And I wonder when it will be time for me to let you go.

Not that you won't always be a part of my heart. I see your face in Gabrielle's every day. Her eyes light up like yours in a way that takes my breath away.

But I wonder if I need to let Gilles further into my life. If I have less of a use for this diary, for these letters. Not that I won't feel a need to come and share from time to time. But these days are short and life is full of the uncertain. I should hate to miss something in the present because I cannot loosen my grip on the past.

I love you, dearest, and I will always love you.

November 1943

Dearest,

Henri came into this world last week. He is quite bald, but aside from that, he looks just like Gilles. Gilles cannot decide whether to walk taller and prouder because he has a son, or more stooped with concern — so truly, he has remained much the same. He loves this new child tenderly, just as he loves me, Gabrielle, and Anouk. We are a strange little family, but a family just the same.

May 1945

Dearest Gabriel,

The war is over. At least, that is what they have told us. Allied soldiers have displaced the Axis soldiers, and the war in Europe is over, though it continues in the Pacific theater.

Forgive me if I am not as celebratory as some of the others. There are so many dead, so many fallow fields, so much destruction. The country is still overrun with foreign soldiers.

The girls are now four years old. They run, they chatter, they have such individual personalities and squabbles and passions.

Cécile and I have not yet discussed the future; I believe she's afraid to bring up the subject. I know she has fully bonded to Alice as if she were her own; Alice does not want for love. And Alice is fully bonded with her sisters, Suzette and Elèonore, though she and Gabrielle remain close and, I believe, always will.

My mother, though, is not afraid to approach the subject.

She sat down next to me while I was knitting a sweater for Henri. She asked if we intended to stay at the chateau, to which I replied that Gilles and I hadn't considered otherwise. He has sold his stakes in the Toulouse factories and has enjoyed his life as a farmer, working in the earth, making things grow. It would break his heart to leave.

And when I gave that answer, Maman asked about my plans for the girls.

She pointed out that if we decided to stay, that it would create a scandal, explaining to friends and neighbors that

Gabrielle wasn't Gilles's daughter, and Alice wasn't the child of Françoise's son Luc, that they were actually the twin daughters of a Parisian Jew.

Her words felt like a slap in the face, and in my daughters' faces. I very nearly jumped out of my seat and stormed from the room.

You must know, darling, that I am not ashamed of you. There is no reason for me to be. But there is some truth in her words. If I insisted on claiming Alice as my daughter, she would be viewed with suspicion. Both girls would be. Even if I wore our marriage papers pinned to my clothes, I don't know that it would be believed, not really.

If we went to Canada or America and started fresh, that would be different. But I cannot imagine the heartache of taking the girls — and Gilles — from a home they love so much.

And then there is the simple fact that one night in Paris, German soldiers came to my home to arrest me and the girls, the way that so many others were arrested and murdered. That we were in the neighbor's home when they broke down the door, I do not know why we escaped when so many didn't. I only know that we were in a safer place, and that Nathan's connections got us out of the city.

Who is to say such a thing might not happen again? That in another generation, some madman will decide to blame a Jew for his lot in life?

If I were more courageous, I might say that it is their history and heritage, and the world can hang.

But I am a mother who wants her children to live long, happy lives.

I have only to look outside my window to see the girls playing in the garden. They are happy, secure, and content. Getting what I want — my daughters together in my arms again — means branding my daughters the bastards of a secret liaison. Getting what I want would hurt my daughters, my husband, my son, and my sister — and every other member of my family, by association.

The price is too high.

No. I carried Alice in my womb, and when she was in danger, I made sure she had the best chance for a happy life in a loving family, with people I trust.

The danger has passed; if I must sacrifice Alice, then Gabrielle will return to her birth name. We have called her

Claire these many months, but if we must tell people it's a middle name, so be it. I must have that one thing.

Gilles has no objections. He told me that because of Gabriel, Gabrielle is a part of his life, and if I would like to honor her with her birth father's name, he could not think of disagreeing.

With Gilles, I am blessed. Not every man would be so generous.

As for Alice, as her mother, the most loving thing I can do is let her go. She's not my Alice anymore. She's Cécile's Sandrine, adopted daughter of the estate, biological daughter of a war hero, if anybody asks. She can hold her head high.

I will always, always love her. But I must let her go.

Sandrine took in a gasping breath. "So it's true. It's true. I have been Alice all this time. Alice." Another breath. "And Gabrielle — She was my *sister*."

"It was another time," Auguste told her, his large hand holding Sandrine's delicate one. "At some point they must have dropped the adoption facade."

"Would anyone have believed it? Sandrine looks just as much like a daughter of the house as her sisters or Gabrielle," my father said.

"She lied about my age, my mother did. I am a year older than I believed."

"It was war. There may have been more turnover in the village than anticipated, or the family may have been so isolated at the chateau that few took notice," Caterina suggested.

"They loved us very much," Sandrine said softly, looking down at the blue diary. "My mother loved me and did not want to let me go. My true mother did not wish to disrupt my life or cause me to live in shame. It is a fierce love."

"All of the letters together. The photos tied with the same ribbon — I wonder," I said, "if Cécile meant one day to tell you about your birth. I wonder if she got too sick too soon."

"You think she gathered the letters together?" Sophie asked.

I shrugged. "Somebody did. They were pristine. Having all of the letters, from all of the parties? It had to be a curated collection."

"Grand-tante Joséphine might have done such a thing too," Sandrine added. "We shall never know, and I suppose it does not matter." She shook her head. "Fleeing Paris like that, hiding us away . . ."

"I remember Grand-mère being very concerned during the Cold War," Sophie said. "She felt certain another world war could break out. I remember her saying that she would not let her family be targets, but I didn't know what she meant, not at the time. Why would we have been?"

Chloé, seated next to Sandrine, looked up at the woman she'd thought of as her grandmother's cousin. "So you're my great-aunt, right?"

Sandrine's face softened. "Yes, *mon chou.*"

Chloé nodded. "That's good. I like that."

"Moi aussi, ma petite. Moi aussi," Sandrine answered, placing an affectionate arm around her grand-niece's shoulders.

Neil joined me in our room as I packed my clothes that night. We weren't leaving for another two days, but I wanted to start gathering my things. Really, I wanted something useful to do and it was too late to cook.

"You know what I was thinking?" Neil asked. "You told me that Sandrine came out and helped with your mom's care when she was really sick, near the end."

I nodded. "You're right."

"So even if they didn't know they were

sisters, Sandrine was there and caring for her until the end."

"She was, yes." I swiped fresh tears from my face. "You're right."

"Did she see much of Mireille? As an adult?"

"Not very much. She was busy caring for the chateau, or caring for her mother."

"Taking care of things in a way that I'm sure Mireille appreciated."

"Yes." I nodded. "Grand-mère always spoke highly of her."

"And she had a good life — that's what Mireille wanted for her in the first place."

"Yes." I sighed as Neil's arms looped around me. "So now we know. Now we know about my grandfather, about Alice." I rested my head against his chest.

"And to think that no one would have known unless you'd decided to take your grandmother's cookbook to work."

"Someone might have found the letters or diary at some point, I suppose."

"But you put all the pieces together. And you found Benjamin."

"I'm excited for you to meet him."

"Me too."

Neil pressed a kiss to my forehead. "You should get some sleep."

I tipped my head up, bumping his nose

with my own. "Not with a kiss like that."

"No?"

"Nope."

He slipped his hand to the back of my head, lowering his lips to mine. My toes curled within my woolen socks, and my eyes slid shut. I kissed him back, my heart glad that he was here, that we belonged to each other.

34

Happiness. Simple as a glass of chocolate or tortuous as the heart.

Bitter. Sweet. Alive.

— **JOANNE HARRIS**

There were dozens of lit candles in the sitting room the following evening. Dressed in the green dress I found in town, topped with Mireille's silk jacket and off-white veil, I felt warm and glowing from the inside out.

I wore garments representing two generations of love, and if I couldn't have my mother and grandmother at my wedding ceremony, that was the next best thing.

Chairs had been placed on either side of the room, creating a short aisle. Looking out, I could see my family, with Nonno at the front, and my husband at the center.

I didn't hear many of the words spoken by the priest, but I loved the way they washed over us, blessed us, covered us.

We ate cake afterward, lovingly baked by Sandrine. My father laughed with his father, sister, and brother-in-law, all of them speaking in rapid Italian, egging each other on.

I loved it.

Neil's hand on the small of my back broke my concentration. "Let's step over here," he said. "I have — well, something to tell you."

"What? What's wrong?"

He shook his head. "Nothing's wrong. I hope it's right, actually. You see, when we were apart, taking the Atlanta job made sense. It had no connection to you, so a part of me chose it because I thought it would remind me of you less."

"I'm moving there with you," I said dryly, "so that plan might not work."

He smiled, that lovely, happy, disbelieving smile of his. "Plans changed."

"They did at that," I said, smiling back. "You've just married me for the second time. In a second language."

"If you keep teasing me," he said, "I won't finish what I have to say." He took a deep breath. "After we married, during this trip, Atlanta started to feel . . . wrong." He reached for my hands and held them in his own. "I called Callan," he continued, his voice husky. "There's a place for me there."

I gasped, my hand flying to my mouth.

"I wish there was a place for me in Portland, sweetheart, but there isn't, at least not now. But how would you feel about moving to Chicago instead?"

"This place, this position — is it as good as the job in Atlanta?"

"Yes."

"It's not a demotion of any kind, or a pay cut — because if you're taking a lesser job because you're worried about me . . ."

Neil chuckled. "It's none of those things, and my best friend lives there. Honey, it's the job I should have considered in the first place, but I knew you had a sister somewhere in Chicago and I couldn't stand the idea of running into her."

I pressed my lips together. "Oh really? And Portland was somehow better?"

"It was short term. I thought I could handle it."

"You did," I said, barely suppressing laughter. "Admirably. So, you avoided Chicago to avoid Cat but you came to Portland short term and" — I bit my lip — "I found you."

"My subconscious turned out to be wiser than anticipated," he said. "And maybe — just maybe — we were meant to be." He squeezed my hands. "All that to say, Juliette D'Alisa McLaren, will you move to Chicago with me?"

"Yes," I said, full of joy, catching the swivel of Caterina's head as our words made their way to her ears.

Soon enough the joy in my heart caught fire, spreading around the room, binding us together every one.

EPILOGUE

"What is this made of?" Damian asked, trying to catch his breath. Callan shifted his hold. "Lead. Pure lead."

"Be nice to that table," I instructed from the sidewalk. "It's been through fire. Literally."

"Two more steps," Neil told the men. "We're almost there."

"I think it needs to stay here," Damian suggested. "It would look nice on your front steps. Like a conversation piece."

I repressed a laugh. "Someone might steal it."

"Who? Does the Hulk live in the neighborhood? It's not going anywhere." Callan grunted. "Could be osmium. Denser than lead."

"French oak," I said. "And marble. In case you were actually curious."

Tarissa, standing next to me, shook her head. "I doubt that."

519

"Are they suffering too much?" I asked, watching the three men struggle with the prep table, wincing as Damian nearly dropped his end. "We should have hired movers."

"Builds character," Caterina answered. "Character and muscles, and I like both."

"Should I tell them there's dessert inside?" She threaded her arm through mine. "We'll tell them when it's in your kitchen."

Five minutes later, we stood around the antique piece, now in its final location. Ten minutes after, everyone had a slice of pie on a plate. The others chattered around me — Damian having made fast friends with Callan and Neil in the weeks since we'd arrived, Tarissa and Caterina hitting it off instantly. They could entertain themselves, and while they were occupied I took in the sight of the prep table.

The last piece to be moved in, it was the table Gabriel had made for Mireille. The original keeper of secrets. My inheritance, in so many ways.

Neil broke away from the group, sidling up to me and breathing a kiss against my lips. "Hi, love," he said.

I smiled and kissed him back. "Hi."

"You like it?"

"I do."

"I'm glad," he said. "Welcome home."

READERS GUIDE

1. The story opens with Juliette dealing with the aftermath of difficult life events. What time in your life did you find yourself adjusting to circumstances after a difficult event?
2. Juliette is dealing with grief differently than other members of her family. How do you handle grief? How do your loved ones?
3. Seeing Neil causes Juliette to question her personal life. Have you ever been in a situation where seeing an old friend caused you to rethink a decision? What did you do?
4. How did you feel about Juliette's response to Adrian's party and impulsive question? How would you respond?
5. In Chicago, Juliette is able to make contact with new family members. Do you or does anyone in your family have a story of reconnecting with lost family members?

How did you feel about it? Did you find familial similarities or unusual differences?

6. Juliette's family celebrates holidays differently because of their restaurants. What are your family's holiday traditions? How are they influenced by career and family commitments?

7. After the fire, Juliette has to think on her feet. What do you think she learns through the experience?

8. Juliette's decisions lead to more changes and doing things differently than she planned. Which of your life events happened differently than you'd hoped?

9. As we read Mireille's diary, we see how her relationship with Gilles changes. What are the factors, do you think, that cause her feelings to change?

10. Mireille must make a heartbreaking choice after the war. How do you feel about her decision?

11. Juliette faces more change after the end of the book. What do you hope lies in her future?

12. What foods from the book would you most like to taste? Which recipes would you be interested in making yourself?

ACKNOWLEDGMENTS

This list of thanks and acknowledgments has to start with Sandra Bishop, my agent, who shepherded this book — and the entire series — because that's the person she is. Let's raise a glass to getting this last one out of the gate!

Many thanks to my editor, Shannon Marchese, for her graciousness and patience with (a) this book and (b) me, as well as her confidence in this story.

Giant thanks to Rachel Lulich, who did an early read and editing pass as a friend, and helped to restore my confidence in this book. Not only does she have a keen eye, but she's a great person to explore Atlanta with.

Thanks to Laura Wright and her consistent eye over all three books, making sure each detail matches from start to finish.

Thanks to Kara Christensen, Katie Ganshert, Rachel McMillan, and Melissa Tagg for being story consultants and supporters, and Sarah Varland for reading the manuscript and giving her valuable feedback.

Grazie to Alessandra Gardino for her invaluable Italian language assistance and recipe consultations, and for teaching me to make truly delicious fresh pasta. This book is far richer with her expertise, and I would encourage anyone with a desire to explore Italy to check out one of her tours with Customized Journeys.

Thanks to Aurora Taylor, Jeff Stirling, and Jamie Erickson for answering my WWII France questions, and to Ryan Goettsch for answering questions about fires and emergency response procedures. Thanks to Anna Freedman for answering questions about Jewish holiday traditions. Any and all errors are absolutely mine.

Thanks to Angie Jabine, who hired me as an intern for *Northwest Palate* magazine ten years ago, an experience that inspired this series. I am also thankful for her willingness, all these years later, to answer questions about garden pests.

Thanks to Lisa Chrisman for lending her family's heirloom pumpkin-pie recipe to the book and volunteering to test recipes.

I tip my hat to the ladies of the Portland Heights Hat Club, for reading my books, attending functions, and simply being fabulous in general.

Many thanks to my mom for reading the manuscript and doing an early copyedit pass, and for making sure the bits I didn't think made sense made sense.

Thanks to my family, the one I grew up with and the one I married into. Their care and support has been invaluable through the writing of this series.

And thanks as always to my husband, Danny, for his support and patience during a long deadline season. I couldn't do what I do without you. Let's take a vacation soon!

ABOUT THE AUTHOR

Hillary Manton Lodge loves nothing more than a good story. She is the author of five novels, including the Two Blue Doors and the Plain and Simple series. In her free time, Hillary enjoys experimenting in the kitchen, rearranging her house, and exploring her most recent hometown of Portland, Oregon. She shares her home with her husband, Danny, and their cavalier King Charles spaniels, Shiloh and Sylvie.

The employees of Thorndike Press hope you have enjoyed this Large Print book. All our Thorndike, Wheeler, and Kennebec Large Print titles are designed for easy reading, and all our books are made to last. Other Thorndike Press Large Print books are available at your library, through selected bookstores, or directly from us.

For information about titles, please call:
    (800) 223-1244

or visit our Web site at:
    http://gale.cengage.com/thorndike

To share your comments, please write:
    Publisher
    Thorndike Press
    10 Water St., Suite 310
    Waterville, ME 04901